The Broken

By

George Donald

CHAPTER ONE

She stopped the car a few feet from the two white coloured garage doors and switching off the Aygo's engine, turned to stare with empty eyes at the large, detached five-bedroom house.

A prison without bars.

With a sigh, she reached for the parcel shelf under the passenger's dashboard and lifting the A5 size notebook, opened it at the last entry.

Glancing at the dashboard clock she was about to carefully write the time, but then with a sad smile decided to give herself a few extra minutes for the coffee she'd treated herself to in the adjacent Costa's. After all, she thought, how would he know?

Beside the time she carefully logged the cars mileage and finally the purpose of her trip; collecting the shopping from Sainsbury's Cuerden Way store in Preston's Bamber Bridge district, eight miles away.

Getting out of the car she fetched the two heavy shopping bags from the rear seats of the three door car and placing the notebook on top of one of the bags, made her way into the house.

The notebook she left with the car keys on the top of the small table inside the hallway of the house, from where Geoffrey would collect it and routinely inspect her entries.

She was about to lift the bags from the floor, but hesitatingly stopped to stare at her image in the four-foot mirror on the wall. Leaning close, she stared at her reflection that showed a slim figured woman now fifty-one years of age with shoulder length auburn hair tied back into a tight ponytail, her skin still fresh and clear, but for the slight bruise on her left cheek; a bruise that was fading to a light mustard colour as it healed.

"Come on, Alice, get a grip," she muttered, then stooping to lift the bags made her way into the kitchen to unpack the groceries.

The wall clock in the large, open plan kitchen indicated it was almost two-twenty, time enough she thought to walk the mile and a half to Marcy's primary school, St Clare's in Sharoe Green Lane and closing the larder cupboard door, glanced about her to ensure that everything was in order before making her way back to the front door and donning her light jacket.

It was the highlight of her day, collecting the eight-year-old from school, seeing her face light up at the sight of her grandmother waiting for her.

Locking the front door behind her, she thrust her hands into the jacket pockets and began the walk to Williams Lane and the long stroll on the grassy verge towards the school.

She arrived in plenty of time and wordlessly nodded to a few of the familiar faces, the waiting parents, grandparents and child-minders, stood at her usual spot beside the chain link fence, the best position from which to watch for her granddaughter leaving the side door.

"Hello, Missus Mayhew," said the soft voice from behind her, causing her to flinch.

Alarmed she turned to see the young woman with the short blonde hair smiling at her, one hand protectively on the handle of a buggy in which lay a sleeping toddler while the other reached solicitously towards her. The woman's face was vaguely familiar.

"I'm so sorry, Missus Mayhew, I didn't mean to startle you," the woman smiled apologetically.

"Oh, no, it's quite alright. I was miles away," she shyly returned the woman's smile.

"I'm Lucy Carstairs, Laura's mum. Marcy's classmate," the woman explained.

"Oh, yes, of course. I'm sorry, I…" she grimaced before continuing, "I'm not very good with faces or names."

"Oh, not to worry," Carstairs gushed. "Me neither and you'd think in my job it would be a prerequisite."

"Your job?"

"Yes," Carstairs smiled. "I'm a police officer. I work out of the Preston office," her eyes narrowed, "I think I might have mentioned it before?"

"Oh, sorry, I must have forgotten," but was saved from any further explanation when the bell loudly sounded.

Sighing almost with relief, she was about to move away when Carstairs said, "Had a bit of an accident?"

"I beg your pardon?"

"Your cheek, Missus Mayhew," she pointed. "You're sporting a bruise."

Her hand unconsciously reached to her face and her face reddening, she replied, "Oh, just me being a little foolish and bouncing my head off a cupboard door in the kitchen. Nothing my husband couldn't deal with," she forced a smile to make light of it.

"Ah, yes, of course. Mister Mayhew, he's a doctor, isn't he? The practice in Blanche Street as I recall," Carstairs slowly replied.

The conversation was getting worryingly awkward and now eager to end it, Alice quickly nodded before turning away to loudly call out, "Marcy, dear. Here I am," as she waved at the tousled haired little girl who hearing her name called, run quickly to her grandmother.

"Missus Mayhew…" Carstairs, began, but was suddenly talking to empty space for Alice had walked off and was hugging her granddaughter who walked beside her.

****

"Gran, what's for dinner?" she asked as hand in hand, they began the walk back to the house.

"What would you like?"

"Oh, spaghetti and…" she stopped and her face clouding, she asked, "Will he be there?"

Alice took a deep breath and forcing a smile, replied, "Of course he'll be there and Marcy, that's no way to talk about your grandfather, is it? I mean, what would people think if they heard you ask such a question?"

"I don't really care what people think," she moodily replied. "I just don't want to be around him, Gran. Never, ever, ever."

She stopped walking and bending down onto one knee, ignored the damp grass soaking into her trousers. Holding the little girls face in both hands and staring at her, she said, "We *have* to think about what we say, Marcy, in case people hear us. Your grandfather is an important man. He's a doctor in charge of a medical practice and lots of people look up to him and like him and trust him. Don't you see that?"

She didn't immediately respond, but stared at her feet before slowly replying, "Well, I don't like him very much," then added, "Your trousers are getting wet, Gran."

Alice sighed and raising herself up from the ground, took Marcy's hand in hers and together they continued their long walk home.

****

They had gone just a few hundred yards when a light fall of rain forced them to don the hoods of their jackets and carrying Marcy's schoolbag in one hand, urged the little girl to step lively.

Not for the first time she inwardly cursed Geoffrey's instruction that she not drive to the school, that it was a waste of petrol and good for the little girl to get fresh air, no matter the weather conditions. His reasoning of course was a lie. He just didn't think it necessary she spend money to fetch the child from school.

At last they arrived home and made their way to the rear door entrance that led into the utility room.

Geoffrey didn't like them using the front door, walking into the house with wet clothes and dirty shoes and insisted…no, demanded, she corrected herself, that they use the utility door.

"Right," she shrugged off her jacket and shoes and bending down onto one knee to remove Marcy's jacket and help her take off her shoes, continued, "let's get you out of those wet things. Now, what homework do you have?"

"Can't I watch bit of tele first, Gran?"

"No, Marcy, you know your grandfather's rules. We're not allowed to use the lounge and no television until the homework is completed."

"Please, please, please," she pleaded, clasping her hands together as if in prayer.

"Well," still down on one, knee, Alice glanced at her wristwatch. Geoffrey wasn't due home from the surgery for at least another hour and so, giving in, replied, "Only if you promise not to tell your grandfather and not complain when I switch it off. How does that sound?"

The little girl threw her arms about Alice's neck and softly replied, "I promise."

Alice smiled, loving the rush of affection she experienced when Marcy hugged her, then getting to her feet she nodded that Marcy run off to the lounge. Shaking the damp jackets, she hung them on the wall hooks with newspaper beneath to catch the drips before turning her attention to the shoes.

Cleaning off the mud splatters in the stainless steel sink bowl, she carefully laid the shoes onto a separate sheet of newspaper spread out on the floor by the wall and checked the sink to ensure it was thoroughly clean in the sure knowledge Geoffrey would undoubtedly examine it later.

Making her way into the kitchen to prepare the evening meal, she smiled at Marcy's laughter and the sound of the Tom and Jerry cartoon.

It was when she stood at the sink peeling the potatoes she remembered and almost in panic, dropped the peeler and hastily returned to the utility room.

Grabbing Marcy's schoolbag, she returned to the kitchen and placed that day's homework jotter and reading book onto the kitchen table. Sighing with relief she knew Geoffrey would have immediately spotted the absence of the homework and been angry. No, not just angry, she unconsciously shivered, though why he even bothered about whether or not Marcy did her homework was…no, she shook her head. She knew fine well why Geoffrey bothered.

It was just another of his controlling demands, his instruction that the child did as she was told.

She knew that Marcy's rebellious refusal to address him as Grandfather or even look at him irritated Geoffrey, though of course he would never admit to it. Yes, she inwardly smiled, the child has her mother's spirit.

Satisfied the stew and potatoes were almost ready, she laid the table for dinner and glancing at the clock realised her husband would be home any time now.

"Marcy," she called through to the lounge, "switch off the television and come through to the kitchen, please."

There was no reply. Wiping her hands upon her apron, she hurried through to the room to find the television blaring and the little girl curled up on the sofa, her head cradled on her hands as she slept. Using the remote, she switched the set off and stared down at her granddaughter, a sudden memory choking her and causing tears to form.

"You look so like your mum," she muttered, her hands clasped at her mouth and her lips trembling.

The sound of a car braking on the stone chips caused her to glimpse through the large window to see Geoffrey's white coloured Volvo XC40 coming to a halt.

"Marcy," she whispered and bent down to shake her granddaughter awake. "Marcy, please," a little more nervously she cast a glance at the window and saw Geoff exiting the driver's door.

"What?" Marcy tiredly rubbed at her eyes.

"Quickly, come do your homework," she pulled at the little girl's hand, hating herself but knowing what she was doing was the lesser of two evils.

Exhaling, Marcy allowed herself to be pulled from the couch and led by the hand through to the kitchen, getting there just as Alice heard her husband opening the front door.

Swallowing nervously, she sat Marcy in the chair and whispered, "If your grandfather asks, you're reading your book, okay?"

She tiredly nodded, but knowing they had but seconds and fearing she hadn't really understood, Alice hissed, "Marcy! Read your schoolbook! Please!"

The girl took a breath and using one hand to rub at her eyes, lifted the book with the other and yawned widely.

Alice moved over to the range cooker and pretended to be stirring the stew when her husband entered and glancing around the kitchen, curtly asked, "Is dinner ready?"

Turning, she forced a smile and brightly replied, "Marcy's just finishing her homework and dinner will be on the table in a couple of minutes if you want to change or anything."

Doctor Geoffrey Martin Mayhew, fifty-nine years of age, clean shaven with thinning dark brown hair, stood six-foot-two inches tall and though now showing signs of being overweight still bore the build of his rugby playing youth. Staring at his wife of thirty years his eyes narrowed when he replied, "Why would I wish to change?"

"I'm sorry, I just thought…"

"Perhaps, you stupid woman," he sneered, "you should leave the thinking to me." Barking loudly in a deep voice, he added, "I will be in the lounge having a whisky. Call me when it *is* on the table."

There had been no courteous acknowledgment of his granddaughter, nothing to indicate he had even seen the child sat there at the table with her head bowed.

Guiltily, Alice stared at Marcy and with a slight smile, softly said, "Put your book and jotter back into your schoolbag, dear, then go and wash your hands. We'll finish your homework in your room after dinner."

The little girl's face was pale and drawn and once more her grandmother worried what must be going through her head, what thoughts she must have.

It was important to Alice that Marcy knew she was loved, that the traumatic loss a year previously of her parents, Alice's beloved daughter Gemma and her artist husband Peter…she stopped and muffled a sob.

****

The heartbreak of remembering that day was almost too much to bear, the police coming to the door to inform her of the accident, the multiple car collision that resulted in Gemma's death though Peter had lingered for almost two full days before succumbing to his injuries.

She remembered driving the Aygo to Geoff's surgery, but little of the journey to Hull in his Volvo, arriving hours later at the Royal Infirmary where they found Marcy, then just turned seven, enveloped in a grey hospital blanket, her thin little legs dangling and one bright red shoe missing, numbly sat upon an adult sized plastic chair in the corridor with a young police woman beside her who held her hand and told her over and over that everything would be all right, that her grandparents were coming to collect her.

She recalled seeing the child's neck and shoulders bore bright red bruises where when seated on the booster seat, the car seatbelt had restrained her at the point of impact.

She closed her eyes tightly against the memory of attending at the hospital mortuary where they identified Gemma's bloodied body. She swallowed with difficulty, recalling Geoffrey reminding her that he was a doctor and it was his opinion and insistence that because Peter was in a coma, there seemed little point in sitting by his bed.

Not, she bitterly realised now because it was for the best or the correct thing to do, but because Geoffrey did not and never had liked the longhaired and bearded young man who courted and loved their only child.

It was one of the few occasions in their long marriage she had the nerve to stand up against her husband and refused to return that day to Preston with him, insisting that because Peter had no family, she and Marcy would stay in Hull and wait by his bed.

She recalled standing in the reception area of the hospital while Geoffrey loudly called her a fool for electing to remain before he stormed off in a petulant rage.

Though he blustered he had patients to attend to the following morning, she knew the real reason for his leaving was that the accident and their daughter's death interfered with his evening, his rugby club's formal dinner where it was expected he would be announced as the new club Chairman.

For two days she and Marcy, booked in at the local Premier Inn, remained by her father's bedside; she attempting to explain and amuse the child through the long hours until late on the second evening, the young doctor requested they wait in the corridor outside the ICU where five minutes later, while she hugged Marcy to her, he knelt before them to break the dreadful news.

She remembered the tearful phone call she made to Geoffrey from the hotel room, of informing him that Peter had died without regaining consciousness and of her husband's response.

"Too bad, too bad," he had replied, his voice slurring and betraying his consumption of whisky, then cheerfully telling her, "It's happened. I'm the newly appointed Chairman and believe me, there will be changes around here, just you wait and see."

Stunned at his insensitivity, she had hung up, preferring not to hear more.

Having travelled to Hull in Geoffrey's car, she and Marcy were obliged to return home to Preston by train.

Despite frequent calls from the telephone kiosk in Preston railway station to the house and his practice, he had not responded and frustrated, she had bundled Marcy and with what little possessions that the police removed from the family's accident damaged car, struggled into a taxi for the four-and-a-half-mile journey to Spruce Close.

It was as the taxi approached the house she saw the yellow coloured Mini Clubman drive out of the driveway and race off in the opposite direction, the same car that she now knew belonged to Geoffrey's receptionist, the twice divorced Debbie Pritchard.

He was in the kitchen wearing his dressing gown and in bare feet making coffee when she opened the door. She saw him to be unshaven, his hair in disarray and when close to him, realised he was smelling of not just whisky, but also of another woman's perfume.

It had surprised her then and still did that she did not care that her husband was a philanderer, having for some time had good reason t suspect that Geoffrey was seeing other women. Even now, ten years after they stopped sharing the same bed when she moved into the second bedroom, it did not bother her. Since then the only occasion he visited her at night had been when he was drinking and demanded some sexual relief, but even these few urges for his wife ceased some years previously when he found what he would mockingly boast were more diverting and interesting company.

To her relief, he did not publicly flaunt his extra-martial relationships, but Alice suspected that was more to do with his reputation in the town as a doctor than to spare her feelings.

For Geoffrey Mayhew's reputation was everything to him.

Widely known throughout the Preston area, not least because of his occasional appearances about medical issues on local television and radio as well as his opinion sometimes sought by the local newspaper, he was also known publicly as a vocal supporter of local charities, though again that was more to do with his public image rather than his altruistic character. Seated on the board of several committees, Alice was acutely aware the popular doctor was well liked and highly regarded by his patients too; a fact that he never tired of telling her.

But none of those adoring patients or media people knew the real Geoffrey Mayhew, not as did his wife, his deceased daughter and her husband or his solemn faced granddaughter. They knew him as a self-centred bully; a petulant, middle aged man who hid behind his public persona of righteousness and virtue.

That day when she returned with their granddaughter to the Spruce Close house, he had stared with bloodshot eyes from Marcy to Alice and greeted her with, "Why did you bring her here?"

Clutching the little girl's hand, she had mustered enough courage to challenge him by asking, "She's our granddaughter, Geoffrey. Where else would she go?"

He had not immediately responded, but turned away to pour boiling water into the mug before replying, "As long as she behaves and does what she's told and I mean, what she is told!"

He had then turned back to stare with watery eyes at Marcy before addressing Alice with, "And she's your responsibility. Keep her out of my way."

They had stood together hand in hand in the doorway of the kitchen as he passed them by to return to his bed, the bed she had shared with him till almost ten years previously, the bed that she knew he had undoubtedly shared with his receptionist while she had forlornly sat with the dying Peter, the father of their granddaughter and Gemma's loving husband.

That first three months had been hellish for Alice who alone coped with the orphaned child's terrible loss, the sleepless nights sat by Marcy's bed while she cried and moaned in her sleep and for the first month, the separation anxiety the child endured each day Alice left her at the school gate.

As time passed, Marcy settled down and the nightmares subsided, but none of it was noticed by the uncaring Geoffrey.

And now, she stared down at the solemn faced child, even after a year had passed her husband still refused to acknowledge the little girl, just as he had ignored their daughter through her life and more so when she had met and moved in with Peter.

God, she wondered, where *do* I find the strength?

****

The little girl was fast asleep in her bedroom and Alice, finished preparing Marcy's lunch for school the next day, considered having an early night with a book when Geoffrey entered the kitchen carrying the notebook from the Aygo in his hand.

It was evident he had been drinking again.

"It says here," he held the notebook up, "that you spent the day at the supermarket. Was that all you did?"

"Yes," she flatly replied, then added, "other than tidying the house and collecting Marcy from school."

"These times you've noted for the supermarket. Show me the till receipt."

Her chest felt tight and she knew from painful experience that when drinking, he was unpredictable and it was not wise to argue or question him. Keeping the kitchen's island between them, Alice moved to lift her handbag from the chair and rummaging inside, produced the receipt that she handed to him before stepping back far enough to avoid his reach.

She watched him squint as he read the receipt and choked back a nervous laugh, aware that for years his eyesight was failing, but that he was too vain to admit he needed reading glasses.

Opening the notebook, he compared the times and growled, "Why did it take you longer to get home? The receipt says you went through the till at one-o-eight, yet you didn't get home till two-sixteen. Why did it take you so long? Where else did you go?"

She hesitated and thought, that bloody coffee.

He tossed the notebook onto the kitchen table and took a menacing step towards her, his hand bunching into fists as she backed against the cupboard door.

Her mind racing, with a sob she quickly replied, "It was the roadworks. The temporary traffic lights on the A6. That's what held me up. You know about them, don't you?"

He stopped and leaning over her, stared at her, his face inches from hers and she thought he would see through the lie, that he would strike her.

His fetid breath reeked of the whisky he had drunk and as the foul smell rolled over her, she fought to stop herself from retching.

"The roadworks," he slowly repeated, then nodded. "Yes, the roadworks," he said again and she instinctively knew that he would never admit that she could beat him with a lie and so convinced himself she must be telling the truth.

She flinched in fear as raising his hand, he gently stroked at her bruised cheek then leaning in so close their noses almost touched, he said, "If I ever thought you tried to lie to me, you know what I will do to you, don't you?"

She nodded, but that wasn't enough for him as he snarled, "Tell me what I will do to you. Tell me."

Terrified, she was almost choking with fear, but at last she whispered, "You'll beat me."

"Yes," he smiled evilly at her, "I'll beat you, Alice."

CHAPTER TWO

He gazed at his reflected image in the bathroom mirror and wondered if he should shave? After all, he mentally argued, it's not as if he was going in to the office today. No, he smiled at the mirror, he had far more important things to deal with.

Rubbing at his stubble, he grinned and after brushing at his teeth – his *own* teeth he frequently reminded his pals – slipped off the bathrobe and hung it on the hook behind the door. Turning on the shower he reached a hand forward to check the temperature of the water and was about to step into the wide glass cubicle when the bathroom phone rung.

"Bugger," he muttered and naked, grabbed at a towel to wipe his hand before striding across the bedroom floor.

Grabbing at the phone he said, "Hello."

"Mister Burke?" asked the youthful voice. "It's Shona Mulveigh from the estate agency about the viewing tomorrow morning at Glencloy Road?"

"Oh, aye, Shona. Is there a problem?"

"Oh, no sir. It's just a courtesy call to ensure you still wish to attend."

"Aye, I do. Eleven o'clock if I recall correctly."

"That's right and it will be myself who'll meet you and take you to the viewing."

"Well, it's my intention to catch the train from Glasgow Central to Ardrossan then the nine-forty-five ferry that is due to arrive in Brodick at…" he squeezed his eyes tightly shut, trying to recall the time, then blurted out, "ten-forty."

"So you'll be travelling as a foot passenger then, sir?"

He grinned and said, "Not unless they let me bring my car onto the train with me."

He imagined he could almost hear her blush before she replied, "Oh, that was silly of me. Perhaps then I can meet you off the ferry, Mister Burke?"

"That would be grand, Shona, and as you're being so kind maybe you should call me Tommy. It's a lot easier than Mister Burke, eh?"

"Oh, right then, ah, Tommy. I'll see you tomorrow then at ten-forty?"

"I'll see you then," he agreed and ended the call.

Replacing the phone into it's cradle, he turned and caught his naked reflection in the full length wardrobe mirror. Turning back and forth, he rubbed at his flat stomach and opening his mouth wide, thought, my own teeth and hair so I suppose that's not too bad for a fifty-seven-year-old guy.

Self-consciously grinning at the mirror, he lifted the towel from the bed and made his way back to the en-suite.

****

He finger-combed his shock of wiry red hair and dressed in a pale blue polo shirt, cream coloured chinos with brown brogues on his feet, faced the mirror to critically examine his clothing. Grabbing his wallet, mobile phone and a navy coloured, light rain jacket from the hall stand and lifting the two bunches of flowers that stood in the bucket of water by the front door, he made his way down the stairs of the modern tenement building to the street. At the close entrance, he realised he had forgotten his car keys. However, his daughter Fiona and her husband Phil's home in Whittingehame Drive in the Kelvinside area of Glasgow was just a mile away from his flat in Hughenden Road and though the clouds were threatening rain, decided a brisk walk would do him the world of good. That and he'd work up an appetite for his dinner, reminding himself that Fiona's meals bordered on restaurant quality and mentally vowed that second helpings were not good for his waistline.

On route to Whittingehame Drive, he glanced at two bunches of flowers he carried for his daughter and granddaughter, eight-year-old Cissie and smiled. The girls will be pleased with these, he thought and idly wondered if he should have brought a bottle of wine for the table.

The rain was starting to fall when he arrived at the large, detached home and hurried up the drive towards the front door, reaching the overhead canopy just as the clouds burst.

Rapping his knuckles against the door, it was pulled open whereupon he was immediately assailed by a curly red-headed whirlwind who cried out, "Granddad's here!" before rubbing her cheek against his then complaining, "You face is scratchy."

Hugging the little girl to him, he grinned then stood back and theatrically bowing, replied, "Then maybe granddad can make up for his scratchy face with flowers for Miss Docherty," and handed her a bunch.

"Thanks," she gushed and run back indoors.

Stepping inside, his bearded, prematurely grey headed son-in-law Phil greeted him with a grin and told him, "Tommy. Thank heavens you've arrived. The boss wouldn't let me open a bottle of plonk till you got here."

"Hi, daddy."

At five-feet eight and just two inches shorter than her father, his daughter Fiona, slim and lovely and with a head of curly red hair like her daughter, stepped out from the kitchen to greet him with a hug before grinning at her husband and telling him, "Okay, dude, you can open the wine now."

"Just the four of us for dinner then?" Tommy asked.

"Just the four of us," she confirmed with a nod and took the flowers from him before heading back towards the kitchen and calling out over her shoulder, "Right, if you three want to get to the table, I'll bring out the food."

Half an hour later, their meal finished, Cissie was excused to watch television in her room while Phil fetched a pot of coffee from the kitchen.

"So, what's this thing you want to discuss with us?" Fiona asked as Phil poured three cups.

Tommy took a deep breath and replied, "Well, as you *are* the oldest of my daughters I thought it best to run it past you first. I'm thinking of buying a house in Arran."

"Arran? Why Arran? Oh," her eyes narrowed, "you mean you want to move there?"

"No, not exactly move and besides, where would you get a babysitter as good as me?" he shrugged, then smiled at them in turn. "No, it's not a permanent move or at least, that's not my intention at the minute. I'll keep the flat in Hughenden Road, but now I'm on my own I want somewhere to spend my retirement time and as you know, your mum and I really enjoyed our holidays on the island. Of course, whether or not I'm there, it will also be for use by you guys and your sister's and their families too. That and the ferry at Ardrossan is only an hour away on the train, then fifty-five minutes on the boat. Besides, it's not as if I'd be going abroad and remember how much fun we had there when you and your sisters were children?"

"I remember before your business took off us living in some really dodgy cottages," she grimaced, then turning to Phil continued. "In fact, the first time mum and dad took us there on holiday was to a place called Machrie," but then she stopped and with a grin, shook her head at the memory.

"You're talking about that old rundown cottage a customer had given me the use of when you were what, about ten?"

"That's it," she clapped her hands and shrieked with laughter. "I was about to turn ten, Vicky was almost eight and Jenny was six. God, the place was awful."

Tommy turned to Phil and sighing, said, "I had just started out on my own, my first venture as a self-employed bricklayer. I did a job, built a wall as I recall, for a couple over in Pollokshields. The husband, the customer I mean, told me his mother had died and left him with a cottage on the island at Machrie on the west side. He was so pleased with the wall I had built that he offered me the use of the cottage for a week during the Glasgow Fair holidays. Well, it was a freebie and in those days Moira and I were really strapped for cash, so we loaded the girls into my old works van and headed for the ferry. What the guy didn't mention was that his mother had died about five years previously, that nobody had lived in the cottage during that time and he had rarely visited it during those five years."

"It was a disaster," Fiona interrupted with a smile. "The water had been cut off and so had the electricity and there were no gas canisters to fuel the cooker and the smell of dampness," she shook her head.

"But we had a good time, didn't we?"

She reached across the table to affectionately lay her hand upon his arm and replied, "Yes, dad. We had a great time. So, tell us about this house."

****

He had brought the estate agent's schedule for the property and after Phil cleared the dishes away, laid the four-page document out on the table. Sat closely beside him, Fiona peered at the photographs of the house and asked, "How old is it? I mean, when was it built? It looks pretty new."

"According to the lassie I'm dealing with, the house is three years old and the current owners are packing up and moving abroad somewhere. They're looking for a quick sale, hence the price."

"Nearly four hundred grand, Tommy," Phil mused. "That's a lot of money."

"Aye, well, since I sold the business most of the money has been lying in an investment pot and to be frank, even at that price it won't make too much of a dent in my account and will still leave me with more than enough for what I need."

Phil stared curiously at him before asking, "You intend paying for the house outright?"

"Yes. Do you think that's a problem? I mean, we both know I can easily afford it and after all, why would I bother with a mortgage at my age?"

"What are you now, fifty-seven, fifty-eight?"

"Fifty-eight next birthday."

"Well, I see your point, but maybe you could negotiate a deal if you're paying cash. Particularly if the sellers are looking for a quick sale."

Tommy smiled and replied, "The sellers won't be worrying about where the money comes, Phil. Besides, I've already checked out the prices of the surrounding properties in Brodick and across the island. The price seems fair to me," he shrugged and puckered his lips.

"Okay, okay," Phil held his hands up. "But you know me, Tommy. I never take the first price for anything."

"If I can butt in," Fiona leaned forward to place a restraining hand on her husband's forearm. "Tell me, dad, why do you think you need a four bedroom house?"

"Well, truthfully, I don't but I'm looking for long term usage such as when you and your blisters and their husbands and the weans all come across." He smiled. "It would be nice for all of you to use the place as a family retreat, particularly during the good weather and don't forget, Arran is also known as…"

"Scotland in miniature," she finished for him and shook her head before adding, "If I'd a penny for every time you've told us *that* story."

"A good story is always worth the retelling," he chuckled.

"And when do you intend travelling across to view the property, dad?"

"Well, that's the other thing I wanted to speak with you about, hen. I've arranged to meet the estate agent tomorrow morning off the ferry and was wondering if you've nothing planned…"

"Of course," she smiled at him. "Phil, you can see Cissie off to school and collect her, can't you?"

Phil, a self-employed IT specialist with an office in the house and who worked in the pharmaceutical industry, nodded before replying, "No problem."

"Then it's all arranged," Fiona grinned and reached for her wine glass.

****

The rain had ceased when almost three hours later, Tommy began the walk back to his flat.

He smiled as he walked, counting himself blessed to have such lovely young women as his daughters and the good men they each had married. Now each with their own child, his one regret was that Moira had not shared the joyful arrival of Victoria and Jennifer's sons before she passed.

He still did not know where he had found the strength to carry on and but for the girls might have succumbed to God knows what kind of life.

The year of suffering through her long and debilitating illness had taken its toll on him and though he would never admit to it, Moira's death had in itself been a blessing and saved her from bearing much agony.

His thoughts turned to their marriage and the difficulties they had endured together as he worked long hours to build the business. In truth, as he was fond of telling people, if not for Moira's endurance and sacrificing her own nursing career, he might never had succeeded for it was her support that kept him going.

Leaving school at sixteen years of age, he had been apprenticed to a grouchy old bricklayer called Archie who when the teenage Tommy fouled up whether by chance or design, the old bugger wasn't beyond slapping him on the back of the head for his idiocy. Still, he grinned as he strolled along, the bugger knew his stuff and when five years later Tommy qualified as a bricklayer, Archie gruffly presented his former apprentice with his own bricklaying tools and a pretty penny they must have cost him too, Tommy knew.

The tools, long since disused, lay within their wooden toolbox in Tommy's storage locker at the flats entrance; tools unlikely to be used again, but which he would never part with.

Shaking his head at the memory, he wondered what Archie would make of his former apprentice now, the man who started Whiteinch Construction out of a former grocery shop in Dumbarton Road and who the previous year, sold the company to a national builder for just under fifteen million pounds. A vast sum of money that he determined would not change him nor would the sums of money he gifted his daughters change them either; of that he was certain.

Aye, he thought, Moira and I…he stopped walking and blinking rapidly, took a deep breath.

Gone now these four years and I still think of her as being with me. He slowly exhaled and continued walking on Great Western Road before turning into Hughenden Road towards the flat.

"Bugger," he muttered and shook his head, "I forgot the milk." About turning, he retraced his steps and walking again on Great Western Road, headed towards the Premier shop at the corner of Kirklee Road and while doing so, continued his thoughts of Moira. Dark haired and with a smile that would stop a rampaging bull, he remembered the first time he met the Lewis girl he had come to know and love. He had been a year out of his apprenticeship and working on a building site when after losing an argument with a large slab of masonry, the site foreman, keen to avoid any problems with the Health and Safety people, reluctantly run Tommy with his badly bruised hand to the casualty department of Gartnavel Hospital. After being X-rayed and confirming nothing was broken, the young Staff Nurse had bandaged his wound. Mistaking her lilting accent as Irish, she had gently rebuked him but laughed when he confessed he was just an ignorant Weegie from Partick who had never ventured further than Saltcoats.

A two-minute bandaging turned into a ten-minute conversation that finished abruptly when Moira was called away by the duty Sister, but not before a whispered agreement to meet him for coffee after she finished her shift.

It was months later that he confessed he had stood in the chilly cold outside the casualty department with his arm in a sling for almost two hours waiting for her.

Still living at that time with his widowed mother, Tommy and Moira spent every free hour together until at last he persuaded her that the money she paid for her accommodation at the Nurses Quarters and what he earned as a brickie could together be enough to rent them a flat.

"Are you asking me to move in with you?" she had stared chastely and suspiciously at him.

"No," he had taken a deep breath and remembered how dry his mouth was when he'd replied, "I'm asking you to marry me."

He stopped walking and smiled. So engrossed in his memories he had not realised he was at the shop and pushing open the door, with a smile called out, "Hello, Missus Ahmed. Two litre milk carton, please, and how are the weans getting on these days?"

****

He was opening the secure entrance door to the flats when his mobile phone beeped with an incoming text message.

Swapping the carton of milk to his left hand, Tommy fetched the phone from his jacket pocket and grinned when he saw the text was from his daughter, Jennifer, and simply read: *Phone me now.*

So, he thought, the word is out.

Climbing the stairs to his second floor flat, he pressed the button for her number to be greeted with, "So, what's this about you moving to Arran?"

Redheaded like her older sister Fiona, his youngest daughter was jokingly referred to as the son he never had. Abrupt, sharp tongued and quick tempered, Jenny didn't suffer fools and never beat about the bush.

"I'm not moving to Arran," he grinned as he spoke. "I'm considering buying a house there so that we all…"

"And when were you going to break this news, Pops?"

He sighed and stopped on the half landing to calmly reply, "I wanted to run it past Fiona first, then I was going to let you and Vicky know, okay? So, stop bullying me, you redheaded devil."

"Fiona says she's going with you tomorrow. Can I come too?"

"No. You've the wee lad to see to and with Andy working all sorts of hours the now, I don't want you fobbing Cillian off to anyone else, particularly after he's just getting over that virus."

"I could bring him with me?"

"No, and that's final, Jennifer. When I've seen the house and *if* I intend buying it, there will be time enough for you to travel to the island to see it."

Using her full name, he knew she would realise he was serious, but still she asked, "Have you told Vicky yet?"

"What? You don't think your big blister having phoned you won't already have been on the blower giving her the lowdown too on what

I'm doing?"

"Point taken. So, you haven't spoken with her yet?"

"No," he sighed, "but likely there will be a call before I get to the flat."

"Why? Where are you now?"

"On the half landing downstairs."

"Oh. When will I see you?"

God, give me a break from this role reversal, he tightly smiled as he shook his head and before replying, "Well, I'm off to Arran tomorrow, so how about breakfast on Thursday at that little café in Dumbarton Road, round the corner from your flat?"

"And you'll bring the photos of the house?"

"Yes," he sighed again and smiling, asked, "Can I go now? I really need to pee."

"Too much information, Pops. Love you."

"Love you too," he softly replied, but she had already ended the call. In the flat he switched on the kettle then milked a mug before adding coffee and while it boiled, went to the loo.

Drying his hands, he heard the phone ring and hurrying into the bedroom lifted it from the cradle.

"Dad, it's me," said Victoria. "What's this about you buying a house in Arran?"

He smiled and in his mind pictured his middle daughter, dark-haired like her mother with the same sensuous mouth and brown eyes that sparkled when she laughed.

"I am *not* moving to Arran," he unconsciously shook his head. "Like Fiona undoubtedly told you, I'm travelling over tomorrow to view a house and that's it. If I *do* buy the house, it will be a retirement present to me that we as a family can share. And before you ask, no, you can't come with me."

"Oh, I wasn't going to suggest that. Besides, this wee bugger is still hanging off my breast and it's bloody tiring and wearing me down." She paused and in a soft voice, wistfully added, "I wish mum was here. I mean, my local health visitor is great and she's been very helpful, but still…"

"I know, hen," he interrupted, sensing Vicky was getting a little emotional. "Fergus is what, a couple months now? Maybe you should be thinking about increasing his bottle feeds. You're no use to the wee guy if you're always so tired. What about Mathew?"

"Oh, he's been great. Gets up in the middle of the night to give me a break and to be honest, he's half asleep going through to Edinburgh every other day to the parliament."

Tommy knew Vicky's husband Mathew, the Member of the Scottish Parliament for the Kelvinbridge area of Glasgow, to be a fine young man and utterly devoted to his wife and two month old son.

"What about getting someone in? Maybe a woman to help with the cleaning while you're still nursing the wee guy?"

"Mathew's suggested that, dad, but it's not the cleaning or nursing. I think maybe I'm going through a bit of postnatal depression or something like that. I just feel so tired and fed-up all the time."

He couldn't help but smile and replied, "Look, Vicky, for the last six years you've had a busy job working with the charity and you are always the first to admit you didn't have a lot of social time or time to yourself. Suddenly you find that your one responsibility is wee Fergus; caring for him and nursing him too and you're finding it difficult to relax. It's as if you've been on a high speed train then after giving birth, you're on the slowcoach to nowhere. Give yourself time to come down to earth. Enjoy this time with your son. The weather is about to take a turn for the better and you're living a stone's throw from Kelvingrove Park, so make use of your time and get out walking. The fresh air won't do the wee bugger any harm either and don't forget," he smiled, "I'm always on the lookout for a lunch partner."

"Thanks dad," she replied and he sensed she was a little cheerier. "It always helps when I talk to you. Anyway, on that point, when are you free for lunch?"

"Well, I've arranged to meet with your wee blister on Thursday morning for breakfast at that café around the corner from her flat, the place that does the good food…"

"You mean the St Louis Café Bar?"

"That's it. I like the breakfast there and they do the veggie stuff for you, don't they?"

"They do. Right then it's a date," she cheerily agreed. "I'll speak with Vicky and see you there. Bye."

He replaced the phone and exhaled. From the kitchen he heard the kettle click off as he wondered what he had done in life that was so right it gave him such smashing daughters.

CHAPTER THREE

She was still shaking when she closed the bedroom door behind her and sobbing, threw herself down onto the bed.

God, what have I done to deserve this, she wondered and to her shame, thought she was going to wet herself when he'd threatened her.

She could hear him downstairs, her ears picking up the tinkling of glass as he rummaged through the drinks cabinet.

It was her nightly hell.

She forced herself to be still and confident he was still in the lounge, slipped her shoes off and opened the door. As quietly as she could, she tiptoed along the hallway to Marcy's room and opening the door, saw the little girl sat on the bed, her back against the headboard and her arms wrapped abut her knees that were drawn up to her chin.

"Hello, sweetheart," she forced a smile and went to sit beside the little girl, drawing her into her arms.

"Did he hit you again?" she whispered in Alice's ear.

She choked back a response before replying in a soft voice, "No, your grandfather doesn't hit me, Marcy. I'm just a little careless and keep bumping into things."

"That's not true, Gran and I'm not a silly girl," she bent her forehead down into her knees. "I know he hits you. I've seen him do it."

Alice was at a loss how to respond for there was no answer to this statement that was not a lie.

"It's not quite as simple as what you think, sweetheart," she slowly said. "Your grandfather is under tremendous pressure, looking after people who come to him at his surgery. Sometimes he gets a little angry…"

"When he's drunk," the little girl spat out.

"Well, he does take a little drink, that's true, but…"

"And that's why he hits you, Gran? Because he's drunk or is it because he's a nasty old man and…"

"No, Marcy. You must never say that to him, that he's old."

"But he is old and…"

"Marcy, please," she turned to face the child, her face expressing her concern the little girl might blurt this out, for she better than anyone knew how vain her husband was about his looks and age, still believing himself to be a fit and handsome man though his intake of alcohol was now obvious by the broken capillaries on his face, the visible wrinkling of his skin, the flushed face, the yellowing of his eyes and the peppermints he persistently used to conceal the smell of whisky on his breath.

Only for the fact that Alice daily laid out his clean and ironed clothes and polished his shoes, her husband's personal grooming might have drawn comments from his many patients and colleagues.

However, what she knew was that Doctor Geoffrey Mayhew was considered by his peers and those he knew and the patients he tended to, to be a good and upstanding man, a pillar of the society in which he mixed and though perhaps a little arrogant, in essence an all round good man.

None of those who knew him would ever consider him to be the bully or the self serving egotist that in reality he was.

None would believe that he drove his own daughter from her home because he did not approve of the man she loved.

None would believe him to be a wife beater or disdainful of the orphaned grandchild in his care.

None would believe the good Doctor Mayhew to have an antisocial personality and to be an obsessive individual who exercised such control over his wife that she feared for her safety if she dared to disobey him.

Yet this was the man she was married to. The man to whom she was bound. The man who completely ruled and dominated her, her every action, her life.

And this was the man who now held sway over her granddaughter's life too.

Holding the child close to her, she could not know it, for there was no indication in her body or her mind, but Alice had made her decision.

Geoffrey would not ruin Marcy's life as he had ruined hers.

Of that she was determined and no matter the cost.

****

She had not slept well, hearing the noise of the large screen television from the lounge that was directly beneath her bedroom, the lounge that neither she nor Marcy were permitted access other than when Alice was cleaning the room.

No, several years previously Geoff had decided that the small portable television set in the spare bedroom was sufficient for Alice, that there was no need for her to use the any of the rooms downstairs other than to conduct her domestic duties.

These rooms he informed her, reminding her he being the sole income provider, were his preserve and his alone and so it had been since that time.

Not even the arrival of Marcy had changed his mind, informing Alice that if the child needed to watch TV then the set in her grandmother's room would suffice for them both.

Now, as the wall clock approached seven that morning, she prepared his cooked breakfast and patiently waited for him to complete his toilet before serving him in the dining room.

She heard him plodding down the stairs and hurriedly filled the plate, carrying it and the pot of coffee through to the dining room as Geoff was sitting down.

Wordlessly, he shook out a napkin that he placed on his lap, but as she turned to go he said, "Have that child minded tonight with that woman along the road. There's a function on at the club and wives will be expected to attend. Make sure you wear something decent, not that awful rag you wore the last time."

He stared irately and waved his hand at her before adding, "And do something about your bloody hair. You look like a farmer's scarecrow with that mop of yours," he shook his head.

"Yes, Geoffrey," she acknowledged with a nod and left the room.

In the kitchen she placed her hands flat onto the worktop and fought the urge to scream out loud.

A *function*, as he so succinctly put it, was just another opportunity for him to lord it over his fellow club members. She recalled with distaste the last time, now almost a year ago, when he had taken her to the club. He had not then been appointed Chairman, but almost as they passed through the door he was off making his round of the members to solicit votes for the upcoming election. Feeling abandoned, she had seen the compassionate stares from the other wives, but not because she had been left alone. No, she recognised the sympathy for what it was, for it was widely gossiped and with good reason that her husband was a womaniser, an adulterer who had tried it on with more than a few of the women present and likely, she guessed, succeeded.

The sound of the front door being closed caused her to sigh with relief and made her way through to the dining room to clear away the breakfast things.

That done, she hurried upstairs to Marcy's room to find the little girl already awake, but still in bed and reading a book.

"Morning, sweetheart," she sat on the bed and smiled at her granddaughter. "Sleep well?"

"Not too bad, but I had a funny dream about my mummy," she replied.

"Your mummy?"

"Yes," Marcy yawned. "She was holding my hand and telling me not to worry, that my Gran would take care of me."

Alice felt a lump rising in her throat and unexpectedly fighting back tears, reached forward to envelop the child in her arms.

"Gran," Marcy sighed as only a child can and shrugging her way out of Alice's grasp, asked, "Has he gone?"

"Yes, your grandfather is away to work."

"Good. Can I watch some tele before I go to school? Please?"

"Only if you hurry up, get washed and dressed…" she stopped. "No, tell you what. Go to the loo and get washed and bring your clothes downstairs. You can get dressed while your watching the cartoons, okay?"

"Great!" Marcy excitedly jumped from the bed and grabbing her towel from the radiator, headed for the bathroom.

****

After seeing Marcy through the school gates and waving cheerio, Alice was turning away to return home when she heard her name called.

"Missus Mayhew."

She stopped and was joined by the young faired haired woman, the police officer, she recalled, though again the name again escaped her.

Her face flushed, the younger woman pushed her child in the buggy as she hurried to join Alice and with a smile, asked, "How are you?"

Taken aback, Alice replied, "Eh, I'm fine, Thank you."

"Just heading home?"

"Yes," she replied, keen to be away before awkward questions began.

"Oh, I was wondering if I might treat you? St Clare's Parish Hall does a morning tea and coffee with cake, if you're interested? I was just about to head there myself and," she gushed, "I was hoping you might join me. It would be nice to have some adult company," she nodded with a grimace to the toddler in the buggy who was staring with curiosity at Alice.

"Oh, I'm sorry, but…"

"Please," the young woman pleaded.

She took a deep breath and biting at her lower lip, glanced at her wristwatch. There was no reason why she couldn't join this young woman and Geoffrey need not know.

With a sigh and a soft smile, she replied, "Why not."

As they walked, Alice blushed and admitted she had forgotten the young woman's name.

Smiling, she replied, "Lucy Carstairs. It's DC Carstairs when I'm working but when I'm at home it's Mum, can I get this or can I get that," she grinned.

"Lucy," Alice repeated. "I always liked the name Lucy. It was one of the names we considered for…" she stopped and took a breath before adding with a regretful smile, "for our daughter."

"Would that be Marcy's mum?"

"Yes. Her name was Gemma," she smiled, but her voice betrayed her sadness.

"I don't know anything about what happened, but like I told you, Marcy is friendly with my daughter Laura and she told Laura her parents died in a car accident. Is that right?"

"Yes. A year ago, now. In Hull. It was…dreadful. Poor Marcy was strapped into a booster seat in the rear and according to the police officer I spoke with, was lucky to have survived."

"I'm so sorry. I can't imagine the pain you must have suffered. You and your husband. It's fortunate," she slowly added, "that Marcy has two loving grandparents to care for her."

Alice cast her a sharp glance and wondered; was this young woman, this detective, prying?

However, her suspicions were slightly allayed as helping Carstairs with the buggy up the entrance stairs and pushing through the door into the hall, the younger woman turned and with a bright smile, asked, "Laura has been plaguing me to ask if Marcy can have a sleepover some time, so I was wondering; is that okay?"

"Oh, eh, yes, I suppose so," Alice nodded before admitting, "I've never really been asked that question before. I'm certain Marcy would be very pleased."

They entered the hall where about a dozen women of mixed ages were seated at the folding tables scattered throughout the room. Waiting to be seated they were greeted by a heavyset middle-aged woman with pink permed hair, her face caked with makeup and heavy rouged lips wearing an overly tight, short black skirt and bright yellow blouse that strained at the buttons. Flapping her arms and in a high pitched voice, the parishioner acting as a waitress called out in an obviously phony high pitched and snobby voice, "Please, take a seat anywhere and I'll be right with you."

Carstairs manoeuvred the buggy towards a corner and once they were seated the middle-aged waitress, a notebook in her hand took their order of tea and cake.

When the waitress was out of earshot, Alice couldn't understand why she was so nervous of this young woman and in a faltering voice, said, "You seem very young to be a detective."

Carstairs laughed and replied, "I'll take that as a compliment, Missus Mayhew…or may I call you Alice?"

"Oh, yes, of course. Alice is fine…Lucy," she blushed.

"And to answer your question, I'm thirty and by God there are days when I feel it, isn't there James?" she smiled and poked a finger at her toddler son's tummy who strapped in the buggy, squealed with delight.

"And is your husband a police officer too?"

"Mike? No, thank heavens," she exhaled as though in relief. "I don't think we'd cope if we were both in the job," and grimaced. "Mike's with the council. An architect. He works in their planning department and believe me, Alice, it's great that he's a five-day week worker. I work shifts so between us and my mother, we manage without having to hire a nanny or a babysitter." She stared curiously at Alice, a smile playing about her lips when she asked, "Unless you're volunteering for the job?"

"Me? Oh, no," she waved her hands in front of her, horrified at what Geoffrey's reaction might be if she agreed to be a nanny before realising that Carstairs was joking and smiled. "I do love children, but things are a little awkward at the minute," but immediately regretted her comment when Carstairs asked, "Oh? Is everything okay? Is there anything that I can help with?"

"No, no," she almost panicked. "What I mean is my husband's job, being a doctor. He's in and out of the house at all hours, you know? Tending to his patients. On call, that sort of thing and likes me to be available if he needs me for anything," her voice tailed off as she shrugged and fervently hoped the young woman would not press the issue.

As if satisfied with the explanation, Carstairs smiled in understanding and was about to speak when the waitress returned with a tray bearing the pot of tea, crockery and a cake stand.

"Here we are, ladies," she placed the teapot down onto the table, spilling some from the spout as she did so. "Now, just help yourselves to whatever cakes you want," she fluttered her eyes like a sexually precocious Lolita before clapping her hands and adding, "it's all in the set price." Almost as an afterthought, she added, "And the cakes are made with low calorie sugar because," she winked outrageously, "we girls have to look after ourselves and our figures, don't we?"

Giggling, she waddled off leaving the stunned Carstairs to quietly comment, "Low calorie sugar? If that woman lost six stone she'd still be overweight."

Alice stared wide-eyed at Carstairs, then seconds later burst into uproarious laughter, causing more than a few of the other seated women to turn to stare curiously and wonder what caused such hilarity.

Carstairs began to giggle at Alice who was now bent almost double with tears running down her cheeks.

It took almost a full minute for her to compose herself and dabbing with her handkerchief at her eyes, slowly exhaled before shaking her head at Carstairs and telling her, "Sorry, but I think I needed that. Phew," she exhaled. "You're not wrong, though. If her skirt stretched any tighter, when she moved it would give her friction burns on her backside," she said, her body quivering when she started hysterically laughing again.

"My God," Carstairs grinned at her, "and there was me thinking you were such a stuffed shirt, Alice Mayhew!"

Alice, calm now, exhaled again and smiling at Carstairs, disclosed, "I'm so glad you asked me to come with you. You can't imagine how long it has been since I laughed like that. My only regret is that poor woman was the butt of the joke."

Her unfortunate reference to 'butt' started her off again and she burst into a fit of giggling.

Composed again, she wiped the tears from her eyes and breathless, said, "Honestly, I'm not really like that. I don't take pleasure in someone's else misfortune."

"What, being the whale shape she is," Carstairs replied, but the remark only set Alice off again.

Once more, when Alice finally calmed down, Carstairs poured the tea and handed the bemused James a cake that disappeared within seconds, but left a trail of crumbs and jam across his face.

"Sorry," she shamefacedly smiled at the younger woman.

"Not at all, Alice. Laughter, I understand, is good for the soul so perhaps we can meet again and share another joke?"

"Yes, I'd like that, Lucy," then caught up in the moment of friendship and to her own surprise, recklessly added, "and next time I'll foot the bill for the tea. Now, about this sleepover."

****

It was an hour later, an hour of idle chitchat about everything and nothing, that the two women finally left the hall.

Before retracing her route along Sharoe Green Lane, Carstairs took her leave of Alice at the roundabout junction with Sherwood Way, telling her, "This is me here," and pointing along the road towards the entrance to the modern housing estate.

"Oh, have you always lived there?"

"No, Mike and I moved here about six weeks ago, though we did live in the area. We needed a bigger house but with Laura already at school and loving it there, we decided to stay local." After agreeing that Marcy would stay over with the Carstairs one night the following week and that Lucy would bring the little girl to school with her daughter Laura, the two women said cheerio and to Alice's delight and surprise, Carstairs gave her a parting hug.

"Bye," she waved at Alice as she walked off.

So full of thought about making a new friend, Alice did not notice the blonde haired woman driving the yellow coloured Mini Clubman who slowed to negotiate the roundabout and stared curiously at her as the car passed by.

Several minutes passed before Carstairs, confident that Alice was now well gone, stopped in her driveway to fetch her mobile phone from her handbag and dialled the number.

The call was answered by a female who curtly said, "DI Sandford."

"Ma'am, it's me, DC Carstairs. I've made the contact and it seemed to go well."

CHAPTER FOUR

Much earlier that day and a little over one hundred and eighty miles to the north, Tommy Burke swung his legs from the bed and opened the curtains to find it was a bright and sunny morning.

The digital clock by his bed read almost six-thirty and pushing the button, he smiled with pleasure at beating the alarm.

He had arranged to uplift his daughter Fiona by taxi from her Whittingehame Drive home at seven-thirty to enable them to catch the eight-forty train from Glasgow Central station to Ardrossan Harbour.

Shaved and showered, he dressed in a light blue coloured dress shirt, navy blue tie, a navy blue pinstriped suit and black patent leather shoes. Truth be told, Tommy wasn't comfortable wearing suits these days, not since he had left the boardroom behind, but recognised that if things went as he hoped today, he might be spending a lot of money and wanted to be taken seriously.

"Like it or lump it," he recalled Moira telling him in her quiet Lewis accent, "clothes maketh the man and if you dress like a scruffy git, Tommy Burke, people will treat you like a scruffy git. Not everyone sees the man inside, like I do."

Examining himself in the full length mirror, he nodded in agreement, but more because Moira was seldom wrong.

Pity I can't do anything about this gruff Weegie accent, he thought as he smirked at the mirror.

In the modern and very expensive replacement kitchen, he had a light breakfast of decaffeinated coffee with two toasted slices of wholemeal bread, each with a light scraping of light margarine and topped with half a squashed banana. He'd much prefer to have real butter or even better, a couple of rolls and square sausage, but his last annual physical indicated a slight rise in his cholesterol and so promised his daughters he'd take better care of his health.

His eyes narrowed as he recalled his youngest, Jenny, once tearfully telling him, "I've lost my mum far too soon. I do *not* want to lose you too, so please, for my sake, take care of your health, Pops."

Since then, every time he had the urge to splurge out on a kebab or a full fat cooked breakfast, her warning haunted him like a gremlin sitting on his shoulder.

It was only every now and then, these days, he surrendered to the occasional full fry up.

He glanced at the wall clock. The taxi was due in a couple of minutes and ensuring he had his wallet, the property schedule and in the event he made a speedy offer for the property, his passport for identification, he packed the paperwork into his old, stressed leather briefcase and grabbing his raincoat, headed for the front door.

****

He stepped out of the black hackney cab to open the door for Fiona and involuntarily smiled.

His daughter was a looker, right enough and half turning, saw the young cab driver's eyes widen as he too appreciated the good looking young woman who stooped at the front door to kiss her daughter Cissie goodbye.

Wearing a three quarter length sleeveless emerald green dress, matching green handbag and high heels with her long red hair pinned up into a bun and carrying a bottle green rain coat over her arm, Fiona looked like a young model on the catwalk as she strode down the garden path.

"Morning, daddy," she greeted him with a peck, then rubbed her finger on his cheek to wipe off the lipstick smudge.

Settled in the cab and en route to the railway station, he explained that he'd considered taking his vehicle across on the ferry, but instead decided to be escorted to the property by the selling estate agent, a young woman called Shona Mulveigh who would meet them at the ferry terminal in Brodick.

"Well, I'm glad we're travelling by train," her eyes narrowed. "Why you insist on keeping that old Land Rover, I just do not know. I mean, daddy, you can afford whatever car you want these days."

"I like my old Defender," he smiled at her. "It's just the job for when I go for long walks up to the Trossachs and the Campsies and being a four-wheel drive, it's unlikely I'm going to get stuck anywhere. Can you see a Maserati or a Bentley pulling me out of the mud?" Fiona scowled in pretend disgust and then asked, "How will she recognise us? The estate agent I mean?"

"What? I don't look like a distinguished Glasgow millionaire?" he joked.

"Actually, when you scrub up and shave you do look quite presentable," she nodded at him, "but that doesn't answer my question."

"Oh, we'll recognise *her*. Her photograph is on the schedule," he grinned.

****

The train journey took just fifty minutes before arriving at the Ardrossan Harbour where they collected their pre-booked tickets from the ferry terminal building and with some time to kill, bought cardboard beakers of coffee before making their way outside to enjoy the sunshine and watch the CalMac ferry berth.

The trip across was just under an hour during which time Tommy and his daughter, seated in the ships main lounge area, laughed as they reminisced about their family holidays in Arran, though the memories were tinged with a little sadness when they recognised that Moira had not lived to enjoy not only the wealth Tommy had accumulated during his working life, but their retirement together.

"What do you miss most about mum?" she unexpectedly asked him.

"Whoa, that's not an easy question to answer," his brow furrowed. He thought for a moment then slowly exhaling, shrugged as he replied, "I miss her wit, her down to earth common sense, her love of life and the uncompromising love she had for you and your sisters. And me of course," he added with a smile. "I miss when sometimes a joke would go right over her head and she'd get annoyed because she didn't get it and everybody else did."

"That *was* funny," Fiona smiled. "Mum had a good sense of humour, but woe betide anyone who took the mickey out of her."

"Aye, love her as I did, she could be bloody obstinate and petulant when she wanted to be. When she burst out and started ranting in the Gaelic, I'm almost certain she was swearing at me, but of course she'd never admit to using bad language. And her temper," he shook his head. "I remember once before you were born we'd been married for about a year I think it was when I had earned a big bonus on a building site…" he stopped to explain, "This was before your mum persuaded me to go it alone and set up the business, you see. Anyway, I arrived home having had a really big swally with the lads off the site and pissed as I was, forgotten we were supposed to be going to the pictures that night. Well, after dinner, I mean. Anyway, drunk as a skunk I went in the door to be met by your mum who had finished her shift earlier that afternoon, raced home from the hospital to make a lovely curry and when I didn't show…" he grinned, "I ended up wearing the curry on my head."

"She never did!" Fiona laughed.

"Oh, aye," he nodded. "The full pot. And I ended up having to clean the carpet too!"

He shook his head and smiling, added, "But I do miss her dreadfully."

"Well," she reached for his hand, "you've got us girls to remind you of her and don't you think Cissie is looking a wee bit like her too?"

"Well, apart from the red hair that Cissie and you and Jenny get from my side of the family, she has your mum's eyes but then again, so have you."

The tannoy blared with the message that drivers were to return to their vehicles for through the windows they could see the ship was approaching Brodick Pier.

"When was the last time you visited Arran," she unexpectedly asked him.

"Ah, well, I've a wee confession to make about that. You know how mum

had said when she died she wanted cremated, but she didn't mind where her ashes were scattered and joked they could go in the dustbin?"

Fiona nodded.

"Well," he slowly exhaled, "you might also remember that even though through the years and after the business took off we had travelled abroad on our cruises, then visited Spain, Italy, France and several other places, your mum thought the most beautiful spot in the world was the land and the views from Goatfell Summit in Arran. Strange when you consider it," he wryly grinned. "All those smashing and bloody expensive foreign holidays and her favourite place was just over an hours drive from Glasgow. Anyway, about a month after the cremation I collected her urn and came over here for a couple of days with the Land Rover. I stayed in the Corrie Hotel that night then the next day drove up to the Summit where I scattered her ashes around the cairn."

"I remember you coming over to Arran," her eyes narrowed. "I think at the time the girls and me just thought you needed a few days to yourself."

He glanced curiously at her and asked, "You don't mind, do you? About me alone scattering her ashes."

"No, dad," she thoughtfully shook her head and before continuing, "I've a confession too, for what you don't know is the girls and I had decided that it was too painful for you to deal with mum's ashes and we would collect them, but when Vicky contacted the funeral director he told her that you had already called for them. We knew then that you must have a plan and the three of us made the decision not to interfere. But I'm glad you told me. Mum would have been very happy with that."

He fought back a sob and to cover his embarrassment, blinked rapidly and getting to his feet, held out his hand to Fiona and said, "Right, well, let's get ourselves together and meet this young woman, Shona."

****

Shona Mulveigh, a short, stick thin young woman in her mid-twenties with collar length mousey fair hair and wearing a cream coloured jacket and navy blue flared trousers, stood nervously on the pier clutching a folder to her chest as she scanned for her prospective client among the disembarking foot passengers.

Believing him to be travelling alone, she mentally dismissed the well dressed middle-aged man and the glamourous young redheaded woman on his arm who surprised her when the man reached his hand towards her and said, "Shona? I'm Tommy Burke. Thank you for meeting us."

Startled, she held out her hand and dropped her folder at his feet. Both bending to lift it, they inadvertently bumped heads and she almost fell back, but was grabbed by Fiona who smiling, said, "I'm as shocked as you. My father doesn't usually have that effect on women."

Grinning, Tommy rubbed at his forehead and introduced his daughter who also shook the younger woman's hand, though a little more warily than did her father.

Flustered now, Mulveigh stammered, "My car's just over here," and led them out of the port to a parking bay on the main road adjacent to the pier and almost directly opposite the Douglas Hotel.

Tommy courteously allowed Fiona to occupy the front passenger seat of Mulveigh's rusting, three-door grey coloured Fiat Panda and who immediately apologised for the condition of her car.

"I'm saving up for a new motor," she explained, "and hoping to trade this in."

She'll be lucky to get a fiver for scrap for this wreck, Fiona unkindly thought, but dutifully smiled.

"I'm holding down two jobs to raise the cash," Mulveigh continued, "doing a bit of bar work in the evenings and at the weekends."

During the journey when she turned to glance at him, he raised his eyebrows at Fiona's tight smile, for throughout the five minutes' drive from the pier to where the property was located in Glencloy Road, the young woman never stopped talking, but whether from nerves or she was just a gossip, he couldn't quite determine.

By the time they reached the property, Tommy and Fiona learned the young woman was newly single having broken up a week previously with her boyfriend of two years, owned two cats, lived with her mother who was divorcing her alcoholic second husband and who preferred the cats to him, hated cheese but was partial to vodka, preferred Adele to Rhianna and already had three points on her driving license, though that was a story for another time, she sighed as well as to Tommy and Fiona's unspoken relief.

When she stopped outside the property, she switched off the engine and glancing with a smile at Tommy, told him, "If you give me a minute, please, I'll just confirm the owners have left the house to permit us the viewing."

Watching her walk through the garden gate to the house, Fiona turned and in a stage whisper, said, "My God, does she never stop talking? That lassie should be fitted with a pause button."

Tommy grinned and patting at his daughter's shoulder, replied, "I think she's wee bit nervous, hen. According to the estate agents schedule she sent me, it describes Shona as a recent addition to the team, so I'm guessing this might be one of her first sales."

"Oh, look, she's waving us in," Fiona said and opened the passenger door.

As they walked along the path towards the large, detached house, Tommy could not but be impressed and casting a professional eye over the few areas of exposed brickwork and the roof, wordlessly nodded his approval.

The white painted roughcast walls and black tiled roof, the large but neatly trimmed and low maintenance lawn and the wide path laid out with perfectly symmetrical flagstones led to an impressive entrance porch.

"So far, so good," Fiona murmured beside him.

To Tommy's surprise, Mulveigh opened the unlocked door and then beckoning them inside, began the delivery of her practised speech, walking backwards and arms flailing as she spoke.

"If you recall the layout plan in the schedule, the large entrance hallway has doors that lead to the open plan kitchen with the dining room and a utility room off the kitchen," she waved a hand. "These doors," she turned to indicate them in turn, "lead to the main lounge and to the sitting room with attached conservatory. This door," she opened it with a flourish, "leads to a small lounge currently used as a TV room. This door, to a small but comfortable study and this door to a downstairs loo with walk-in shower."

Fiona peered into the room and lips pursed, nodded her admiration for the brightly tiled room.

"On the upper floor," Mulveigh continued and waved to the white painted stairway, "there are four bedrooms, one of which is currently being used as a sitting room. The master bedroom has an en-suite and two further double bedrooms are also also en-suite." She paused and taking a deep breath, continued, "There is a family bathroom with a walk-in separate shower. Now, Mister…I mean, Tommy. You have the schedule with the rooms dimensions and no doubt you'll want to have a wander about the place yourself. I should add, all carpets, window blinds and curtains are included in the price."

"Really?" Fiona expressed surprise before asking, "Can you tell us why the owners are selling?"

"Eh," Mulveigh frowned, "as far as I'm aware, Mister and Missus Campbell are moving abroad. She's a Canadian and I believe they intend retiring out there."

Leaning closer as though divulging a great secret, her voice lowered when she added, "The word is their daughter and son-in-law and their children emigrated a year ago and Missus Campbell misses the kids. Anyway," she sniffed, "that's what I heard."

"I'm guessing it's a very quiet road outside, Shona, and the schedule said there's a detached garage?"

"Oh, yes. We can see that later when you view the grounds. It's a double garage too and there's a tool shed at the back fence."

"A double garage should be big enough for your old Land Rover, dad," Fiona smiled.

Tommy returned her smile then turning towards Mulveigh, said, "If the owners don't mind us having a poke about, hen, why don't you relax while Fiona and I have a look around."

****

It was while they were in the roomy master bedroom that Fiona said, "I read recently that buying a house is the biggest outlay that most people make, yet spend the shortest time inspecting the property before making that decision. So, what's your gut feeling, dad?"

He didn't immediately respond, but slowly nodded and casting a glance about him, moved to stare through the panoramic window. Though the house was built on the level and overlooked the road outside, the shrubbery filled ground on the other side of the road swept down in a gently slope towards the harbour area to present a spectacular view of Brodick Bay.

To the rear of the house and beyond the property fence line, the land gently rose towards the hills and was covered in dense forest.

He and Moira had struggled in their early years, then when the business took off were financially secure to purchase holidays and luxuries they had never dreamed of. Still, he had learned from her that to buy in haste was to regret at leisure, yet there was something about this property, some inner sense telling him he should make it his own.

"I like it," nodding, he softly replied at last. "You know, hen, never in my wildest dreams when your mum and I were first together would I ever imagine being able to afford a house like this. It's beautiful and being modern, there's nothing needing done to it. Even the décor," he waved a hand towards the walls, "is bright and fresh. It's in a real move in condition, isn't it?"

"Well yeah, I can see the owners have certainly spent a lot of money on it and…" her eyes narrowed. "Wait a minute, dad. You're not *really* thinking about moving here full time, are you? I mean, I know you said…"

He raised a hand to stop her and smiling, replied, "Like I told you, I'm looking for somewhere to spend some of my retirement time. Somewhere we can all share as a family."

"Anyway," he teasingly asked, "even if I did come over to the island full time, it's not as if I'd be a million miles away. Heavens, it took us what, under an hour on the train and less than an hour on the ferry to get here. I mean, if you wanted me back in Glasgow to mind Cissie, I would leave first thing on the ferry and be with you before eleven o'clock."

"You are thinking of moving over here, aren't you?" she accused him. "Admit it."

"No," raising a hand, he smiled at her persistence. "I'm telling you, I haven't made up my mind yet, but it is a thought and besides, look at this place. It's lovely, isn't it?"

"Yes, it is," she sighed.

"Right, let's get downstairs and have a wee chat with Shona…"

"You mean Miss Motormouth?"

"Now you're being cruel," he smiled, "though you're not far wrong."

****

To the younger woman's delight, he asked her to drive to the Douglas Hotel across the Shore Road from the harbour where Tommy insisted she join them for lunch.

Desperately keen to obtain a decision, Mulveigh asked, "So, am I to assume you like the property?" Her eyes bright and seated opposite Tommy, she was unaware that a tiny sliver of potato was slowly working its way from the corner of her mouth to her chin.

"I do like the house, yes," he nodded, fighting a grin and conscious that sat on his left, Fiona desperately wanted to tell the younger woman about the flake of potato, "and I have a couple of questions that I would like you to pass to the owners. Now, you mentioned they plan to emigrate to Canada?"

"As far as I'm aware, yes," she nodded, wondering where this was going.

"If so, what's their intention regarding their furniture?"

"Their furniture? I'm sorry, what do you mean?"

"What I'm asking, Shona, is it seems obvious to me the owners have good taste. If I were to buy the house I would need to furnish it, however, other than personal items like their wall prints and bedding, things like that, if they intend disposing of their furniture I'd be happy to offer them a price for the house and the contents. It would not only save me a great deal of trouble, but the purchase could be a kind of lock, stock and barrel buy, if you see what I mean?"

She unconsciously laid her cutlery on to her plate and brow furrowed, said, "I've never been asked that kind of question."

Probably never sold a bloody house either, Fiona unkindly thought and unable to resist it any longer, irritably lifted her own napkin to wipe at Mulveigh's mouth.

"Sorry," she grimaced, "but us girls have to look after each other, don't we?"

Mulveigh hardly noticed Fiona's wiping of her mouth, so engrossed was she with Tommy's suggestion, but then replied, "I'll certainly ask. Can you give me a couple of minutes?"

Scraping back her chair, she lifted her handbag from the floor and hurried out from the restaurant to the hotel reception area.

"You didn't get to ask the other question, dad. What is it?"

"I was going to ask about the time frame for the purchase, but we'll see how she gets on with that question first."

CHAPTER FIVE

She didn't return immediately home, but continued towards the mid-terraced house in the affluent Middleton Road, a short five-minute walk away.

Her knock on the black painted wooden door was answered by grey haired Doris Chisholm, a stoutly built woman in her late sixties with flushed cheeks who smiled and said, "Alice, how nice to see you again. Come in, please, come in," she ushered her through the door.

Alice breathed in the smell of home made bread and with a nervous grin, said, "Actually, Doris, I'm here to ask a favour of you."

"Let me guess," the older woman raised a hand to her chin as though in thought before brightly replying, "You need a babysitter for that lovely young granddaughter of yours."

"Just overnight, if it's not too much trouble. Geoffrey sprung it upon me before he left for the surgery this morning. Some sort of function at his club," she sighed.

"Yes, of course my dear, I'll be happy to keep Marcy overnight, but I seldom drive my old jalopy these days unless it's an emergency or something, so you'd need to collect her for school in the morning." Doris grasped Alice's hands in her own before adding, "But I'll keep her only if you stay for a cuppa. I've just lifted a freshly baked loaf from the oven, so we can have some nice toast."

****

Seated at Doris's scrubbed wooden kitchen table, the two women were enjoying their tea and toast when Alice nodded to a small oil painting framed in dark wood wood that hung on the wall and with a smile, said, "I've always liked that picture. The scene seems so, oh, I don't know, tranquil I suppose is the word I'm looking for. Is it a real place or an artist's vivid imagination of what a lake and the hills should look like?"

"Actually, it's not a lake, dear. It's a loch and it *is* real. It's Loch Tanna on the island of Arran in Scotland. My husband bought me that almost fifty years ago, when we were on honeymoon."

Alice smiled with surprise and said, "I didn't realise you honeymooned in Scotland. I thought, oh I don't know why, that you and Stephan went off on some sort of glamourous adventure, trekking across the Arabian desert or fighting your way through a jungle in the mysterious far east. You just strike me as being that sort of person," she continued to smile.

"Oh, let me assure you, Alice, Scotland has it's own glamour. Stephen and I spent several weeks touring in an old caravan we bought for sixty quid from his uncle and my God," she laughed, a real belly laugh that brought tears to her eyes, "the bloody thing was held together by string and tape and what a time we had, island hopping on the tightest of budgets. Yes," she took a breath to calm herself and exhaling, wistfully stared at the painting, "those were the best of times."

They sat in silence for a few seconds, lost in their own thoughts, but broken when Doris quietly asked, "And speaking of husbands, how is the good Doctor Mayhew? Still lording it over all and sundry?" Alice was aware of her friends opinion of Geoffrey and being the only confidante she had, more than once confessed to Doris about his bullying and dominant behaviour against Alice.

"Oh, he's not changed," she replied, trying to avoid sounding bitter, but failing miserably. "Still won't acknowledge Marcy and ignores her very presence. It's heart-breaking to watch, but what can I do?"

"You can leave the bugger, is what you can do," Doris snapped back, but realising she was sounding too simplistic, that they had been over this ground countless times before, reached across the table to gently hold Alice's hand and continued, "A good lawyer would take him apart in a divorce court, love. And you know that even though you have no family, you needn't have to worry about you and little Marcy finding somewhere to live. My God," she grinned and theatrically waved a hand about her. "This is a three-bedroom house and I only need one and with the added bonus that Marcy needn't change school."

"He would never agree to that," Alice sighed.

"Agree to it?" Doris sat bolt upright and thundered, "He wouldn't have any say in it. You pack your bags, my girl and walk out on him. See what his wife leaving him will do for the bugger's reputation and let's face it; that's a pretty important issue for him around here."

"Oh, I don't know, Doris, it all sounds to simple and besides," her face was etched with worry, "he's far too smart for me. I would be the villain, taking his grandchild from him. You just don't know him like I do."

"You'd prefer to remain and have him terrorise you? Use you as a punch bag when it suits him?" Doris's face was studiously pale. "You know that eventually you'll be so cowed the thought of leaving will never occur to you. You'll become like one of those dogs, you know, one of the dogs that Russian psychiatrist experimented on. Running about after him every time he clicks his fingers."

Alice smiled. "I think you mean Pavlov and he was a physiologist, not a psychiatrist and he didn't click his fingers; he used a bell."

"Whatever, but I didn't mean Pavlov, I meant Geoffrey and you," Doris icily replied, then waved away her explanation before continuing. "Anyway, you know exactly what I'm talking about, my girl."

Alice visibly sagged in her chair and shaking her head, softly replied, "You're right, of course, but you don't understand how hard it is, what you're asking of me."

"I'm sorry to be so blunt, my dear, dear friend, but it's not you that I'm wholly concerned about, Alice. You are a mature woman who deals with this man day in and day out. You cope, though why still confuses me," she softly sighed. "It's your granddaughter who concerns me. And you need to consider the effect his treatment of you is having on Marcy."

"What do you mean?"

She didn't immediately respond as she sought the right way to present her argument, then said, "Children will pick up on emotions a lot quicker than an adult. Marcy's what now, eight?"

Alice nodded.

"Well, my experience is that about her age children are already developing their sense of self worth and as they mature, develop more complex emotions such as shyness, embarrassment, shame, elation and so on. I haven't seen or spoken with Marcy for several months, but I'm in no doubt that during that time and likely since she began living with you and…and him," she almost spat the word out, "she will have seen the way he treats you. Not just his cold attitude, but the violence too. I have little doubt that what she witnesses will impact upon her fragile mind and if not immediately, must surely have some long term consequence." Her eyes narrowed as she asked, "have you noticed any recent changes in Marcy? Her behaviour or anything out of the ordinary?"

"Doris," a cold hand clutched at Alice's heart and she could feel her throat tighten, "you're beginning to worry me."

"Well, I believe you should be worried, Alice. Like it or not, you have the responsibility for a child's upbringing and development and that's nothing to be taken lightly. In one fell swoop, that little girl lost both her parents and as the only remaining family she has, her grandparents should be supportive and concerned for her welfare. But let's consider what she does she have. Yes, a grandmother who loves and cares for her, but according to what you have related in the past, you are a wife who lives in fear of her husband who not only physically neglects you and abuses you, but also shuns his only grandchild too. My God, Alice, *what* must be going through the little girl's head?"

"We've been through this before," she glanced at her watch.

"You're doing it again," Doris tightly smiled with a shake of her head.

"Doing what?"

"As soon as I get under your skin about leaving that monster of a husband of yours, you're clock watching and looking for an excuse to leave."

"I am not," Alice pretended indignation.

"Then stay for dinner here, with me. Fetch Marcy from school and use my phone to call him and tell him to stick his club function up his fucking arse, that you refuse to go with him."

"Doris!" she pretended outrage at the old woman's language.

"But you won't," Doris sighed and slowly shook her head.

They sat in silence for a moment before Alice rose from the table and said, "I'd better get home. I've the place to tidy and my hair to do and…" she stopped and leaning across the table, pressed her hand to that of Doris's and said, "Thank you, for being concerned. You're the only true friend I have."

"Then, if that's true, Alice dear, start *listening* to me."
****

Though the time spent with the young police woman and her friend Doris was pleasant, Alice realised it threw her routine out of synch and hurrying home, began in earnest to clean the already clean house. She knew the carpets did not really require to be hoovered, however, though he had been unaware, years earlier she had seen Geoffrey deliberately drop a small piece of piece of lint on the lounge carpet near to the wall and upon his return home that evening from the surgery, warily watched as he marched straight to the lounge to where the lint was dropped to check if the carpet had been hoovered. It was also his daily practise to run his fingers along skirting boards and door lintels to check for dust.

Hanging her coat in the closet, she shivered at the memory some months previously when he discovered dirt stains in the utility sink after she had cleaned Marcy's school shoes.

The discovery had earned her not just a rebuke, but her head held firmly in his grasp by her hair when he shoved face down into the sink and snarled, "If I can see the fucking mud stains, so should you!"

She did not make that mistake again.

Weary but satisfied the house was at its usual high standard of cleanliness, she made her way upstairs to her room to decide what dress she would wear to that evenings function.

Laying out her wardrobe, she shook her head at the poor choice. While Geoffrey regularly treated himself to new suits and shirts to accommodate his ever increasing waistline, for several years Alice had not been permitted to purchase any new clothes.

"I'm not made of bloody money," he would growl at her.

His only reluctant concession was the pitifully small allowance he permitted her, much of what she used in the Preston town centre charity shops to purchase clothes for the growing Marcy and necessary garments for herself. What he did not know was that the food budget sometimes permitted her to siphon off a few pounds that she carefully saved and concealed in an envelope in her underwear drawer.

Holding the dresses one by one against her body in the full length mirror, she thought it fortunate that even at the age of fifty-one, her figure had hardly changed over the years. Repeatedly trying the dresses one by one, she dithered on which to choose, but finally settled upon a red coloured floral pattern satin swing midi dress that she had bought three years previously in a Cancer Research charity shop and hoped that none of the female guests at the function were the donor.

Drained but continuing to stare at herself in the mirror, she sat down heavily onto the bed.

Her mind was a jumble of thoughts, but at the forefront of these thoughts was the conversation with Doris.

What if she did work up the nerve to leave Geoffrey, she wondered. Would he pursue her? Beg her to return? No, she shook her head. Geoffrey was many things, but he'd never lower himself to beg her for anything.

And yes, while undoubtedly Doris was kind, living with her could only be a short term measure, for Doris had her own grandchild, a young student Alice had not met but was aware often arrived unannounced to stay for weeks on end.

And as for Marcy.

Would Geoffrey be vile enough to demand the return of the child, even if he didn't really want her. How could she fight him in court with no money, no job prospects and not even a home to call her own? Besides that, he was a respected figure in Preston. Nobody knew or could guess that the man who was the senior partner in his practice, chaired his local rugby club and sat upon the committee of several local organisations was…she drew a sharp breath and unconsciously nodded; a bully and a wife beater. A man who privately disowned his daughter when she made the mistake of falling in love with a young man of whom he disapproved, no matter that Peter Benson was a loving husband and father to their daughter. The struggling young artist was on the verge of success when the tragic accident occurred that claimed his and Gemma's life.

And what do I owe him, she wondered? After all these years skivvying for him, what do I *really* owe him?

She closed her eyes to fight the tiredness that threatened to overcome her, resisting the temptation to fall backwards onto the bed and sleep and decided that a coffee was the caffeine she needed to stay awake and focused.

****

She had decided not to bring the little girl home, but instead took a plastic bag with overnight clothes for Marcy when she collected her from school.

She watched as her granddaughter, arm in arm with a fair haired girl she recognised as Laura Carstairs, hugged her friend goodbye before running to greet Alice.

Walking hand in hand, Marcy saw the plastic bag Alice carried and being told it was pyjamas and clean school clothes for the following day, was immediately excited to learn that she was staying over with Doris and even more excited when her grandmother asked, "How would you feel about an overnight stay some time with Laura?"

The little girl's enthusiasm tugged at Alice's heart that even though she had been deprived of so much, the simple pleasure of staying away for the night excited Marcy.

Arriving at Doris's house, the maternal woman greeted Marcy like one of her own and after a hurried farewell with Alice, run off to Doris's kitchen to help make yet more bread and as a special treat, fairy cakes.

 Stood at the door, Doris smilingly told her, "She'll be fine. Don't worry and try to have a nice evening. "I'll give you a call if…" she began to add, but stopped and grimacing, continued, "Sorry, I forgot. He won't let you have a mobile phone, will he?"

Alice wryly smiled before reminding the older woman, "Say's I don't need one, that if he needs to get me I'll always be at home unless I'm out shopping for groceries. Even then he times me," she sighed.

"Oh yes, the notebook in the car. Have you given any thought about what I said? What we discussed?"

"Every waking minute, Doris, and thank you, but we both know it won't happen."

She glanced at her wristwatch and saw she had just an hour before Geoffrey arrived home earlier than usual to ready himself for the function.

"I'd better be off. I'll be here first thing in the morning to get her to school. Thanks again, Doris," she hurried away before her friend again tried to persuade her to leave her husband.
****

She had showered and washed her hair and towel rubbing it dry, was wearing just her dressing gown when she heard the front door open and close.

Hurrying downstairs, her heart raced when she realised that Geoffrey was home even earlier than she expected and reaching the ground floor, called out, "Can I get you something, dear? A tea or coffee?"

She saw him place his leather medical bag on the floor under the hall table and slipping off his jacket, quietly replied, "Come here, Alice. I wish to have a word," before turning and walking into the lounge.

It was his quiet voice that filled her with dread, recognising it as his preamble to a complaint or worse, his rage.

Nervously, she wrapped the towel about her head and meekly followed him into the large room where she saw him take up a stance by the fireplace.

"Yes, Geoffrey?"

He didn't immediately reply, but then asked, "Tell me about your day."

"My day? Oh, there's really not much to tell," she forced a smile, conscious that her throat was constricting and suddenly finding it hard to breathe, her arms by her side and hands tightly gripped into fists as she forced her body to stop shaking.

"Tell me anyway," he smiled humourlessly and she sensed something was wrong.

"Well, I dropped Marcy at her school and called on my my friend Doris to arrange that she take Marcy overnight because of the function at your club, then I came home and like you told me, tried to do something with my hair," she tried to laugh, but even to Alice her voice sounded strange and squeaky.

He moved slowly towards her and she knew now something was definitely wrong.

"So that was your whole day then, Alice. Nothing else?"

"No, nothing that I can think would interest…"

His hand snaked suddenly up to seize her jaw in a vicelike grip, drawing her cheeks painfully together. She lifted her hand to prise his fingers off, but he was too powerful and all she could do was flail at his wrist.

"You're lying and I know you're lying," he hissed, his breath smelling of raw onions and without warning pushed her away.

She stumbled backwards and unable to prevent herself from falling, landed heavily onto her backside on the carpeted floor.

He stepped forward to bend over her and snarled, "You were seen speaking to a woman with a pram at the roundabout on Sharoe Green Lane. Who was she and why are you lying?"

Lips trembling, she stuttered, "She's just one of the mothers at the school. Her daughter is Marcy's friend. She took me for a coffee in the church hall, that's all it was. I didn't think…"

"No!" he loudly interrupted her, "You never fucking think! When I ask you a question, I want the truth, do you hear me? The truth, else you know what will happen to you, don't you?"

"Yes, Geoffrey," she remained flinching on the carpet, her head down and expecting a blow and knowing from bitter experience she dare not look at him when he was in this kind of mood, that he would see it as insolence.

"What's her name, this woman?" he turned away to lean his hands on top of the fireplace.

"Lucy," she softly replied, "I mean, Missus Carstairs."

"Carstairs?" he turned back towards her, his eyes narrowing, his voice lowering when he asked, "What's her husband's name?"

"I don't know…no, wait," dreading being caught out again with a lie. "She *did* tell me. It's Mike, Michael, I think. He works for the council."

"Ah, yes," he nodded in recognition. "Mike Carstairs. Scrum-half, good man," and then without looking at her, snapped, "Fetch me a coffee then go and get yourself tarted up for tonight. I don't want you embarrassing me and looking less than your best."

She shuffled to her feet and with a sob, her hand trying to ease the ache in her jaw, scrambled from the room.

****

He was too astute to risk driving to the club when he knew by the
end of the night he would likely end up drunk, so instructed Alice to
order a taxi to uplift them from the house.

Wearing his dinner suit, he stood impatiently by the front door and
idly played with his shirt cufflinks while in the downstairs bathroom,
Alice clipped on the silver earrings and critically examined her
reflection in the mirror above the wash hand basin. Leaning towards
the mirror and though she had applied make-up, she imagined she
could still see his thumb and fingerprints outlined on her cheeks.

"Taxi's here!" she heard him bellow and taking a deep breath,
unlocked the bathroom door and collecting her charcoal coloured
coat from the hallway coat stand, made her way downstairs to join
him.

The ten-minute journey with Geoffrey in the front seat was spent
mainly in silence, other than when the elderly driver asked if they
wished to book a return journey at the end of the night.

To her surprise, Geoffrey replied, "Yes, good idea, old man. Be at
the front door by ten, if you don't mind, to bring my wife home."

Turning in his seat, he said in a solicitous voice, "That suit you,
dear?"

She nodded, recognising that he was trying to appear to the taxi
driver to be an attentive husband, but Alice knew what ploy was
going through Geoffrey's head. She supposed he had already made
an alternative arrangement for the night, likely with the new woman
he was courting and if she guessed correctly, it was the blonde
receptionist at the practice, Debbie.

She caught the driver's eye in the rear-view mirror and smiling, he
replied, "I'll be there at ten, Missus Mayhew. Count on it."

"Thank you," she automatically smiled.

****

Their arrival through the front door of the plush club was greeted
with a round of applause and much back-slapping and handshaking
for Geoffrey, with a drink almost immediately pressed into his hand.
Grateful that she was ignored, Alice quietly slid into the rear of the
crowd and removing her coat, handed it to the young woman who
manned the small room where the coats were checked in.

On her way out, she hesitated as she glanced about her at the clusters
of men and women and was unaware of the interest she drew from a

group of five women and of the whispered comments her appearance provoked.

"That's her, isn't it? Geoffrey Mayhew's wife," asked one stocky, fifty years-old woman.

"Yes, that's her," agreed another. "Don't usually see her at these sort of things. I heard she keeps herself to herself and isn't very sociable."

"My God, what's she wearing?" sniffed another who stared disdainfully at Alice's dress, before mockingly adding, "That styles year's old."

"Not a bad looker, though," murmured a fourth with a candid comment that drew her some sceptical glances. "Good figure, clear skin and quite pretty for her age."

"How old do you think she is?" the youngest of the group hesitatingly asked.

"Oh, I'd heard he'd married a younger woman so I'm guessing she's what, mid forties perhaps? Certainly a few years younger than me," the stocky woman huffily offered what she believed was her expert opinion.

They would have been surprised had they known that Alice was in fact a year the woman's senior.

Stood alone among the crowds, she was embarrassed and though conscious of the stares and polite smiles from those around her, no one approached to speak with Alice; not until she felt a nudge at her arm and turned to see Lucy Carstairs smiling at her.

"Alice, how nice to see you here. I was under the impression," she continued in a stage whisper, "that this sort of thing wasn't quite your cup of tea."

As the clear and obvious interest in her faded away, Alice sighed with relief before replying, "I don't usually come to the club functions, no, but Geoffrey insisted. But what are you…" she stopped in understanding and nodding, said, "It's your husband, Mike. He's a player, isn't he?"

"Well, he is for the minute, the foolish man, but when his knee finally gives up on him…" she sighed. "He's in the second team. That's him over there," she turned and pointed to a tall and squarely built man with dark curly hair standing among a group of laughing men that surrounded Geoffrey Mayhew who clearly was holding court.

The bell rang for the club members and their guests to take their seats in the dining room.

"You'll be sitting with Geoffrey," Carstairs smiled, "but once we've risen from the table, I'll meet with you and we can have a drink, okay?"

She scurried off before Alice could explain that Geoffrey didn't like her drinking.

****

The meal lasted a little longer than was expected and mainly due to Geoffrey Mayhew's longwinded speech; a speech that drew much handclapping and many cries of *'Hear, hear'* and *'Good show'* from the increasingly drunken members when, as their new Chairman, he guaranteed success in the both the local league and county cup, then thumping a fist on the dining table and loudly called out "…at any cost." He received further cries of support when he individually called upon the club's up and coming young stars to stand-up to be recognised and led the thunderous applause.

Alice ate little and smiled on cue, but as the evening progressed was acutely aware of her husband's flushed face and slurred voice and privately pleased he was unlike to arrive home that night.

To her relief, the dinner concluded as the members returned to the main lounge to continue their drinking and the commencement of their raucous behaviour while the ladies, carrying their drinks, were ushered through to the smaller lounge for tea and coffee.

It was there that Alice met again with Lucy Carstairs who idly chatted, but caught her unawares when she remarked, "I see your bruise is healing."

Instinctively raising her hand to her left cheek, Alice smiled and replied, "Yes, I'm getting a little clumsy in my old age."

"Old age? My God, woman, look at you," Carstairs expressed surprise. "When was the last time you looked in a mirror, Alice Mayhew? You're what, forty-eight, forty-nine? God, woman," she shook her head and sighed. "I wish I had your skin. It's as clear as a bell, not a wrinkle to be seen and your hair, not a grey one in sight. How do you do it?"

Flushing with pleasure at the compliment, Alice leaned a little forward to confess, "Actually, I'm almost fifty-two, but to be honest these days I feel a *lot* older, believe me."

"No," Carstairs drawled unbelievingly at the admittance and with a sly look around her, continued in a low voice, "You won't know this, Alice, but you're the talk of the club. The gossiping busybodies here all believe you to be in your forties and a bit of a snob."

"A snob? Me?" she was surprised.

"Yes, well, because your husband usually arrives alone, the wives are of the opinion that you don't like the club…" she stopped and stared thoughtfully at Alice. "But that's not true, is it? It's nothing to do with you. It's him, your husband. He's the reason you aren't a regular here."

Taken aback and suddenly uncomfortable with the way the conversation was going, Alice glanced at the large decorative clock above the small bar and seeing it was quarter to ten, lied, "I'm sorry, Lucy, my taxi will be here any minute now. If you don't mind," she leaned across the younger woman to place her glass of orange upon a nearby table.

"Alice," Carstairs held her hand up and shaking her head, said, "I'm sorry. Please, that was inappropriate of me. Look, there's no need to rush off. We can share…" but tight-lipped, Alice shook her head and wordlessly turned to leave.

Carstairs bit at her lower lip and sighing, took a gulp of her wine. That did not go the way she intended and inwardly rebuked herself for being too pushy, aware that when she reported back to the DI there would be raised eyebrows.

Alice was shaking with annoyance when she collected her coat from the attendant, though not at Carstairs, but at how she failed to properly handle the probing question. Thanking the young cloakroom girl, she made her way through the brightly lit foyer to the front door.

Stood outside the front doors with her breath making a small cloud of vapour in the chill of the night air, she was buttoning the coat when she heard voices to her left.

Her eyes narrowed when ten metres away at the corner of the building and stood beneath a security light, she saw her husband in an apparent heated conversation with a tall, young blonde haired man she recognised from the dinner; one of the talented rugby players who had been praised and applauded during Geoffrey's speech.

Archer was his name, she vaguely recalled. Yes, certain now. Jonathan Archer.

Her eyes widened when she saw Archer place his hand of her husband's arm as though pleading with him, only for Geoffrey to roughly push the arm away and then with his other hand on the younger's man chest, thrust him back against the club wall.

She strained to hear what was being said, then thought she heard Archer hiss, "If you want to win," she lost the middle bit, but then when Archer's voice excitedly raised a pitch, clearly heard him say, "…and you're the only one who can get them for me."

She didn't fully catch Geoffrey's response, but believed she heard him reply something like, "…when I tell you, so you *will* do as I say."

She shivered and was about to step back into the foyer when she was caught in the headlights of the approaching taxi that stopped in front of her.

The driver wound down his window and cheerily said, "I'm a little early, Missus Mayhew, but if you're ready?"

Opening the rear door, she turned to glance to where Geoff and Archer stood, but saw that they were gone.

CHAPTER SIX

Tommy Burke and his daughter Fiona were on the return ferry to Ardrossan when his mobile phone chirruped with an incoming call.

"Hello, Tommy, it's Shona Mulveigh. Can you speak?"

"Aye, Shona, but give me a minute till we go out on deck so that I can put this on speaker for Fiona to hear too."

Pushing their way through a heavy door to the deck, Tommy said, "Right, Shona, that's us. How did your meeting with Mister and Missus Campbell go?"

"Well, it's good news all round," she gushed. "They were delighted with your offer and more so when you suggested taking the furniture as part and parcel of the deal. Missus Campbell actually said it solves one of their problems, not having to worry about selling the furniture. Of course, there are some personal items, such as paintings and ornaments that they will retain, but likely you will be wanting to provide your own wall coverings anyway. Would I be correct in thinking that?"

"Aye, of course, hen, and I'll also be ordering new mattresses and bedding to be delivered, so if the owners can dispose of their own, I'll be grateful. Now, what's the time frame for their emigration?"

"Well," she slowly drawled, "they told me they were very flexible on that score. Said their intention is to stay with their daughter while they look around for their own place in the town they're going to. Chandler, I believe the town is called." He heard her snigger as she added, "Mister Campbell even joked they can be on an Air Canada flight tomorrow because Missus Campbell is already packed."

"So," he glanced at Fiona, seeing her eyebrows raised and patiently repeated the question, "did they give you any idea when they can settle the deal?"

"Actually, when I told him about you and that you were a cash buyer, Mister Campbell suggested you phone him direct to discuss it with him. That and agreeing on a price for the house contents. Will that be okay with you?"

He smiled for he guessed the young woman enjoyed being the middle man in the deal and was probably miffed at being cut out in the final stage.

"That's fine, Shona, so if you text me his number, I'll do just that. Now," he winked at Fiona, for he was about to brighten the young estate agent's day, "can I call upon you again, Shona? I know the Campbell's will probably leave the place in good condition, but I'll want a cleaning team to go in before I take occupancy and maybe look to hire a cleaning lady on a regular basis. That and probably a painter to touch up the walls where they've had photos and paintings up. You being a local lassie, I'm sure you will have all the necessary contacts. Of course, I'll be very grateful and likely you'll send me a bill for your services."

"Oh, of course, Mister…Tommy," she corrected herself and he imagined her excitement at being retained to help the transition; that and the obvious delight at what was probably her first major house sale.

"Good, then after I speak with Mister Campbell I'll have my lawyer contact his to proceed with the purchase. Thank you, Shona," he ended the call.

He glanced at Fiona and smiled. "You've something on your mind, so spit it out."

"I'm just a bit concerned, dad," she defensively raised her hands, "and I know you've said this house is a retreat for you and for my sisters and me, but I'm still not convinced," she slowly said and stared at him with her piercing green eyes. "I'm worrying that you're spinning me a line, that you really intend coming across to live in Arran full time," she nodded towards the island that was disappearing as they approached Ardrossan, "that you'll lock yourself away over there for good."

"And would that be a bad thing? I mean, it's not a million miles away, Fiona. I'll be keeping my Glasgow flat on and travelling back and forth to visit you and your blisters and the weans on a regular basis. That and you'd be coming across regularly to see me."

"But not daily and that's what worries me," she shook her head. "Right now you're seeing me or Vicky or Jenny at least every day or every second day for lunch or just a chinwag or to take the kids for a walk in the Botanic Gardens. And you'll miss meeting your old brickie cronies in Weatherspoons every Friday and then there's your pal, uncle Peasy. You'll miss your lunches and pints with him, too. You won't have that contact if you're a hundred miles away."

"Actually, it's less that fifty miles," he smiled again.

"You're being pedantic," she frowned, "and you know fine well what I mean, you old bugger."

He knew she was worried about him and nodding, he raised his hands in surrender.

"Okay, okay, I understand your concern, sweetheart, but seriously, I do intend spending time there, but not the whole year. I was thinking more of a couple of months at a time," then before she could argue, added, "during which time of course I would travel across the water to visit you lot. Then I could be back in Glasgow for a couple of months with you and your blisters, catching up with people."

"Blisters," she irately shook her head and scowled, "Sisters, dad, my sisters. Enough with the juvenile talk."

God, he thought and choked back a laugh; she's her mother's daughter right enough. Even her quick temper reminds me of Moira.

"It's been nearly four years now, dad," placing a hand on his arm, her voice lowered as she hesitantly broached the subject. "The girls and I were talking, you know? I mean, we're not suggesting you take off somewhere and, well, you know, find yourself a girlfriend or anything, but…" she exhaled.

He reached for her and enveloping her in his arms, held her tightly. "But you're worried about your old dad being lonely. I get that," he smiled and nuzzled her hair. "The thing is, your mum was all the woman I really wanted and I've never given much thought to, well," he shrugged, trying to find the right word, "replacing her, hen. Not unless big Sigourney Weaver gives me a phone call."

"Dad, she's six feet and too tall for a midget like you," Fiona growled.

"Hey, I'm five feet ten and that's tall for a Weegie," he sniffed. "Besides, if I'd a chance with big Sigourney I'd wear heels," he quipped, then added, "But you liked the house?"

"You're going off track to change the subject."

"Sorry. The house?"

"Yes," she sighed, "I *liked* the house and I also liked the idea you had about buying the furniture. I have to admit, the couple do have good taste," she mused.

"And you can see yourself, Phil and Cissie spending time there?" he teased.

She gave in and smiling, replied, "Yes, dad, I can see my lot and me and my sisters and their lot coming over to spend time with you."

"Excellent," he nodded. "Now, why not phone Phil and have him hold dinner. I feel like taking you guys out tonight to that wee Italian place in Byres Road."

****

They sat in the restaurant till just after nine o'clock that evening, until finally Fiona pointed out that Cissie needed her bed.

"Do you want dropped off?" she asked her father as they exited onto Byres Road.

"No, thanks," he shook his head and glanced up at the clouds. "It's a fine night for a walk and I'll get home before the rain starts."

He took his farewell of his daughter and her family and with just a mile to his flat, decided to walk home via Great Western Road. Turning up the jacket of his coat, he set off at a brisk pace.

As he walked he made the decision that the following morning, he would phone Mister Campbell, the owner of the Arran property and finalise the deal.

When that was done, he would contact his lawyer and make him aware of the transaction and with a bit of luck and if there were no hiccups, he smiled, he could be moving in within a week or two.

Curious, he thought, that after all these years I can still get a little excited at a deal.

His thoughts turned to his late wife and he wondered what Moira would make of all this.

Probably think I'm off my head, he grinned and at a point of just over halfway home, turned his face to the sky to feel the first drops of rain splash down upon him.

Bugger, he shook his head and continued to hurry home.

****

The following morning, Thursday, dawned bright and fresh with the streets glistening from the rain throughout the night.

It was almost eight o'clock when Tommy, getting out of bed, dressed in his old worn tracksuit and grabbed a glass of fresh orange juice before hitting the street for his daily jog.

He had his set route that took him along Great Western Road to the Botanic Gardens, then twice round the periphery of the Gardens; an estimated three miles at a pace that got his heart pumping, then at a slower pace jogging west on the north side of the Great Western Road to Anniesland Cross which added another four miles to his route before he turned about and headed back to Hughenden Road on the south side of the main road.

He stopped at last outside his building to draw breath and turned when his name was called.

"You should know better at your age, Tommy. You'll do yourself a mischief one of these days," said Harry Bates, his ground floor neighbour who scoffing good-naturedly was descending the front steps to street level and shook his head.

"What, and end up a wreck like you if I give up?" he grinned at the younger, but portly man.

"Aye, but this is all bought and paid for," Harry patted at his large waistline.

They stood for a few minutes exchanging craic before Harry, glancing at his watch, said, "Must go. I've a meeting in an hour in Paisley," and headed towards his car.

Tommy waved cheerio and legs still shaking from his exertion, began to make his way upstairs to his second floor flat.

A brisk shower and he was ready for a coffee, but aware he was meeting with his two daughters in an hour's time at the café, decided against toast.

Dressing casually in chinos, navy blue polo shirt and black coloured brogue shoes, Tommy took his coffee through to the lounge and setting himself down in a comfortable chair, dialled the number texted to him by Shona Mulveigh.

His call was answered by a woman who he greeted with, "Missus Campbell? My name's Tommy Burke. I understand your husband might be expecting a call from me or shall I deal with yourself?"

"Oh, Mister Burke," the woman hesitantly replied. "Bob's just finishing his shower if you can hold on for a moment or can I get him to call you back?"

"No, I'll hang on," he said and detecting a slight accent, socially asked, "I understand you are a Canadian. You must be quite excited about returning home."

"Well, yes and no, Mister Burke."

"Please, Tommy," he insisted.

"Tommy," she repeated before continuing, "Well, please call me Grace. As for me returning home, my daughter and her family are over there now and I miss them so very much. But that said, I *will* miss Arran. I've had very many happy years here on the island."

"So the house you're selling isn't your first property on Arran?"

"Oh no, Tommy. We've lived in, what, three houses before this house was constructed. A cottage in Sannox and two properties in Lamlash. I've been very happy here, believe me."

"Well, Grace, let me tell you I am very impressed by your home and you can trust that I will make it my own and care for it as you so lovingly have."

"Oh, oh," he had obviously taken her unawares by his comment and thought he heard her sob before she sniffed, "Thank you, Tommy. Now, here's Bob."

Tommy's conversation with Robert Campbell lasted almost an hour during which the man was gratified by the offer Tommy made for the house and contents. Following their exchange of their respective lawyers details and Campbell's agreement to dispose of certain household effects that would be replaced by Tommy, they agreed that subject to the transfer of the funds the property would be occupied by Tommy in two weeks' time.

"Now, I want you to assure me that such a short time will not inconvenience you, Bob?"

"No, not at all," the man gruffly replied. "We've made all sort of arrangements and," his voice lowered almost to a whisper, "if truth be told I'm keen to get going. She's been moping about the house for weeks now so likely she'll be counting the days, if not the hours, before we're off."

Their conversation concluded with both agreeing to phone should there be any hiccups, but confident there would be none, Tommy wished Campbell a good journey.

****

He arrived minutes before his two daughters.

Jenny, carrying a backpack, entered the café leading two years old Cillian by the hand while Vicky guiltily apologised as bumping against legs and banging into chairs, she manoeuvred her baby Fergus in his buggy that was laden with a changing bag, through the tightly knit spaces between the tables. At last they settled around the table with Cillian clamouring to get onto his granddad's knee, but was instead thrust heavily into a high chair by his mother who snapped, "Stop it right now, dude, or me and you will fall out!" provoking a fit of giggling from the toddler.

Shaking his head, Tommy smiled and said, "My God, with the amount of gear you two carry it's like a military operation going anywhere. I don't remember your mum and me carrying so much stuff when you girls were wee."

"Probably because you were never around, dad," Jenny grumpily replied. "Mum used to tell us you were always working."

"Aye, building up the business so you buggers could have an easier life," he retorted with a grin.

"Maybe if you two can give it a rest for two minutes," Vicky interrupted, "I can get some breakfast. I'm starving."

After ordering their food, Jenny asked, "Did you bring the schedule?"

Tommy handed it to her and for the next five minutes, the three discussed his prospective purchase of the Arran house.

"Fiona believes you might live there permanently, Dad," Jenny said. He sighed, knowing the three girls had been telephoning each other and shaking his head as though tired of explaining, raised his hand and replied, "I've been over this with her. Please, that's *not* my intention. After all," he reached across to the IKEA high chair to ruffle Cillian's hair and added, "Can you see me giving up this wee guy or Fergus or Cissie, full time? At the minute, though admittedly

I love the place, nothing will persuade me to stay permanently in Arran."

"At the minute?" repeated Jenny.

"Well, not unless big Sigourney takes up residence there."

"What is it with you and Sigourney Weaver," sighed Vicky.

"Listen, hen, if you had been a man and seen that big dolly bird in her underwear in the Alien film," he solemnly nodded, "you'd know."

****

He'd enjoyed his time with his daughters and his grandchildren and promising to let them know how things went with the purchase, bid them cheerio and began his walk home.

Approaching Hughenden Road, his mobile phone activated in his pocket and smiling, saw on the screen the caller to be his old pal, Peasy Byrne.

"How's it hanging?" he greeted the former detective.

"Fine so far, but I haven't had a look for a while," Byrne quipped.

"I'm calling to ask if you fancy a lunch sometime next week for a catch up? Say, twelve o'clock on Wednesday at the Counting House in George Square?"

"Can't think that I've anything on that day so aye, suits me," he unconsciously nodded.

"Right then, see you there," Byrne ended the call.

Smiling, he returned the phone to his pocket and thought about Peasy. Their relationship had begun shortly after Tommy had started out on his own when a mutual friend suggested Tommy as the brickie to build Byrne's lengthy, rear garden wall. After that first meeting and extremely pleased with Tommy's workmanship, Byrne had in turn recommended him to his police colleagues and so had begun an enduring friendship that was now into its thirtieth year. Retired from the police some years previously, Byrne had almost immediately been hired as the head of security for the Glasgow Hilton Hotel and just recently again retired for a second time, from that job. Now, with time on his hands, he spent much of it on the golf course improving his handicap.

Though not himself a player, Tommy knew of at least seven golf courses on Arran that would interest Byrne and could not wait to tell his old pal about his purchase of the Brodick house.

CHAPTER SEVEN

Five weeks had now passed since the Alice had attended at the rugby club dinner with Geoffrey.

Five weeks during which she dutifully tended to her housewifery chores and to his increasingly unreasonable demands.

Five weeks during which time Marcy had enjoyed a sleepover at her friend Laura's house while Alice skilfully avoided any time alone with the little girl's mum, Lucy the detective.

Five weeks during which time Alice gave much thought about Carstairs attempt at friendship and particularly about the questions she had asked, the information she had try to solicit.

Five weeks when her one visit during that time to her true friend Doris provoked yet another attempt by the elderly lady to persuade Alice to leave her husband.

Five weeks during which time she discerned a change in her husband's demeanour as increasingly he became even more secretive than usual.

Five weeks of almost nightly phone calls at strange hours until he angrily ordered that she was not to respond to any of the calls to the house, that he would himself deal with them.

Five weeks during which she had noticed too that Geoffrey was spending more time at the rugby club and though first presumed it was his duties as the Chairman that caused this break in routine, come to realise the club wasn't open during all the hours he was supposedly there, so wondered what was going on that kept him out till late at night.

Finally, she stoically decided it was likely his adulterous relationships and yet was grateful for the diversion that kept him away from the house.

Not that she could possibly to complain, she inwardly sighed, for to do so would only provoke his rage.

That day that would forever remain with her, she had just returned to the house after walking Marcy to school and decided before she tackled the ironing she would treat herself to a coffee.

Switching on the small television that was hung on the kitchen wall, she was idly spooning the granules into a mug when the local news started. It was the mention of the name Archer that caused her to turn and to her surprise, saw a photograph of the young man from Geoffrey's rugby club on the screen. She had missed the opening comments, but when the broadcaster continued "…and police are treating the death as unexplained," her mouth fell open.

The news continued, but Alice was no longer paying attention.

Dead?

Yet he was just a boy, no more than nineteen or twenty, she recalled. She had no idea what had happened to the unfortunate young man and Geoffrey strictly instructed she should not use the desktop computer in his study; not that it would do her any good anyway, for even if she did have access to it she wouldn't know how to operate it.

Impatiently, she realised she must wait for the hourly news on the radio if she was to learn more.

Or perhaps, her brow furrowed, she might speak with Lucy Carstairs if it was she who that afternoon was to pick up her daughter Laura from school.

****

Her housework completed, she decided to have a quick shower before attending at the primary school to collect Marcy.

As Alice was about to go upstairs, the phone in the hallway rung. She hesitated, mindful of Geoffrey's warning, but suspecting it might be him calling to check she was at home lifted the receiver and said, "Hello?"

There was silence for a few seconds before a man's voice hissed, "I want to speak to Doctor Mayhew."

"I'm sorry," she stuttered, taken aback at the gritty intensity in the man's voice, "but my husband is at his practice. May I ask who's calling and take a message?"

"No, you don't need my name and he's not at his bloody surgery. Put him on the phone!"

"But he's not here and…"

"Then where the hell *is* he?"

"I'm sorry, but…"

The line went dead.

Stunned, she stared in confusion at the at the phone before slowly replacing it into the cradle.

Now, she wondered, what was that all about?

****

Walking to the school and mindful of her recent rebuffing of Lucy Carstairs, she run different scenarios through her head as to how she might approach the younger woman and open a conversation.

As it turned out, when she arrived at the school she saw Carstairs exiting a red coloured Ford Focus and walk ahead of Alice to the school gate, but without her toddler son.

Forcing a smile, Alice strode towards her and tapping her on the shoulder, brightly said, "No James today then?"

Turning, Carstairs seemed surprised before shaking her head and politely replying, "No James. My mother's visiting, so she has him at home while I collect Laura. How are you, Alice?"

"Me? Oh, just the usual," she continued to smile, but sensed that the detective was already guessing her intention before she asked, "I saw it on the news. About that young boy. The rugby player from the club. Tragic, isn't it?"

Carstairs stared keenly at her before slowly nodding, then exhaling as though unburdening herself, replied, "More so for his parents. Nineteen he was. Just a child, really. So, it was on the news?"

"Yes," Alice was now swallowing with difficulty, forcing her voice to be neutral. "The television news, I mean. Was it an accident?"

She didn't miss Carstairs glance about them before she quietly replied, "No, Alice, it wasn't an accident. It was someone older and who should know better taking advantage of his youth and persuading him that taking pills could enhance his rugby playing." Her voice filled with vehemence when she added, "And it's my job to find that individual and arrest them."

Pale faced, Alice could only stare at the angry woman who then visibly relaxed and herself forced a smile before she said, "But I know it's nothing to do with you, Alice, and I also know that you and I will keep this conversation between us two, won't you?"

Alice was no fool and recognised the implied warning that she was not to recount or discuss what Carstairs told her with anyone; not even her husband.

Her husband.

Her eyes remained locked onto Carstairs as she slowly raised her hand to her mouth.

Surely to heavens Geoffrey…no, he wouldn't, couldn't. After all he was a doctor, for God's sake.

But a doctor who beat and bullied his wife and…

As if in a daze, she turned away from Carstairs who watched her walk off.

"Gran. Gran?"

She glanced down to see Marcy staring curiously at her and taking the little girl's hand, without explanation hurried her away from the school to make their way home.

****

Her head was a jumble of thoughts as she almost dragged Marcy along the road to Spruce Close.

Once in the house, she turned to the little girl, but before she could speak, Marcy asked, "What's wrong, Gran? Has he been hitting you again? Is that what it is?"

Stunned, she replied, "No, of course not, sweetheart, what made you…"

"Don't lie to me, Gran!"

"I'm not lying, dear. What made you think that?"

Huffily folding her arms, her face grave, Marcy stared up at Alice before replying, "Because when you're worried or sad like this, it's because that's what he's done. He's hit you again. You think because I'm eight if I don't see it, then it's not happening? Well, I *know* it's true and even though you tell me it's not, it *is* true and I know it's true because I've seen it."

Almost as if she were sitting on Alice's shoulder, her friend Doris Chisholm's warning rang in her ears; her caution that Geoffrey's behaviour towards her would eventually impact upon Marcy's young fragile mind.

She shivered, not from the cold, but from the realisation that she alone was raising a child in a house where bullying and violence had become the norm.

Kneeling down, she embraced her granddaughter and held her tight before whispering in the little girl's ear, "No matter what you see, no matter what you hear, I will never let any harm come to you."

Marcy braced herself and slowly pushing herself from Alice's arms, stared with sad eyes at her grandmother before replying, "But how can I protect you, Gran?"

****

It was a night without homework, so she sent the child to Alice's bedroom to watch the television and began to prepare that evening's meal. She expected Geoffrey home at his usual time between five-forty-five and six o'clock which give her time to switch on the wall-mounted kitchen television to catch the local five-thirty news bulletin.

The first item featured a fatal road accident that had occurred earlier in the day, however, the second item commenced with the photograph of nineteen-years-old Jonathan Archer who had collapsed while training during a rugby practise match at his college, but been pronounced dead upon his arrival at the Royal Preston Hospital. As Alice continued to watch the reporter related that Jonathon, an accounts student, was an only son who lived with his parents and a younger sister. The reporter added Jonathon was a promising young rugby player with the local Fulwood Martyrs Rugby Club and had been tipped as a starter for the England under twenty-one's upcoming match with Wales. The screen flashed to a still photo of a mid-terraced house somewhere in Preston as the reporter added the family were too upset to be interviewed.

And why wouldn't they be upset, she numbly thought.

The reporter concluded her item by intimating the police were treating Jonathon's death as unexplained and an autopsy was to be held later in the week.

She heard the sound of tyres on the gravelled driveway and quickly switching off the TV glanced at the wall clock to see Geoff was home earlier than usual.

Uneasily, she checked the pots heating on the cooker and patting a nervous hand at her hair hurried into the hallway to greet him.

When the front door opened, her first impression was he'd been drinking as he bent to irately kick his leather medical bag under the hall table, then straightening up he squinted as he stared at her.

Her first impression had been wrong. His hair was in disarray, his face flushed and his tie undone and she realised he hadn't just been drinking, he was drunk.

"Bloody day I've had," he snarled at her then taking a deep breath, said, "Has there been any phone calls?"

She thought it might be a trick question, that he was trying to find out if she'd answered the phone against his instruction, but decided to reply, "A man. I thought it might be you, that's why I answered it."

"What man?" he growled, his eyes narrowing in suspicion.

"I don't know," she stammered. "He didn't give his name. Asked for you and when I said you were at the practice, he told me you were not at the practice…no, not the practice," she corrected herself, "he said the surgery, and demanded to know where you where. He didn't sound happy that you weren't at home, Geoffrey."

"Did you tell him where I was," his fists bunched and he took a step towards her.

Fearfully, she replied, "No, Geoffrey, of course not. I thought you were at the practice. I didn't know where you where. How could I?"

He rapidly blinked as he took in her response and then as if understanding she was telling the truth, slowly nodded and slurred, "Had to leave early, had some business to attend to. Anything else?"

She didn't know how she could raise the subject of the young man's death without enraging him and shook her head.

"Sure?"

"Yes, Geoffrey, nothing else."

"If this fellow rings again, don't answer the phone," he wagged a finger at her.

She was about to reply if she didn't answer the phone, how will she know it's him, but thought better of antagonising her husband and so instead, simply nodded.

He walked past her and she raised a hand as if to remind him about dinner, but stopped when she realised he had other things on his mind.

Returning to the kitchen, she switched off the gas under the potatoes and the veg and was about to switch off the oven when the phone rung.

She startled, knowing that she should not answer it, but was curiously keen to do so.

As quietly as she was able, she moved to the kitchen door.

Her husband was in his study, but the door was ajar. Heart pounding in her chest, her hands clenched so tightly her nails dug into the skin of her palms, she slipped off her slippers and slowly moved across the hallway to the open door, then stood perfectly still.

Hardly breathing, she heard Geoffrey's swivel desk chair squeak as he turned back and forth. Satisfied he was sitting down at the phone on his desk with his back to the door, she swallowed her fear and took a further nervous step towards the door.

Listening intently, she heard him growl, "And I'm telling you, you gutless bastard, there is no way this will come back to us, do you hear? We didn't force him, did we? It was his bloody decision!"

She frowned, wondering to whom he was speaking, then heard him continue in an angrier voice, "They know nothing and suspect even less, so I'm telling you…no, *you* listen to *me*! You *will* keep your mouth shut! Do you know what will happen to us if they find out?"

She almost fainted with shock when from behind her, Marcy asked, "Gran. What *are* you doing?"

Placing a forefinger against her lips to hush her, Alice quickly ushered the little girl into the kitchen and closed the door behind her, praying that Geoffrey hadn't heard them.

For a precious minute she stood tense, holding Marcy to her and waiting for him to barge through the door, but at last she sighed and realised he mustn't have heard after all.

"What were you doing, Gran? Were you listening to him?"

She exhaled with relief at her narrow escape and nodded, saying, "I was, but that's our secret, isn't it?"

A slow smile spread across Marcy's face before she grinned widely and nodded, then asked, "What was he saying?"

Alice's brow creased in thought before she replied, "You know what, sweetheart, I'm really not sure."

****

He remained for most of the evening in his study, leaving it only to fetch another bottle of whisky from the cabinet or use the cloakroom toilet.

She worried he would create a fuss if she were not immediately on hand to provide his dinner, so Alice remained in the kitchen, sitting on a stool at the island and trying to concentrate on the fifty pence novel she had purchased from a charity shop, but her mind was on other things.

Through the course of the evening she twice heard him on the phone, but other than his voice becoming increasingly louder, could not hear what was being discussed in the call.

A little after eight o'clock, Marcy, rubbing tired eyes and wearing her Paddington Bear cotton pyjamas, came down from Alice's room to ask if she could spend the night in her grandmother's bed.

"Of course, sweetheart," she smiled and hugged the little girl. Alice was secretly thrilled for since her arrival at the house, this was one of the few occasion that she had asked to spend the night in her grandmother's bed.

Taking Marcy by the hand, she led her upstairs and after ensuring she brushed her teeth, tucked her into the narrow bed.

"Will you fit in too?" Marcy yawned as she asked.

"You bet I will," she replied, determined that nothing would stop her from cuddling her granddaughter. "In fact, I'll nip back down to the kitchen to fetch my book and join you in five minutes, okay?"

"Okay, Gran," Marcy yawned again and sleepily closed her eyes.

She leaned across the bed to stroke at the little girl's hair and kissed her on the top of her head, telling her, "Just in case you're sleeping before I get back."

Switching on the side light and then switching off the ceiling light, Alice hurried back downstairs for her book, but as she reached the hallway, she heard a definite snore from the study.

She bit at her lower lip and sneaking across the carpeted floor, risked a glance through the partially open door to peek into the study.

Geoffrey, his head thrown back and one arm dangling over the side of the three-seater leather couch against the far wall, was fast asleep. An almost empty bottle of whisky was on the desk.

She was about to close the door then startled when he suddenly grunted and expelled some wind, but still he slept.

Exhaling with relief through puckered lips, she quietly pulled the door closed.

Turning, she was about to enter the kitchen when for some unexplainable reason, her attention was drawn to his old, leather medical bag that lay askew where he had flung it under the hall table. Instinctively reaching to straighten the bag, she saw the top catch was undone and pulled the bag out from under the table to properly close it. When she did so her eyes narrowed when she saw the small, white and rectangular cardboard packets within. Her curiosity was aroused for she had never known Geoffrey to carry any medicines. Indeed, he had often boasted and was vainly fond of telling people that he was "…a proper doctor, not a bloody pharmacist. As a doctor I *prescribe* medicines. It is not my job to dish them out, that job belongs to lesser beings."

Her curiosity got the better of her and with a cautious glance to the closed study door, she opened the bag. Glancing inside her brow furrowed for she could see about a dozen of the cardboard packets.

With trembling fingers, she lifted a packet from the bag and opening it saw it contained four strips of aluminium foil, blister packs she knew them to be called. Withdrawing a blister pack she examined it and saw it contained eight small, reddish brown tablets.

Turning the white cardboard packet over, she frowned when she saw the print was not in English, but in a foreign language and slowly tried to pronounce *povysheniye proizvoditel'nosti.*

Alice had no idea what language she was reading, but some instinct told her that there was something wrong, something amiss with Geoffrey's possession of the tablets.

Her nerves were shredded for she could not help but think of the young man, Jonathan Archer. Her stomach tightened and recalled the argument at the rugby club and thought she was going to vomit for in her heart she knew that her husband, in some way she could not yet explain, knew something or worse, had something to do the young mans death.

Hastily she tried to place the blister pack back into the packet, but the fragile aluminum foil bent and then eyes widening, she realised something had changed; she could no longer hear him snoring.

Panicking, she shoved the blister pack and the opened packet into her trouser pocket and hastily closed the bag before pushing it back under the table.

Fearfully, she again glanced at the door, but to her relief heard a loud sigh and then a grunt.

Rising to her feet, she collected her book from the kitchen and ensuring the doors were all locked, turned out the kitchen and hall lights and made her way upstairs.

****

Lucy Carstairs kissed her daughter cheerio and shouting to her husband that she would be back in an hour or so, left the house for her meeting at the Preston police office in Lancaster Road.

The late evening traffic was light, enabling Carstairs to arrive at the office in fifteen minutes,

Turning from Craggs Row into Singleton Row, she parked her Ford Focus in an empty bay by the rear yard entrance and used her pass to open the security gate.

Hurrying through the yard to the main building, she again used her pass to permit entry to the back stairs and made her way to the CID suite on the second floor.

Taking a breath, she rapped on the glass paneled door and heard a woman's voice call out that she enter.

Sat behind her desk, Detective Inspector Julie Sandford, with complete disregard for Lancashire Constabulary's prohibition on smoking anywhere on police premises, held a lit cigarette with the filter torn off between the forefinger and middle fingers of her left hand and greeted Carstairs with, "You're late."

"Sorry, Ma'am, I had to wait for my husband to return home from work before I could get away."

Sandford nodded to the chair opposite and when Carstairs was seated, tersely asked, "Anything to report?"

"Nothing other than Alice Mayhew spoke with me today when I was collecting my daughter from school. As I previously told you, I got the impression that she has been avoiding me, so I was rather surprised when she did speak to me."

"Was she aware of the death of the young lad Archer?"

"Yes and actually, it was Missus Mayhew who opened the conversation about it. Told me she had seen the item on the television, that she had recognised him from the function at the rugby club and asked if it was an accident."

"An accident," Sandford slowly mused before asking, "Did she seem to think it might have been?"

"I'm not certain, Ma'am. What was obvious to me was that she seemed a little nervous."

"So, do you think she was probing, trying to find out from you what the police know about his death?"

"I'm not certain, Ma'am, perhaps," Carstairs slowly nodded. "However, like I've told you, I believe that Alice Mayhew is an innocent in all of this. She strikes me as a woman who has lost her confidence and unsure who she can trust. When she speaks to me, her eyes are constantly glancing about her, as though she's worried about saying the wrong thing and maybe being overheard. You will recall that several weeks ago I saw a bruise on her face. If my suspicions are correct, she didn't suffer an accident with a kitchen door like she told me. I think she was struck and likely by her husband."

"That's quite a leap, DC Carstairs. Without knowing anything of their relationship or having any evidence, you're accusing the good doctor of striking his wife," she retorted, though Carstairs detected a hint of cynicism in her response.

"It was just my thought at the time, Ma'am," the younger woman blushed.

Sandford didn't immediately respond, but glanced down at the file on her desk and turned over a sheet of paper. Her eyes narrowed as she read the entry.

Now forty-four years old, twenty of Sandyford's twenty-five years as a police office had been spent in the CID and as a woman from a mixed race background, it had not been easy achieving the rank she now held. Perhaps, in the privacy of her thoughts, this was the reason she was so curt with her colleagues.

She glanced up at Carstairs and pointing with an ebony finger at the file, said, "This item here, the night the Mayhew's granddaughter had a sleepover at your house; you gathered from speaking with the child that she has no relationship with her grandfather and you were of the opinion the grandmother is afraid of her husband. Correct?"

"Yes, Ma'am. I sent my daughter to do homework and engaged the little girl in conversation while I made dinner. She's a bright child and I quickly realised I had to be careful with my questioning."

"Orphaned, if I recall."

"Yes, Ma'am."

Sandford inhaled deeply on her cigarette and flicking the ash into a glass ashtray on her desk, turned her head to blow the smoke towards the nearby partially ajar window.

"How do you see your relationship with the woman Mayhew developing? In fact, let me rephrase that question. Is it worth continuing a relationship, trying to gain her trust? I ask because if as you believe Alice Mayhew has no knowledge of her husband's activities, what can we learn from her that might be useful to our investigation?"

Carstairs hesitated before replying, "Several weeks ago when I met with her at the rugby club, we seemed to be hitting it off. However, when I mentioned she was not often seen out in public and when I inferred that perhaps it was her husband who was the cause, she quite literally took fright and that's when she cut off all contact with me. Until today, that is."

"You think that from what the little girl told you and from what you discerned, she's frightened of her husband?"

"Yes, Ma'am, I do."

"Can you use that fear to invoke her to inform on him? Gain her trust to enable her to provide us with information?"

"I'll work on it, Ma'am, if you give me time."

Sandford stared at the younger woman and with a resigned sigh, replied, "Time, DC Carstairs, is probably a luxury we do not have. However," she dismissed her with a nod, "do what you can meantime."

CHAPTER EIGHT

Following the conclusion of the purchase of the house and its contents, Tommy had spent several days travelling back and forth to the island to supervise the interior painting and spending time there, awaiting delivery of the new mattresses and items of furniture that he wished to replace in the Glencloy Road house.

The estate agency young woman, Shona Mulveigh, had proven as good as her word and now after satisfactorily checking out the references of her candidate for the job, here he was comfortably seated in the lounge of his new home interviewing the slightly nervous fifty-year old Mary McKay for the position of his part-time cleaning lady.

Offering her tea and cake, the prematurely grey headed, rosy cheeked woman patted at her stocky figure and politely declining the cake, jokingly said, "Do you not think cake is the last thing I need, Mister Burke? I'm on a permanent diet these days."

"So, Missus McKay, you're an islander then?" he asked, pleased that the woman had a sense of humour.

"Aye, born and bred, Mister Burke," she smiled.

During the half hour interview he learned she was married to Malcolm, or Malky as she called him, and proudly intimated that her son and daughter were currently away studying respectively at Stirling and St Andrews Universities. At last he nodded and told her, "I'm sure you are exactly who I'm looking for Missus McKay. How does three days a week suit you? Say, Monday, Wednesday and

Friday? Anything else we can come to a mutual arrangement."

He could see she was pleased and even more so at the salary he offered.

Following a short discussion and agreement on her duties, he asked, "And does Mister McKay work here on the island?"

Her face fell slightly and she hesitated slightly when she replied, "Malky lost his left leg below the knee a number of years ago working on the fishing boats, Mister Burke. He has a prosthetic now, but he gets around okay and even drives our wee automatic car, wreck that it is," she sighed. "He had to give up full time work though and now tries to find odd jobs here and there. We get by though on both our incomes," she nodded, "though I have to admit it's not easy these days, what with trying to help out the children at Uni, too."

He had a sudden thought and glanced through the window at the sizeable lawn that already showed signs of needing weeded and mown and was surrounded by heavy foliage that required to be cut back.

"Can I ask where Mister McKay is right now?"

Her brow creased at the odd question and she slowly replied, "Oh, he's at home."

"And how far away do you live from here?"

"From here?" her face registered her surprise before she replied, "We have a wee semi-detached bungalow in Brathwic Place. It's about, oh, I'm guessing, a mile and a half maybe? Ten minutes in the car, no more. Can I ask why you want to know where Malky is right now?"

"Well," he slowly drawled, "young Shona…"

"My niece," McKay said, but suddenly blushed as though disclosing a secret.

"And that explains the referral for the job then," Tommy smiled in understanding. "Anyway, Shona did a good job during my purchase of the house and organised a local company to come in and give the house a good once over clean, as well as a couple of guys to do the bit of painting I needed. However, there are a couple of jobs that I still need doing and I'm looking for someone to keep an eye on the garden, maybe do the outside windows as well, that sort of thing. Do you think your husband might be interested in some regular, part time work?"

She took a breath and eagerly nodded, saying, "I walked here, so he has the car and I can have him here to speak with you in ten minutes, if you're serious."

"Oh, aye, I'm serious, Missus McKay, and while you give him a phone from the hallway there, why don't I put the kettle on again."

****

Fifteen minutes later, the balding Malky McKay proved to be as thin as his wife was stout, but with a cheery demeanour and a firm handshake.

Within minutes of meeting him, Tommy decided he liked the younger man and had no reservations about hiring him as a handyman.

Walking around the large garden with them both, Tommy admitted he was not green fingered and though he enjoyed a well kept garden had no real interest in tending to it, so was pleased to discover Malky McKay was an enthusiast. While both inspected the large garden shed, his first instruction to Malky was to purchase whatever tools or equipment he required to keep the garden in such good shape as it was.

Later seated with them in the lounge, Tommy explained he had one firm rule. As they had the run of his house, they were to call him Tommy, not Mister Burke and in turn requested he address them as Mary and Malky.

They sat for a good half hour with Tommy explaining his background, that he was a retired widower and anticipated that he and his daughters and their families and likely some friends too, would make good use of the house.

"I'll give you your own key," he told them, "both for when the house is empty and to ask that if any of the girls or myself are coming over to stay, Mary, you might run by and stock the fridge for us arriving. Otherwise, if you both just generally keep an eye on the place and do what needs to be done as you see fit."

She turned to glance at her husband seated beside her and unconsciously reached for his hand before replying, "I'm grateful for the trust you're placing in us, Tommy. We won't let you down. Now, when do you want us to start?"

He pursed his lips and smiling, said, "As far as I'm concerned I consider that coming here for your interviews is a working day so you've already commenced working for me. All I need now is your bank details to deposit some money for what you need to purchase, Malky, and for you to tell me what day you want your wages deposited."

****

After the McKay's had left, he wandered around the house, pleased that they seemed such a genuinely nice couple and that he had the means to hire them.

Moving from room to room, he found himself again admiring the interior of the house, the bright décor, the freshly painted walls, then finally stood at the panoramic window in the master bedroom looking down the hill towards Brodick Bay.

A sudden thought occurred to him and realising what the room lacked, went downstairs to the small bedroom he had decided was to be the study. Seating himself at the old fashioned mahogany desk, he switched on the Apple desk computer.

Opening the Amazon search engine, he typed in the word 'telescope' and browsed for half an hour. Coming to realise he knew absolutely nothing about telescopes, he finally chose and purchased one that seemed to have the magnification to enjoy the view from the window in the master bedroom.

With a satisfied smile, he glanced at his wristwatch and decided it was time to prepare dinner.

****

Fiona Docherty lifted her mobile phone to find the caller was her sister Victoria.

"Any word from dad?" Vicky asked.

"I spoke yesterday with him and he seems to be fine. He told me he intended interviewing a woman today about being a part-time cleaner, so likely I'll hear from him tonight sometime. But that's not why you called, is it?" she guessed.

"I'm just a bit concerned that no matter what he tells us, he's going to settle over there. What do you think?"

"Could be worse," Fiona shrugged, "he could have buggered off to Spain or somewhere like that. I mean, Arran's only what, an hour in the car and an hour on the ferry," she inwardly smiled when she realised she was repeating what her father had told her and thought, my God, I'm getting more like him every day.

"I suppose you're right," Vicky exhaled.

Fiona heard the sound of her nephew crying in the background, then Vicky telling her, "The wee bugger wants fed again. Speak soon, bye," and she was gone.

However, the call prompted Fiona to call Tommy on his mobile phone.

"Hi, dad. How did the interview go?"

"Fine, hen. I've hired Missus McKay…Mary… and her husband Malky as a part-time handyman to keep the garden tidy and any other odd jobs that might need done. How are things at your end?"

"Oh, same old, same old. Vicky was on the phone asking after you. Maybe you can give her a call?"

"Can do," he replied, before adding, "I'm spending the night here to get a feel for the place, then I'll be home, say midday tomorrow. I want to go to IKEA tomorrow and get some things to bring back over on Friday. Think you can pop up to my flat and stick some milk and something for my dinner in the fridge?"

"No problem. I'm making lasagne for dinner tomorrow, so I'll leave you some in a container," but then involuntarily shaking her head, said, "No. Here's a better idea. Why not come to us for dinner tomorrow? Cissie will want to see her granddad."

"Good idea. Give Cissie a hug from me and tell her I'll bring her some rock from Arran. Bye."

After he'd rung off, she stood and wondered what it was in his voice that sounded a little different, then surprised herself by smiling when she realised he sounded happy; really happy.

****

Wednesday morning dawned bright and sunny and pulling his old tracksuit from the overnight bag, Tommy decided to try and find a route for his daily run.

Finishing a glass of orange juice before he set off, he commenced his run down Glencloy Road to the A841 then turning south and running parallel with the golf course in the direction of Ormidale Park, he decided to veer right onto the narrow Auchrannie Road in the general direction of the Auchrannie Resort.

Having completed just under a mile and a half and realising the road was unfamiliar to him, he wondered where the hell he was before laughing at his stupidity and decided to retrace his route, vowing to buy a local map before venturing out again.

Arriving back at the house he saw he had an hour before the ferry departed.

Showered and changed into a clean red plaid shirt, jeans and hiking boots, he was about to pack his shaving gear when he stopped and grinned. Glencloy Road was now as much his home as was the flat, so decided to purchase a second shaving kit when he arrived in Glasgow.

Locking the door behind him, he smiled when he recalled Mary McKay's surprise at him handing her a key when bemused, she stared at him and said, "But nobody locks their doors in Arran, Tommy."

Now that, he shook his head, was something he must really get used to.

Throwing his overnight bag into the rear of the ten-year old, five-door Land Rover Defender, he drove the short distance to the ferry terminal.

****

Just under an hour later after disembarking from the ferry, Tommy was driving on the busy M8 towards Glasgow at a sedate fifty miles an hour.

His daughters and his sons-in-law had all at one time tried to persuade him to give up the Defender, reminding him that with the money he made from the sale of the business he was now a multi-millionaire and could afford to purchase any car from a Maserati to a Rolls Royce. However, Tommy loved the rust coloured Defender and joking it was just like him, a little battered and bruised, resisted all attempts to get him to part with it.

"I'm a kind of down to earth guy and besides," he had contended, "can you see a Maserati or a Roller pulling me out of the mud?"

"Aye, but there's not many muddy fields in the west end of Glasgow," his daughter Jenny had retorted, "and the only off road driving you do, Pops, is when you park on the pavement at your flat."

No, he had resisted their arguments, he was definitely keeping the Defender.

As he drove his thoughts turned to his daughter Fiona, recalling their conversation some weeks previously when she confessed that she and her sisters had been discussing Tommy and their concerns that he had not, since their mother's death, formed any attachment to another woman.

He sighed for during the discussion he had felt bad for…well, he reasoned with himself, he had not quite deceived Fiona, but neither had he been entirely honest with her, having decided some time ago that what the girls didn't know would not in any way hurt them.

It had been just over a year and a half previously and some months after he sold the business. With Moira gone almost three years his daughters, who were deeply concerned about how much he had thrown himself into the business, had persuaded Tommy to take a break and try to wind down from what had been a busy working life. He smiled for they had not *persuaded* him, they had literally bullied him into taking the break, the three of them arriving one wet and winter night at his flat with a carry out curry, a plastic bag full of holiday brochures and determined looks on their faces.

He remembered how they had almost forcibly sat him down at the dining table and while Jenny in the kitchen set out the plates and the food, Fiona and Vicky spread out the glossy brochures and reminded him that affluent as he then was there seemed little point in having money if he was going to be a miserable bugger and not spend some of it.

"Besides," he recalled Vicky telling him, "the way you're moping around you're causing us heartache, so do us a favour, dad, and get your arse away for a fortnight in the sun. That way we don't have to spend a fortune calling each other behind your back telling each other how miserable we all are worrying about you."

Not one to mince her words, his youngest daughter Jenny called out from the kitchen, "She's right, Pops. I've cried at night worrying about you, so why don't you do me a personal favour and bugger off for a while?"

In the end he had reluctantly given in and after a couple of hours of examining the brochures and at their suggestion, booked himself a Far East cruise; or rather, the cruise was booked for him.

All he did was surrender his MasterCard and provide his passport details.

A week later he found himself being dropped off by Fiona at Glasgow Airport with two packed suitcases full of summer clothes and booked on an Emirates flight to Dubai where he joined the P&O cruise ship, Arcadia, for a seventeen-night cruise bound for Hong

Kong, embarking at Dubai and calling at a number of ports along the route
****

Growing up in the two-bedroom council tenement flat with his widowed mother in the Partick area of the city, Tommy had stood on the dockside and stared in awe at the massive cruise ship that was to be his home for a little over two weeks. Once aboard and directed to his port side cabin, he was stunned at the both the opulence and the services offered on board the luxury liner.

Arriving at his mini-suite with its outside balcony, he discovered his suitcases had already been delivered to the ship and unpacked and his clothes hung or stored away by Crisanto, the cheerful and effervescent Philipino steward responsible for his welfare and the domesticity of his cabin.

For several hours after his arrival and prior to the Arcadia's departure, he wandered aimlessly around the ship, good-naturedly introducing himself to the stewards and crew he met as well as shaking hands and waving away their formality, insisting they call him Tommy and unwittingly becoming a firm favourite with them all.

The first night at sea he had self-consciously donned his new dinner suit with black bow tie for the introductory meet and greet with the Captain in the VIP dining suite and with a smile recalled that, being more used to wearing open necked shirts and casual trousers, felt overdressed and likened himself to a stuffed penguin.

What he hadn't then realised was the Maître D', having access to the passenger list, tactfully placed Tommy at a round table of eight passengers comprising of three couples and a woman travelling alone.

Barbara.

Escorted to the table by the smiling Italian, he had been last to arrive and was seated next to the glamorous woman with the blonde, curled hair that cascaded down to her shoulders who wore a tightfitting, sleeveless red dress with a low cut cleavage that showed off an ample portion of her milky white breasts.

However, it did not escape his attention that she also wore a wedding band beside a large diamond engagement ring.

Conversation at the table for the first few minutes was stilted, but as their wine and champagne glasses were frequently refilled, introductions were soon made as they continued at every opportunity to toast each other through the meal. It quickly became apparent that two of the couples were regular travellers together while the third couple were delighted to share that they were being treated by their family to their retirement trip.

"And you, Mister Burke," Barbara had smiled at him, "You're travelling alone, too?"

"It's Tommy, please and yes," he had replied. "I'm here at the insistence of my daughters who almost at gunpoint told me if I didn't take a break from work, they were disinheriting me." He'd grinned when he'd added, "Though I'd always thought disinheriting was a parental thing."

Being a social drinker rather than a regular imbiber, he later considered perhaps it was the wine that loosened his tongue or maybe the convivial company. Whatever the reason, he felt comfortable sitting with Barbara and his fellow diners, exchanging details of their lives and was so captivated by the attractive blonde he hardly noticed the departure of their fellow diners until at last he realised they were the last couple seated within the restaurant. Retiring to one of the ships many lounges, they sat till almost midnight during which time he learned she was then forty-seven, owned and managed an upmarket lingerie shop called 'Intimate' within the Lanes Shopping Centre in her native Carlisle, was married but had been estranged for over a year and had a twenty-five-year-old son she loved dearly. As if testing Tommy, she slowly intimated her son Mark was in a relationship with his long time male partner; however, admitted her husband Philip found it difficult to come to terms with his son's homosexuality. Following many heated arguments over the preceding year, Barbara recounted that both she and Philip agreed to a trial separation while they reassessed their marriage, hence her trip to take time to relax and contemplate what decision she intended making.

"And how do you feel about gay people, Tommy?" she had suddenly asked, taking him completely unaware as her light blue eyes searched his face with interest.

Even then he knew he had to be careful how he must respond, but throughout his life Tommy had never been comfortable with anything other than the truth.

"I've never really given the question much thought and I'm not really aware if I know any gay people," he had honestly admitted, "but the chances are that I do, though can't say I have ever had anyone who has openly admitted it to me. No, that's not quite true," he had shaken his head. "I do know a gay woman. My daughter Vicky has a best friend who is gay, but I've never really given her sexuality any thought. I don't see Jean as anything other than a nice, smart lassie. I've known her for so long," he slowly nodded, "I believe I can call her my close friend too, for if truth be told she's like one of my own. By that I mean if she's visiting me, she's raiding the fridge without asking, just like the other buggers," he smiled. "Jean has been around the family since she and Vicky were kids at secondary school, so I've watched her grow up and frankly, I've never even thought about her being gay. She's just our Jean," he shrugged, "if that makes any sense."

He sighed and continued, "You also have to understand, Barbara, I worked for most of my early life on the building sites where the majority of the workforce are male and have this," his face screwed in thought, "how can I describe it, macho image of themselves. Building sites can be rough and ready places and guys will pick up on anything they think they can good-naturedly or otherwise, abuse each other about," he shook his head. "Whether it be religion, football allegiance, race or anything, whether they're fat of thin, take Marmite or cheese on their pieces, they'll find some reason to make a derogatory comment."

She had smiled and asked, "So, you're not prejudiced against gay people?"

"I'm prejudiced against bullying, Barbara, not someone's gender choice, their race or their creed. If anyone abuses an individual because of their particular persuasion, whatever that might be, then *that* bloody annoys me." He had grinned, then added, "Unless it's the English national football team, because they're fair game for everybody," a comment that earned him a pretend scowl.

Having disclosed something of her life, he had in turn told her about his daughters and sons-in-law, of his then two grandchildren and more hesitatingly, of the loss almost three years previously of Moira. "May I ask, how did she die?"

"Well," he inhaled deeply before slowly exhaling through pursed lips as though the memory were painful, "it started with what seemed to be rudimentary surgery to remove a mole on her breast. Following the operation, she suffered what the doctors call a venous thromboembolism or more simply, a blood clot that worked its way to her heart."

He paused, his brow furrowed and contemplated what he was about to relate before continuing. "I'd like to say that if there was someone to blame, someone to rant and rave at, someone to whom I could point a finger at, it might have made my anger at losing her easier to cope with, but the sad truth is she received the best of care in the hospital and there was nothing they could do until it was to late to do anything. At the time I didn't understand my anger when really I should have been heartbroken, but by God I *was* angry; angry at the unfairness of it, I suppose, that she was a healthy and vigorous woman who was taken far too early. I didn't just lose my wife and my best friend, you see. My daughters lost their mother and their children lost their grandmother. It just seemed so…so bloody *wrong*! Anyway, I plunged myself into my business and worked all the hours that God sent and really," he turned and slowly smiled at her, "that's why I'm here now. Under strict instructions from my girls to relax and enjoy myself."

"I'm sorry for your loss," she had reached a hand to hold his.

He remembered her touch as though it occurred just moments ago, of staring down at her hand, at the smooth skin and perfectly manicured nails and of curiously thinking, since Moira died this is the first physical contact I have had with a woman who is not my daughter, not a relative and of the strange, tingling sensation he experienced of desire.

They had parted in the early hours, he escorting Barbara to the door of her inside cabin, both promising to meet that morning for breakfast and then hesitantly as she stood on her toes, of her soft lips brushing his cheek and softly whispering goodnight.

****

The following day with the ship now sailing in the Arabian Sea towards their first port of Mormugao in the Indian state of Goa, they met as arranged then spent the morning exploring the ship; he delighted with her cheery company, her blonde hair tied back into a girlish ponytail and dressed in her tight yellow coloured tee shirt, equally tight black coloured shorts and blue deck shoes and seemingly oblivious of the admiring glances she drew from both passengers and crew alike.

A light lunch was followed with a swim on the open deck pool and when Tommy watched Barbara remove her white, cotton robe to reveal her black, one-piece costume, he glanced about him with quiet pride and a soft grin to see that she was the focal point of interest for the dozen or so men and women who sat or lay on the surrounding deckchairs.

Following their swim, they sat for an hour together basking in the sun; not conversing but simply happy to be in each others close company.

Later that evening and again wearing his dinner suit, he escorted her from her cabin to dinner, impressed by the plain black, strapless midi dress she wore that clung to her, her hair piled up on on her head and her high heels raising her to his eye level. Arriving together in the dining room and though not commented upon, it occurred to Tommy that curiously, he and Barbara had been subtly accepted as the fourth couple at their table.

Their meal concluded, they attended at the three-tier theatre where they took in a show. Tommy was delighted to find the main entertainment was Elaine Grey, a noted Scottish singer whom he read in the theatre programme originated from Bothwell and who wowed the crowd with her performance, receiving a standing ovation at the conclusion of her act.

A late night drink in the bar saw them being joined by the retired couple from their table before the two couples bid each other goodnight.

In silence, their hands entwined, he had walked Barbara back to her cabin, both knowing that what was happening between them had its predictable conclusion.

At the door, he glanced along the empty corridor and heart beating rapidly, took a deep breath and leaning close, took her face in his hands and tenderly kissed her.

Neither could foretell the passion that the kiss unleashed and as she fumbled with the door handle at her back, they almost fell into the cabin where both burst into helpless, embarrassed giggles.

Panting heavily yet still with their bodies and lips pressed together, they waltzed into the cabin where he fumbled at the rear zip of her dress while she shrugged his jacket from him to fall to the floor and slipped his braces from his shoulders.

Breathlessly, she'd raised her hand and said, "Wait. Let me use the en-suite to get out of this," and without waiting for him to respond, turned and closed the door behind her.

Taken aback and a little uncertainly, Tommy had stripped off his clothes and throwing them onto a nearby chair, turned down the cabin lights before slipping between the sheets.

Moments later, Barbara opened the en-suite door and his eyes had almost popped for framed in the doorway with her blonde hair falling to her shoulders, one arm demurely covered her naked breasts while wearing just a black coloured, silk thong that she later disclosed was her own design.

Their first attempt at lovemaking again had them in fits of laughter, but slowly and inevitably, desire overcame their nervousness.
****

For the remainder of their voyage, that was to be their routine, every moment spent together and alternating their nights and often their afternoons between their respective cabin beds.

In short, Tommy had no need to use the ships marvellous fitness centre, for not only was he getting all the exercise he needed, but with Barbara's enthusiastic and lustful assistance, happily ended three years of enforced sexual abstinence.

As the days passed and the Arcadia docked at the foreign ports, they often went ashore, occasionally with a group or more often as a couple.

It was a few days after their first night together that Tommy had worried that somehow he was being unfaithful to the memory of Moira. One afternoon as they lay entwined in his cabin bed and almost in a fit of remorse, he confessed his thoughts to Barbara.

To his surprise, she was unperturbed and reminded him, waving her forefingers like quotation marks, that she was still a married woman and knew exactly how he must feel.

Yet no matter their doubts, their desire for each other overcame their concerns.

At last, on the evening prior to the cruise concluding the following day at the Hong Kong pier and at the final ball, Tommy confessed he needed to see Barbara again, that they must not lose touch, that if she was agreeable, they could make a life together, that he was willing to quit Glasgow and live wherever she chose.

He guessed she was torn between returning to her husband and a new life with him, but Tommy had found what he believed to be a second opportunity at happiness, a second chance and had begged her to take that second chance with him.

However, he had seen the hesitation in her eyes and knew in his heart she did not have the same feelings for him as he did her, that a life together was not to be.

They had parted at Hong Kong International Airport; he to return via Dubai to Glasgow while Barbara's flight, two hours earlier, was with KLM; first to Schiphol Airport and thereafter the short hop across the North Sea to Newcastle Upon Tyne International Airport.

But that was not the last time he saw and met with her.

In response to an e-mail a few days after his return and in the mistaken belief she might have had a change of heart, he had driven to meet with her at a Carlisle hotel.

Within a room booked by her for that afternoon, she tearfully disclosed that upon her return home and following a meeting with her husband, she decided to try to work things out; it was, she told Tommy, her own and Philip's second chance at saving their marriage.

Devastated, Tommy had with a heavy heart accepted Barbara's decision and returning on the M74 to Glasgow, stopped at the Abington service station where for almost an hour he sat numbly, staring through the rain splattered windscreen and contemplating what might have been.

Yet though he believed then his heart was broken, as the days passed he came to realise that his relationship with Barbara was what women's magazines called a whirlwind romance, that the short time they had spent together was not real life and finally accepted his feelings were more physical desire and not as he thought, real love.

Waited upon and confined to the ship for those short weeks, they had not endured any ups and downs that couples must bear to strengthen their relationship; they had not undergone hardships as he and Moira endured, the ups and downs of family life, the scrimping and saving in the early days of every penny and the sacrifices each had made to further their relationship; he working long and difficult hours on the building sites in the worst of weather and she giving up her nursing career to raise their children and establish their home.

Still, she remained in his thoughts and for a long time, he did wonder what might have been.

He had since that time kept his relationship with Barbara his secret, but for one individual in whom he finally decided to confide; his old friend Peasy Byrne.

****

It was about three weeks after his return from Carlisle, he had met with Byrne where one rainy afternoon, closeted in a booth in the Horseshoe Bar in Glasgow's Drury Street, he finally unburdened himself to disclose the full details of his cruise and relationship with the enigmatic Barbara.

If Tommy had been expecting some form of sympathy or compassion from his closest friend, he was to be rudely shaken.

"Ya lucky wee bastard," was the big man's initial and unexpected reaction, shaking his balding head, before he continued, "The next time you go on one of them fancy cruises, take me with you. Please."

"But you're missing the point," Tommy had tried to explain, but been cut off when Byrne raised a hand and interrupted with, "Look, Tommy, you lost your wife and you were lonely for female company. That's a given, okay? Now, you'd spent what? Nearly three or four years alone since Moira died…"

"Just over three, actually," he sighed. "Me and Moira didn't, you know, during the time she was ill."

"Okay then, numb nuts. So it was just over three years without your Nat King Cole. It stands to reason that when a good looking birds shows up and takes an interest in a wee scabby and ugly git like you, you're going to fall hook, line and sinker, aren't you?"

"But Peasy, what I'm trying to tell you is…"

"Before you go on, tell me this. Did you at any time allude to this woman that you were worth millions?"

"No," he had shrugged. "There didn't see to be any reason to. I suppose she thought I was worth a bob or two because of the cabin I was in, yes, but I didn't want to boast or have her think I was trying to impress her or anything. I only told her I was a retired brickie who'd made a few quid, not what I was worth. Now, what I'm trying to tell you is…"

"Good," Byrne had raised a hand to interrupt him, "well that explains why she didn't try to hang onto you, then. Look, ya dunderhead, I know what *you're* trying to tell me, but what *I'm* trying to tell you is this. You're a smart guy when it comes to business, there's no denying that, but though it pains me to admit this you're also a decent looking wee man too, with your own hair and teeth," he grinned. "Now, think outside the box here for a minute, will you? This woman you're telling me about, this Barbara. A good looking blonde with nice tits and on a cruise by herself, she told you, because her and her man have split for a time to reassess their marriage, yeah?"

"Yes," he slowly agreed.

"So there you are, Tommy, she finds herself sitting next to a decent looking guy and a genuinely nice man, if a little naive when it comes to the women."

"Now hold on there…"

"Don't interrupt when I'm trying to explain as best I can," again Byrne held his hand up, before continuing, "As I said, there you are at the dinner table sitting next to this blonde with nice tits and suddenly, you're spellbound. You have a couple of swallies and everything she tells you makes sense, yeah?"

"Yes."

"Did you not stop to think that maybe, just maybe, this woman was on a cruise because she was looking for a bit of Mills and Boon, a wee romance with a bit of rumpty-pumpty thrown in? Heavens, Tommy, if indeed she *is* married, then she's having a great time to herself without her husband ever likely to find out she's away shagging in the Far East."

"Well, I suppose if you put it like that…" his face fell. "But what do you mean about me being naive around women? I am not," he sourly said.

"Really?" Byrne's eyes narrowed as he smiled at Tommy. "Let me tell you this, boy. I love your weans like they were my own, but those lassies have you wrapped around their little fingers. Think about it. God rest her soul, but without Moira here to protect you and your business acumen aside, since she's been gone do you *ever* make a personal decision without first running it by the girls?"

Tommy thought for a few seconds and then slowly grinning, sheepishly replied, "I suppose not."

"See? Now, about this bird, Barbara. This meeting you had in the hotel in Carlisle. Now that interests me," Byrne rubbed at his jaw. "Just my humble opinion, but she's likely had a good time shagging you on her trip abroad, so to avoid any complications, like you trying to track her down then moping after her and pleading for her to marry you," his face betrayed his scorn at this idea, "she's invited you down to this hotel and given you a sob story about getting back with her man. Remember, she's under the belief you're just a retired bricklayer spending your pensionable lump sum on the cruise, not," he grinned and made quotation marks with his forefingers, "a playboy multi-millionaire, yeah?"

"Yeah," Tommy slowly nodded.

"So, as far as this bird is concerned, her giving you the heave-ho puts an end to a pleasant trip she had with no complications. Do you agree?"

"I suppose so, yes."

"Now, this place of business that she told you about, 'Intimate,' you said she called it. Ever check the Internet to see if it exists?"

"No. I didn't think that…"

"Hang on," he raised a hand to stop Tommy speaking. Fetching his mobile phone from his pocket, Byrne mumbled, "My eldest showed me how to use Google on this bloody thing, so give me a minute." Minutes later he turned the screen towards Tommy and said, "No trace of a lingerie shop called 'Intimate' anywhere in Carlisle. Sorry, old pal, but it seems you've been had."

Tommy inhaled and nodding, his face red, said, "I'm an idiot, aren't I?"

"What? You need *me* to confirm that fact?"

Byrne grinned and then with a wicked smile, asked, "Did you have a nice time with this Barbara? I mean, do you feel you've had…" he shrugged, "what you might call, a stimulating experience?"

Tommy paused at the question, then smiled at the memory of her svelte body before replying, "I had a wonderful time."

"Then nothing was lost other than a wee bit of your pride."

Sipping at his vodka and diet coke, Byrne licked his lips and banging down the empty glass, said with a roguish wink, "It's your round, Tommy boy, and when you come back to the table, you can tell me again in better detail about this Barbara. She does sound like one foxy lady."

CHAPTER NINE

Alice had replaced the foil strip of tablets into the cardboard packet and hidden it under her mattress.

Still uncertain why she was so agitated about the discovery of the tablets, she wished not for the first time that she had access to and been able to operate a computer and the Internet to research the strange labelling on the packets.

All night or as much as she remembered, she had lain awake wondering about Geoffrey's phone call and the mystery man who had demanded to know her husband's whereabouts.

Was he a patient, she wondered, but knew in the heart he was not.

Did it have anything to do with the young man Jonathon Archer's death?

God, she silently prayed, I hope not.

Yet the notion persisted and glancing at the wall clock, decided there was one person who could help her, her only friend, Doris Chisholm.

She reached for the wall phone.

****

Arriving early at his surgery that morning with a headache so severe it caused him to squint, Geoffrey Mayhew passed through the busy waiting room with a fixed smile, nodding a greeting here and there to the smiling patients waiting for their appointments.

Behind the reception desk, Debbie Pritchard, wearing a low cut black silk blouse and a tight grey coloured pencil skirt, flashed him a professional smile and said, "I have the patients' files for their appointments, Doctor Mayhew. I'll be right in with them when you're settled."

He was about to nod in acknowledgement, recognising her comment was a prelude to a brief sexual encounter in his examination room. However, today he had other concerns on his mind and stopping, turned and replied, "Don't bother Missus Pritchard, I'll just take them in with me."

Surprised and feeling a little rebuffed, she handed him the thick pile of files as he added, "Give me ten minutes before you send in the first patient. I've a couple of calls to make."

She stared after him and furiously wondered what the hell had gotten into him? The shadow of a doubt crossed her mind as she thought, was he blowing her off? After all his promises and what she had done for him, was he trying to end their relationship before she had the opportunity to close the deal?

In his office with the door closed and headache continue to thump from his previous nights' intake of whisky, he filled a glass with water from the tap at the sink and fetching a packet of Paracetamol from his desk drawer, popped four from the blister pack and swallowed them one after the other before drinking the full glass of water.

Slumped behind his desk, he slowly exhaled and wondered how the hell he had got himself into this bloody position.

That the lad had died was bad enough though it was the stupid bugger's own fault for being so careless, but what made the whole situation worse was that Geoffrey was not the only individual who knew what he had done.

If, God forbid, Teddy Meiklewood opened his stupid bloody mouth, they were both for the high jump. High jump? His head slumped down to his hands as he stared unseeingly at the desk pad. Christ, it was worse than that. They'd both go to prison and the bloody key would be thrown away. Even the hint of a scandal and he'd be ruined, his license to practice medicine withdrawn, the practice closed down and without an income, his home and car repossessed. He'd lose everything.

First things first, he'd need to get rid of those bloody tablets and with a sudden sense of purpose, stood up from his desk and walked to the coat stand to lift his medical bag from the floor. Placing the bag onto the desk, he opened it and took out the cardboard packets, counting them as he did.

His brow furrowed, for he had made a mistake. He had counted eleven packets, not twelve.

He recounted the packets and the bag and emptied the contents onto the desk, watching as his stethoscope and other medical instruments fell from the bag.

Rummaging a hand among the items, he then peered into the now empty bag.

Confused, he counted the packets again, but saw he had not been mistaken.

The twelfth packet was missing.

"What the hell…" he murmured, his mouth suddenly dry.

There was definitely no mistake.

A packet was missing, but where the hell could it have gone to?

The door knocked and was almost immediately pushed opened by Debbie Pritchard who began to say, "That's Mister…" but got no further when he furiously screamed, "Get out!"

She jumped back in alarm, her hands shaking, her face red with embarrassment and quickly closed the door. Turning to the elderly patient stood behind her and her eyes flickering uncertainly, she stammered, "I don't think Doctor Mayhew is quite ready for you yet, Mister Ainsworth."

Returning to the waiting room with the elderly patient, her body shook with fury.

She had put up with him for almost six months now. His lacklustre performance in bed, his outrageous sexual demands and on occasion when he was in a mood, felt his wrath on her cheek, then accepted his groveling, repentant gifts when he blamed stress.

Put up with it all because of his halfhearted promises that he would leave his insipid wife and move her into the big house in Spruce Close, then when the time was right, inferred marriage.

Put up with it because of the prestige of being married to a doctor and not just any doctor, but Geoffrey Mayhew, Chairman of the local rugby club and popular personality in Preston.

Put up with it because she was sick of living on a basic income in a shitty flat when she knew that Geoffrey was sitting on a pile of money.

Her eyes brimming with unshed tars, she slammed the door of the staff toilet behind her and hands resting on the sink, stared at her reflection in the mirror.

She tossed her head and watching her blonde hair bounce, forced a smile. She was still a good looker and there were plenty of men out there who would appreciate her; plenty of men with money who knew how to give a woman a good time.

Taking a deep breath, she made her decision.

Smoothing down her skirt and with a final glance in the mirror, she swaggered out of the staff toilet to fetch her jacket and handbag from the staffroom.

Making her way back through the reception area, she loudly called out to her fellow receptionist, "If he's looking for me, tell Doctor *fucking* Mayhew, I'm out to lunch."

****

Detective Inspector Julie Sandford, her left hand supporting the elbow of her right arm, inhaled deeply on the cigarette held between her fingers as she stood beneath the canopy at the rear door of the Royal Preston Hospital mortuary, sheltering from the rain.

She hated autopsies, hated the antiseptic cleanliness of the white tiled room, hated the smell of Formaldehyde but most of all, hated the sight of a body being dissected.

Dressed in a white coloured paper Forensic suit with nitrile gloves on her hands and her thick, black hair tied in a tight bun, the passing ambulance crew smiled and nodded as they walked by, but were then slightly miffed that she totally ignored their civility.

Courtesy, had they known, was not one of Sandford's endearing qualities.

"Ma'am?"

She turned to see DC Lucy Carstairs stood behind her, similarly dressed in a Forensic suit with one hand holding open the door while the other held a small, white coloured plastic lunch-size box with a carrying handle.

"That's me got the samples and just about to head off to to the college with them."

It was fortunate, Sandford thought, that for speediness Preston College had agreed their Science Department would conduct Forensic tests on the body samples taken from the deceased Jonathan Archer.

Sandford nodded in acknowledgement before thoughtfully replying, "Use your charm with the head of the laboratory there and ask that they treat the samples as urgent. Play the sympathy card and tell him that the family need to know why a healthy and virile young man as Archer was so suddenly collapses and dies at a rugby practice match. Ask that they get the result to me as soon as possible to permit me to inform the grieving family, okay?"

"Got it," and was about to turn away when Sandford asked, "Any further news about Missus Mayhew?"

"Nothing, Ma'am, but I've arranged to collect my daughter from school this afternoon so I'm guessing I'll see her there and hopefully engage her in conversation. I'll try to invite her out again for coffee."

"Do what you can," Sandford dismissed the young detective with a nod.

In the mortuary changing room, Carstairs tore off the paper Forensic suit and with the sample box, made her way to her Focus in the car park.

The short drive from the mortuary car park to the college campus took Carstairs but a few minutes. Arriving at the main door, she parked her car in a visitors' bay and headed upstairs to the Science Laboratory where she spoke with the Professor in charge of the department and relayed Sandford's request.

As it happened, the white bearded man was aware of the media reporting of Jonathon Archer's death and promised he would have a result for Sandford by late afternoon at the earliest or possibly first thing the following morning.

As satisfied as she could be with his response, Carstairs phoned Sandford with the information and was instructed to return to meet the DI at her office.

****

Doris Chisholm opened the door at Alice Mayhew's knock and ushered the younger and very nervous woman through to the kitchen.

"My, but you're very pale, dear," she sat Alice down at the scrubbed wooden table that was already set for afternoon tea.

Laying the teapot on the mat between them, she asked, "Now, what's this all about? This thing that has so upset you?"

Alice took a swallow and replied, "I need your help with something," then in a rush told her of receiving the curious phone call from the man who would not give his name, of overhearing Geoffrey's conversation on the phone, of finding the packets of tablets with the strange writing and lastly, of her deep and anxious suspicion it had something to do with the young man Archer's death.

The elderly woman smiled and though it pained her to say anything contradictory about her opinion of Geoffrey Mayhew, softly said, "Perhaps, dear, you're letting your imagination run away with you. I mean, the phone call you received might have been from a rude patient and as for overhearing Geoffrey on the phone. I'm certain there must be times when he has to be firm with his patients, impolite even, don't you agree?"

Alice visibly relaxed, for Doris's explanation now made the phone calls seem so trivial, not the conspiracy she imagined.

She continued, "And much as I loathe your husband, I really can't believe he would be so foolish as to involve himself in a young man's death. I mean, he is a doctor after all. As for the tablets, well; while I accept that perhaps he doesn't as a rule carry prescribed medicine with him, I'm sure there must be occasions when it is necessary, perhaps when he is visiting a housebound patient, eh?"

"You're right, of course," Alice felt very foolish and breathed a sigh of relief.

"Anyway," she carefully poured the tea into the china cups, "you mentioned the packet of tablets you found had strange writing upon them. Have you any idea at all what the language is?"

Almost guiltily, Alice reached to her jacket that was hung on the back of the chair and from the pocket, produced the packet she had retained.

"Oh, you've brought it with you," Doris smiled then bidding Alice remained seated, left the kitchen to fetch her Apple iPad.

A moment later she returned and switching the IPad on, took the packet from Alice.

Her eyes narrowed as she read the writing on the packet and murmured., "I'm not of course certain, dear, but I do believe this language is Cyrillic.

"Cyrillic?" Alice slowly repeated.

"Well, Russian, if you prefer," she replied and carefully typed in *povysheniye proizvoditel'nosti.*

Her eyes opened wide and turned the screen towards Alice to permit her to read the translation: enhancement performance.

She stared curiously at Doris before pointing to the translation and asking, "What do you think this means?"

"I can't be certain, of course," Doris stared thoughtfully at the foil strip with the eight small, reddish brown tablets, then continued, "You said this young man who died, Jonathon Archer. He was a rugby player at Geoffrey's club?"

"Yes. At the dinner I attended, Geoffrey was raving about how talented the young man was, how he would turn around the clubs' fortune in the league and the cup matches. A star player, was how Geoffrey described him."

"Oh, he was an athlete, then. My dear," Doris, her brow creased in thought and face pale, she reached across to hold Alice's hand and said, "I believe you might be on to something after all."

****

Just as he was being discussed in the kitchen of the house in Middleton Road, Geoffrey Mayhew was now almost in a state of panic.

He held his head in his hands as he desperately tried to remember, but he could not for one minute imagine where the missing packet of the enhancement tablets had got to. Worse, he knew if they fell into the wrong hands and if for some unaccountable reason the police came into possession of them, it was likely his fingerprints and most certainly his DNA would be on the foil strips for when he had acquired them he had taken the precaution of checking every packet contained four strips of eight tablets.

Damn!

It had seemed so simple. Purchase the tablets, then two for young Archer before every match would ensure a victory for the club that would lead to winning the league and securing the county cup too. He would have been the club's most successful Chairman ever.

If only that stupid boy had did as he was told.

Well, there was nothing for it now but to cover his tracks and the only other individual who knew of Archer's enhancement drug-taking was the club's coach, that bloody has-been, Teddy Meiklewood, he snorted.

But how, he wondered, could he ensure that Meiklewood would never betray him?

****

Carstairs knocked upon her DI's room door and was called in to find Sandford at her desk while the seven detectives assisting with the inquiry were seated or stood against the wall.

"Ah, DC Carstairs, here at last," her voice tinged with sarcasm. "We were just about to go over what we know so far. DS Goodwin?" she turned with eyebrows raised to a portly man in his late thirties with thinning fair hair and a scruffy fair beard who wore a stained, black coloured 'Black Sabbath' tee shirt and whose belly hung over his baggy jeans.

"Ma'am," DS Terry Goodwin acknowledged her with a nod. "Well, in the last three months, we know that there has been a dramatic rise in the distribution of a batch of Russian made drugs nicknamed the Brown Speeders. Forensic examination has concluded these tablets," reaching across to the desk, he lifted a foil strip of six of the reddish brown tablets that he held up as an example, "are on sale right across Lancashire and have also been discovered in North Yorkshire too." He paused to return the foil strip to the desk, before continuing, "To date there has been five recorded deaths of youths and young men aged between fourteen and twenty-three, all of whom Forensic examination has concluded popped these tablets prior to their death. It has been assessed that the tablets which were pharmaceutically produced, are designed to enhance fitness by increasing lung capacity and stamina. All shite, of course," he sighed. "In reality, what they do is when taken prior to any form of physical exercise, whether that be sport or sex…" he grinned at the burst of laughter, before Sandford raised a hand and loudly called out, "Quiet! Cut out the bullshit, DS Goodwin. Just get on with it."

Humour it was generally known, was also not one of Sandford's endearing qualities.

"Anyway," Goodwin continued in a more sober voice, "the official statement from the pharmaceutical company was that there were side effects to the use of the drug and it was withdrawn from the market. It seems the tablet increases the blood flow to the heart to such a forceful rate and, as it was explained to me in layman terms by a pathologist, quite literally explodes the heart in the chest. Needless to say the drug was quickly banned in Russia, but not before a lorry load of boxes containing the drug was stolen from the pharmaceutical laboratory in Saint Petersburg, where it had been developed. Some of the boxes were recovered in European cities, namely Paris and Marseilles, then Madrid and recently Amsterdam, but we're now finding that some have made their way across the water to us here in England. Now," he glanced at his fellow detectives, "you might think that Preston is a curious place for the drug to end up, but intelligence from our Met colleagues at Scotland Yard tells us that Preston and the surrounding area is a trial run for the local production of the drug here in England. So, boys and girls, it's our job to find out who's distributing this shite and put a stop to it."

He turned to Sandford. "Ma'am?"

Her eyes darted around the room and she asked, "Questions?"

"Any intel about when and how this drug got into the country and who the local supplier is here in Lancashire, Terry?" asked a young dark haired woman wearing a navy blue coloured trouser suit who throughout the meeting incessantly chewed gum.

He shook his head before replying, "The Met's best bet is by lorry via the Channel Port, but of course that's their standard response when they haven't got a fucking clue," he grinned. "However, if that *is* how the drug is getting into England, when and what lorry," he shrugged, "is anybody's guess. As for a local supplier. We've turned a few dealers and that's how we came across the Brown Speeders," he held up the foil strip as an example. "A couple of dealers gave up the name Monty Reid, who likely you will all know or had dealings with."

This was acknowledged by a general groan, for Montgomery 'Monty' Reid was not only a well documented drug supplier, but since his spectacular rise in the North of England illegal drug trade and despite some expensive undercover operations against him, the Lancashire Constabulary and those of several neighbouring counties had been unable to procure a successful conviction against the highly successful drug supplier.

"As you can imagine, while some of these buggers dealing the stuff are happy to fire Monty into us in exchange for a favourable report to the DPP, not one will give a *statement* or is willing to appear as a witness against him."

"Hardly surprising, Terry," quipped a whippet thin bald detective who grinning, added, "unless they know how to hold their breath under water with ten feet of chain wrapped about them and a masonry block attached to the other end."

"Thank you, DC Hargreaves," Sandford moodily nodded, but before she could continue, her desk phone rung.

"DI Sandford."

The team watched as she grabbed at her pen and began writing on her desk pad.

Moments later she returned the phone to its cradle and said, "That was the Forensic Department at the college. They've done us a great favour by timeously examining the stomach contents and blood samples from Jonathon Archers body and now confirm that as we suspected, he did die of some kind of drug abuse, though they are unable to determine from their MIMS what the drug is. Hardly surprising it's not in the MIMS," she scowled, referring to the database of both prescribed and generic drugs, "seeing as how the bloody Russians quickly took it off the market after they discovered it kills people. Anyway," she sniffed, "the pathologist concluded that young Archer's heart was increased far larger than normal for a man his age. So, together with the evidence of drugs in his body and from this," she pointed to a clear plastic evidence bag containing a foil strip with six Brown Speeders, "discovered in his locker in the changing room, we must assume he has ingested the Speeders. However, the blood sample will be sent to our own Forensic Department at Headquarters in Hutton where I'm confident our suspicions will be confirmed."

She was desperate for a fag and had she been alone in the office, would have undoubtedly gone ahead and lit up, but with her office so overwhelmingly crowded, was forced to exercise some patience. Nevertheless, she reached into her drawer and withdrew her cigarettes and lighter that she noisily slapped down onto the desk; the subtle hint that she was about to wrap the meeting up.

Taking a deep breath, she begun, "We know that Archer was the rising star player of the Fulwood Martyrs Rugby Club and that he was being individually coached by Teddy Meiklewood who two years previously, featured in a drugs ring that was supplying enhancement drugs at Meiklewood's former club. Unfortunately, though we knew of Meiklewood's involvement, there was insufficient evidence to arrest him at the time.

We also know that Meiklewood is associated with Monty Reid and that a year ago he featured as a bit player in the unsuccessful operation against Reid."

She paused, her fingers involuntarily reaching for the packet of fags. "We also know that the local and much respected Chairman of the club, Doctor Geoffrey Mayhew, was not just Archer's local GP, but also doubles as the club doctor."

She paused again, her lungs aching for an infusion of nicotine. "What we do *not* know, ladies and gentlemen, and what we must prove," she stared morosely at her team, "is if Meiklewood did supply Archer the Speeders and if so, where did he procure them? We also need to know if Doctor Mayhew had any knowledge of Archer's use of the Speeders or indeed if he *did* know, if the good doctor condoned Archer using the performance enhancement drugs." Her fingers drummed at the desktop while her right foot tapped rhythmically on the linoleum floor as her urge for nicotine was now almost overwhelming.

"Go and find me evidence," she bluntly dismissed them.

****

In his mind, he retraced his steps since placing the tablets from the plastic shopping bag into his medical bag.

Six weeks previously he'd collected fourteen packets in the plastic bag from Meiklewood of which, he screwed his eyes tightly closed to remember, he gave two packets to young Archer with the instruction to take two tablets before each match.

His eyes snapped open as he guessed that likely the police will have what is left of Archer's packets. Mentally counting the rugby games Archer had played in, Geoffrey calculated if the young fool did as he had been instructed, there should be two full foil strips of eight tablets each with a third foil strip containing four tablets remaining. What he could not know was that contrary to the strict instructions, his protégé Jonathon Archer had in fact consumed far more tablets than he had been told by Geoffrey, that only six tablets instead of twenty tablets remained.

Again, his main concern was not the death of a young man with a brilliant athletic career ahead of him, but his own survival when as they undoubtedly would the law came looking for the man who had provided the tablets.

He stared at the pile of patients files lying on his desk, realising that almost like an automaton, he had dealt with almost a dozen patients yet could not recall speaking to a single one. With a sigh he pressed the buzzer for his receptionist, Debbie Pritchard.

Returned from an extended lunch just minutes earlier, the blonde first knocked then entered his office, her face pale and drawn and icily asked, "Yes, Doctor, what can I do for you?"

"Ah, sorry about earlier, Debs. I've a lot on my mind at the minute," he faked a smile before asking, "Anymore patients I've to see?"

"Missus Hill was the last patient fifteen minutes ago," she sharply replied. "Is there anything else?"

He sat back in his chair and leering at her, said, "Well, perhaps that gives us time to…" but got no further when Pritchard held up a hand and abruptly told him, "I'm sorry, Doctor Mayhew, but my working hours are dictated by my contract. I'm due to finish in a couple of minutes so, if there's nothing else?"

Stunned, he could only shake his head as she turned but then stopped and staring at him, snapped, "Give my regards to your wife!" then slammed the door on her way out.

His astonishment lasted mere seconds, but was then replaced by embarrassed rage.

Angrily, he swept the patients files from his desk to scatter on the floor and standing, his hands clenched in to fists, turned to kick at the files, but then stopped as a sudden flashback crossed his mind. His brow creased and his eyes squinted as he tried to recall kicking something, then it came to him.

He turned to where his medical bag lay on the cabinet by the window. That's what he had kicked, but where?

With a sudden flash of inspiration, he remembered. The hall table. Recalling now that he had been pissed the previous evening when he'd got home, he'd kicked the bloody bag under the hall table.

He slumped down into his desk chair, unconsciously nodding and wheezed a sigh of relief.

The missing packet must have fallen from the bag when he'd kicked it.

He reached for the phone, thinking he'd instruct Alice to get herself under the bloody table and find it for him coming home, but his call rang out and cursing, remembered then he'd told her not to answer the phone.

He'd need to get straight home and find it himself.

Locking his desk drawer, he ignored the spilled files and headed out towards the reception area.

"Good evening, Doctor Mayhew," the elderly cleaner called out to him, but he didn't respond, surprised to find the reception desk was unmanned and that as she had threatened Debbie Pritchard had already gone home.

Bloody woman, he inwardly snarled. About time she got the heave-ho anyway, he thought. Getting too uppity for her own good and what was that crack about giving her regards to Alice?

Leaving the practice through the front door, he indicated the cleaner close it behind him. Walking to his car he knew what had been going through the blonde's mind.

Jealousy, for more than once she had urged him to leave Alice, that she would make a far better companion.

Spouse, more likely she meant, he sneered.

As if he would entangle himself with a woman with such a reputation.

No, he already had it as good as it needed to be.

A wife for the domestic duties and to pull out of the cupboard every now and then for public social functions, then glancing in the rear view mirror, smirked at his reflection. And a stock of local women all keen to bed the good Doctor Mayhew.

Grinning, he started the engine and prepared to drive home.
****

She had collected Marcy from school, but was still in a daze, almost a walking coma while she tried to come to terms with what she had learned.

Her good friend Doris had been in no doubt that after hearing about the telephone calls and the discovery of the packet of tablets, Geoffrey must be mixed up in some sort of criminal enterprise, or that's what Doris had called it.

"But what are you going to do about it, Alice?" she had asked. "Will you take what you know to the police?"

"I can't," she had vigorously shaken her head. "I mean, what will I tell them? That I suspect my husband might somehow be involved in a young man's death? For God's sake, Doris," she was on her feet, her arms flailing and a headache coming on as she walked the floor of the kitchen. "What if Geoffrey has the drug for some sort of…of…I don't know! A patient who needs that type of prescription!"

"What?" the ridicule evident in Doris's voice. "He popped over to a pharmacy in Moscow at his lunch break to get them?"

Alice knew when she was being mocked; Christ, hadn't she suffered enough derision over the period of her marriage?

"I get enough bloody sarcasm at home, Doris Chisholm, without having to take it from you!" she snapped back.

"Then do something about it!" the older woman slapped a hand down onto the kitchen table. "For God's sake, Alice! For once in your life stand up to the bastard and do what you know is right! As we stand here arguing over this, a family is grieving and we both know that your husband might possibly be the cause!"

They had stared at each other in angry silence until Doris had walked round the table and taking Alice in her arms, continued in a soft voice, "Look, it wouldn't do any harm to at least speak to the police and if he has not done anything wrong, no harm done. Besides, I'm sure if you were to ask the police to keep what you tell them confidential, they will and Geoffrey need never know."

She had lifted her head from Doris's shoulder and staring at her, replied, "I know a police woman. A detective. Perhaps I should have a word with her. Over a coffee. As friends, you know?" she tried to smile, seeking assurance that this was the correct thing to do.

Doris had smiled and said, "Now, that's a good idea."

Well, it had seemed like a good idea, but when Alice arrived at the school, it was Lucy Carstairs who approached her, but try as she might she could not find the courage to tell Carstairs anything and without even a smile, turned away from the younger woman.

Now here she was at home, the table set and dinner prepared, Marcy in her room completing her homework and her legs began to shake when she heard the sound of Geoffrey's car arriving in the driveway.

CHAPTER TEN

Tommy Burke had risen early hoping to get an early start and after his morning run, changed into a casual shirt and jeans before heading out in the Defender to the IKEA store at Braehead.

He had made a list rather than trying to remember everything in his head and humming along to the radio, turned into the large car park and parked in a bay as close as he could near to the store exit.

Collecting a trolley, Tommy examined his idiot list, as he called it, and spent over an hour collecting household items from throughout the store.

He was loading the Defender with his purchases when his mobile phone activated and saw on the screen it was the Arran housekeeper, Mary McKay.

"Good morning, Tommy, I had a message last night on my answer machine to call you."

"Morning, Mary. Just to let you know that as it's Friday, I'm coming over sometime early evening evening for a few days on the island and was wondering if you could maybe buy me some essentials and pack the fridge with some foodstuffs. You know, milk and bread and …" he stopped and grinned. "Sorry, Mary, I'm forgetting myself. You've been a housewife for a long time now, so why am I telling you what groceries I need?"

"Aye, well," she cheerily laughed, "I've an idea what a strapping man like yourself will want to eat, Tommy, so I'll go up there this afternoon and get the fridge filled. One thing I'd warn you about, though. It's a holiday weekend so traditionally at this time of the year the island is packed solid with visitors and likely most of the holidaymakers coming across to the island will be off Friday. That means the ferries will be packed solid so if you intend driving over it might be prudent to book your vehicle onto the ferry right away."

"Good point," he unconsciously nodded as Mary added, "Anything else you need done?"

"Nothing I can think of, so I'll give you a phone when I'm at the house," he replied and ended the call.

****

Geoffrey had kept her awake that night till the early hours of the morning, noisily stomping about the house before finally making his way to his bedroom, but thankfully was gone in the morning without breakfast and before Marcy awoke.

Returning to the house after walking her granddaughter to school and now making Marcy's bed, Alice Mayhew froze when to her surprise, she heard the sound of her husband's car stopping on the gravelled driveway. It wasn't like him to be home during the day and so patting at her hair, she rushed downstairs to meet him.

She forced a smile and stood demurely as he walked through the front door, but his face gave him away.

He was angry about something, evident by the way he flung his medical bag to the floor.

There was no greeting or acknowledgment of her other than him crooking his finger at her and growling, "I want a word with you. Come here," and stepped through the door into the lounge.

Her heart beating frantically in her chest, Alice timidly followed him into the large brightly lit room and when he turned to face her, she hesitantly asked, "Yes, Geoffrey?"

From his wax jacket pocket, he produced a small cardboard packet and her eyes widened when she recognised it as the same type of packet that she had hidden under her mattress upstairs.

Her surprise wasn't lost on her husband whose own eyes narrowed as he took a step closer to her.

"It had been my intention to ask if you had seen a small packet such as this one," he returned it to his pocket, "but clearly, you have and that will be the one that is missing from my medical bag. I've wasted all last night and much of this morning looking for the bloody thing when all I had to do, it seems, was ask you. So tell me, Alice my dear," he took another step towards her, his face red and his hands bunching into fists, "Where exactly is the packet now?"

She swallowed with difficulty and stammered, "I haven't seen anything like it, Geoffrey. Truly."

He took another step and now was so close she could feel his rancid breath upon her face, his eyes bright and his teeth gritted as she flinched from his stare.

"You're lying, Alice, and we both know it. Now, what happens to you if I suspect you're lying to me? Remind me, my dear."

She could hardly breath for such was her terror, but at last she replied, her voice almost a whisper, "You'll beat me."

She turned her head down and her face away from his stare then eyes tightly closed, braced herself for his fist.

But it was not his fist.

It was so unexpected that she had no time to react, but suddenly his large right hand was at her throat and he was pushing her back against a heavy wooden sideboard, the force of which when her lower back struck the edge was enough to cause her pain and to knock over the hefty, ceramic vase on top.

He was far too heavy and far too strong for her to fight him off. Grabbing at his wrists to try and ease the pressure on her throat as he strangled her, she thought she was going to faint.

His face was inches from hers with small bubbles of saliva collecting at the corners of his mouth, he hissed, "Where is the fucking packet!"

She was terrified and now with both his hands at her throat, knew that he really intended hurting her this time, but more than that, in the briefest of heartbeats some inner sense, some instinct told her that he was as frightened as she was.

It was the missing packet. That's what scared him, she suddenly realised.

He was beyond control now and his grip tightened.

She couldn't breathe, could feel the veins in her head throbbing and knew she was seconds away from passing out.

Panicking, she released her right hand from his wrist and groped behind her for something, anything, to stop him choking her.

Her hand fumbled at the vase that had fallen over, a thick, ceramic, multi-coloured bottle vase with a wide base that fluted to a narrow opening. Her hand grabbed at the vase, feeling her fingers wind around the narrow top and with all her might swung it at Geoffrey's head.

He went down as though poleaxed and with his grip released, she struggled for breath, gasping and wheezing like an eighty-a-day smoker.

He lay on his side on the wooden floor in front of her, the shards of ceramic lying about him.

Stunned, she saw that she still held the broken neck of the bottle in her hand and in horror, threw it from her and watched it skid across the floor to the opposite wall.

The left side of his head began seeping blood and she was about to reach down towards him, but stopped when he groaned.

Relieved that she had not killed him and realising he needed medical attention, she turned to make her way to the phone on the side table, but then stopped.

In that terrifying few seconds, a dramatic change had come over Alice.

Drawing upon some inner strength, a reserve of courage she never realised she had, she slowly turned to stare at him as though he were a stranger. She saw not the beguiling young doctor who had wooed her, but a menacing beast who had bullied and terrorised her almost since the beginning of the marriage; a fleshy, drunken adulterer she no longer considered to be her husband, but someone for whom all affection had died a long time ago.

While he was still unconscious, her eyes narrowed as with mixed emotions she thought, my husband tried to strangle me and yet I'm about to phone for an ambulance for him?

A mad, crazy idea came to her and as hurriedly as she could, Alice sprinted into the kitchen and grabbed a handful of plastic shopping bags from the cupboard.

The bags in her hand, she raced upstairs first to Marcy's room where she emptied the little girl's drawers into two of the plastic bags then into her own room where she stuffed some clothing and underwear into the remaining two bags before finally retrieving the packet from under her mattress.

She stopped, wide-eyed and listening intently.

Was that Geoff coming up the stairs after her?

Heart beating wildly, she sneaked out into the hallway, but the stairs were empty.

Making her way back down to the lounge, she saw with relief that he had stirred and now lay on his back; however, he remained unconscious.

She dropped the four bags at the front door and as slowly as she dared, returned to the lounge where reaching into his wax jacket pocket she lifted out the packet of tablets.

A thought occurred to her and gritting her teeth, she turned him towards her and almost collapsed when he grunted and expelled some trapped wind. Taking a deep breath and with her hands shaking, she fetched his leather wallet from the inside pocket of his suit jacket and grabbed the currency notes from within before throwing the wallet across the room.

With a final glance at him to ensure he was still breathing, she rose to her feet and resisted the urge to kick him in his face.

Grabbing her jacket from the coat stand and the plastic bags from the floor, she took a final glance inside the house before slamming the door behind her.

****

Seated at her desk, Lucy Carstairs went over it again and again in her head.

There was no other way to explain it. Yesterday at the school gate, Alice Mayhew had deliberately ignored her and did so again this morning.

She irately shook her head. There was no telling what kind of mood the bloody woman was in. Eyes closed, she shook her head, remembering DI Sandford's instruction she get close to Missus

Mayhew and learn what she could about the doctor's movements and callers to the house.

How the hell was she going to explain that she was being snubbed for as the DI was fond of saying, she didn't accept excuses, only results.

A sudden idea came to her, a way to confront Alice in such a way that she could not ignore Carstairs.

Grabbing at her handbag and car keys, she knew exactly how she'd get to speak with her.

She'd visit Alice at her house.

****

He came to very slowly and wondered why he was lying on the floor. He tried to turn his head and almost immediately moaned in pain and fought a wave of nausea. Still lying flat, he raised a hand to his head and felt the stickiness of drying blood.

What the…his eyes flickered.

She'd hit him. The bitch had struck him with the vase. He turned on his side and with his left hand, reached for the leg of the sideboard with the intention of pulling himself upright, but his right hand pressed down onto a splintered piece of the broken vase and almost immediately felt the splinter digging into the soft skin of his palm at the thumb. Crying out in pain, he fell backwards as a gush of blood spurted from the wound. Reaching into his trouser pocket with his left hand, he withdrew his handkerchief and pressed it against the flow of blood.

Awkwardly, his head throbbing, he turned and managed to get to his knees then using the uninjured hand on the sideboard, pulled himself to his feet.

His rage knew no bounds.

Staggering through to the kitchen, he run his hand under the cold water tap and reached for a dishcloth that he used as a makeshift bandage.

He knew she was gone, had fled the house though other than that old cow who she had befriended, also knew she had nowhere to run to. She didn't even have use of the old Toyota because he only permitted her the keys of it when it was shopping days. However, a doubt crossed his mind and glancing through the lounge window his mouth tightened until he saw the Aygo parked in its usual spot.

She'd be back at some point, of that he was certain and then, he snarled, there would be a reckoning; he'd make her pay for what she did.

Satisfied the bleeding was for the minute stemmed, he made his way through to the hall and collected his medical bag before heading upstairs.

It was half an hour later that he discovered that not only had Alice removed his wallet from his jacket, but the packet of tablets was gone too.

****

Doris Chisholm hurried to her front door, slightly alarmed at the way it was being pounded to find a wild-eyed Alice Mayhew stood there, her face chalk white, her eyes wide and staring and clutching plastic bags in both hands.

"My God, dear, what the…" but was almost rudely pushed to one side when Alice pushed by her.

"I need your help," she gasped.

Doris could see her friend was close to tears and reaching for her with hands outstretched, said, "Whatever it is, you know you can count on me. Come in, come in," she ushered Alice through the hallway towards the lounge and took the plastic bags from her. "Sit down, please," she almost pushed the younger woman into a chair. "Now, tell me, what's going on?"

If she expected an immediate explanation, it wasn't to be for Alice burst into tears, her body shaking and her face in her hands as bent over in the chair, she hysterically sobbed.

Patting her gently upon her shoulder, Doris said, "Sit here and compose yourself. Whatever is wrong, whatever has happened, you're safe here. I'll put the kettle on and while I'm doing that and when you're ready, go upstairs and use the bathroom to wash your face."

In the kitchen, Doris knew it had to do with Geoffrey Mayhew and furiously shook her head. She knew that man was well thought of in the town and it angered her that nobody could see him for the real bastard he actually was.

While the kettle boiled, she prepared two mugs and heard the upstairs toilet flushing, the sound of Alice coming down the stairs then joining her in the kitchen.

"Sorry," she said, her arms folded and her eyes red from weeping.

"For what? I'm your friend, dear, if you can't come to me in times of trouble, who can you turn to?"

Doris Chisholm had never really been a tactile individual, but suddenly found herself crushing Alice to her.

"Now," she forced a smile, "sit yourself down and tell me what has happened."

It took Alice just five minutes of non-stop talking to relate what had occurred.

"So, he's alive then," Doris wryly commented.

Aghast, Alice stared at her, but then burst into laughter, before replying, "Yes, Doris, I haven't killed my husband," she sighed before muttering, "more's the pity."

"What's in the plastic bags?"

"Clothes for Marcy and me."

"Clothes?" Doris was puzzled. "Why not use a suitcase?"

"Because the suitcases are locked in the garage and only Geoffrey is permitted the key," she slowly shook her head.

"What a ridiculous situation," Doris almost laughed, but then stopped and staring curiously at Alice, continued, "I assume if you have fled the house with clothes for you and Marcy, you have no intention of returning?"

"No, none," she vigorously shook her head. "I've had enough and can you imagine what he would do to me if he catches me."

"Why not go to the police?"

"And do what," she laughed humorously. "Tell them I cracked a vase across my husband's head?"

"Yes, but only because he was trying to strangle you. I mean look," she pointed to Alice's reddened neck. "There's proof."

"I don't think so," she twisted her neck to relieve the ache. "I think the police would say I did it myself to back up my allegation against him, Doris, and even if I did go to the police and if I did tell them of my suspicions about Geoffrey and the young man Archer's death. Look at me," she shook her head. "I'm the wife of a respected doctor. He would merely make some excuse about the tablets being for a patient and fall back on his Hippocratic oath not to divulge the patient's name. The police would have no proof and I'd be seen as a hysterical woman and they'd probably ask *me* where I got the bloody tablets! What do I tell them? I *stole* them from my husband's medical bag? Besides," she shook her head at the unfairness of it all, "you know his reputation in this town. Who do you think the police would believe?"

Doris didn't immediately respond, but then softly replied, "You are right, of course. But that begs the question, Alice. What do you intend doing?"

She raised a hand before Alice could reply to add, "You know that you and Marcy are welcome to stay here with me, but this will be the first place he looks. If I am to offer you any advice, it's this. Get as far away from him as you can. London, Cornwall, somewhere he wouldn't think to look for you."

Alice, her hands curled round the mug of tea, had never in her life felt so insecure and raising the mug to her lips, her eyes fell upon the painting on the wall and a thought occurred to her.

"I'll need to collect Marcy from the school, make some excuse about a doctor's appointment or something. Can you run me there and then take us to the railway station in Preston?"

"Yes, dear, of course," Doris frowned, "but what are you planning to do? Where do you intend going?"

Alice didn't answer, but laid the mug down onto the table and from her jacket pocket, fetched out the creased currency notes she taken from Geoff's wallet. Counting them out, she said, "I have almost two-hundred and fifty pounds here and the bank card he gave me for the shopping. There's about fifty pounds in that account. That will need to do me till we get where we're going and I get some kind of job."

"Where you're going? Wait a minute," Doris left the kitchen, returning a moment later with her handbag. Rummaging in her purse, she produced four twenty pound notes and said, "Here, take this. It's not much but it will help."

"Thank you," replied a grateful Alice.

"Another thing, dear, I've an old suitcase you can have. I loved it when I used it, but haven't used it for donkey years and it's in a bit of a state. To be honest, I really thought about throwing it out, but you can have it for it's better than you hauling plastic shopping bags of clothes around with you."

Alice sighed and nodded her grateful acceptance of the offer.

"The bank card you use for the shopping," Doris's eyes narrowed. "We'll need to draw the money somewhere local before you go to the station, then destroy it."

"Why?"

"Because if you use it wherever you are going to, Geoffrey can find you. All he has to do is contact the bank and concoct some excuse to find out where it's being used."

Alice's eyes widened in understanding as she slowly nodded and said, "There's an ATM at the shop down from the school. We can stop there and I'll empty the account."

"But you haven't said where you are going?"

She smiled and replied, "Like you said, it needs to be somewhere Geoffrey won't think to look for Marcy and me."

She nodded towards the painting and grimly added, "I'm taking her to your island. We're going to Arran."

CHAPTER ELEVEN

DC Lucy Carstairs turned her Ford Focus in through the gates of the house in Spruce Close and stopping the car, stared curiously at the old Toyota Aygo parked beside the large white Volvo. She guessed the Toyota was probably Alice's car yet had never seen her driving to school in it, even in the worst of weather when most if not all the parents and grandparents used their vehicles to drop off or collect their children.

Glancing at the dashboard clock she saw it was almost eleven o'clock and mentally crossed her fingers that Alice was at home. Getting out of the car, she took a breath and walking along the path to the front door, adopted a cheery smile before ringing the doorbell. There was no immediate reply and she was about to ring again when the door was snatched open by Geoffrey Mayhew.

It was apparent he had suffered some sort of injury to the left side of his head that bore a large sticking plaster and his right hand was bandaged too. She didn't need to be a detective to realise that something was amiss, that someone had caused his injuries.

"Doctor Mayhew," she brightly smiled, "I'm Lucy Carstairs, Mike Carstairs wife?" she added in the belief her husband's rugby playing for the club might perhaps break down any barrier. "I was wondering if I might have a quick word with Alice, please?"

He didn't respond, but stared curiously at her before grunting, "She's not here right now."

"Oh, I'm sorry I've missed her. Can you tell me when she'll be back?"

"No, and if you don't mind, Missus Carstairs, I am rather busy at the moment."

"Oh, right," she stepped to one side and took a quick glance inside, but he realised what she was doing and closed the door over a little further before adding, "As I said, Alice is not at home. Now, if you don't mind?"

"No, of course," she backed a step away and was about to turn towards her car, but then to her surprise, he stared keenly at her and asked, "You *are* the police officer, that's correct, yes?"

"Yes, I am," she continued to smile.

He didn't respond, but merely nodded in acknowledgment and closed the door.

Inside the house, Geoffrey stood with his back to the closed door and bit at the knuckle of his closed left fist.

Was her visit to Alice for information about him? Could it simply be coincidental that Carstairs wife was a police officer or was it something more sinister, that Alice had told her of his possession of the Brown Speeders? But that would mean Alice knew what they were and…but, how could she know, he reasoned. She had been a trainee teacher when they met and had no medical or pharmaceutical training. There was no way on God's earth she could know about the tablets being used to enhance an athlete's performance and, his eyes narrowed, she could not possibly connect the tablets to the death of that idiot Archer.

However, the unexpected visit of the police woman seeking to speak with Alice and her theft of the packet of enhancement tablets had in Geoffrey Mayhew's mind, unwittingly sown the seed of doubt.

Teeth now gritted, he knew that only way he could really be safe from any police attention or prosecution was to retrieve the tablets from her and, he swallowed with difficulty at the enormity of what he was considering, make sure she could never tell anyone about them.

****

While Doris Chisholm waited in the old Peugeot estate car by the main gate, Alice buzzed for entry at the main door of the primary school and explained to the secretary who opened the door that she was there to collect her granddaughter Marcy for a doctor's appointment.

"I'm sorry, Missus Mayhew," the secretary frowned, "I don't have anything in today's calendar for Marcy."

"Oh, that husband of mine," Alice glibly lied with a smile and sighed as though in disappointment. "I ask him to do one thing and make the arrangement with the school and he's forgotten."

"Oh, well," The secretary returned her smile. "Doctor Mayhew is a very busy man, isn't he? I'll just run along and fetch her for you if you wait here, please."

It seemed to an anxious Alice that the secretary took far longer than usual and she kept nervously glancing through the window into the car park, half expecting to see Geoffrey's white coloured Volvo haring into the car park.

At last, the secretary arrived back at the reception foyer holding Marcy's hand.

"Am I going to the doctor, Gran?" the little girl asked, her face betraying her curiosity.

"Just for a check-up, sweetheart," Alice tightly smiled and thanking the secretary, ushered Marcy through the door and down to the waiting car.

Seeing Doris sat in the driving seat, Marcy squealed with delight and called out, "Auntie Doris. Are you coming to the doctor's too?"

Doris cast a quick glance at Alice before replying with a reassuring grin, "Even better, little one. You and your Gran are going on an adventure."

****

Doris turned into Butler Street and driving to the end on the one-way street, circled the tight roundabout before coming to a halt outside the main railway building.

In the rear seat, Marcy's head swivelled back and forth as she excitedly called out, "Are we going on a train, Gran? Is that the adventure?"

"Yes, sweetheart, something like that," Alice, her heart beating like a drum, tried to curb the child's enthusiasm before adding, "I'll tell you all about when we get on the train, okay?"

She got out of the passenger seat and while Doris helped Marcy from the car, Alice grabbed the old and very battered brown coloured suitcase from the boot.

"Be careful with the handle, dear," Doris warned her, then apologetically continued, "I'm sorry it's so old, but it's the only one I have."

"Tell me again about how I get there," Alice grunted as she heaved the case onto a trolley.

With Alice pushing the trolley and Doris leading Marcy by the hand as they hurriedly made their way to the ticket office, she replied, "Well, remember Stephan and I drove there and it was a very long time ago, but according to what I read on the Internet, you catch a train to Glasgow Central Station and from there get a connection to Ardrossan Harbour and the ferry terminal."

"Central Station, Ardrossan Harbour, ferry terminal," Alice nodded as she repeated the instruction.

"Where's Ard…Add…that place?" Marcy piped up.

"It's in Scotland, dear," Doris smiled down at the little girl, who's eyes widened as she repeated, "Scotland," then asked, "Is that a foreign country?"

"They think so," quipped Doris with a grin to Alice.

To Alice's surprise, the cost of her and Marcy's one-way ticket was just under thirty-eight pounds for the journey that the smiling ticket seller said would take just over two hours and fifteen minutes.

She knew the little girl had missed lunch when she took her from the school, so quickly bought a sandwich and juice at a kiosk and a couple of children's magazines for the trip.

Returning to Doris with tears in her eyes, she hugged her and promised to phone as soon as she was settled.

Bending to the little girl, Doris took her in her arms and whispered in her ear, "Look after your grandmother for me. She's a very special lady."

"I will," Marcy sombrely whispered back.

****

On the road back to her office, Lucy Carstairs was puzzled.

She was too professional to question Geffrey Mayhew on his own doorstep and ask how he had come by his injuries, but suspected the wounds he sported were somehow significant. Besides, she argued with herself, she had gone to the house ostensibly to see his wife Alice, not as a police officer.

And where was Alice, she wondered?

Certainly, if she was not using the Toyota or the Volvo vehicles she had seen parked on the driveway, she must be out on foot somewhere. It was just approaching lunchtime, so not at the school, she reasoned.

A cold chill swept through her.

Geoffrey Mayhew's injuries. Could it be they were inflicted during a fight between him and Alice? Was it possible, her stomach clenched, that Alice *was* in the house and perhaps injured or worse?

She unconsciously stepped on the pedal, keen to speak with DI Sandford and inwardly prayed that Alice was not harmed, that she was still alive.

****

As the Virgin train headed north towards the Scottish border, Alice, sat facing Marcy, watched the little girl finish the sandwich and juice before quietly telling her, "We might not be going home again, Marcy. Would that upset you?"

She stared curiously at her grandmother before replying, "What, never?"

"Hopefully not," Alice smiled tightly.

"Is he coming with us to Scotland? Will he be there?"

"No," she shook her head. She decided to be as honest as she could be with the little girl and continued, "Your grandfather will be staying in Preston. It will just be you and me. It won't be easy though," she sighed. "I'll need to find somewhere for us to live and a job and you will need to go to a new school."

"Do they speak like us in Scotland or will I need to learn to speak Scottish?"

"No," she supressed a smile at the serious question, "Scottish people speak English like us."

"But if they're not English like us, why *don't* they speak Scottish?"

Across the aisle, an elderly man and woman, presumably his wife Alice thought, could clearly overhear the conversation and began to laugh. Turning towards them the man said in a broad Glasgow accent, "Don't be worrying too much, young lady. We all speak the same language, though you might have a wee bit of trouble to begin with because of the Scottish accent. Now, if you can take my advice, if anyone says something you don't understand, just ask them to speak a wee bit slower. Okay, hen?"

Marcy solemnly nodded her head and hesitantly replied, "Okay," though was a little confused as to why the old man thought she was a hen and not a girl.

Turning back to her grandmother, she asked, "Where will we live, Gran?"

"Well, the place we're going to is an island called Arran and to begin with, we'll need to find a guesthouse or maybe…" she saw Marcy seemed puzzled and explained, "A guesthouse is like a small hotel where we can get bed and breakfast. Yes?"

"I think so, yes," the little girl slowly replied.

"Then I'll get a job and we'll find you a school."

As Marcy settled back into her seat to read her magazines, Alice stared thoughtfully through the window at the passing countryside. It all sounded so easy, finding a guesthouse, getting a job and a school for Marcy.

Doubt clouded her eyes and she wondered not for the first time; am I doing the right thing, running from Geoffrey and pulling Marcy from school?

Tears formed in her eyes, but not wishing to upset Marcy, pulled her handkerchief from her trouser pocket and pretending to blow her nose, wiped at her eyes.

She sensed she was being watched and turning, saw that while the elderly man across the aisle seemed to be dozing, his wife with female intuition realised that something was amiss and smiling, softly said, "I'll keep my eye on the wee girl if you need a couple of minutes to go and freshen yourself up, hen."

Alice inhaled and not trusting herself to speak, nodded before making her way to the toilet at the end of the carriage.

In the privacy of the small loo, she sat on the closed lid of the toilet and cried for almost five minutes. Her face and hands washed, she felt slightly better and was returning to her seat when she heard the tannoy inform the passengers that they were approaching Carlisle.

"Gran, where were you?" the relief in Marcy's voice was evident. "I thought you'd got lost."

"Now," she smiled, her eyes sparkling, "how could I possibly get lost on a train?" then turning to the elderly lady, mouthed 'Thank you.'

****

DC Lucy Carstairs found DI Sandford standing at the rear door of the police office, her customary fag in one hand and a Costa beaker of coffee in the other.

"Ma'am," she greeted her and proceeded to relate her visit to the Mayhew's house.

"You did what!" Sandford's eyes blazed with anger. 'What the *fuck* possessed you to go to their house?"

Her face red and aware of the two passing uniformed constables who were pretending not to hear, she replied, "I went as Alice Mayhew's friend, not as a police officer."

Sandford inhaled then slowly exhaled before asking, "So, he didn't seem rattled that you went to his door?"

"No, Ma'am, not at all. I mean, why should he?" she replied, wisely deciding that she need not mention that Geoffrey Mayhew had already asked that question, thinking she had screwed up enough and not wishing to incur more of Sandford's disapproval.

Taking a breath then shaking her head, Sandford stared keenly at her before she asked, "What's your take on it? His injuries I mean?"

"Well," she thoughtfully replied, "He's been struck with something, of that I'm certain and the wound on his right hand; defensive, maybe?" she shrugged. "However, my main concern is he might have hurt his wife, that she is in the house."

"But we have nothing to indicate she *is* in the house and no evidence to crave a warrant, even if we wanted to," she bit at her bottom lip. "How badly was the bastard hurt?"

"Hard to say, Ma'am. Certainly he had a fresh sticking plaster on the left side of his head and I could see even though he'd tried to wash it off, there was some dried blood on his ear. As for his right hand," she shook her head, "all I could see was a fresh looking bandage that looked as though he'd put it on himself."

Sandford drew deeply on her unfiltered cigarette before continuing, "But your main concern is that you think Alice Mayhew might be in the house, perhaps even injured?"

"Yes, Ma'am."

Sandford glanced at her watch before asking, "Who is picking your daughter up from school, today?"

"My daughter, Ma'am? Eh, my husband. He's an early finish on a Friday."

"Right, here's what you're going to do," she dropped the butt end and stood on it, ignoring the tin bin that was screwed to the wall to collect cigarette ends. "Phone and cancel your hubby. You collect your daughter and that will give you the opportunity to find out if Alice Mayhew attends to collect her granddaughter." Her eyes narrowed when she asked, "I take it she is the only person who collects the child from school?"

"As far as I'm aware, yes, Ma'am. I can't say for certain, but I've never seen her husband collect the child."

"Right then, get that done and phone me the instant you have that information. If the wife is not there collecting the child, we'll reassess our options."

****

"Fiona," Tommy greeted his daughter on the phone. "Just to let you know, hen, I've been to IKEA to pick up a few things and I'm packed for a weekend stay over in Arran so if you need me for anything," he paused to permit her to respond.

"Okay, dad, just be careful and let us know if…" she stopped and asked, "Is the landline phone connected there yet?"

"I got a text from Missus McKay to tell me the engineer was in on Wednesday, so that's both the telephone and the Internet up and running."

"Do you have the house number?"

"Not yet. I'll text it to you when I get there. Give Cissie a big hug from her granddad and let your blisters…your sisters, I mean," he corrected himself with a smile, "know where I am, okay?"

"Okay, dad," she ended the call.

He was curiously excited about spending the weekend in the house and already had a schedule of his weekend planned for he intended visiting some of the local pubs and restaurants to check out their menus with the idea that when his daughters and their families or invited guests arrived to stay over, he would know the best places to take them to dine, for Tommy fully expected that the Arran house would see many visitors.

He would never describe himself as a genuinely nice and generous man, but that was how others saw Tommy Burke.

When he started out as a one-man business, he quickly made a reputation for himself throughout the city as a good worker who charged a fair price. As time passed and he recruited an apprentice and apprentices thereafter, he also gave of himself; teaching the young bricklayers their trade and as the business grew, soon was hiring them as time served tradesmen to work with him who in turn tutored their own apprentices.

Even during the winter months when site work was sometimes curtailed by foul weather, Tommy never laid off any of his crew, but conscious most were family men, would find them work indoors. When an employee suffered injury or ill health, Tommy would be at their door ensuring their family did not face hardship until such times the employee returned to work. Such care for his people endeared Tommy to them and though there was the occasional individual who tried to take advantage of his good nature, Tommy's wife Moira was always there like a guardian angel on his shoulder, putting him wise to the individual's shenanigans.

Then Moira passed and his heart was no longer in the business and when the multi-national company came calling, he ensured that the sale of the business safeguarded the jobs of the numerous employees who to his pretended surprise, held a farewell party in the ballroom of the Glasgow Central Hotel, where he and his daughters and their families were guests of honour.

However, typical of Tommy, he had of course learned about the party beforehand and spent much of the night handing out plain white envelopes to his people, each envelope containing two fifty pound notes, telling them, "Get a wee thing for the weans Christmas, from me and Moira."

Satisfied that he had switched off the gas and the standby on the TV, he had a final look around the flat, before grabbing his bag and heading downstairs towards the front door of the close.

CHAPTER TWELVE

The Virgin train arrived on time at Platform One in Glasgow Central Station.

Helping Marcy on with her jacket, Alice decided to wait till all the passengers had left the carriage before manoeuvring the old brown suitcase from the rack by the exit door. She glanced at the fraying threads holding the handle together and hoped it would last until at least they arrived at some accommodation in Arran.

Getting off the train, she was struggling with the suitcase until a Virgin employee stood on the platform raised his hand to stop her and said, "Let me get you a trolley, hen."

While the young man went to fetch the trolley, Marcy grinned and said, "He called you a hen, Gran."

Alice returned her grin and explained, "He doesn't mean I'm a hen like the bird that lays eggs, Marcy. I think it's what men in Scotland call ladies and girls. Remember the man on the train calling you hen?"

That set the little girl off into a fit of laughter and Alice watched as she bounced around the platform and pretended to be a chicken.

The young man returned with a trolley and a smile.

"Can you tell me where the ticket office is, please?" Alice asked him.

Pointing through the gate into the busy station concourse, he asked what train she intended connecting with?

When Alice replied the train to Ardrossan Harbour, he informed her there was one within the next twenty minutes, if she hurried.

Within ten minutes, their tickets in hand, Alice and Marcy were on platform eight awaiting the arrival of the Ardrossan Harbour train.
****

The Paracetamol had kicked in and his head didn't hurt as much. Making himself coffee he thought again of where Alice might have gone to and decided that likely she would be staying away until he had calmed down.

Well, she was in for a rude shock because he had no intention of calming down.

No, he grimly watched the kettle boil, he had every intention of beating her senseless for what she had done to him.

The kettle clicked off and he was about to lift it, but stared at his bandaged right hand before lifting the kettle with his left hand. After he filled the mug, he gently touched at the side of his head.

How dare that fucking woman assault me, he thought, his head filled with visions of how he would make her suffer.

His thoughts turned to the packet of tablets she had stolen from his jacket pocket and he wondered again, why had she taken them but more importantly, what did she intend doing with them?

She couldn't go to the police for she would have to explain how she came by them and as a respected doctor, he would simply deny any knowledge of them and also wonder where Alice got them.

But his heart sank when he reminded himself he had touched all the foil strips and if the police were thorough in their examination of the foil strips, they would find his DNA on them.

His brow furrowed.

But then again, how would they know it was *my* DNA, he wondered, for they don't have any comparable sample from me.

Then there was that blasted woman coming to the door; Mike Carstairs wife, the police officer.

Not a bad looker, he leered and again wondered about her relationship with Alice.

He sipped at the scalding coffee and knew that he would get no answers until he spoke with Alice and if necessary, if it had to come to it, he'd beat the truth out of her.

He glanced at the wall clock and again wondered where she had got to.

He was undecided if he should jump in the Volvo and go to look for her, but where would he start?

There was that old harridan she sometimes visited over in Middleton Road, but if she was there he guessed the old bitch would deny it and refuse to let him in.

That's when it came to him.

At three o'clock, she'd be at the school for no matter how frightened of him Alice might be, she would not permit Marcy to walk home alone.

Yes, he sipped again at his coffee, he'd go to the school and be his charming self, bring them both home and after he sent Marcy to her room…he sniggered, relishing the idea of his revenge.

Well, Alice, then it would be time for our little chat.
****

After dropping Alice and Marcy at the railway station, Doris Chisholm returned home but could not settle for worrying about her friend.

More specifically, she worried that somehow Geoffrey Mayhew would in time find her and harm Alice.

On the drive home she had considered contacting the police herself, but thought, what would she tell them?

It was hardly likely that they would take any statement from Doris, but would ask where Alice had gone to. Though Doris had no reason to mistrust the police, Geoffrey Mayhew had such a good reputation in the town so, she reasoned, who was to say he didn't have his own friends among the constabulary?

There was one thing she could do, though.

Setting the kettle to boil, she fetched a pen and her diary from her study and seating herself at the kitchen table, began to write.

****

Arriving at the ferry terminal, Tommy Burke handed his printed ticket to the gatekeeper and was directed to join the queue of vehicles waiting to board the ferry that he could see in the distance, was approaching the pier.

****

The train arrived at the Ardrossan Harbour just over hour after Alice and Marcy boarded it in Glasgow.

Alighting from the train, she carried the suitcase awkwardly, aware that leather handle was fast becoming loose but fortunately found a trolley lying to where near the carriage had halted.

Pushing the trolley through the covered walkway, she and Marcy followed the large crowd of passengers towards the ferry terminal building.

It didn't escape her attention that few if any of her fellow travellers had to carry their suitcases, that most were wheeled and towed behind their owners while still others carried backpacks and many of the travellers were dressed for hillwalking.

Maybe I'd have been better off with the plastic bags after all, she wryly grinned to herself.

Setting Marcy down to sit on the trolley while she purchased their tickets, she asked the woman behind the counter if the crowd travelling over to the island was usual for this time of the year, but the woman smiled when she replied, "No. It's a holiday weekend here in the West of Scotland, so most businesses are closed on Friday through to Tuesday. If you've not booked accommodation on the island," the woman grimaced, "you might find it a wee bit difficult to get a room for the weekend."

Her stomach tensed at the thought that she and Marcy had come all this way, yet might not find anywhere to stay.

Forcing a smile, she decided not to dampen the little girl's enthusiasm and brandishing the tickets like a prize, brightly told her, "Fifteen minutes and we'll be on the ship. Are you excited?"

"I've never been on a ship," she replied, "Does it have big sails?"

"No," Alice softly laughed and pointing to a large photograph on the wall, added, "That's what the ship looks like, there. It's actually called a ferry and it takes cars and vans too. Now, shall we head out to watch it as it comes in?"

The main door from the building was no more than forty metres to the gangway they would use to board the ship, but Alice's heart sank.

She could not take the railway trolley with her and would have to carry the case, but worried about the handle. If it snapped as it threatened to, it would be a large and awkward thing to carry.

Gritting her teeth, she inwardly mumbled a prayer and with Marcy walking beside her, made their way with their fellow passengers to the where a crew member stood at the bottom of the gangway checking boarding tickets.

As she struggled with her case, a young man and his girlfriend, she assumed, offered to take it from her, but she smiled and declined, then later wondered why she was being so defensive.

It's living with Geoffrey for nearly thirty years, that's why, she decided.

In the lounge they made their way through the crowd of cheery passengers towards the stern and found a table with bench seats against the bulkhead.

"Can we go outside and see the water, Gran?" Marcy excitedly asked her.

"Let's get settled and wait till the ships underway, Marcy," she replied, then grinned and thought, listen to me; *underway*. I sound like a sailor.

While they waited for the ferry to set off, Alice was about to suggest they go outside, but the rain began to batter off the windows and she decided that if they did venture outside, not only would they be soaked but it was likely their seats would be occupied when they returned to the lounge.

That and Alice didn't really feel like carrying the suitcase with her so instead, leaned down and whispered to Marcy, "Maybe we'll just keep our seats here and save our strength for when we get to Arran, eh?"

Tired, the little girl nodded and leaned into her grandmother.

****

Tommy acknowledged the crewman's wave and slowly drove the Defender up the ramp, taking his route from the second crewman within the bowels of the ferry who using both hands, directed him to a position behind a campervan then used his hands in a cutting motion to switch off the vehicle's engine.

Getting out of the Defender, Tommy was amazed to see there was literally centimetres between his vehicle and the campervan and joked, "You'll have done that a few times, eh?"

"Aye," the bearded crewman grinned, "but I still get a few nudges from them that don't keep their eye on me and think they know best."

Making his way to a gangway, Tommy headed up the stairs to the lounge deck to find it crowded with foot passengers.

The cafeteria had just opened and if the crowd was anything to go by, he guessed it would soon be busy and purchased himself a coffee in a polystyrene cup. That done, he strolled through the lounge to search for a seat where he could settle and read his Kindle.

A woman, in her mid-forties he guessed, with shoulder length auburn hair wearing a dark coloured anorak was sat beside a young girl with collar length brown hair on a bench seat in front of a table and with a shabby brown suitcase in front of them.

Tommy could see there was just enough room to squeeze himself in beside the little girl and the bulkhead and politely asked, "If nobody's sitting here, do you mind if I squeeze in beside your daughter?"

Though she didn't say anything, the woman tightly nodded and turned her head away as he sat down.

Miserable faced bugger, he thought and catching the little girl's eye, winked at her.

She returned his wink with a shy smile and smiling in return, he opened his Kindle.

****

Lucy Carstairs arrived early to collect her daughter Laura and getting out of her car, scanned the waiting crowd, but failed to see Alice Mayhew. As she smiled and acknowledged some of the greetings

from other parents, she turned and to her surprise, saw Geoffrey
Mayhew sitting in his Volvo a little further along the road.

Now, she wondered, why has he come to collect Marcy and not his
wife?

The bell rang and as she furtively kept her eye on Mayhew, also
wondered why he remained in his car.

The horde of screaming children that excitedly exited the school
doors run to the gate and their waiting parents and grandparents.

Carstairs daughter Laura, her school bag nonchalantly carried across
her shoulder, walked towards her mother with a big grin.

"Hi, darling," she greeted her daughter then continuing to smile,
asked, "Not walking with Marcy today?"

"Oh, Marcy's gone," Laura disinterestedly replied.

"Gone? Gone where?"

"I don't know," the little girl shrugged. "She got taken out of
classroom and didn't come back in. Can I watch the TV when we go
home? I've no homework tonight."

With a fixed smile, Carstairs knelt down and pretending to button
Laura's jacket, asked, "Who took Marcy out of the classroom?"

Her daughter stared at her as though she were mad and sullenly
repeated, "I don't *know*, mum. The woman who works in the office,
she came into the classroom and spoke to Miss Timmons then Marcy
went out with her."

"When was this, love?"

"Mum! I don't *know*!"

"I mean," she patiently asked, "was it before or after your lunch?"
Sighing as if the question was too difficult, Laura replied, "Before
lunch. Yes, just before the bell went. Can we go home now, *please*!"

Carstairs nodded and getting to her feet, turned and startled, for
Geoffrey Mayhew stood directly behind her.

"Missus Carstairs," his voice oozed charm, but his eyes bored into
hers. "It seems that I've missed my wife and granddaughter for I was
hoping to take them from here straight to dinner in the town, this
being Friday," he chillingly smiled. "Haven't seen them, have you?"

She was in no doubt he must have overheard her questioning Lara
and stuttered, "No, I haven't, Doctor Mayhew. I was hoping to see
Alice to arrange another sleepover with Laura, wasn't I dear?" she
gently stroked at her daughter's hair.

The little girl stared at her mother in surprise, but Carstairs widened her eyes and pinched Laura's arm to warn her not to reply. That was when it occurred to her and she asked him, "As I've missed her here at the school, Doctor Mayhew, you wouldn't have her mobile number? I can give her a call to make the arrangement," she gushed with a bright smile.

"Oh," taken aback, his face fell when he replied, "Alice doesn't have a mobile. Doesn't like them," he forced a smile.

It was a blatant lie and they both knew it, but Carstairs had no recourse other than to nod and respond, "Well, perhaps I'll just see her on Monday when she brings Marcy to school."

"That's what to do. Right then," he smiled again. "I'll be off. Cheerio."

She watched him turn and head back towards the Volvo and an unaccountable chill went through her.

It seemed apparent that he had no idea where his wife was and now that their granddaughter was also apparently gone too, it begged the question; to where?

****

Alice was uncomfortable with the man seated so close to Marcy, though realised that with the large and noisy crowd aboard the ship there really was nowhere else to sit.

He glanced down at the case that prevented him from extending his legs and taking a breath, asked, "Excuse me, but do you mind if I shift your suitcase a wee bit to the side to give me a bit more legroom here?"

"Go ahead," Alice nodded.

"Thanks, that will be grand," Tommy replied and reached down to lift the suitcase by the handle.

To his horror, when he lifted the suitcase the handle snapped and it thumped back down onto the deck.

He turned to stare wide-eyed at Alice who, tired and hungry, scowled and said, "Well, that didn't work, did it?"

"I'm so very sorry…" he began, but she raised a hand and interrupting, icily snapped at him, "Please, don't concern yourself. It was bound to happen anyway. It's an old suitcase."

"Aye, it certainly looks like it," he cheerfully replied, trying to lighten the moment, but his comment completely backfired when Alice angrily retorted, "Yes, it might be old, but it's all we've got!"

The passengers who stood or sat about them quietened, sensing that some sort of argument was brewing.

Embarrassed and red-faced, Alice continued in a flat voice, "I'm sorry, but it just makes it that more difficult for me to carry it now, doesn't it?"

Tight-lipped at being so publicly rebuked, Tommy arose from his seat and walked off.

Irritably, Alice stared at the old suitcase, seeing its corners frayed to expose its wiry, metal frame, the scuff marks on the edges and the threads that held the handle together now lying loose and damaged beyond repair.

Despair overcome her and continuing to stare at the suitcase, she thought, it's just like me; worn out, shabby and broken.

She felt guilty about snapping at the man and wondered what kind of bad tempered woman she had become when Marcy said, "Look, Gran, that man's forgotten his little computer."

He glanced at where Tommy had been sitting to see his Kindle lying on the seat.

"Oh, Marcy, run and see if you can find him…" she began, but then saw Tommy returning with something held in his hand.

She was about to reach for his Kindle to hand it to him when he brusquely said, "I got these for you," and bending down, he undid the packaging from three broad and bright rainbow coloured luggage straps.

As she curiously watched, he fitted and tightened two straps vertically around each end of the suitcase then used the third strap to form a makeshift handle between the two vertical straps.

Getting to his feet, he pointed to the suitcase and said, "That should hold you, missus, till you get to wherever you're going," then reaching down for his Kindle, began to walk off.

"Wait," she called out and as he turned, said, "What do I owe you? For the straps."

He raised his hand and shaking his head, curtly replied, "Call it quits, hen," and made his way through the crowd.

She was conscious of the pitiful looks she was getting from the other seated passengers and head down, shrunk into her seat and hoped the ferry soon docked.

****

The call for drivers to return to their vehicles saw Tommy heading down the gangway to the Defender. Within ten minutes he was driving down the ramp through the slight fall of rain and heading along Brodick's Shore Road for the turning that would lead up the hill towards Glencloy Road.

Arriving at the house, he drove to the garage and after donning his jacket and a skipped hat against the sudden fall of rain, began to unpack the vehicle, dumping his IKEA purchases inside the house at the kitchen door.

He was still bristling at the bloody woman's bad-tempered attitude on the ferry, but more at himself for he was honest enough to admit that he had been no better, ignoring her when she tried to pay for the straps.

Humping the bags and boxes into the house, he muttered, "I definitely didn't handle that very well," then found himself smiling at his inadvertent pun.

****

Getting off the ferry among the throng of foot passengers, Alice was dismayed to see that the rain was falling. Carrying the suitcase by its improvised handle, she was surprised to find that the man had made a good job of it and the broad strap acting as a makeshift handle made the case far easier to carry. Leading Marcy to the shelter of an arched overhanging entrance to some nearby shops, she set down the suitcase and opening it, rummaged around to find something to keep the rain off, finally settling for two thin cotton scarves that she tied around their heads.

"I'm hungry, Gran, and I'm tired too," the little girl said, rubbing at her eyes.

Forcing herself to sound cheery, Alice replied, "Well, let's me and you go and find somewhere to stay and then somewhere to eat. How does that sound, sweetheart?"

Marcy nodded and reached to assist in carrying the suitcase, but with a strangled sob at the little girl's attempt to be helpful, Alice shook her head and told her, "I'm fine, dear. Really I am. Now," she pointed towards across the main road at the bright lights outside the harbour and said, "that looks like shops over there so let's go, eh?"

It seemed to Alice the further she walked, the heavier the suitcase got and as she and Marcy left the harbour area, she saw a hotel across the road. Drawing closer she brightly said, "Look, the Douglas Hotel. Shall we see if they have any rooms?"

It was only when they drew even closer that Alice could see the hotel was a large, fine building and conscious of her limited funds, seriously doubted that she could afford to spend more than a night there, let alone a week.

However, needs must she told herself and with Marcy in tow they made their way to the entrance and into the large and opulent foyer where a young man stood behind the reception desk.

If he was surprised to see her holding an old and tattered suitcase with a brightly coloured luggage strap as a handle, he didn't react and smiling, politely greeted her with, "Yes, Madam, how may I help you?"

"Do you have any rooms available?"

His face fell and glancing at the tired Marcy, sorrowfully shook his head and replied, "I'm afraid not, Madam. We're solidly booked for the weekend. It's a holiday weekend, you see."

"Yes, so I heard," she glumly replied, then added, "Do you know of anywhere close by that might have a room available?"

"Hang on, I'll ask my boss," he smiled encouragingly and disappeared through a curtain.

Minutes later he returned accompanied by an older woman who shaking her head, said, "I'm sorry, but I can't think of anywhere at all," then eyes narrowing, added, "but you might think about asking at the Shorehouse. Out onto the main road and turn left, past the Crazy Golf and you'll find it on the left. It's signposted," she helpfully smiled.

"Gran, I'm hungry," Marcy complained by her side.

"We'll find something, sweetheart," Alice confidently replied and thanking the young man and his boss, left the hotel to find the Shorehouse.

It was still raining as they trudged along the main road and worried now, Alice began to consider that running off with Marcy might not have been her best idea.
****

It had gone six o'clock and still Alice and the child had not returned home.

Growing angrier and hungrier by the minute, Geoffrey stormed about the house then had an idea.

He went upstairs to Alice's room and began searching through her things, looking for any indication as to where she might be.

She had been limited in her choice of clothing to take for both her and Marcy and being unaware of exactly what clothing she owned, it never occurred to Geoffrey that some of Alice's clothes were missing. Besides, he reasoned, the suitcases were locked in the garage and he held the only keys to the doors so decided she couldn't have gone too far.

But frowned when he thought, where the hell is she?

****

At the teams evening meeting in DI Sandford's room, Lucy Carstairs reported her findings and concluded, "If my daughter is correct and I've no reason to believe otherwise, Geoffrey Mayhew received his injuries some time before his wife Alice arrived at the school to collect their granddaughter, so it's doubtful that she was lying injured in the house when I called there."

"So, after spiriting the girl out of the school, it seems that her husband is looking for Missus Mayhew and if what he told you is true, he has no idea where she is?"

"Ma'am," Carstairs nodded in agreement, then added, "Curiously too, when I asked for her mobile phone number, he told me she doesn't have one, that she didn't like them." She pursed her lips and shaking her head, added, "I got the feeling he was lying."

"DS Goodwin," she turned to the detective, "just as a safety precaution and while I realise it's out of hours and it's now the weekend, contact the school janitor and try to obtain the phone number of the girl's teacher. Find out why she was taken out of school and if the teacher has any information about her whereabouts."

"And if the teacher asks why the police are inquiring about an eight-year old pupil?"

"Be creative," Sandford scowled before turning to Carstairs and asking, "What about you. Do you have any idea where she might be? When you had coffee together did she mention any friends or relatives?"

"No, Ma'am," she shook her head, before adding, "In fact she shared with me that she has no family, that both she and her husband were an only child and other than their deceased daughter, they had no other children."

Sandford's eyes narrowed and she stared at the team in turn, before telling them, "Let's be clear here. Alice Mayhew has not figured in this inquiry as a suspect, but as a possible source to report on her husband's activities. However, if she has now fled with her granddaughter, there is likely to be a good reason." She turned towards Carstairs and asked, "You said you saw two cars in the Mayhew's driveway?"

"Yes, Ma'am. The Volvo Doctor Mayhew uses and an old Toyota Aygo."

"We've the registration number of the Volvo, but we didn't know about the Aygo, did we DS Goodwin?"

"No, Ma'am, we didn't," he confirmed. "What I'll do is take a run past the house, clock the reggie number and add it to our watch list. If Mayhew is using the Aygo, we'll catch him on the ANPR as he moves about the county."

"Yes," Sandford nodded, "but it strikes me as curious if Missus Mayhew has use of the Aygo too, why is it still there? Why hasn't she taken the car if as we suspect she has taken off with her granddaughter?"

There was a few seconds of silence before Carstairs replied, "Perhaps she's on the run, Ma'am."

"From us?"

"No, Ma'am, I was thinking of her husband. We know from previous reporting that he is quite a dominating man, narcissistic and forceful. Perhaps he carries that attitude back home with him."

"Maybe," Sandford mused, then coming to a decision, told her team, "Okay then, here's what we will do. For the time being we will monitor the situation and if by Monday the child is returned to school, nothing lost; however, if the child is not returned to school, you DC Carstairs with the pretext of arranging a sleepover with your daughter, will contact Mayhew to ask where his wife is. If he still cannot provide a suitable response at that point we will review Alice Mayhew's status as a possible source and treat her as a potential witness to her husband's behaviour and actions. If Missus Mayhew is still unaccounted for, I am of the opinion that this woman has not simply taken off for no good reason, but might have information that we can use. Any questions?"

The team had none, so Sandford dismissed them with, "Continue with your inquires meantime and we will resume here midday tomorrow."

CHAPTER THIRTEEN

Tommy pulled open the door and grinned.
Mary McKay had surpassed herself for the fridge was filled with a selection of meats and other foodstuffs as was the freezer beneath. He glanced again at the note in the neat handwriting on the table informing him that holiday weekend or not, Mary would be in on Monday to give the house a onceover.
He did briefly consider telling her not to bother, that there was not much chance of him dirtying the house that much it meant her giving up her holiday weekend, but shaking his head guessed that Mary McKay would have her set routine and be unlikely to change it just because her boss said so.
He was about to reach into the fridge to grab himself a meat pie, but stopped and smiled.
No, he'd drive to the golf club in Lamlash where he knew the food to be excellent and with a bit of luck and if the place wasn't too busy, get himself a table and treat himself to a slap-up dinner. Deciding not to bother getting changed, he pulled on his jacket and grabbing his old and worn skipped hat, made his way out into the darkness and falling rain towards the Defender.
****
The staff at the Shorehouse were sympathetic, explaining once more it was a holiday weekend and regretting there was nothing available for Alice or Marcy, suggested they try the guesthouse a little further along the main road.
Fifteen minutes and two guesthouses later, Alice realised that there was little point in trying any more of the hotels or guesthouses for it was evident they were all fully booked. That and little Marcy was exhausted.
Tired and demoralised, she realised they had little option but to return to the harbour and take shelter for the night in the arch covered area of the shops and await the early morning ferry back to the mainland. In the covered area they would at least be partially sheltered from the rain and she would try as best she could to construct some sort of warm bed for Marcy from the clothes in the

suitcase. In the meantime, she would purchase some food and water from the brightly lit Cooperative they had passed.

Approaching the supermarket, she was dismayed to see the lights going out and the staff leaving or driving off in cars.

She stopped and turning her face to the sky, the rain fell onto her as tears began to form while she come to accept the hopelessness of their situation.

To make matters worse, Marcy tugged at her hand and said, "I need to go to the toilet, Gran. A number two."

Alice felt like crying, but adopting a brave face, replied, "Yes, well, once we get to the harbour we'll see what we can do, eh?" and lifting the suitcase, struggled on.

****

The rain had come on heavy and with the windscreen wipers going full pelt, he was just about to pass by the Cooperative supermarket when he glanced to his left and saw two figures walking on the pavement. He might have ignored them, but suddenly realised that the taller of the two was carrying a suitcase around which were bound brightly coloured luggage straps.

Braking, he stopped the Defender some thirty metres in front of the figures and glanced in the side mirror, but it was rain soaked and he couldn't make them out. Judging by their difference in height though, he was convinced it was the woman and the child from the ferry.

"Bugger," he muttered and for a heartbeat almost considered it was none of his business and he would drive on.

But then the little girls face jumped into his head and inwardly cursing his deep-rooted good manners, grabbed his skip hat from the passenger seat and got out of the vehicle.

Approaching the woman, he could see in the faint glow of the overhead street lighting that she and the little girl were soaking wet, their hair plastered to their faces and they looked exhausted.

The woman faltered and eyes staring suspiciously at him, stopped in mid stride then with her free hand, ushered the child behind her.

He didn't know how to open a conversation so with both hands defensively raised, said, "Hello. My name's Tommy Burke, I think we met on the ferry. I'm the man who put those on for you," he pointed at the straps on the suitcase.

"What do you want," she fearfully asked, her voice trembling.

"I'm guessing that as it's this time of the evening and," he pointed upwards, "it's piddling down, you haven't found anywhere to stay?"

"Why do you care?"

God, he thought, she's really making this difficult.

Behind her, the little girl peeked out from behind the woman to stare curiously at him.

"Look, There's nowhere that I know of on the island where you will get any accommodation at this time of the evening and it's a…"

"A holiday weekend, yes, I know," she nodded then brusquely added, "Everyone keeps reminding me of that."

"Yes, well," he took a deep breath to calm himself then opened his hands wide again. "I have a room that you can use for the night until you find something tomorrow. You're welcome to it."

Alice didn't immediately respond, but stared suspiciously at him before replying, "Why would you do that? Offer us a room?"

He almost countered with, because I'm a bloody idiot inviting a rude woman into my home, but forcing himself to remain calm, instead replied, "I can see you're both soaked through and I have a granddaughter about your daughter's age and it's not right a wee girl like her should be out wandering the streets in this bad weather."

"She's not my mum," the little girl giggled with a hand over her mouth, "she's my Gran."

"Oh, sorry," he resisted the urge to laugh and again asked, "Do you want the room or not?"

Aware that she could not have Marcy sleeping rough on a night like this, Alice had no choice but to agree and nodding, her voice a little more forceful, said, "I'll pay."

"Why don't we discuss that later, but right now I think we should get you to the house and dried off, eh?"

He took a step towards her, his hand reaching for the case, but she instinctively drew back and sighing, he raised his hand yet again and said, "Look, missus, I'm not going to steal your suitcase. Call me an old fashioned bugger, but I only want to put it into the back of the vehicle for you, okay?"

Feeling a little foolish, she nodded and allowed him to take the case from her.

"Right then," he nodded to the Defender and pulling open the rear door, added, "let's get you back to the house."

****

She sat in the back seat with one arm wrapped around Marcy, the warmth of the heater blowing through the car making her drowsy and staring suspiciously at the back of the head of the driver. Through the front windscreen she could see in the bright beam of the headlights they were now travelling up a dark, hilly road with gradually fewer houses on either side.

Was it good fortune or had she made a bad decision allowing this strange man to persuade her into his…she glanced curiously around her at the inside of the Defender, his jeep thing. Did he really have a spare room and where was he taking them?

A wave of panic swept across her and she was about to call out that he stop the jeep, that she let him and Marcy out, that he could keep the suitcase, but just let them go, when Marcy nudged her and said, "I *really* need to go to the toilet, Gran."

Before she could reply, Tommy turned the jeep though a set of wooden gates and into a wide driveway that led to a modern, white painted house with bright security lights illuminating the front and both sides of the house.

"Here we are," he said and turned with a smile towards them. "I heard the wee girl saying she needs the loo. The front door's open and there's a visitor's toilet on the right as you go through the door. On you go in and I'll fetch your suitcase from the back of the car."

She helped Marcy out of the back seat then taking her hand, hesitantly made her way to the front door.

It was just as he said, the front door was unlocked and opening it she ushered Marcy into a spacious and brightly lit hallway.

"That will be the toilet," she indicated a door and was about to join Marcy who scowled and said, "I *can* go myself, Gran. I mean, I'm eight now."

She fought back a smile and nodding, replied, "I'll just wait here then."

Marcy closed the door as Tommy, carrying the suitcase, entered the hallway and closing the door behind him with a forced smile said, "I'm glad this strap thing worked. Maybe I'll patent it, eh?" but when he saw Alice's face, the joke fell flat.

"Thank you for your hospitality, Mister…I'm sorry, I didn't catch you name."

"It's Tommy Burke. And your name is…?

"Alice…" she hesitated just for a heartbeat before adding, "Benson. Alice Benson."

"And the wee girl, your granddaughter she said?"

"Marcy Benson."

Tommy nodded, but the woman's slight pause caused him to be a little suspicious and while he could not explain it, shrugged in acceptance and said, "At the landing upstairs, Missus Benson, you'll find the first door on your left is an en-suite room with twin beds, if that's okay with you. I'll just take your suitcase up there now."

As he finished speaking, they heard the toilet flush and Marcy opened the door. Staring at them in turn, she frowned and asked, "Were you listening?"

Stifling a smile, Tommy quickly turned away as Alice bent down to embrace her and said, "No, not at all sweetheart. Mister Burke was just telling me about our room."

Glancing at them both in turn, Tommy nodded towards the stairs and said, "If you want to follow me, I'll take you up there now."

****

Pushing open the door, Tommy laid the suitcase on the floor just inside the room that Alice could see was bright and airy.

Indicating the en-suite, he said, "You'll find fresh towels for you both in there and a I'll leave a hair dryer outside the door for when you're finished showering. If you bring your wet things when you come downstairs, I'll hang them to dry in the utility room. Now, have you eaten?"

Before Alice could reply, Marcy called out, "I'm starving!"

"She seems to have got a new burst of energy, then," he smiled at the little girl and turning towards Alice, said, "I'm no gourmet cook, Missus Benson, but if you're okay with oven cooked fish and chips I'll give you half an hour to get yourselves sorted and have it on the table for you downstairs in the kitchen."

Turning then to Marcy, he saw her staring curiously at her Gran for though he couldn't know it, the little girl didn't understand why the man called her Missus Benson.

Tommy continued to smile and catching Marcy's attention, asked, "Peas or beans?"

"Beans," she grinned at him.

"Tea or Lemonade?" then turned to Alice and grimacing, added, "If lemonade's okay with your grandmother."

Alice nodded as Marcy replied, "Lemonade, please."

"Thought so," he nodded.

"Please, you needn't really put yourself to any trouble," Alice began, but he waved a hand in dismissal and nodding to Marcy, said, "If she's anything like my granddaughter, she'll be wanting double portions."

He was gone just a moment when Marcy, about to speak, stopped when her grandmother raised a warning forefinger to her lips.

"Why did he call you Missus Benson, Gran?" she asked in a stage whisper.

"Because I don't want anyone finding us here, sweetheart," she quietly replied, "so for now I'm Alice Benson and you're still Marcy Benson. Okay?"

"Okay," she nodded.

Alice glanced about her at the brightly furnished room then sighing, told the little girl, "Right now, lets get you out of those wet thing and into a hot shower.

****

In the kitchen, Tommy inserted a 'Lighthouse Family' CD into the radio/CD player then pulled on a IKEA green cotton apron before heating the oven.

There'd be no golf club dinner for me tonight, he sighed and fetched out the frozen fish and frozen chips from the freezer.

Humming along to the music, he set the table and brewed the tea before filling a glass of lemonade for Marcy. With a smile, he fetched a can of beans from the larder unit and popped them into the microwave, ready to be cooked.

Almost to the minute, the kitchen door opened to admit Alice, her auburn hair still slightly damp from the shower and tied back into a tight ponytail and dressed in a sleeveless, plain, green coloured midi dress, brown coloured soft leather shoes and carrying their wet clothes and jackets.

Marcy, her hair dry and curly, was wearing pink coloured cotton pyjamas and pink coloured Barbie slippers.

Tommy couldn't help himself, but stared at Alice as though seeing a different woman to the one who had walked through his door.

Pretending to clear his throat to hide his surprise, he took the wet clothes from her before dumping them for the time being onto the worktop in the utility room.

"Just in time," he jovially greeted them and indicated they sit at the table.

"You're wearing an apron," Marcy greeted him with a squeal.

"Marcy!" her grandmother scolded her, but Tommy waved away her protest and smiling at the child, replied, "Don't you know all the best cooks wear aprons?"

"Now," he raised a forefinger to his lips and pretending that he'd forgotten, asked, "You did say peas, didn't you?"

"No," she giggled with her hand to her mouth, "I said beans!"

"Just as well I made beans then, eh?" grinning, he scooped a pile onto her plate.

Watching them devour their food, he guessed they hadn't eaten all day and when Alice saw him staring at her, she blushed and said, "I'm sorry. You must think we're gluttons, the way we're stuffing our faces."

"Not at all, I'm just pleased that you're enjoying my cooking, basic though it is," he smiled.

He was pouring Alice a second mug of tea when she asked, "You're eating with us. Isn't your wife at home?"

"My wife?" he was for a second, taken aback, then with a glance at Marcy who was still eating, replied, "Actually, Missus Benson, I'm alone here."

"Oh," she frowned as her eyes dropped to his hand. "When I saw the wedding band I thought…"

"I *was* married," he tightly smiled, "but I lost my wife four years ago to a…a sudden illness."

"I'm sorry, I didn't think…" she began, but he waved away her apology and said, "Please, you couldn't have known. Now, as you've cleared your plate I have some ice-cream in the freezer…" but stopped when Alice nodded towards Marcy who though still holding her cutlery, had her eyes closed as her head drooped towards her plate.

"If you don't mind, Mister Burke, I'll get her up to bed," and rising from her chair, moved round to lift her granddaughter in her arms.

"Do you want me to carry her up for you?" he quietly asked.

"No, I'll be fine," she replied a little more curtly than she intended.

"Okay," he slowly drawled, but didn't miss the sharp response and raising his hands, genially continued, "It's not yet nine, so if you aren't yet ready for bed, I'll stick the kettle on again while I'm clearing up here."

As he turned away she lifted Marcy from her chair and with the little girls arms about her neck, stopped and briefly glanced at him as she wondered; have I misjudged this man? Is he as kind as he seems?

Yet some inner sense told her that after living all those years with Geoffrey, the only men she ever mixed with were his rugby associates, his type of man, he was fond of saying; so were they really all the same she wondered and decided it would be foolish to let her guard down.

Nevertheless, he was correct for now showered and fed, she felt rejuvenated and was still on a bit of a high. Nodding, she politely replied, "Yes, thank you. Another cup of tea would be lovely."

****

In the bedroom, she gently laid the slight figure of Marcy onto a bed before turning the sheets back on the second bed. Lifting Marcy again, she laid her down and covering her, bent to kiss her goodnight.

She stood for a moment gazing down at the sleeping child and involuntarily shivered.

Like it or not, if it hadn't been for the kindness of Mister Burke she and Marcy would be sleeping in the open under the arch of the shops at the harbour. Maybe I'm being too harsh, she folded her arms as she stared down at the sleeping child and sighed.

Maybe I'm too ready to believe him to be like Geoffrey.

No, she vigorously shook her head; not like Geoffrey.

There wasn't anyone like Geoffrey.

At least she hoped not.

Switching on the side light, she reached down to stroke gently at Marcy's hair, then leaving the room, quietly closed the door.

She stopped on the landing and gazed back at the hall table that was against the wall between the two doors at the end of the landing.

She hadn't noticed before that upon the table was an array of framed photographs.

Peeking over the bannister, she could hear him moving about in the kitchen and tiptoed towards the table.

There was a half dozen photographs, three of which were young brides and their husbands. Two photographs were of children, a laughing boy with an unruly mop of hair who seemed no more than a toddler and a photograph of a red-haired girl about Marcy's age who grinned at the cameraman.

The last photograph showed a smiling, younger Tommy Burke standing behind a pretty, dark haired woman, his hands resting on her shoulders and who Alice thought must be his wife.

She felt a lump in her throat for the one thing that all the photographs had in common, she could see, was the happiness of the subjects.

Taking a breath, she made her way downstairs to find him just finishing clearing up.

"I said tea, but I have coffee or if you prefer, some wine," he said.

"No, tea will be fine, thank you," she smiled, though he saw the smile didn't reach her eyes.

"Right well if you head on into the lounge, I'll bring it through," he cheerfully replied.

"The lounge?"

"Oh, sorry, yes. Straight through the hallway and it's the door facing you."

Pushing open the door to the lounge, she was startled to see how lovely it was and walking to the panoramic window and even though it was raining heavily, could see across the water to the lights shimmering on the mainland.

The door opened to admit Tommy who had removed his apron and carried a tray with mugs, a pot of tea and a plate of biscuits that he laid down onto the coffee table in front of the suite of chairs.

"Here we go," he smiled and poured tea into both mugs. "Milk only, yes?"

"Yes," she nodded and sat on the settee opposite him.

She had mentally prepared her speech and was about to begin, when he raised his hand and said, "Hang on. This time of night there's nothing like a bit of Frank Sinatra."

Makin his way over to a small compact CD player, he pressed a couple of buttons and soft music began to play from four hidden speakers.

"Mister Burke," she began, "I'm very grateful that you stopped and offered Marcy and I accommodation for the night." She bit at her lower lip and to her surprise, thought she was about to cry. Taking a breath, she continued, "If you hadn't stopped and offered us a room in your home, well…" her head dipped for she found that her practised thank you was too much for her.

He let her compose herself and then said, "Missus Benson, I'm not offering you charity. The room is going to cost you a bottle of red wine."

Confused, she stared at him as he continued, "You told me that you intended to pay for your room. Well," he pretended aloofness, "there's a nice wee bottle of Beaujolais the Cooperative supermarket down in the town is selling for five-ninety-nine and I'm partial to a glass of the old vino, now and then."

She smiled for real this time, for she realised she was being teased and replied, "Just the wine, Mister Burke? No cheese to accompany it?"

"Naw," he shook his head and joked, "I've never been that partial to cheese unless it's on lasagne or maybe a MacDonald's Big Mac. But the wine? Yes, but only if it's not beyond your means."

"Oh, I think Marcy and I might manage a bottle of red wine, Mister Burke. But I really must insist on paying you something for our night here. And the food, of course."

He sighed and shaking his head, replied, "No, a bottle of plonk will do me nicely and another thing. When I was working, I was sometime called Mister Burke, but these days I'm just plain old Tommy. Would that be too much to ask?"

She smiled and repeated, "Tommy. Well, I'm Alice."

"Pleased to meet you, Alice," he toasted her with his mug.

"And I'm pleased to meet you too, Tommy," she returned his toast. They sat in comfortable silence for a few minutes, but then the phone in the hallway rang.

"Excuse me," he left the room.

She could hear him speaking through the partially open door, but could not hear what was being said.

He returned to the room a few minutes later and sighed, "That was my oldest girl, Fiona. Seems I'm in trouble for not phoning her right away when I arrived on the island. It's what I think they call role reversal. We care for them and worry about our children when they're growing, particularly when they're out and about, but then when they're adults, we answer to them as to our whereabouts."

He smiled at her and asked, "What about you, Alice. The phone's there for you to use if you need to call anyone."

She swallowed with difficulty, wondering just how much she should disclose, but then realised that there was no guile in his question, that he was simply being gracious.

"No," she shook her head. There's just Marcy and me," she swallowed tightly at the lie before quickly adding, "My daughter, Gemma, Marcy's mother, was killed just over a year ago along with her husband Peter in a road accident."

"My God," he was genuinely shocked. "I'm so sorry. I can't imagine what it must be like, losing a child and that poor wean, to lose both her parents like that," he shook his head and groaned.

To the best of her recollection, other than in television programmes Alice had never actually met any Scots before and eyebrows raised, she hesitantly asked, "Wean?"

Tommy smiled, but with a tinge of sadness when he explained, "Child. It's local West of Scotland vernacular and means a child." There was another short silence between them, broken when he asked, "If you're on your own with the wee girl, I'm guessing there's no Mister Benson?"

"No," she firmly shook her head, "there's no Mister Benson." When she didn't explain further, Tommy assumed Alice was either divorced or widowed and decided if she wanted to tell him, she would, that it wasn't his place to press her for information.

Frank Sinatra was just winding up his hit song, *I Won't Dance* when Alice finished her tea and said, "Thank you for the tea and everything, Tommy, but if you don't mind, it's been a very tiring and stressful day."

He rose as she did and nodding, replied, "I hope you get a good night's sleep, Alice, and thank you for sharing with me about Marcy's parents. I imagine it must be very difficult for you to talk about."

She stared at him and though he couldn't know it she wondered at his perception for that was exactly the right thing to say. Choking back a response, she nodded and tightly smiling, left the room.

He sat for another few minutes and decided he too would have an early night.

He hadn't told Fiona he had overnight guests and smiled at what his eldest daughter might have said. Knowing her, he rightly guessed, she would have told him he was too soft hearted, but like her mother would have agreed he had done the right thing.

Collecting the mugs and the tray, he took them through to the kitchen and ensuring everything was switched off, made his way to his bedroom.

****

She couldn't fall asleep right away for her mind was still racing with thoughts of the day.

By now, she thought, Geoffrey would have realised she wasn't coming home and likely drunk himself into a selfish stupor.

She still couldn't believe she had the nerve to leave him, but in her heart knew it was the right thing to do. If she'd stayed any longer he surely would have subjugated her to the point she would have no free will at all.

Doris was correct, she thought. Marcy is my first and only concern. I couldn't have her living in that house any longer.

She turned to stare at the sleeping child and smiled. No matter what she had to do, no matter what lies she had to tell, her granddaughter would grow up without fear or intimidation being part of her daily life.

Glancing at the room about her, her thoughts turned to Tommy Burke and briefly wondered, should she place a chair against the door?

Smiling at her doubt, she decided against it.

He was a very nice man and as her eyes closed, for one brief moment wondered what her life might have been like, living with someone like him.

CHAPTER FOURTEEN

Alice awoke to the bright sunshine streaming through a narrow gap in the curtain and stretching, for a few seconds wondered where she was. Lazily, she turned to stare at Marcy, but her heart raced when she saw the quilt cover pulled back and the bed was empty.

Panicking, she sprung from the bed and pulling open the door, frantically raced downstairs where she saw Tommy, dressed in a maroon coloured polo shirt and brown coloured corduroy trousers, standing at the kitchen table with a mug in his hand and reading a letter.

"Where is she! Where's my granddaughter!" she shrieked.

Stunned, he stared wide-eyed at the panic-stricken Alice and saw her to be barefooted, her hair in disarray and wearing a knee length, navy blue coloured nightdress.

Raising his free hand, he replied, "Calm down. She's fine. She's in the small lounge, watching the television. Across the hallway," he pointed behind her, "on the left."

Turning, Alice run to the door and pushing it open, saw Marcy sitting cross-legged on the couch, a tartan blanket wrapped about her shoulders and a bowl of cereal on her lap.

"Morning Gran," she greeted Alice and returned to watching the adventures of Tom and Jerry.

Alice thought her legs were going to give way and holding onto the door for support, could only stare at her until from behind, Tommy quietly said, "The wean got up earlier and didn't want to wake you. When she came downstairs she was a wee bit chilled so I put her in here to watch the tele with a blanket round her shoulders. She's had some cereal, if that's okay with you?"

Still shaking with anxiety, Alice could only nod as Tommy continued, "It's almost ten o'clock. You've had a right good lie-in this morning. Now, much as I appreciate seeing a good looking woman in her nightie," his mouth twisted as he tried not to grin, "maybe you'd be better going back upstairs and freshening up. I'll give you fifteen minutes," he glanced at his watch, pretending to be firm, "then your tea and toast will be on the table, okay?"

She could only numbly nod and conscious she was naked beneath the nightdress, pulled it together at the front opening and slid past him to make her way back to the room.

Inwardly seething at her stupidity, she was in the shower when she remembered what he'd said.

He'd called her good looking.

****

Just over ten minutes later, showered and refreshed and dressed in an old beige coloured sweatshirt and faded jeans with her hair again tied fiercely back into a ponytail, Alice made her way down stairs. She hesitated at the kitchen door and seeing Tommy at the range cooker with his back to her, lightly knocked on the open door.

Turning, she saw he wore the apron and nervously smiling, said, "I'm sorry about earlier. I got a fright when I woke up and found Marcy gone."

"Totally understandable," he raised a hand and nodded before adding, "Sit yourself down. I've decided against toast and taken the liberty of preparing you a breakfast. After all, if you're spending all that money on a bottle of wine you deserve the very best this hostelry has to offer, Madam."

Smiling, she slid into a seat and saw he had set the table for three, but then he told her, "Marcy's elected to stay in the small lounge and have her breakfast through there watching the cartoons, if that's okay with you?"

"Yes, of course, but what if she makes a mess?"

He stared curiously at her before replying, "She's a child, Alice. It's a requisite part of their growing up. Jammy fingers on the chairs, spilled drinks on the couch, crayon marks on the walls and crumbs kicked into the carpet. Don't worry, she won't do anything that can't be cleaned up. Now, how do you like your eggs?"

Taken aback by his tolerant response, she hesitated before replying, "However they come, thanks," then sighing as if in apology, continued, "I'm sorry I slept so late. I can't remember the last time I lay in till almost ten in the morning. Thank you."

"No worries," he cheerfully replied. "You looked last night like you were done in, utterly exhausted and needed the sleep. Did you sleep well?"

"Like a log," she smiled and realised yes, she really did.

Ten minutes later, their fry-up finished, she burped and blushing turned to him, but before she could apologise, he grinned and said, "Well, I'm glad you enjoyed breakfast."

"Here," she tried to rise to her feet, "let me clear up, please."

"No," he raised a firm hand and continued, "I've a better idea for you."

From the worktop he collected a handful of brochures and removing her plate set the brochures down in front of her.

"This is a selection of information about Arran that I picked up a while back from the information office at the harbour. This one here," he pointed to a double sided sheet with a colourful map of Arran on one side and local maps of Brodick, Lamlash and Whiting Bay on the reverse side, "has a list of places of interest and also of hotels and guesthouses. What I suggest is I've put a chair out at the hall table for where you can use the phone to call round and inquire if there are any vacancies. I'll clear up here and get us another cuppa going, okay?"

"Okay, thank you," she nodded.

Making her way into the hallway, she stopped to glance into the small lounge where she smiled at Marcy who still wearing the tartan rug on her shoulders, was now slumped onto a pile of cushions watching the television, her empty plate on the breakfast tray on the small table in front of the couch.

"Hi, sweetheart. Enjoy your breakfast, did you?" she softly called.

Yawning, Marcy turned and gave Alice a thumbs up before returning her attention to the cartoons.

****

Seating herself at the hall table, Alice dialled the first number on the brochure Tommy gave her, but the lady who answered apologised and regretted all her rooms were taken, adding the first that would be available was on Wednesday.

Almost one hour and seventeen calls later that included a 'glamping' camping site, Alice replaced the handset and admitted defeat. There simply was no accommodation to be had on the island for the holiday weekend.

Lifting her empty mug, she took it through to the kitchen where to her surprise, she saw Tommy and Marcy, who still wearing her pyjamas was stood upon an IKEA two step-stool and like Tommy wore an apron, though hers had been tucked up several times to enable it to fit. They were at the kitchen island, their hands and aprons white with flour and kneading dough into a large plastic bowl.

"We're making Scottish scones, Gran," Marcy grinned, the tip of her nose white with flour.

"How did you get on?" Tommy asked.

Her face registered her surprise at his bond with her granddaughter and placing her mug onto the worktop, shook her head.

"It was the same story at all the places I tried, booked solid because of the holiday weekend," she sighed.

"So, what do you intend doing now?"

"There's nothing else for it. You've been very kind, Tommy, but if I can impose one more time and ask that you drop us back to the ferry. With luck I might be able to get something over in Ardrossan."

"Yeah, of course," he nodded. "Look, as you'll have guessed, I'm a right tea-jenny. Must be something to do from the days I worked on the building sites. Why don't you stick the kettle on for a brew and let Miss Cheeky Nose and me finish up with our scones…"

"Hey, I'm not Miss Cheeky Nose," Marcy giggled. "You're Mister Cheeky Nose."

"Aye," he pretended to be stern and replied to the little girl, "Any more of your nonsense young lady and I'll put you into the oven with the scones!"

She giggled again as he winked at Alice before continuing, "Once these are in the oven, why don't we sit down and look at your options."

"Okay," she slowly agreed.

****

Permitting Marcy to watch some more television, Alice sat with Tommy in the kitchen with the tantalising smell of baking scones about them.

"Tell me, Alice, if I'm not being too intrusive, why did you come to Arran?"

She thought about her response and reluctant to lie to this kind man, replied, "I just upped and left because I wanted a new start for Marcy and me. I honestly didn't think it out," she shook her head, "and naively thought I'd get somewhere for us to rent and a job for me."

"A job? What kind of job?"

"Anything," she softly smiled. "Anything that would earn us enough to live on. Then I could enrol Marcy at a local school and, well," she hesitated and pausing, sighed. "But it doesn't seem as though it will happen now. Tell me, what's Ardrossan like? Is there job opportunities there, do you know?"

He stared at this sad woman and though she obviously couldn't see it, wondered if she realised how attractive she was. He couldn't know Alice's age, but with her clear skin and soft features, guessed her to be in her mid to late forties. Yet, Tommy was no fool and suspected he wasn't getting the whole story from Alice.

Yes, he thought, there was definitely something about her, something mysterious; something that she wasn't disclosing.

His head dipped as he shook it and replied, "No, I'm sorry. Other than passing through I only know that before the foreign holidays became affordable for the working man, Ardrossan and its near neighbour Saltcoats were the summer holiday destination for thousands of Weegies."

"Weegies?" she smiled, her eyes betraying her curiosity.

"Sorry, Glaswegians."

"But surely they must still cater for holidaymakers? Hotels or guesthouses and what about places to rent?"

"I suppose there is," he shrugged, "but I can't say for definite."

"Hmm," her brow furrowed as she was lost in thought.

"Tell you what," he glanced through the kitchen window and cheerfully said, "It's almost twelve and it's a beautiful Saturday morning. Why don't you and the wean get ready and I'll take you on a tour of the island. Maybe when you're out in the fresh air you'll see things a wee bit different and it might give you the opportunity to clear your head. What do you say?"

His enthusiasm was infectious and lifted her from her despair. Nodding, she smiled and said, "I'll get Marcy ready."

****

He opened his eyes and almost immediately, the throbbing headache started.

His mouth felt as though he'd sucked on a week old sock and taking a breath, swung his legs over the side of the bed, idly noting that he was still fully clothed and even wearing his shoes.

He was about to call out, but couldn't get any spit in his mouth and working his lips and tongue eventually produced some saliva and shouted, "Alice! Alice! Get in here!"

He waited for a response and wondered why she didn't come running, then realised.

The bitch hadn't come home after all.

He forced himself to his feet and swaying, reached his hand to the wall to steady himself before staggering to the bedroom door.

Pulling it open, he loudly called again, "Alice! Get up here!" but it was as before, no response.

He swallowed and knew he needed Paracetamol to counter the drumbeat in his head and carefully making his way downstairs, wondered how he'd got home last night from the club.

A taxi, that was it. His eyes narrowed as he fought to recall then remembered being shoved into a taxi by a laughing crowd of the members.

In the hallway, he stared down at his jacket lying abandoned on the floor, his car keys beside it and recalled driving to the club.

Bugger, he thought, I'll need to get a taxi to collect he bloody motor. One hand on the banister, he slumped clumsily down onto the third step and sat there, wondering where the *hell* she had got to.

She had no money of her own and would not survive for long on the couple of hundred quid she'd stolen from his wallet. Then he remembered, there was fifty odd pounds in the shopping account. He smiled, but without humour. He'd contact the bank and find out if the money was still in the shopping account and if she tried to use it or withdraw the money, he'd demand to know where she used the card or from what ATM.

Yes, pleased with himself, he nodded; that's what he'd do.

And when he found her…

****

Tommy's oldest daughter Fiona lifted the mobile phone to see on the screen the caller was her younger sister, Jenny.

"Any word from Pops?"

"I phoned him last night and he's fine. I'll text you his new landline number for the house. What you up to, today?"

"Nothing much planned," Jenny replied. "As it's the holiday weekend, Andy and me were thinking about taking the wee dude over on the ferry as foot passengers and surprising Pops, maybe staying overnight. Besides, I'm dead keen to see the place too. What do you think?"

"What, not driving? I didn't realise you knew you had legs, sis."

"Aye, very droll. Anyway, what are you and Phil doing this weekend?"

"Not sure, but I was speaking earlier with Vicky and because it's such a nice day, she and Mathew are having a picnic in the Kelvingrove Park."

"Really? I fancy the idea of that. Are you joining her?"

"I was considering it," Fiona's lips pursed, before continuing, "To be honest, sis, I got the idea when I spoke with dad that he fancied a quiet weekend to himself. I don't want to put you off or anything…"

"But you're telling me anyway," she sighed. "Okay, hint taken. I'll give Vicky a phone and ask if she won't mind the company and see you in the park. What you bringing to eat?"

"Probably a portable barbeque and sausages and stuff. That suit you?"

"I'll bring a sweet and tell Andy to get some drinks. See you there," Jenny ended the call.

Fiona laid the mobile back down onto the worktop and thought about her father.

She had been candid with her sister and knew her dad needed some time alone.

A week previously her husband Phil had been quite forthright when he told her that sometimes he thought Fiona and her sisters smothered her dad, that Tommy shouldn't be at his daughters' beck and call as much as he was.

She argued that Phil was wrong, that neither she nor her sisters were like that, but it had sown the seed of doubt and the more she thought about it, the more she realised her husband was right; they did take their father for granted and just like their mother, often tried to steer him in the direction they believed he should go.

Yes, her father was a strong minded individual when it was work related issues, but he was now retired and she admitted, far too genial with his daughters when often, Fiona was coming to believe, he should raise his hand and so no, I'm too busy or no, it doesn't suit.

She knew in her heart that part of her wished Jenny would go over on the ferry to confirm he was okay, but suggesting she didn't visit, she now realised, was the right and proper thing to do.

She smiled at her own decision and making her way through the house, called out, "Cissie, sweetheart, do you fancy going to the park today?"

CHAPTER FIFTEEN

Alice and Marcy's jackets had dried overnight, but the weather had taken a turn for the better and they didn't need to wear them.

"Besides," Tommy held Alice's thin jacket in his hand, "this is hardly Scottish weather wear so if you don't mind wearing this old thing."

He handed her a dark green coloured, quilted waterproof jacket with a corduroy collar and frayed cuffs. "I know it's past its sell-by date," he smiled, "but it's a lot comfier that this wee thin thing you were wearing."

"However," he continued, "this is Scotland and the only predictable thing about the weather up here is it's unpredictable, so we'll stick them in the back anyway."

"What kind of jeep is this?" Alice asked, strapping Marcy into the rear seat behind Tommy then climbing into the front passenger seat and closing the door.

"Actually, it's not a jeep, it's a Land Rover Defender," he grinned and patted the dashboard. "It's getting on in age now, but I love it and always have."

"How old is it?" Marcy asked from the rear seat.

"Older than you," he chortled. "In fact, it's almost ten years old now. Right, here we go."

He drove down the hill towards the main road, then turned left with the sea to their right.

"How big is Arran" Alice asked.

"Let me see. If memory serves correctly, it's roughly twenty miles long and about ten miles wide at it's widest point. The drive around the island is about fifty odd miles, fifty-six or seven I think and takes us through some lovely scenery. Of course, you can cut through the island on the inner roads, but I like to keep the sea beside me," he turned briefly to grin at her, then asked, "Do you drive?"

"Yes, I do, but I've never driven anything as big as this Defender," she nodded at him.

As they drove, Tommy enjoyed his task of guide and pointed out the places of interest, seeing in the rear view mirror Marcy's expression of surprise when passing through Corrie, they saw a pair of seals sitting upon a rock thirty metres out into the sea. He stopped the vehicle in a layby and suggested the little girl to run to the edge of the water and call to the seals.

Stood watching from the side of the vehicle, he and Alice smiled at the little girls wonder as the seals called back to Marcy.

They continued their journey and when passing through Sannox, he pointed to the Gowanlea guesthouse and related the story of the time he and his wife Moira had stayed there with the very funny and amusing Missus June Warburton and her husband Chris who she insisted on calling, 'him indoors.'

Continuing onwards past Arran's only distillery, he asked if Alice enjoyed a dram?

"A dram?"

"Whisky."

"No, not at all," she shuddered, but Tommy could not know that her aversion was not to the golden liquid itself, but of the memory of her husband Geoffrey's consumption and his bullying attitude that seemed to surge when he had been drinking.

Tommy sensed he had stirred up some bad memory and to lighten the atmosphere, called out to Marcy, "Are you ready for a cuppa or a juice, Miss Cheeky Nose?"

She giggled and replied, "Juice, please."

"Then juice it is," he said and turned the Defender in through the gate of the Stags Pavilion tea room.

Getting out of the car, Tommy reached into the boot and brought out a leather carrying case that contained a pair of binoculars.

Handing them to Marcy, he pointed to the hill behind the tea room and said, "Look up there. Do you see the deer?"

It took the little girl a moment to focus on the herd of a dozen deer, but then her jaw dropped and she cried out, "Gran! I can see deer! Look! There!" she pointed her forefinger towards the hill.

The tea room was crowded with visitors, some who had stopped in their vehicles but a large number of whom were clearly walkers, Alice judged by the number of backpacks and rucksacks piled at the entrance.

They found a table directly under the large chalkboard menu on the wall that offered all the foods available.

It was when they were seated that Marcy, her eyes narrowing, peered at the chalkboard and asked, "What's ven-i-son," she slowly read out the word.

Alice, her eyes widening, glanced a warning to Tommy who quickly replied, "It's a kind of meat, like a sausage. I don't think you'd like it," he made a face and shook his head.

Alice flashed him a grateful smile and he grinned.

The young waitress who attended at the table with her notebook cheerily asked, "What can I get you?"

Tommy replied, "Orange juice for Miss Cheeky Nose here and one of your famous scones."

The waitress smiled and continued, "And for you and your wife?"

Taken aback, he glanced inquiringly at Alice, who remained pokerfaced and said, "Ah, latte for me, please."

Finding his voice, Tommy agreed with, "Two latte's then and a couple of scones, please."

When the waitress walked off and giggling behind her hand, Marcy said, "She thinks you two are married."

For some unaccountable reason, Tommy felt his face redden and replied, "Yes, well, *she* thinks you're called Miss Cheeky Nose, too."

They sat in a slightly uncomfortable silence for a moment until Alice brightly said, "You seem to have an excellent knowledge of Arran, Tommy. How long have you lived here?"

"Lived here? Oh, I only bought the house about six weeks ago. It's supposed to be my bolt hole, my retreat. I've a flat in Glasgow that's my full time home. That said, my wife and I used to bring our daughters to the island on holiday and," he grinned, "we stayed in some crummy places too, all around the island. The house is a palace to some of them."

"Your house *is* lovely," she smiled at him.

"Yeah, it's not at all bad, is it?" he warmly agreed.

"Gran," Marcy interrupted. "Can I go outside and look at the deer again?"

"Tommy?" she turned to him.

"She'll come to no harm, but only if you promise," he wagged a warning forefinger at the little girl, "to stay at the back of the building and do *not* go out the front to the car park. Deal?" he extended his hand to her.

"Deal," she grinned at him and shook his hand.

Handing her the binoculars, they watched her scamper off through the door, then turning to Alice he said, "This is Arran. She'll come to no harm here."

"So, how long are you here for at the moment?"

"Well," he inhaled, "because I'm retired, my time is my own. I did intend spending the holiday weekend here, but we'll see what the weather brings. I might consider staying on if the sun continues to shine."

Again there was that awkward silence until Alice said, "Maybe we should consider moving on if we're to see the rest of the island and Marcy and I are to catch the ferry, later."

"Right," he slowly drawled, then taking a breath, bit at his lower lip. "I was thinking," then raised his hands and continued, "just if you agree, that is, that you and Marcy might want to stay over for another night. The only reason I'm suggesting it is…"

"Yes, please," she interrupted him, then hesitated and wondered if he thought her too eager.

"Oh, right then," his eyes fluttered in surprise. "Ah, what I *was* going to suggest was there seems little point in dragging Marcy and that wreck of a suitcase around Ardrossan this evening looking for places to rent when instead you can use my computer to search for accommodation on line, then phone for more details. That way you'll have somewhere to go to rather than take pot luck, yeah?"

"That seems like a better plan, Tommy," she smiled with relief, but a little embarrassed to admit she had never before used a computer.

"Tell me, where the heck did you get that old suitcase anyway?"

Her smile fixed to her face as she replied, "That's a long story, but maybe for another time."

"Oh, right," he guessed that was a question too far and then adopting a serious expression, said "You do realise that another night's accommodation at Casa el Tommy will cost you a further bottle of my favourite red?"

"About that," she slowly replied, "Grateful as I am for your hospitality, I really do think you should let me pay something for our keep."

He grinned and said, "Alice, without going into details let me assure you, I really do *not* need payment for your keep."
****

Collecting the excited Marcy, they continued their journey past Lochranza and on to Pirnmill with Tommy pointing out the local landmarks and features.

"Like I said," Alice nodded, "you do have a good knowledge of this island."

"If you think I know my way about," he grinned, "you should meet my cousin Gerry McGoldrick and his wife Alison. Alison and her family have been coming to Arran since she was a wee girl and she has an almost encyclopaedic knowledge of the island. I keep telling her to write a visitors' guide, but will she listen?" he shook his head. Approaching the Kinloch Hotel, Tommy glanced at the dashboard clock and called to Marcy in the back, "How are you getting on, Miss Cheeky Nose."

There was no response and it was only when Alice turned in her seat that they realised the little girl had fallen asleep.

"Bless her," Alice smiled to which Tommy quietly responded, "Why don't we leave the rest of the journey for another day and take her home."

As they continued in silence, it was moments later that Alice wondered was Tommy's comment 'for another day' and 'take her home' a slip of the tongue or was she reading into something that wasn't there?

****

He gently lifted Marcy from the rear seat and carried her up to the room where after leaving her grandmother to take the little girl's coat and shoes off, went downstairs to wait for Alice.

When he heard her tiptoeing down the stairs, he beckoned her to follow him into his study and switched on his Apple desktop.

She grimaced and admitted, "I've never actually used a computer before."

Though Tommy thought that was unusual, he made no comment and instead said, "You've drawn money out of an ATM, haven't you?"

"Yes," she stared curiously at him.

"Well then, you have used a computer, only this one is a little more sophisticated."

Bringing in an extra chair, he sat Alice down and in the chair beside her guided her hand on the mouse and taught her how to open the search engine.

Her heart beat a little faster as his hand closed over hers for other than Geoffrey, she had never known another man's touch.

Within fifteen minutes, she was confidently searching the web and with a huge grin, turned with eyes sparkling and said, "I never realised how easy this is."

"Well, you'll find a pen and paper in the desk drawer for taking a note of phone numbers of properties to let," he told her, "so while you're searching Ardrossan for accommodation, I'll stick the kettle on for a brew."

In the kitchen after switching on the kettle, Tommy stood leaning against the island and wondered; what the hell am I doing? This woman and her granddaughter are passing through my life and will be gone in the morning. Bloody hell man, didn't you learn your lesson with Barbara? How many times must you get kicked in the balls before you realise you're on your own and that's just the way it is.

He sighed and turned to the cupboard to fetch out two mugs, then pouring the tea made his way back through to the study.

"How are you getting on?" he laid her mug onto a coaster on the desk.

"Oh, there's plenty of guesthouses and places to rent," she sighed, "but I've limited funds and…well, frankly I'm at a loss what to do." She turned towards him and he inwardly prayed, please don't let there be tears; I won't stand a chance if she starts weeping, but saw that her eyes were glistening and she was close to crying.

It was then he heard a noise behind him and stepping out into the hallway saw Marcy standing at the bottom of the stairs, her hair tousled and rubbing the sleep from her eyes.

"When do we go for the ferry, Gran?" she tiredly yawned.

Taking a deep breath, Alice arose from the desk chair and subtly rubbing at her eyes walked to the study door and replied, "We need to stay another night here with Mister Burke, sweetheart. Is that okay with you?"

Tommy wasn't prepared for the little girl's reaction when she screamed, "Yippee!" and running towards him, threw her arms around his waist and with her head against his stomach, said, "Thank you, thank you, thank you."

He couldn't help but smile and told her, "I only made the offer. It's your gran you should be thanking. She made the decision to stay another night."

Marcy reached for her grandmother's hand and staring up at Alice, said, "Thank you, Gran."

"Well," Tommy coughed to hide his embarrassment, "if you let me go Miss Cheeky Nose, I'll see about getting dinner ready."

"Would you mind if I cooked dinner tonight?" Alice asked.

"What, fed up with my cooking already?" he grinned at her.

"No, not at all, I just want to repay your kindness by cooking you a meal."

"Well, in that case when dinner's ready, Missus Benson," he winked at Marcy, "you'll find Miss Cheeky Nose and me in the small lounge watching cartoons."

He was about to step away, but paused, then turned and said, "And if you're sticking the kettle on…?"

****

Sitting on the floral patterned armchair in the small but comfortable lounge and surrounded by photographs and ornaments collected throughout her life, Doris Chisholm, lifted her A3 sized diary from the oak coffee table in front of her to read what she had so far written.

It was only when she put pen to paper her thoughts turned to the type of life her friend Alice had endured.

Geoffrey Mayhew was nothing but a big and blustering bully, her lips tightened. The way he treated his wife was absolutely scandalous and people who believed him to be an upstanding man and respected doctor should know what kind of man he really was, she thought.

But how would she go about it?

She raised the diary and reread her most recent account of the revelations made by Alice about her life with Geoffrey, his penny pinching and demands she retain every shopping receipt for him to peruse. His refusal to permit Alice to use a car for anything but shopping or even to have a mobile phone; his absurd refusal to accept eight-year old Marcy as his granddaughter because he disliked the little girl's father.

But more worryingly, his past and increasingly violent conduct towards his wife, whether he had been drinking or not.

My God, Doris shook her head, how in heaven did Alice manage to tolerate living with such a beastly man all those years. She laid the book down onto her lap and thought again of the story Alice had recounted, of the time her spirited daughter Gemma boldly announced she was leaving home to marry her boyfriend Peter, of Gemma's demand her mother come to and of Alice's shamefaced admittance she was too frightened of Geoffrey's reaction.

Doris recalled how she had gently coaxed the real reason from Alice who confessed that if she had gone with her daughter, Geoffrey would never have permitted Gemma and Peter any peace, that he would have hounded them until Alice returned.

"So," Doris had asked, "you stayed with him to protect your daughter, even though you knew what kind of man he was?"

"What else could I do," Alice had softly replied. "She deserved a life of her own and besides, mine was already over. As my mother used to tell me when she was alive," she had sighed, "you made your bed, now you must lie in it."

Eyes closed as she sat back in the comfortable chair, Doris mentally composed the next chapter of her narrative; Alice's discovery of the packet containing the little brown tablets that Doris suspected were performance enhancement pills and her friend's suspicion that in some way Geoffrey was connected to the young rugby player's death.

She reached for her pen, but then the doorbell rang.

****

Seated on the couch with Marcy beside him and engrossed in the adventures of Merida in the animated Disney film 'Brave,' the door opened and turning, Tommy saw Alice pop her head in and who said, "I wonder if I might ask another favour of you?"

"Of course," he smiled.

"May I use the phone to call a friend?"

"It's there anytime you need to make a call, Alice; you don't need to ask."

In the kitchen she set the stew and the potatoes on the range cooker at a low gas, then with a glance at the ornamental clock on the wall, decided she had time to phone Doris and let her know that they were safe, that they had made a friend.

Tommy had already returned the chair from beside the hall table into the study, so Alice stood as she dialled the number for Doris's house. She could not know that when the phone rang in the hallway of the house in Middleton Road, her friend was standing fearfully a few feet from the enraged Geoffrey Mayhew, who wearing his green coloured wax jacket and brown leather driving gloves, had pushed the old woman back from the door that he slammed behind him and now stood glowering at her in the hallway.

"I'll ask you again," he snarled, his eyes shining bright with menace, "where is my wife!"

"And I told *you*," she mustered enough courage to snap back at him,

"I don't know!"

He glanced at the ringing phone and eyes narrowing, suspiciously asked, "Is that her?"

"No, no," Doris vigorously shook her head. "It will be my granddaughter and if I don't answer, she'll worry that I've fallen or something and be round here in a minute. She only lives round the corner," she lied, her throat tightening and her legs trembling.

"Well, let's see if it *is* your granddaughter, shall we?" he made to reach for the phone, but Doris bravely pushed at him only to be grabbed by the front of her blouse and brutally shoved hard against the wall for she had little chance of stopping a large and powerfully built man like Geoffrey.

Lifting the phone from the cradle and keeping a watchful eye on Doris, he didn't speak, but listened.

"Hello?" said Alice. "Doris? Can you hear me? Doris?"

He was about to reply, but was taken by surprise when Doris lunged at him and her mouth dry with fear, in a choked voice cried out, "Help me! I'm being attacked!"

Grappling with her, he let go the phone that fell to the floor, dragging the cradle with it.

On the other side of the line, Alice had heard only the scuffling noise and cried out, "Doris! Is that you? What's happening? Who's there with you?" but the line suddenly went dead for unknown to her, Geoffrey had torn the cord from the wall socket.

Stunned, Alice immediately ended the call and quickly redialled Doris's number only to hear the constant tone that indicated the line was disconnected.

She didn't understand what had happened, but stomach clenching, knew it was something bad.

In the hallway of the house in Middleton Road, Geoffrey lost all control after Doris's futile attempt to attack him and grabbed the elderly woman's throat in both hands. Choking her, he pushed her backwards, forcing the panicking woman through the open door of the small lounge before brutally shoving her away from him.

He did not intend that she fall so heavily, but simply wanted to frighten her into submission. However, the action of the large and heavily built man that he was against the smaller and frailer Doris caused her to land heavily onto her back, striking the left side of her head on the corner of the oak coffee table as she fell.

To Geoffrey's horror the impact of her skull against the solid wood resulted in a spray of crimson blood that when her skull fractured scattered across the nearby armchair and the carpet.

Mortally wounded, her body lay limply on the carpet and as he watched, her head rolled to one side before she gave a gentle sigh, then stared at him with unseeing eyes.

Stunned, Geoffrey could only gape at the blood that rapidly seeped from beneath her head and was about to move towards her when he stopped.

There was no saving her, of that he was certain. What he had to do now was save himself.

Taking a breath, he stared around the room, but then thought if he began a search he would undoubtedly leave some trace evidence of himself for the police to find so with a final glance at the dead woman, retraced his steps into the hallway.

He was about to step over the phone lying on the carpeted floor towards the front door, but then a thought occurred and bending down, with shaking hands plugged the cable back into the socket and replaced the phone onto the small table.

Fetching a pen from his inner jacket pocket, he took a deep breath and readied himself. Licking at his suddenly dry lips, he dialled one-four-seven-one and listened as the last phone number was digitally repeated.

He didn't recognise the STD code, but noted the incoming phone number on a piece of paper from his pocket.

That done, he replaced the phone into the cradle and with a hesitant glance moved aside the net curtain on the square window set in the door. His nerves now shredded, he first checked the street outside was clear of any passers-by then left the house, quietly closing the door behind him.

CHAPTER SIXTEEN

In the colourful animated film, Merida had just bested the huge bear and was protecting her mother from the spears and arrows of her Clan when Marcy leaned close into Tommy. Squirming up so that her mouth was against his ear and with her hands cupped, she whispered, "Can I tell you a secret?"

He inwardly smiled and marvelled that in such a short time he had apparently earned the trust of the little girl.

Nodding, he stifled a grin and quietly replied, "As long as it's a real secret and you're not trying to persuade me to talk your grandmother into letting you stay up late, tonight."

She drew back a few inches and staring at him, replied, "No, it *is* a real secret and you're not to tell anyone. Promise?"

Wise in the ways of small girls, he solemnly asked "Is this a pinkie promise secret?"

Marcy nodded and holding up her right hand, made a fist with the small finger extended.

With three daughters of his own and a granddaughter Marcy's age, Tommy was no stranger to pinkie promises and gravely did likewise, wrapping his small finger around Marcy's.

That done, she leaned in close and softly whispered, "We've run away from him and we're not going back."

Tommy half smiled, not quite understanding and turning to face Marcy, stared curiously at her when he quietly repeated, "Run away? Who have you run away from?"

Marcy in a low voice, replied, "Him, my grandfather."

The simple statement hit Tommy like a slap in the face.

Alice had lied.

She was not as she had inferred, widowed or divorced or at least that's what he had assumed when she had told him, 'no husband.'

Jesus, Burke, he momentarily closed his eyes and gritting his teeth in anger, mentally chastised himself and thought, when will you learn not to trust women?

A cold fury swept through him that he was again being deceived and had to physically resist the urge to march into the kitchen and confront her with the lie.

Instead, he forced himself to inhale then slowly exhale to relax his body before softly asking the little girl, "And why did you run away?"

Her brow furrowed and the tone of her response was as if his question was silly, but then she whispered, "Because he hits my Gran and shouts at her and makes her cry even though I'm not supposed to know."

Stunned, his anger dissipated almost immediately as he stared wide-eyed at Marcy then without thinking, wrapped his arms about her and without resistance drew her protectively close to him.

Though he did not know Marcy, he instinctively realised there was no deceit in the little girl, that what she had disclosed was the truth as she knew it and he wondered that this wee lassie should have witnessed such violence at her tender age. He also realised that while he was reluctant to question her further, it was not her place to provide Tommy with the real truth of why she and her grandmother were on the island.

No, his brow furrowed, that was Alice's job, but how did he go about disclosing what he had learned?

He glanced down at the tousled head and decided that albeit the little girl was just eight years of age, if he betrayed her trust he might never again redeem it.

But then again, he reasoned, she and her grandmother were likely to be gone in the morning and asked himself; why should I care?

He answered his own question when tight-lipped he thought, because I'm a bloody idiot that hates men who assault women and besides, he glanced again at Marcy and could not help but smile, this wee girl trusts me.

The door opened to admit Alice, wearing his green apron and who pale faced and wringing her hands on a dishcloth, stuttered, "Dinner's ready," then hurriedly left the room again.

Did she hear Marcy tell me, he wondered or is there something else that's happened because of her phone call?

****

Though there were just a dozen or so steps from the small lounge to the kitchen Tommy experienced a wave of emotion that see-sawed from anger at Alice's lie to sympathy for what seemed to be her dilemma; an abusive husband.

He allowed Marcy to lead him by the hand into the dining kitchen and wordlessly took his seat.

Alice stood with her back to him spooning out the food onto the plates that lay on the worktop beside the range cooker. When she turned he could see she was still pale-faced and close to tears and any vestige of his anger quickly faded.

Rising from his chair, he told her, "Why don't you go and wash your face, hen. I'll finish putting the dinner out."

"No, thanks, I'll be fine," she sniffed.

Marcy immediately picked up on her grandmother's distress and sliding from her chair, rushed over to throw her arms about Alice's waist, asking, "What's wrong, Gran? You can tell me and Tommy." She lowered her voice and in a stage whisper, added, "He knows we're running away."

Alice's head jerked up and she stared at Tommy, her expression changing to one of panic.

"What did you say! What did you ask her!" she loudly demanded, pulling the now scared little girl tightly to her.

"Now hold on," he remained standing by his chair, "I didn't ask Marcy anything…"

But Alice ignored his explanation and, placing both hands on Marcy's shoulder, she stared into the frightened little girl's eyes and snapped "Run upstairs and put our clothes into the case!"

When she saw Marcy hesitate and glance towards Tommy, she snapped again, "Now Marcy! Go on!"

"Alice!" Tommy harshly called out and when she turned to him he could see the fear in her eyes.

"Please! Calm down," he lowered his voice, slowly waving his hands up and down, the palms out flat as he continued, "I did *not* ask Marcy anything. She told me it was a secret and I respect that. It's your business what you do and why you're here on the island. If you choose to leave now, that's fine," he nodded, "but think of your granddaughter. You made the decision to stay here at my home because of her welfare. I know you are a loving grandmother, I can see that, but *please*, consider her welfare first."

He paused to let his comment sink in and seeing that Alice was listening, that she was visibly relaxing, then added, "Whatever or whoever you're frightened of, let me assure you; you and the wee girl are safe here. If you need one more night to consider your next move," he extended his hands wide, "that's fine. But I urge you, do not make a hasty decision that will cause you and Marcy hardship."

They faced each other across the width of the kitchen, Alice's arms still holding her granddaughter tight, then she said, her voice a murmur, "I lied to you."

"I know that and you must have had a good reason to do so, but for what it's worth," he slowly smiled and quietly added, "you're not the first woman to tell me a fib."

She closed her eyes, her mind racing at the enormity of being caught in the lie and ashamed after Tommy had been so trusting and so kind.

At last she stared sadly at him and said, "You can't possibly tolerate us…me, being in your home; not after what I told you."

He pointedly sniffed the air and resuming his seat, waved that Marcy sit down before replying, "Why don't we discuss that after dinner and before the food gets cold."

****

He had parked his Volvo in the adjoining street and starting the engine, nervously glanced about him, but saw no one before driving off.

His throat was tight as he drove and a rivulet of perspiration run down his spine.

Stupid, stupid, stupid, he hammered a fist off the steering wheel. However, Geoffrey's anger was directed not at himself, but at the foolish old woman, convincing himself as he drove that it was she and she alone who was responsible for her death. He had simply wanted to know where his wife was, yet Doris Chisholm had refused to disclose where Alice had gone and even had the gall to challenge him. Him! He gritted his teeth at her bloody insolence.

Deep in thought the short distance to Spruce Close passed so quickly that Geoffrey drove automatically and was turning into the driveway before he realised he was home. Getting out of the car he glanced at the roadway behind, fearfully wondering if his vehicle had been spotted when parked near to the woman's house or if he had been seen driving off.

Approaching the front door of the house he saw the letter box was stuffed with junk mail and realised that Alice still had not returned home.

Where the hell can she be, he wondered and idly cast the junk mail onto the hall table.

As he did so, he saw there was a message recorded on the answer machine and pressing the play button, heard a man's voice say, "It's me. Where the hell are you, Geoff? You can't keep ignoring my calls. Get in touch pronto or else."

He gritted his teeth, for he hated his name being abbreviated, being called 'Geoff.'

Playing the message a second time he heard the man again say 'or else' and that, Geoffrey bristled and decided, is a threat.

He had a sudden feeling the walls were beginning to close in on him and even before taking off his coat, he was reaching for his mobile phone and jabbing a stubby finger at the name in the directory, then listened for the call being answered.

When the voice said, "Geoff, it's about time…" he interrupted with, "Who the *fuck* are you to threaten *me*, Meiklewood! You forget your place, you halfwit!"

"Look, Geoff," the man's voice was almost pleading, "I've had the cops sniffing about my house, asking my missus where I am and trying to coax me down to the station for an interview about young…"

"Don't say his name on the phone!" Geoffrey snapped before adding, "Are you stupid as well as incompetent?"

"Incompetent? What the hell do you mean by that?" Meiklewood was outraged.

Geoffrey inhaled deeply before hissing, "You were supposed to be careful what he took, but oh no," he vigorously shook his head as though emphasising the point, "you allowed the bloody fool to consume far more than was safe, didn't you?"

Geoffrey's caution about speaking on the telephone was forgotten in his rage and he continued, "I told you, didn't I? Two tablets before a match and no more. Four tablets would undoubtedly cause cardiac arrest and six, well," he sighed, "six are fatal, aren't they?"

"How the hell am I supposed to know all that," Meiklewood blustered. "You're the doctor and besides," he began to whine, "I *did* warn him no more than two before a match, but he just wouldn't listen. You know what John-jo was like. Thought he knew best, he did."

Geoffrey didn't immediately respond, but rubbed at his aching head with his free hand before telling Meiklewood, "We need to meet. There's a few things that I need to clear with you."

"Are you out of your mind? We can't meet. It's too dangerous."

"What the hell are you on about?"

There was a loud and very audible sigh before Meiklewood replied, "Have you not considered that one or perhaps both of us might be under surveillance? The police aren't stupid…"

Not like you anyway, Geoffrey harshly thought.

"…they'll soon connect the dots and cross the T's. They'll know that my…*our* supplier," he corrected himself, "will be importing the Speeders and they'll connect him to me. Once they've done that, then ergo, they'll connect me to you."

A cold chill run through Geoffrey and he felt his throat dry and his bowels constrict. This then was the threat from Meiklewood out in the open. He was the link between the drug dealer, he thought. The supplier, this man Monty Reid he boasted was his friend - and me.

"Yes, of course you're correct, Teddy," he soothingly said before adding, "though I would like to meet you one final time, agree face to face so there is no dubiety what we might say if indeed the police do wish to interview us, yes? Now, here's a thought," he was thinking fast before Meiklewood began to have doubts, "even if the the police are watching one of us, it's highly unlikely they will have a budget to carry out their observations through the night, don't you agree?"

"Well, yes I suppose so," mumbled Meiklewood before asking, "What are you thinking?"

"You know the Hills and Hollows Nature Reserve on Fulwood Row?"

"Yes," he slowly replied.

"Let's say we meet there at three o'clock tomorrow morning when it's dark. We can meet in the car park at the entrance to the nature reserve where the road is closed to traffic and can sit quietly and discuss what we will say if we are interviewed and required to provide statements. Do you agree?"

He held his breath, hoping Meiklewood wouldn't suspect anything. "Bloody hell, Geoff, it's a hell of a time on a Sunday morning."

"But safe, Teddy, and that's the important thing, so I'll see you there, then," and ended the call before Meiklewood could disagree. Returning the mobile phone to his jacket pocket, he stared down at his shaking hands, aghast at what he was considering, but realised that it was necessary if he were to survive this awful mess. He glanced at his car keys to ensure the garage keys were still attached to the metal ring and thought about what he would need to get from the garage before he attended his meeting with Teddy Meiklewood. But first, there was something he had to do.

Fetching the slip of paper from his pocket he cast off his coat onto the hallway table as he walked, then made his way to his study and seating himself in his leather swivel chair, switched on the desktop computer.

"Come on, come on," he impatiently muttered as the computer warmed up.

At last the screen burst into life. Bringing up the search engine page, he glanced at the slip of paper and typed in the full number he had written down.

Nothing came back, but when he typed in the STD code, the result made him stare curiously at the screen.

"Arran," he muttered, vaguely aware that it was somewhere in Scotland. "What the hell is she doing in Arran?"

****

They had finished their meal in silence that ended when her voice breaking, Marcy said, "I'm very sorry Gran. It was me that told Tommy about us running away."

Alice forced a smile and reached across the table to take her granddaughter's hand in hers and with a shake of her head, replied, "No, it's not your fault, Marcy. It's mine. It was me who told Tommy a lie," she cast a glance at him, "and for that I'm very sorry. Now I have to make up for that by telling him the truth so if Tommy doesn't mind, perhaps you can go and watch some television while I speak to him."

Reluctant to go because she feared some argument would develop, she was about to protest, but stopped when Tommy said, "Your grandmother's right, Marcy. You go and watch the TV and I promise you," he smiled and with the forefinger of his right hand made an X sign across his chest and said, "with all my heart that we'll sort things out, okay?"

"And you'll not hit her?" the little girl's lips trembled.

Stunned, his mouth fell open and he got out of his chair. Kneeling beside Marcy and laying his hands gently on her arms, he vigorously shook his head before quietly telling her, "I would never, ever, *ever* hit your grandmother or any lady. Please believe me, Marcy. Some men are not very nice, I admit that, but you have to know that not all men, not all dads and granddads are like that. I *need* you to believe me. I have three daughters and a granddaughter and they would tell you the very same thing. I am *not* a bad man and would not let anyone hurt you or your gran."

He smiled reassuringly and raising a clenched hand with the small finger extended, added, "Pinkie promise."

Reassured, Marcy nodded and wrapping her own small finger around Tommy's, repeated, "Pinkie promise."

He turned to glance at Alice and saw that her hands were at her mouth and clasped together as though in prayer and her eyes glistened with unshed tears.

He didn't say anything, but turned back to Marcy and said, "Now, away you go wee one and your gran and me will have a wee chat and when we're finished, we'll come and tell you what your gran has decided, okay?"

"Okay," she nodded and left the kitchen.

"Thank you," Alice said, her voice breaking.

Getting to his feet, Tommy asked, "Do you feel fit enough to have a wee chat?"

Nodding, she rose from the chair and replied, "Let me wash my face first."

During the few minutes Alice was gone to the cloakroom toilet, Tommy cleared the table and packed the dishwasher. When she returned he told her, "Let's take our tea into the big lounge."

Seated opposite each other in the two comfortable armchairs, he started with, "Before we say anything else, Alice, you made a phone call that seemed to upset you. Is everything okay?" Holding up his hand he added, "I don't intend to pry, but…"

"No," she abruptly stopped him. "You have every right to ask. Every right," she sighed before continuing, "I have one friend in this world, Doris, and that's who I phoned. But when the call was answered," she frowned, "someone was there, I'm sure of it, someone listening, but nobody said anything. Then I thought I heard the sound of…"

She paused, her eyes narrowing at the memory, "I really don't know what I heard, but it sounded like a struggle and maybe someone shouting, then the line went dead."

"You phoned back, though?"

"Yes, almost immediately, but you know that tone you get when the line's disconnected? That constant tone?"

He nodded.

"I phoned again a moment or two later, but though it sounded as if the line had been reconnected, there was no reply. I phoned three or four times, actually," she blushed.

"Would you consider phoning the police? Ask them to go round to check if your friend, this woman Doris, is okay?" He pursed his lips and added, "Maybe tell them that you think she might have had an accident or something."

"I hadn't thought about that," she admitted, then glancing down at her feet, raised her head to stare at Tommy and said, "It would be a lie, of course. I seem to be getting good at lying these days."

He couldn't help himself, but smiled and replied, "Give yourself a break Alice," then staring keenly at her, said, "I'll ask you this one time. Did you lie to me to con me, pretend you weren't married to take advantage of me?"

Shocked, she forcefully shook her head and defensively raising both hands, palms towards him, burst out, "No, never! As God's my witness, Tommy, I didn't!"

"So that wee fib was to protect yourself and Marcy?"

"Yes, truthfully," she vigorously nodded. "I didn't know you, didn't know how kind you were, didn't realise you would be so generous in letting us stay here …"

"Stop right there, you're starting to give me a big head," he grinned at her, before adding, "Don't forget, you're paying through the nose for it with two bottle of my favourite red."

The icy atmosphere now dissolved, she sat back in her armchair and sighed.

"What am I to do, Tommy? How will I find out if Doris is okay?"

He stretched his legs out in front of him and with a wistful look, replied, "Perhaps, Alice, if you were to begin by telling me why you're here on Arran and about this man, your husband I mean," he corrected himself, "who has so frightened you and that wee girl through there that you were willing to take off with a few possessions in a crummy old suitcase to a Scottish island with no place to live and no job prospects."

She stared at him, her head telling her that she should not disclose anything, but her heart desperate to believe in this kind-hearted man and so she said, "You cannot imagine how difficult it is for me to trust anyone, Tommy. Not after what Marcy and I have been through."

And voice faltering as she began, but growing stronger and without holding back, she did tell him.

Everything.

CHAPTER SEVENTEEN.

Over an hour had passed since Alice began her story during which Tommy sat quietly and without interrupting, if not spellbound, then certainly shocked by her account.

When she finished, she bravely smiled and concluded, "So, that is how we ended up here on this lovely island. I saw a painting on my friend's wall and thought it was the one place in the world Geoffrey would not find us."

He took a breath and rubbing at his chin, slowly exhaled before asking, "Would you mind if I asked you a couple of questions? No," he shook his head, and his brow creased, "more than a couple."

"No, of course not."

"Why did you stay all those years with him? I mean, after he drove your daughter from the house, wouldn't that have been the time to leave?"

"There's no easy answer to that question, Tommy," she sighed. "You would not believe how many time I've asked myself that same question, but I suppose the only answer is that Geoffrey controlled me, every aspect of my life and like I told Doris, if I left he would have hounded Gemma and her new husband Peter, perhaps even went out of his way to make life difficult for them. He is just that sort of man. As for me," she sighed, "I wasn't an independent person, I was someone who believed…" her brow furrowed, "I don't know, perhaps that I needed him to continue, I suppose is the only way I can describe it."

She paused, gathering her thoughts.

"Apart from Doris, who he only knew of when he gave me permission to visit her, I was not permitted friends. The only people I met socially were his rugby club friends and even then, I was always warned beforehand not to open my mouth unless I was spoken to, not to engage anyone in conversation. If someone spoke with me, he wanted to know what was said and what we discussed." She shrugged. "I had no income of my own, only what Geoffrey permitted me when I needed to purchase, you know, feminine items," she blushed, then added, "and if I required to buy something new, say for one of his club functions, up until the last few years when he no longer had any kind of interest in me, he would inspect my clothing to ensure that the old clothes were too worn before permitting me some money to purchase new clothes; clothes that I usually bought in charity shops. God," she shook her head, "what a fool I've been."

Tommy said, "I can't believe he checked your mileage and only permitted you the use of the car when you needed to go shopping." She glanced suddenly at him, but he raised a hand and apologetically added, "No, what I mean is I believe *you*, Alice. What I *can't* believe is that any man would do that sort of thing."

There was a brief, awkward silence, then Tommy took a breath and asked, "When he assaulted you, did you consider at any time reporting him to the police?"

She smiled tolerantly and replied, "You have to understand, Geoffrey is a pillar of the community, very well regarded locally, Chairman of the rugby club and often features on local television when the programme requires a response to a medical issue; so no, I didn't consider reporting him every time he struck me," she replied, a little sharper than she intended.

"Sorry," she passed a hand across her brow where a strand of hair had come loose from her ponytail.

"You said you were young when you met?"

Alice nodded. "I was just about to turn twenty and at teacher training college. Geoffrey had just qualified as a junior doctor a year previously and to be frank," she sighed, "he swept me off my feet. I quickly came to realise that being Geoffrey's girlfriend came with certain conditions and boundaries, but I was young, naive and more than a little foolish and wouldn't listen to my parents or friends. By that I mean he told me he would take care of me, I had to do nothing but care for him and keep house and slowly but very surely, I dropped friends he didn't approve of, lost touch with my parents, quit my course and finally moved in with him."

She smiled sadly and said, "I became pregnant with a son and we quickly married, but the baby died in childbirth and to this day, I believe Geoffrey never really forgave me. After Gemma was born he paid scant attention to her, particularly when the obstetrician broke the news that I could have no more children."

A thought occurred to him and he said, "A very personal question, I know, but how old are you, Alice?"

Startled, she gave a short laugh and replied, "I'm fifty-one, almost fifty-two. Why do you ask?"

"Fifty-one? Really?" he inhaled as his face registered his surprise. "I figured you to be in your, what, mid to late forties at the most maybe?"

"You flatter me, Tommy," she blushed.

"I don't do flattery, Alice, and I don't tell lies either. I'm kind of old fashioned that way. Fifty-one, eh? Well, lady," he grinned at her, "you're looking good for your age."

Seeing her relax a little, more soberly, he continued, "About your friend, Doris. I'm guessing that you think Geoffrey paid her a visit, but do you really think that some harm might have come to her? Isn't there anyone else you could contact to find out for you? What about the young police detective you spoke about, the mother of Marcy's friend? Do you have her number?"

"You forget, Tommy, I was never permitted the use of a mobile phone so I had no need to take Lucy's number. Besides, if she did go to speak with Doris and everything is fine, Doris wouldn't hold back; I know her. She detests Geoffrey and I've no doubt she would try to persuade the police that he is in some way mixed up with or responsible for the young man Archer's death. It could cause problems for Doris if Geoffrey *is* innocent and, I don't know," she shrugged. "Knowing what he's like he'd probably sue her for defamation or something. No," she shook her head, "I'll need to return to Preston and find out for myself that Doris is okay."

They turned at a timid knock on the door and saw Marcy's poking her head into the room.

"Is everything all right?" she asked, glancing at them in turn.

Smiling, Alice held out her arms wide and the little girl run into them.

"When you didn't come in to see me, I thought you might be arguing. Are you?"

"No, sweetheart. Tommy and I are not arguing. In fact," she raised her eyebrows to him, "I think we'll take up Tommy's kind invitation and stay another night. What do you think?"

"Yes, please," Marcy eagerly nodded, then without prompting turned to Tommy and quietly said, "Thank you."

He couldn't trust himself to reply, so just smiled and nodded.

"Now," Alice turned Marcy back to face her grandmother, "ten more minutes of television then it's off to bed, young lady."

There was no protest, the relief on the little girls face evident to them both.

When Marcy had left the room, Tommy said, "I really don't think it's a good idea you going back down to Preston, Alice." His brow knitted in thought as he continued, "Would you mind if I suggested something?"

****

DC Lucy Carstairs finished work later than she expected and though she hated working Saturdays, looked forward to the long lie the following morning when her husband Mike would rise early, feed the kids and then take them out to the local park for a couple of hours.

Driving home, she wondered what Mike had prepared for dinner and not for the first time was grateful she had married a man who enjoyed cooking.

The road was quieter than expected for that time of the evening and as she drove she wondered again where Alice Mayhew and her granddaughter Marcy had gone. Or rather fled, she corrected herself for if the subtle hints that were reaching the investigation teams ears were anything to go by, the credibility of the good Doctor Mayhew was now in serious doubt.

Conducting their inquiry among the local area, it was the little things the team were learning about him that started when young Jonathan Archer's parents, admittedly grieving and seeking someone to blame for their son's death other than Jonathan himself, hinted that Mayhew persistently pressured Jonathon into upping his training routine. For the good of the club, he had told the young man.

"He was training far too hard," Missus Archer had wept. "We tried to tell him, but he wouldn't listen. All he would say was that Doctor Mayhew said this and Doctor Mayhew said that," she almost spat the name out, "and Doctor Mayhew was keeping a close eye on him."

"No," his father had shaken his head, "Jonathon had no history of drug taking and in fact was a health fanatic, choosing to purchase his own healthy and nutritious food and drink rather than the meals his mother prepared."

When asked, neither parent had any knowledge of Doctor Mayhew prescribing their son any medicines and both declared that as far as they were aware, their son was in excellent health.

And yet, Carstairs thought, the young man ingested a highly toxic performance enhancement drug. Now, why would he do that if he was so intent on maintaining such a fitness regime?

With the rest of the team, she could only surmise that Jonathon had been informed by the individual who supplied the drug that it was harmless.

Could that be Doctor Mayhew, she wondered and not, as the team believed, Teddy Meiklewood.

Then there was the anonymous phone call to Crimestoppers from a woman, who was recorded as saying, "I'm on about your campaign on domestic violence and no, I won't give my name, but if you look at Doctor Geoffrey Mayhew who works out of the practice in Blanche Road surgery, you'll find he isn't as squeaky clean as he pretends to be. Likes his women submissive and docile, does Geoffrey and not above giving out the occasional slap now and then and I should know!" she had bitingly said before abruptly hanging up.

Normally that type of call would have been dismissed as either a crank or from one of Mayhew's aggrieved infuriated patients or perhaps as it's content suggested, from a scorned woman. However, it was fortunate that as an associate of Teddy Meiklewood, Mayhew's name had been added to the watch list by the team and the DC who monitored the recordings to Crimestoppers had as a matter of course passed the information to DI Sandford. That and the woman's casual use of Mayhew's forename seemed to infer she was acquainted with him.

"Nothing really to go on and of no use to the investigation," Sandford had told the team as she flipped the report into a basket, "but perhaps just another titbit to add to the profile of Mayhew."

Turning into her driveway, Carstairs felt in her bones that Alice Mayhew was somehow the key to the inquiry. She'd tried to explain her gut feeling to Sandford who to be fair had listened, but without any evidence to implicate Mayhew there really was nothing to go on. That and Teddy Meiklewood had been keeping a low profile, avoiding his usual coaching sessions at the rugby club and again, without any evidence there was no reason to subject him to a formal interview.

She was about to switch off the radio when the local news hour commenced. With her finger hesitating on the button, she listened for the headline, then her eyes opened wide.

Late that afternoon the body of a seventeen-year-old girl had been discovered in Witton Country Park in the suburbs of the nearby town of Blackburn. According to the reporter at the scene, the unnamed girl had been a promising long distance runner and was training for a European marathon and while there was no other person suspected of involvement in the teenage girl's death, local police have not ruled out a drug overdose.

The remainder of the news was lost on Carstairs as she wondered; the girl apparently was an athlete so could this be another Brown Speeders death?

She locked the car and staring up at the darkening and cloudy sky, her thoughts turned again to Alice Mayhew and she wondered; where the devil are you?"

****

He waited till Alice had gone upstairs with Marcy before making the call.

Pressing the number on his mobile phone, the gruff voice answered, "I'm sitting watching a recording of Celtic hammering Rangers in the League Cup Final, so this better be good."

Tommy grinned and replied, "And hello to you, too, Peasy."

"I know you're not at home because I was talking earlier today with Fiona. She's a tad worried about you, Tommy. Thinks you've taken yourself off to Arran and intend settling there. That right?"

"No, well, it's not a decision I've made yet, though when you come over for a visit I know you'll be blown away with the island. That and the golf courses that are here."

"Golf courses? Now you're talking my language. So, other than disturbing my fitba' what prompts you to ring me on a Saturday evening because I know you're too far away to meet for a swally."

Tommy took a breath and grimacing as though expecting a lecture, said, "I might need a hand with a wee problem I've got or more truthfully, a friend of mine has."

After a pause, Byrne replied, "And this friend, does she happen to be a female friend?"

"Yes, but it's not what you think."

"How the hell would you know *what* I'm thinking other than me thinking, my God, don't tell me he's got himself involved again."

"Look, Peasy, you're my best mate and if I'm going to turn to someone for help, it's you. I know it's an imposition, but is there any chance at all that you might speak with Alice. Her name's Alice," he unnecessarily added.

There was that pause again, Tommy thought, before Byrne replied, "I'll speak with her for your sake, Tommy. You know you only have to ask."

"Okay, well, if I was to bring her over to the mainland tomorrow. Her and her granddaughter. Have you anything on?"

"Granddaughter? Bloody hell, wee man, what have you got yourself into?"

Tommy inhaled before replying, "Better Alice tells you herself, Peasy. So, is that okay with you then?"

"Well," Byrne drawled, "it means I won't be able to drive my daughter and her weans to the shopping mall at Livingstone, so, oh joy. Yeah, no problem, however, save yourself a trip; I'll come across to the island and it will give me a chance to have a look at the house you've bought, too. Aye, it will give me a wee day out to myself. I'll get the train from Motherwell into the Central Station and then down to catch the ferry at Ardrossan, probably earlier rather than later. Can you pick me up at the harbour?"

"Text me what time your boat docks and I'll be there. Thanks, Peasy."

"No problem, wee man. I'll see you tomorrow."

Ending his side of the call, Peasy Byrne sat back and reflected on the phone call.

Though the retired brickie didn't know it, had Tommy asked Byrne to come immediately, he would have done so for Byrne owed his mate a debt of gratitude that could never be repaid.

Seven years earlier and prior to his divorce three years later, Byrne and his wife Lorna had been devastated at the news their youngest daughter discovered a lump on her leg that after examination by an oncologist, was thought to be cancerous.

Learning of the bad news and without intimating their intention, Tommy and his wife Moira arranged for the Byrne's and their daughter to be flown the following day to London where not only had accommodation been arranged for them at an upmarket hotel, but a private consultation booked for the following day with a Harley Street specialist. In a remarkably short time, the biopsy was conducted that confirmed the lump was not as first diagnosed, cancerous.

Refusing any form of thanks, Tommy and Moira remained firm friends with the Byrne's and their divorce, amicable though it was, did not change that relationship for while Tommy and Peasy continued to regularly meet, so did Moira and Lorna.

Following the death of Moira, Peasy's friendship with Tommy and his daughters continued as did Tommy's very occasional city centre lunches with Lorna, though when she formed a new relationship, their meetings finally tapered off.

He glanced at the paused screen and with a quiet smile, reached for his phone to call his daughter and inform her the shopping trip was off and ask that sometime tomorrow, she call in to his house and walk wee Chic, his Westie dog.

****

When Alice returned to the lounge, Tommy thought she seemed a little nervous.

"What's wrong?"

"Oh, nothing really. It's just that…well, you've been so good to us both and I don't know how I'm going to repay you."

"You did promise me two bottles of red wine," he reminded her.

She pretended to scowl and replied, "You know fine well what I mean, Tommy."

"Well then, have I asked for any repayment?"

"No, but that's not the point," she persisted. "I'm involving you in something that has nothing whatsoever to do with you."

He didn't immediately respond, but then said, "While I know we have only known each other for a couple of days, would you consider me to be your friend?"

"Yes, of course, but…"

He held his hand up and smiling, continued, "Then, other than Doris, you now have two friends and correct me if I'm wrong, but is there some sort of limit on friendship?"

She didn't know how to respond to that and shook her head.

"Well then, as your *friend* I'm happy to help you when you need it, Alice. You and that adorable wee girl upstairs."

"She is something isn't she?" Alice smiled.

"Oh, aye, she's something," he agreed with some feeling, then continued, "I spoke with my mate Peasy. He's arriving tomorrow morning on the ferry. I'm sorry, but rather than trying to explain on the phone, I believe it's better coming from you."

"I can do that," she confidently nodded. "Look, it's been a bit of an exhausting day. Would you mind if I went to bed?"

"No, of course not."

She rose to her feet and was about to turn towards the door, but hesitated. Her heart thumping, and her mouth dry, she stepped towards where he was seated in the armchair and nervously bent down to lightly kiss him on the cheek.

"Thank you, Tommy, for everything," she stared at him.

Surprised, he could only nod and smile at her.

Leaving the lounge, she was slowly walking up the stairs when she began to smile. Lightly touching her tips of her fingers to her lips, she realised she had been wanting to do that all day, but had not the nerve to do so.

She stopped at the bedroom door her hand on the handle and blushing furiously, held her face in her hands and thought, God, what was I thinking! What must he think of me?

****

It was just after one in the morning.

Geoffrey Mayhew glanced out of the lounge window into the darkness and saw the clouds threatened a heavy downpour of rain. He had dressed in dark jeans, a black sweater and heavy black brogue shoes. On the chair ready to be worn was a black coloured rain jacket and his brown leather driving gloves.

The plastic bag and the twenty-inch crowbar within lay on the floor by the chair.

He poured himself a second whisky, but just as he was about to throw it back, he hesitated and shook his head. This is foolish, he thought. I need to be sharp tonight.

His plan was simple, or so he believed. He would depart earlier that was necessary and drive the small, black coloured Aygo to the meeting with Meiklewood instead of the highly visible white coloured Volvo, then park the Aygo a little distance from the arranged venue.

In his head he had gone over his plan a dozen times and each time satisfied himself that what he intended was the right thing to do.

He couldn't let a wastrel like Teddy Meiklewood drag him down.

No, it was out of the question and besides, he couldn't trust the dolt to hold his tongue if the police did choose to interview him.

It has to be this way, he decided.

Ensuring the house was locked up, he made his way to the small Aygo and uncomfortably settled his bulky figure into the driving seat.

It had been some time since Geoffrey had driven a manual car, having through the years much preferred the option of automatic Volvos.

Crunching the clutch a half dozen times before he had travelled a mile, he cursed loudly, the focus of his anger being Alice for rather than admit his own inability to smoothly change gears, instead blamed her for somehow wrecking the bloody gearbox.

Just another thing he would make her pay for.

At last, he settled down to a reasonably smooth ride and though the meeting place was just under two miles from his house, Geoffrey decided to take a circular route in the off chance he encountered a police vehicle.

He arrived at the venue ten minutes after leaving his address and switched off his main beam headlights. The sidelights were so faint he had cautiously slowed to almost crawling speed. The overhanging branches from the trees that paralleled the narrow, unlit road were shrouded in a ghostly mist as he leaned forward to peer ahead.

He shivered, not from the cold but with the expectation of what he intended.

Judging himself to be roughly two hundred metres from the car park, he stopped the Aygo and switched off the engine. It was unlikely, he thought, that any traffic would pass along the road at this time of the morning and before squeezing himself from the driver's seat, awkwardly reached into the rear floor of the car and fetched out the plastic bag.

As quietly as he could, he began to walk towards the car park.

However, some fifty metres from his destination, his heart jumped when he saw what looked like a light on the opposite side of the road. As slowly as he dared, he continued walking and to his annoyance, saw the light was a porch light above the door of a bungalow house in a field opposite the car park.

Damn, he thought, for though he had visited the reserve in his youth, he was not familiar with the area and had not considered that someone might live close by.

He stopped and listened, but could not hear any sound from the house.

Bringing his wrist up to his eye, he could see that it was now fifteen minutes to three and decided to hide in the bushes nearby.

His hands within the leather gloves were moist with sweat, his mouth dry and to make matters worse, his stomach rumbled and he realised he needed to shit.

After what seemed like an interminably long time, he heard the sound of a car engine and a moment later, saw the headlights of a vehicle approaching him from the opposite side of the car park entrance. As the car turned into the car park, the beam swept across him, causing him to involuntarily duck down and almost fall onto his arse.

Cursing, he continued to watch and saw it to be a light coloured, old style estate car.

It was Teddy Meiklewood's car, of that he was certain.

He began to move through the shrubbery, irritably tearing his feet out of the soft, clinging mud and unable to avoid the grasping thin branches that tore at his arms and his jacket and painfully whipped at his face.

As he stepped forward towards the car park, he removed the crowbar from the plastic bag, stuffing the bag into his jacket pocket.

He wouldn't need the bag again for the crowbar was not coming home with him.

Intent on one thing only, he saw that Meiklewood remained seated in the car.

Geoffrey stopped when he saw a sudden flaring light as Meiklewood lit a cigarette.

Now he was just a few metres from the car, approaching it from the rear on the passenger's side.

He was breathing heavily now, willingly himself to go on, his right hand firmly gripping the crowbar.

Taking a deep breath, he rounded the back of the car and sidling up to the driver's door, wrapped his gloved knuckles on the window. He almost laughed out loud when he saw Meiklewood startle and drop the cigarette onto his lap.

The door was suddenly pushed open and Geoffrey blinked rapidly as the interior light came on, brightening the area around him.

"Jesus, Geoff," Meiklewood cried out, his head down as he sought to recover the dropped cigarette from the floor at his feet. "You scared the shit out of me, you idiot!"

Geoffrey's plan depended on getting Meiklewood out of the car and his mouth suddenly dry, he fought to get some spit, then croaked, "Let's go over there to my car and we'll have a chat."

"Why, what's wrong with talking here?" Meiklewood squinted up at the darkly dressed figure, then turning his head, stared behind Geoffrey into the darkness before asking, "Where is your car, anyway?"

"Over there," Geoffrey vaguely pointed, but then decided that he was getting suspicious and with his left hand, grabbed at Meiklewood's collar with the intention of pulling him from the car. Tall and bulky as Geoff was he had not foreseen the difficulty of what he attempted, that it is no mean feat trying to grab a reluctant man one-handed from the seat of a car, notwithstanding that Meiklewood himself was five feet ten inches tall and a former rugby player, well used to the rough and tumble on the sports field.

"What the fuck!" Meiklewood strongly pulled back against Geoffrey's hand, reaching with his right hand to grab at Geoffrey whose assault on Meiklewood was not being as cleanly executed as he had planned in his head.

It was then more by chance than design that Geoffrey, panting heavily with exertion and suddenly realising the situation was getting beyond his control, used the crowbar as a stabbing weapon and by a sheer fluke caught Meiklewood in the face, the rough edge of the metal tearing the skin at his left eye.

Meiklewood cried out in pain and instinctively tried to protect his face with both hands, giving Geoffrey the opportunity to grab him more firmly by the collar and yank him bodily from the car.

As Meiklewood's torso fell to the tarmacadam ground with his legs still inside the car, Geoff lost all control and raising the crowbar above his head, brought it down onto Meiklewood's shoulder, missing his head by a few inches.

Meiklewood screamed in pain and with one foot caught twisted in the pedals of the car, tried to turn onto his back and bring his legs out of the car, but realised he didn't have the time to do so and instead raised his forearms in an attempt to ward off the next blow.

He failed.

With blinding speed, the crowbar came down from above Geoffrey's head and landed squarely on Meiklewood's face, bursting his nose and his right cheekbone. The blow caused blood to spray over Meiklewood, who made a gurgling noise, as well as splattering Geoff and the surrounding square metre of ground.

In the next few seconds, Geoff lost count of the number of times he raised then viciously smashed the crowbar down onto the head and body of the now lifeless Meiklewood.

Aghast at what he had done and gasping after his unaccustomed exertion, he dropped the crowbar and staggering back from the body, leaned with his back against the car to recover his breath.

Even in the faint interior light of the car, it was plainly obvious to Geoffrey that Meiklewood was dead for he had stopped twitching and his face had literally disappeared under a dark blanket of blood. Geoff anxiously looked around him, but there was nobody about and he could hear nothing either.

Hands and legs shaking and breathing hoarsely, he staggered away from the car and with a final, nervous glance at Meiklewood, hurried off to the road to make his way back to the parked Aygo.

CHAPTER EIGHTEEN

If anyone travelling that bright and sunny Sunday morning on the Arran bound, early ferry, had given the tall, rugged face man seated on the chair on the open deck a second glance, they would correctly have guessed him to be a fit looking, strongly built individual in his mid-fifties, around six feet tall and seen him to be clean shaven with a ruddy complexion. His balding strawberry blond hair was hidden under a blue knitted tammy and he wore a black coloured three-quarter length rain jacket buttoned to the neck with blue denims and stout, brown coloured walking boots. On the seat beside him was his khaki coloured shoulder bag that contained his Kindle, the Sunday morning edition of the Sun newspaper with, in his opinion, its excellent coverage of the weekend sports, a notebook with lined pages that was bound by a thick rubber band, a variety of pencils and pens and a silver metal litre sized flask, now empty.

While Charles 'Peasy' Byrne did not fit the description of the archetypical police detective so beloved by the television scriptwriters, the retired Detective Sergeant and former head of security at the prestigious Glasgow Hilton Hotel was considered by most of his peers and to their regret, many of Glasgow's noted criminals, to be a shrewd and determined CID officer with a wealth of investigative experience in crime detection. Highly regarded by his bosses at the former Strathclyde Police Force, the quietly spoken Byrne had served in a number of specialist CID departments where, aside from his quick humour, his tenacity and perceptive aptitude had placed him at the forefront of a number of high profile investigations.

Watching Brodick Harbour approach, Byrne grabbed at his bag and began to make his way towards the gangway that would lead down to the deck from where he would disembark.

With practised skill by its Captain, the ferry was docked within a few minutes and striding down the covered walkway to the dockside, Byrne smiled when he saw Tommy Burke waving at him.

"Glad you could come, Peasy," Tommy greeted his friend as they began to walk towards the Defender, parked in a bay just outside the Harbour.

"Aye, well, you might not be so glad when I meet this woman, Tommy. I've been wondering all night what you've got yourself into this time," Byrne shook his head.

Tommy supressed a smile as they walked before replying, "Time enough for Alice to explain, but have you had any breakfast?"

"Just toast before I left this morning and a flask of coffee on the train that I finished on the ferry."

"Good. Alice is cooking up a storm in the kitchen, so after introductions we'll eat and then you can decide if you want to help her."

Byrne stopped and pulling at Tommy's arm, firmly told him, "We need to get this straight and right now, Tommy. If I'm going to help, then I'm helping you, not some woman you've know for what, a couple of days? You also need to know if I decide that what she tells me is a load of shite, I'll be telling her so and I don't want you falling out with me because of it. You know I wouldn't lie to you and even if it's to save your feelings, I'm not about to start now." Tommy nodded and quietly replied, "I know that, Peasy, and I appreciate your honesty. No, I don't see me and you falling out over a woman, but just hear what she has to say and whatever you decide," he raised a hand in submission, "I'll respect that decision. Okay?"

"Fair enough," Byre nodded, then pulling open the passenger door of the Defender, added in a voice dripping with cynicism, "Let's see if she can cook as well as spin you a story, ya dunderhead."
****

Seated at the table in the dining kitchen, Byre was conscious not only of the edgy atmosphere but also of the sly glances he was getting from the little girl, Marcy.

Finally, resting his cutlery on the cleared plate, he turned to her and not unkindly said, "I know you're dying to ask me something, so what is it?"

In a faltering voice, she replied, "Tommy told me that you're a detective and you catch bad people and put them in prison. Is that true?"

"Why do you ask?"

She glanced at her grandmother and Tommy in turn before asking, "Are you going to arrest my grandfather for hitting my Gran?"

"Marcy!" Alice raised a warning hand towards her, but Byrne stopped her when he said, "I need to speak to your grandmother first, Marcy, and find out what has been happening."

He squinted at Tommy before turning back to the little girl and sighing, continued, "I *was* a police detective and yes, I did catch a lot of people who did bad things, Marcy, but it was the judge who sent them to prison. Do you know what a judge is?"

"Is it like someone on the X Factor that picks out the best singers?"

Byrne stifled a laugh and nodding, smiled when he replied, "That's right. A judge is someone who makes a decision, but the judge I'm talking about is not like the X Factor judges. The judge I'm talking about decides if someone has done something wrong or bad and then makes up his or her mind if that person should go to prison or not.

Does that make sense?"

"I think so," her brow furrowed. "So, you'll speak with my Gran and when she tells you about how bad my grandfather is, you'll catch him and a judge will send him to prison?"

Byrne took a deep breath, but before he could respond, Alice stood up from her chair and interrupted with, "Marcy, why don't you go and watch some cartoons."

Turning to Byrne and Tommy, she added, "I'll just clear up if you men want to take your tea into the big lounge."

"No," Tommy got to his feet and shook his head, "I'll clear up, Alice. You and Peasy go and have your chat."
****

He sat on the armchair facing Alice and as an opening statement, with a smile said, "It's a beautiful home, isn't it?"

"Yes," she turned her head to stare out of the panoramic window at the bright day.

Her hair fell loose about her shoulders and her face was devoid of make-up. Wearing a lemon coloured polo shirt over dark casual slacks, he wasn't to know they were charity bought clothing and the second last clean change of clothes she had, in the back of her mind mentally told herself she'd need to get a wash done.

Staring at her, he could see she was clearly nervous and wrung her hands on her lap. He could also see why his wee pal was captivated by her for she was indeed a good looking woman.

He began, "Tommy is my best pal, Missus Mayhew, and I would never see him hurt. He's also a bloody magnet for sob stories, but seems to think that you're *not* a sob story, that you need help. Do you need some help, Missus Mayhew?" he stared keenly at her.

"It was Tommy's suggestion that I speak with you, Mister Byrne," she defensively replied, "but it was *my* idea that I tell you my story, not his. He told me are a very cynical man or rather, you can be. I don't need you to believe me, but I made a promise to him that I would tell you what I told Tommy. Yes," she glanced down at her hands then raising her head, returned Byrne's stare, "I know how kind he is." She paused before continuing, "God knows what I would have done on Friday night if he hadn't taken Marcy and me in. But know this, Mister Byrne, I will *not* hurt him and I will leave this house this very minute if you were to think or decide otherwise."

He pursed his lips at her candour and said, "The wee girl seems to think or rather I should say, disclosed your husband hits you. Has she seen that happening?"

Alice closed her eyes in painful memory before opening them again and softly replying, "Marcy saw and heard things that at her age, she shouldn't have. I don't know how I can possibly make it up to her and that's why we're here, on Arran I mean; why I left my husband."

He sat forward, his clenched hands in front of him and preparing to give her the benefit of the doubt until he heard her story, said, "Okay, Missus Mayhew, tell me from the beginning."
****

In the early hours of that morning, the first thing Geoffrey did when he returned home was undress in the utility room and stuff all his clothes, including his shoes and the leather gloves that he tightly wrapped in his shirt and jeans, into the washing machine. He had never actually operated a washing machine before, but thought how hard can it be?

Searching for the soap powder he had finally found it in a cupboard then after sprinkling a liberal amount of the powder into the machine frustratingly spent the next five minutes pressing buttons, opening and slamming shut the door, trying to get the bloody thing to operate and cursing that this was Alice's job, not a trained professional like him.

At last to his relief the drum began to slowly spin round, the bundle of clothes slapping against the sides of the metal drum, then with a sigh decided he'd better shower just in case any droplets of blood had settled on him.

His hair damp and dressed only in his robe, he had returned downstairs to fetch the whisky to settle his nerves and downed at least a half bottle before going to bed.

Maybe it was the whisky, but more likely it was the memory of killing Teddy Meiklewood, for his sleep was punctuated by bouts of abrupt wakefulness to find that he was perspiring heavily and both the sheet and quilt cover were soaked in sweat.

At last he must have drifted off into a deep slumber for here he was, still in bed, his head aching and the digital clock indicating it was almost eleven o'clock.

His body felt as though he had been through a dozen rough scrums and rising from the bed, slipped his feet into his slippers and reached for his robe. In the en-suite, he made his toilet then bending at the sink to wash his hands, glanced into the mirror.

His brow creased for that's when he saw the faint scratches on his face.

Tentatively raising a hand to touch gently at them, at first he wondered how he'd came by them but then scowled, realising they must have been caused by the bloody branches when he was making his way through the shrubbery.

Holding the bannister while he slowly and tiredly staggered downstairs he fetched his medical bag from the hallway then with a small bottle of iodine and cotton buds, went into the cloakroom toilet to use the mirror, dousing the cotton buds in iodine then dabbing them on his face.

As he treated the scrapes a thought occurred to him and he made his way through to the utility room. The washing machine had stopped hours previously and opening the door, he pulled the bundle of damp smelling clothing and shoes out onto a wrinkled mess on the floor.

Unwrapping the sodden cothing he stared disgustedly at the heap, at the brogue shoes and the leather gloves, now water damaged and completely ruined as well as badly stained from his overuse of the soap powder. As for the rest of the clothing, he had already made up his mind. It might be that the blood was washed away, but if there was even the slightest chance that any of Meiklewood's blood remained adhered to the clothing, anything from which the police might be able to extract DNA; well, like the shoes and gloves, everything was going into a bin.

But not his own bin. No, he'd find a bin some distance from the house and dump the stuff there.

In the kitchen he glanced at the clock and reached for the radio, switching it on just as the music heralded the start of the midday news.

He unconsciously held his breath then his eyes widened and he found himself swallowing with difficulty when the announcer opened with the story about the discovery of a body in a local nature reserve.

The announcer introduced a female reporter who was at the scene and who breathlessly began, "I'm here in Hills and Hollows Nature Reserve on Fulwood Row where police have sealed off a public car park. I'm standing by the blue and white police tape that cordons off the area and about fifty metres away I can see a white tent has been erected and partially covering a black coloured estate car. According to the detectives here at the scene, a man's body has been discovered in what they describe as suspicious circumstances. There's no more information forthcoming at this time, but what I have learned from local passers-by is that the blood-stained body was discovered by a group of Sunday morning walkers from a local club. With me here is Mister Blakely who…"

But Geoffrey had stopped listening.

They had found him and for some unfathomable reason, his body began to shake.

****

Alice finished relating both her account of her life with Geoffrey and the reason she had fled with her granddaughter Marcy, to Arran.

"Can I assume you have tried again to contact your friend, Missus Chisholm?"

"Several times last night and again this morning," Alice confirmed with a nod.

"Yet still no reply to your calls?"

She shook her head and he could see the worry reflected on her face. For a few seconds, Peasy Byrne stared thoughtfully at her, then said, "Wait here, Alice. Can I call you Alice?"

"Yes, of course," she stared curiously at him, wondering what was going through his head.

He tightly smiled and left the room, but returned a minute later carrying his khaki coloured shoulder bag from which he extracted the notebook and a pencil. Laying the bag onto the carpeted floor by his chair, he resumed his seat and opening the notebook, said, "Give me all those names again, Alice, and where you can remember, their addresses. Let's start with your husband's home address and his practice address."

****

Tommy sat on the couch with Marcy's head resting against his arm, watching the cartoons, but his mind was elsewhere, wondering what was happening in the big lounge, what was being said.

Restlessly, he gently levered the little girl off his arm and with a smile, placed a cushion under her head and said, "Just going to pop the kettle on, hen. You stay here and watch the tele, eh?"

"Okay, Tommy," she replied, but her attention was focused on the comical antics of the 'Penguins of Madagascar.'

In the kitchen he busied himself doing nothing, impatiently waiting for Alice to finish the retelling of her story and turned when he saw Byrne opening the lounge door.

"Everything okay?" he asked.

His old pal smiled and giving him a thumbs up, told him, "I've just got to get my bag then we'll be in for a cuppa if you get the kettle on."

Unconsciously breathing a sigh of relief, Tommy exhaled through puckered lips and preparing the tea, set out three mugs. Minutes later he was joined in the kitchen by Alice and Byrne who sat at the table as he poured the tea.

"Alice had quite a tale to tell," Byrne began.

Surprised, Tommy noticed Byrne's use of her forename and guessed the previous formality between them had been dropped.

"It seems to me, however," Byrne continued, "that she would be foolish to risk returning to Preston so while I'm open to suggestion, here's what I propose." He sipped from his mug, before continuing.

"I'll get myself back home and pack a bag and prepare to travel down south first thing tomorrow morning. Shouldn't take me more than say, three hours to drive to Preston. When I get there I expect it might take a couple of days to get the information I need, so I'll find digs then call in on Missus Chisholm to let her know that Alice and the wean are safe and find out if she's any idea what Alice's husband is up to, if he's looking for her or what. Of course, the only way she'll know that is if he's been to visit her. That done, I'll try to speak with this detective Alice mentioned, Lucy Carstairs, and see if she'll be happy to hear what I have to say about Alice's suspicions. The only thing that concerns me is that it's worrying Missus Chisholm isn't answering her phone, but there could be any number of reasons for that, so until I find out why, there no need to unnecessarily worry and I do not want us to jump to any conclusion, understood?" he stared pointedly at Alice who nodded.

Continuing, he said, "I'll also need to take those packets of tablets with me, hen, to hand over and corroborate your story. The likelihood is that if this detective Carstairs woman is on the ball, she will want a statement from you about finding the packets and it might mean a local detective here in Scotland speaking with you to take the statement. The worst case scenario is that at some time in the future, you might have to attend court. Are you okay with that?"

"Yes, Peasy, I'm fine with that," she answered, though the truth was the thought of attending court and facing Geoffrey almost made her want to throw up.

"Okay then," he smiled, then turning to Tommy, thoughtfully asked, "Alice shared with me that she's a bit strapped for cash right now, Tommy. Do you think you'll be able to put her and the wee girl up for a couple of more days while I make the inquiry down south?"

"That's not a problem, Peasy," he nodded in reply, then added, "I'm very grateful to you for what you're doing."

"I'm not doing it for you, ya dunderhead," he cheekily grinned, "I'm doing it for Alice and the wean."

"Thank you, Peasy," Alice smiled. "I didn't realise that I would make such good friends when I arrived here."

"No bother, hen," Byrne's face reddened. "And another thing. Tommy was right about the breakfast," he nodded. "You're not a bad cook."

****

Lucy Carstairs arrived at the murder locus to find the place swarming not only with uniformed police and detectives, but also around a dozen or so of the usual rubberneckers desperate to get a glimpse of what was going on with their mobile phone cameras at the ready. Them and the media who stood prepared with their cameras and notebooks to snap the inappropriate photograph or catch the unguarded comment from an imprudent police officer. Parking her Focus at the direction of a uniformed Police Community Support Officer, she first fetched a packaged Forensic suit from the boot of the car that she donned before making her way towards the white Forensic tent.

A female cop she knew smiled and lifted the blue and white tape to enable Carstairs to duck under, quietly cautioning her as she did so, "Watch yourself, Lucy. Ma'am's in a foul mood."

Is she ever anything else, Carstairs thought, but acknowledged the warning with a grateful nod.

She made her way to where DI Julie Sandford stood in conversation with DS Terry Goodwin, both similarly dressed in Forensic suits and though Sandford saw her approach, chose to ignore her for a moment before turning to icily greet her with, "Nice of you to join us, DC

Carstairs."

She bristled, but calmly replied, "Only received the phone call twenty minutes ago, Ma'am. Seems there might have been a breakdown in communication. What have we got here?"

"DS Goodwin will fill you in," Sandford abruptly replied then strode off to speak with the casualty surgeon who was just exiting the tent.

"Morning, Lucy," Goodwin nodded, but his head was slowly shaking at Sandford's ill-manners as he watched her walk off. Turning back to Carstairs, he said, "That woman really needs to get herself a man. Right then," he cheerily began. "The body. A group of walkers making their way into the nature reserve stumbled across the car and its driver, one Teddy Meiklewood of this parish, done to death."

"*Our* Teddy Meiklewood?" she gasped.

"The one and only," he grinned with graveside humour at the victim's death. "Someone took a crowbar to his head and left the crowbar at the scene. Not much left of his ugly mug, but enough to recognise him. That and some personal ID we found on him and the car's registered to him, too."

"So, it's not a suicide then," she said with her own hint of humour before asking, "Any suspects?"

"Well," he slowly drawled, "according to Ma'am, the first suspect who comes to mind is Monty Reid or at least one of his team. Personally, I can't see Reid being so indiscreet as to leave Meiklewood's body lying around. If he's true to form from what we hear, he usually disappears his victims to a watery grave or the concrete foundation of a new building," he sniggered.

"Then who do *you* think is responsible, Terry?"

He slowly shook his head and brow knitted, replied, "We've got to ask ourselves, who benefits most from Meiklewood's murder? We *suspect* Meiklewood to be the man supplied by Reid who then dealt the Brown Speeders to Jonathon Archer, so did someone in Archer's family know about it and is it a revenge killing by that individual or is it someone else, who knew what he did? Or is it a scorned lover or perhaps even the husband of a mistress? Or as Ma'am firmly believes, it is drug related and its Reid disposing of Meiklewood because he's the connection between Reid supplying the drugs and Meiklewood dealing them to Archer. Take your pick," he drily added.

"What can I do?"

"Right now, nothing really. The rest of the team arrived here shortly after the call went out so they've been dispatched to inform the victims wife and take the walkers who found the body back to the station to note statements and obtain elimination fingerprints. What we *don't* yet know is if Ma'am will take the investigation on or if headquarters will send a DCI down to take charge of the murder while we continue with the drug inquiry."

"So," she gave him a wry smile, joked, "are you telling me I'm surplus to requirement, that I could have had another hour or two in bed?"

He didn't immediately respond, but after a thoughtful glance then said, "I didn't get the opportunity to take a run past the doctors house to get a note of his second cars registration number, the Aygo you saw. Maybe you could do that and then by that time we'll likely be back at the station for a briefing from Ma'am, so you can meet us there, okay?"

"Yeah, okay," she nodded.

****

In the mid-terraced house in the quiet suburban Middleton Road in the Fulwood area of Preston, several times that quiet Sunday morning the phone rung, causing the young woman calling to wonder where her grandmother was.

Unfortunately, Doris Chisholm, the elderly occupant of the house was in no position to respond to the frequent ringing, for she remained where she had fallen, lying in the small lounge on her side, her hair and one side of her face matted with dried blood while she stared unseeingly at the legs of the solid oak table on which she had struck her head when so savagely pushed to her death by Doctor Geoffrey Mayhew.

CHAPTER NINETEEN

DS Terry Goodwin poked his head into the station refreshment room and cheerfully called out to the detectives stood or sitting around a table, drinking coffee, "That's Ma'am returned from Headquarters, so you lot are to get your arses into her room for a briefing."

Minutes later the team squeezed into DI Sandford's room where she sat glowering at them as they filed in.

Second last into the room, DC Lucy Carstairs stared at her boss's downcast face and thought; oh, oh, she is *not* a happy woman.

Nor was she for when the team had settled, Sandford grimaced and opened with, "The murder of Teddy Meiklewood indicates to me that this damned situation is getting out of hand. I've had words with the Area Commander and the brief version is that Teddy Meiklewood's murder is being taken from us. In the AC's short-sighted wisdom and being a wooden top with no CID experience," she scowled her opinion of the AC, "he has warned me off investigating Meiklewood's murder and decreed that the DCI in charge of the Force Major Investigation Team will arrive shortly with his clipboard carrying door-knockers to show us how a murder is solved. As if," she slowly shook her head in further wordless comment of her opinion on the matter.

Wisely, none of the team made any response, but continued to listen as Sandford said, "Nevertheless and his murder aside, Meiklewood still figures in our Brown Speeders inquiry as a person of interest so we will continue to make investigation into his movements and whereabouts prior to his demise and pull in for interview all the buggers he associated with. Any questions so far?"

There was a couple of half-hearted shaking of heads, a shrugging of shoulders from another or no reaction from the rest of the assembled detectives as Sandford went on, "I intend to bring in Monty Reid for interview. I am aware that he is usually surrounded by a group of hired muscle to protect him from his competition rather than us, so to avoid any…" she paused, then evilly smiled, "unpleasantness, we will enlist the cooperation of some of our bulkier colleagues from the Operational Support Unit."

The detectives as one smiled, for all knew that the officers who were recruited to the OSU were a knuckle dragging, hardnosed bunch trained primarily for public order events as well as firearms and a host of other skills, some of which were legally debatable.

However, her attention was taken by Terry Goodwin who she could see was unhappy.

"You have a problem, DS Goodwin?"

"I think it's a mistake, Ma'am, going for Reid."

There was a definite chill in the room, broken when Sandford asked, "How so?"

"Well," he slowly replied, "for one, the AC has warned you off investigating Meiklewood's murder. How the hell do you propose to interview Reid about his relationship with Meiklewood without questioning him about the murder? You simply can't ask him about his drug-dealing and the Brown Speeders," he shook his head, "without discussing the murder. You risk the AC pulling you off the investigation into the Brown Speeders deaths and that would fuck up our whole inquiry."

"I take on board your concern, DS Goodwin, and I also understand your concern about the AC's directive. Needless to say, if he finds out I've circumvented his direct order then yes, I do risk being disciplined and pulled from the Brown Speeders investigation, but to get Monty Reid," she stared hard at Goodwin, "that's a risk I'm willing to take. However, I accept that where mud is flung, it doesn't always stick just to the target, so I'll ask you this. Do you wish to be stood down in this investigation?"

He didn't immediately respond, but returned her stare, then slowly shook his head before replying through gritted teeth, "No, Ma'am, but again, I urge caution."

She slowly nodded in acknowledgement then staring at each of the team in turn, said, "DS Goodwin is correct. Having informed you of the AC's directive, I cannot order any of you to continue against his order, so I leave the choice to you. If you wish to return to normal CID duties then please do so and, though you may not wish to believe me, you have my word I will not think any less of you." There was a slight shuffling of feet, but nobody moved towards the door.

A minute passed then Sandford, in a rare mood of gratitude, said, "Thank you."

"When do you propose going for Reid, Ma'am?" asked Goodwin. She stared at him for a few seconds then with a slow smile, replied, "I've nothing on this Sunday afternoon, DS Goodwin. Have you?"
****

Alice Mayhew had elected to stay behind in the house to catch up on laundering the few items of clothing she had managed to bring with her while Tommy and her granddaughter walked Peasy Byrne down to the harbour. Now, leaning on the Ferry's guardrail, he waved to them as they stood on the Harbour and grinned at the sight of the little girl Marcy leaning into Tommy.

Unconsciously shaking his head, he stared at them both and thought, you are well and truly hooked, wee pal. That woman and her granddaughter have, in the space of a couple of days, become part of your life, yet surprised himself for being happy for his lifelong friend and fervently hoped it worked out between Tommy and Alice.

With Brodick slowly disappearing in the wake of the ferry, Byrne decided to go downstairs to the lower deck and grab himself a seat where he could while the time away catching up on his Kindle.

However, a few minutes later with the Kindle opened on his lap, his thoughts wandered to the promise he had made to Alice, having told her that the next day that he would set off from his home and drive to Preston to find and confirm that her friend Doris Chisholm was fine.

With at least one comfort break, Byrne didn't thing the trip would take much longer than three hours. Besides, as he had told her, he enjoyed driving and looked forward to giving his new BMW estate car a good long run.

All he had to do now, he inwardly sighed, was break the news to his daughter that he was off on a little jaunt for a couple of days and ask her to continue to look after wee Chic for a day or two.

****

That Sunday morning and feeling much better with a good hearty breakfast in him, Geoffrey Mayhew wiped his lips on a paper towel then loudly burped before dumping the dirty plate and cutlery into the kitchen sink to join the greasy frying pan.

Refilling his mug from the teapot, he carried it through to the lounge and sitting himself down onto the wide couch, used the remote to switch on the television for the midday news.

Frustrated that there was no local news he sat through almost twenty minutes of UK wide news before the reporter announced that following the early morning discovery of a body of a man, Lancashire police were investigating a suspicious death.

The screen switched to a local reporter who wearing a Barbour coat, stood facing the camera with his back towards what Geoffrey recognised as the Hills and Hollows Nature Reserve car park.

Unconsciously leaning forward in his seat, he stared wide eyed at the white Forensic tent and partially covered black coloured estate car in the reporter's background. Within seconds, while the reporter continued speaking, the cameraman zoomed in to the white tent where Geoffrey could see figures working at the scene.

Using the remote he paused the picture then laying his mug down onto the carpet, approached the fifty-inch television screen on his knees and stared silently at the tent and the figures clad in Forensic suits frozen around it.

He didn't mean to, couldn't explain why, but suddenly found his fingers raised and tracing the images on the screen.

Feeling a little foolish, he shook his head as though to clear it and returned to sit on the couch. Using the remote he restarted the news item and listened intently as the reporter more or less repeated what Geoffrey had already heard earlier on the radio; the blood-stained body had been discovered by a party of walkers, police were treating the death as suspicious and there was no information yet as to the identity of the deceased.

His thoughts were elsewhere as the reporter ended his story and handed back to the studio.

Nothing about that old bitch Chisholm, Geoffrey wondered then considered, perhaps her body had not yet been discovered. He wracked his memory, trying to recall what Alice had said about her, whether she was married or lived with family, but nothing came to mind.

It didn't occur to him that even though Alice might have disclosed these details, it was his habit to tune her out when she spoke unless the information was of interest to him.

His eyes narrowed.

He had gone to Middleton Road simply to speak with the woman, ask her about Alice's whereabouts, nothing more.

He hadn't planned to kill her…then stopped, his mouth opening wide and his chest tightening.

He didn't kill her!

No, he involuntarily shook his head; it was her own stupid fault! *She* had attacked *him*, or that was certainly his recollection of the event. Her death had been an accident, nothing more, he unconsciously nodded in agreement with himself. But what worried him now was, he had left her house in a hurry. Was there anything he had missed, his eyes narrowed; some evidence that might lead the police to identify him?

He slowly lowered his head to stare at his hands.

Thank Christ he had worn gloves, so there was no way he might have left fingerprints. The gloves themselves, now ruined by immersion in the washing machine, were with his shoes and the rest of his clothing in the black bin bag outside the back door, tied at the top and waiting to be dumped.

A reckless thought passed though his head. Perhaps he should take a drive back to Middleton Road, see if the police were in attendance there. If they were, then that meant the body has been discovered.

If there is no sign of the police, should he take the opportunity to re-enter the house and ensure he had left nothing that might identify him?

He remembered pulling the door to close behind him.

Was it a Yale lock or was the door locked by a key?

No, dammit, he couldn't remember.

Frustrated and now worrying himself that he had not left the house as cleanly as he had planned and executed the death of Teddy Meiklewood, he once more inadvertently sowed the seed of doubt in his mind and hands clenched into fists, decided that if nothing else, he would drive to Middleton Road to check if there was a police presence at the woman's house.

****

Vicky had just got baby Fergus off to sleep in his cot when to her exasperation, the phone in the bedroom rang.

Grabbing at it, she snapped, "Hello!" then glanced at the cot and sighed with relief. The wee bugger was still sleeping.

It was her sister Fiona who in a voice dripping with sarcasm, said, "And hello to you too, sis. What's with the attitude?"

"Oh, sorry, I thought it might be another of those bloody PPI calls. I've been plagued with them over the last week and I've just got Fergus off to sleep," she explained.

"Oh, those buggers. I just interrupt them and ask if they have God in their life," Fiona chuckled. "You'll be surprised how fast they finish the call. Anyway, is the wee dude still getting you up through the night?"

"Oh, only every hour or so," she exhaled. "How's things anyway? Heard from dad today?"

"Well things are fine and no, I haven't spoken with him since he told me he arrived safely on Arran. And that's why I'm calling. I was wondering because tomorrow being Monday and it's a public holiday, Mathew will be off work to watch Fergus. So, if you fancy a wee trip across to visit dad? Sort of surprise him?"

Vicky shook her head and replied, "What you really mean is you want to check up on him and have a look at what he's done to the new house since you were over there."

"Well, that too," Fiona coyly said. "Anyway, are you up for it?"

"I don't know, sis. You know dad can sometimes be funny about turning up at his door if we haven't called first," then softly laughed when she added, "I mean, what if he's got a woman there or something?"

"Aye, like *that's* going to happen," Fiona smiled on her end of the line.

"Have you asked Jenny about going over with you?"

"I thought I'd run it past you first then give her a call. So again, are you up for it?"

"Let me speak to Mathew when he gets home and I'll give you a call tonight, okay?"

"Okay. By then I'll know if Jenny fancies coming to. Anyway, I know Jenny will definitely come because she's done nothing but talk about the new house. We can make it a girls' day out, leave early and catch the evening ferry back. I'll need to bring Cissie with me, though, because it's not a holiday for Phil. He'll still be working through the day."

"Right," Vicky turned as Fergus grunted in his sleep. "I think my son's filling his nappy so I'll give you a call later," and ended the call.

****

En route to Burnley, DI Julie Sandford turned from the front passenger seat to address the two DC's in the rear seat and nodding to Terry Goodwin who was driving, said, "DS Goodwin and I will meet with the OSU personnel in Padiham police station and brief them on what I want done." Staring at the male DC she said, "Find yourself a computer and a printer and make at least half a dozen copies of the local area around Monty Reid's house in, eh," she glanced down at the file in her hand and added, "Healey Court. According to the file it's a large five bedroom detached Victorian villa set in an affluent area and the house is accessed via a lane off Healey Court. If previous reporting is correct," she glanced again at the file, "he's usually got at least two or three heavies in the house in case any of his competitors come calling without an invitation." She glanced at Lucy Carstairs and speaking directly to her, continued, "While he's gathering the maps, DC Carstairs, I want you to phone the weekend duty clerk at the DPP's office and ask that the search warrant for Middleton's house be delivered ASAP to us at Healey Court. I don't want to be caught out hanging around there and give him and his mates in the house the opportunity to flush everything down the lavvy."

"Ma'am," Carstairs acknowledged with a nod.

"Right," she turned back towards Goodwin, "Have I forgotten anything?"

"Can't think of anything, Ma'am," he shook his head.

"Okay then, put the foot down and let's get to the Padiham nick."
****

Of course, no one knew where the leak came from, whether it was a paid informant within the ranks of the police or it was overheard from a loose-tongued officer or whether when they were informed, a member of the Meiklewood family had themselves informed the media. However, the news was broken that afternoon on the local radio that the murdered man had been identified as Edward 'Teddy' Meiklewood, the coach for the Fulwood Martyrs Rugby Club. Coming so soon after the death of one of the team's star players, it was soon hinted by the media that Meiklewood's murder and the recent drug related death of Jonathan Archer might somehow be connected.

Of course the police refused to comment or speculate on any hint of a correlation between the two deaths, but still, it was enough to cause the press to hover outside Meiklewood's home address in the hope of soliciting a comment from the family.

However, the presence of the press caused the local Area Commander to unwisely station a marked police car with two uniformed officers at the house to protect the family from unwanted intrusion and thus unwittingly confirmed the media's suspicion regarding Meiklewood's identity.
****

As it was a fine and sunny late afternoon, Tommy Burke decided to treat his guests to a slap-up Sunday dinner at the Kildonnan Hotel on the south side of the island.

"How long will it take to get there?" Marcy asked as he helped her into the rear seat of the Defender.

"This is Arran, hen," he grinned as he buckled her in. "There's nowhere on the island that isn't within a forty minutes drive away. As for Kildonnan? Well," he narrowed his eyes in thought before continuing, "it's only about eleven or twelve miles away, but we're in no hurry and the table's booked for us in," he glanced at his watch, "thirty-five minutes. Are you hungry?"

"Starving," she gleefully nodded.

He glanced at the front door and asked, "Where's your grandmother got to?"

"She's just getting changed," Marcy giggled, then added, "She told me not to tell you," she giggled behind her hand, "but she wants to look nice for you."

"Oh, she does, does she?" Tommy smiled and closed the door. He was about to get into the driving seat when the front door of the house opened and he stared.

Carrying her jacket and handbag in one hand, Alice wore her auburn hair lying loosely on her shoulders and had changed into a black coloured, long sleeved blouse, a knee length, pleated lemon skirt and plain, black block heeled shoes. She worried that the clothes were past their best having been purchased in a Preston charity shop, but Tommy saw none of this.

Moving to the passenger's door and chivalrously opening it, saw she had applied lipstick, but could not know that it was the only item of the few cheap cosmetics she owned and had thought to bring with her when she and Marcy fled from Preston.

"You look, well, amazing," he smiled at her.

"Thank you," she blushed and took his hand as he helped her into the seat.

Making his way around the front of the vehicle to the driver's door, he glanced in the back to see Marcy wearing a huge grin and pretended to scowl at her.

As he had told Marcy, there was no hurry and once again Tommy took on the role of tour guide, calling out when they passed places of interest.

Sitting back comfortably in her seat, Alice sighed and staring at the scenery, the forested rolling hills and the sea beyond, she thought how beautiful the island was and daydreamed that she could live here and never leave.

Travelling through Lamlash, Tommy stopped the Defender in a lay-by and fetched the binoculars from the boot. Passing them to Marcy he directed her attention to the Holy Isle that lay just a short boat ride off the coast of Arran and told her something of its history; of the holy well that was supposed to have healing properties, the hermits cave of the sixth century monk Saint Molaise and of the Buddhist community who not only own the island, but have settled a community there. He told her of the nuns who also have a retreat on the island.

"What's a retreat?" she asked.

He smiled thoughtfully before replying, "It's like a place where people go to think, to pray and to be safe."

"To be safe," she slowly repeated, her eyes narrowing as she stared into his, then to his surprise she innocently added, "Like your house? Like with you?"

He felt his chest and his throat tightening and resisted the temptation to glance at Alice, before he replied, "Yes, wee girl. Like my house. Like with me."

Marcy nodded and turning away, lifted the binoculars to her eyes. Tommy turned towards Alice and softy smiling, said, "I think we'll be on our way, eh?"

****

The police vehicles, both marked and unmarked CID cars, departed from Padiham police station in convoy with a local detective directing the lead CID car to Healey Court.

Wisely, DI Sandford had accepted the Padiham nick's duty DS's advice where to plot up the vehicles until the arrival of the search warrant.

Ten minutes later, with all the vehicles reporting they were in position, DC Lucy Carstairs phoned from Padiham to inform Sandford the warrant had arrived and she would join them shortly. However, mindful of the old adage that 'the best laid plans of mice and men often go awry' Sandford was dismayed to hear from the detective in the local CID car who had eyeball on the lane adjacent to Reid's house, that a Bentley motor car registered to Reid was about to depart and there were at least three males aboard.

Conscious that her planned raid on the house was about to go to hell, she swithered for a brief second on what to do.

"Fuck it," she growled then teeth gritted and fingers mentally crossed the warrant arrived soon, hissed into the radio, "Go, go, go." There was a screech of tyres as the six vehicles deployed around the house raced towards the lane, then the radio burst open with the detective who had eyeball, screaming, "They've stopped the motor, they're reversing…wait! They're out the motor and running back to the house!"

With Terry Goodwin driving and Sandford bracing herself with both hands on the dashboard, the CID car turned sharply into the monoblock turning area in front of the house to find three uniformed vehicles and a CID car already come to a halt.

One of the uniformed vehicles, a double wheeled Transit van, was disgorging officers dressed in the bulky protective riot clothing and helmets with face masks down who were running towards the closed front door.

A bear of an officer carried the 'Enforcer,' the name given to the metal battering ram used to force entry to premises. As Sandford and Goodwin exited their vehicle, they saw the officer draw back the solid steel battering ram and after a couple of blows, make short work of the wooden door that permitted the OSU to pile into the house, loudly calling out warnings as they did so.

The CID officers present stood back to permit the uniformed officers to secure the occupants of the house and moments later the OSU sergeant in charge, her helmet carried in her hand, appeared at the door grinning widely and giving them a thumbs up.

Walking towards the house, it briefly occurred to Sandford that the occupants mad dash to escape the police could only mean one thing. They had been tipped off, but there was no way of knowing if by a police tout in Padiham nick or a nosy neighbour who had seen the police vehicles plotting up around the area.

"Three males and one woman, Ma'am, all secured in the kitchen," the sergeant reported. "No violence offered to us," she added.

Goodwin suspected the sergeant was a little disappointed there had been no resistance and commented, "The big guy who put the door in," he glanced pointedly at the damage that had been inflicted. "I wouldn't like to get on the wrong side of him."

"I'll let The Midget know you're pleased," the sergeant continued to grin.

"The Midget? You call a guy that size The Midget"

"Yeah, only *Bridget's* a woman and as you're the CID, I'll let you work out how she got her nickname," she mischievously grinned at Goodwin, then added with a smirk, "but don't even suggest to her you thought Bridget was a man, not if you want to keep your balls."

"Point taken," he replied with a shiver, wondering how much pain a woman like Bridget the Midget could inflict when she got started.

Sandford's first impression of the décor in the house was one of poor taste by the occupant. Though it seemed obvious there had been money spent, nothing seemed to match and she idly thought regardless of their cost, she would not give house room to the flashy paintings and tasteless ornaments that adorned every wall and stick of furniture; that and the thought that drug money likely paid for them.

The OSU sergeant led the way to the kitchen where the four detainees were seated on chairs, their hands bound in front of them with Flexicuffs.

Though the men remained silent, the young woman, a dyed blonde in her late teens or early twenties wearing a knee length, black silk negligee and short, black coloured silk dressing gown that hung open at the front to expose her deep cleavage, loudly and persistently verbally abused the officers present.

The woman turned to watch Sandford and Goodwin enter the kitchen and then began to berate them too with language so ripe and obscene it caused Sandford to request the woman's removal from the room.

"Gladly, Ma'am," grinned the blonde, cropped haired officer known as The Midget who grabbing the woman by the back of her dressing gown, hauled her from the chair to her feet. Unfortunately for the incensed woman and to the amusement of the officers' present, the dressing gown bunched in the Midget's grip and caused the negligee to fully part at the front, permitting her ample breasts to literally bounce free of the thin material as the Midget led her, still loudly uttering explicit and profane threats against the police, from the room.

Within seconds of the kitchen door closing, the woman's taunting cries were silenced, though none of the officers dared to offer an opinion as to why the woman had suddenly gone quiet.

Staring down at the three seated men, Sandford addressed the man in the middle with, "Hello, Monty. Long time no see. How have you been?"

Montgomery Charles Reid, forty-six years of age, his blonde hair neatly combed to his shoulders and wearing a navy blue pinstriped Saville Row three piece suit, his black shoes polished to a high sheen, sneered in return before replying, "Well, well, well, if it's not my favourite darkie, DI Sandford."

Beside her, Sandford could almost feel Goodwin bristle, but refusing to be baited, laid a restraining hand on his arm before continuing to smile and said, "I have a warrant to search this house, Monty. Now, before I set my troops about their business, anything you might wish to tell me about? Any loose drugs lying around? How about a murder weapon? Anything like that?"

She didn't miss his eyes narrowing and the tightening of his throat. "Murder weapon? So, that's what this is about then? Teddy Meiklewood getting himself murdered," he laughed, a deep uproarious laugh before continuing, "You put my door in, detain me and my associates, ogle my bird's tits and all because you think I've got something to do with Meiklewood's murder? You fucking idiot!" he tried to lunge at Sandford from the chair, but she realised it was a half-hearted effort to impress his two thuggish pals and he was quickly restrained and shoved back down onto his backside. "I'll have you for this, Sandford! You see if I don't, you fucking bitch!"

Before she could respond, the kitchen door was opened by Lucy Carstairs who catching Sandford's eye subtly nodded she had the warrant.

Turning to the OSU sergeant, Sandford pointedly ignored Reid and said, "Leave some of your people with these three, Sergeant and have the rest of your troops come with me," then added with a quiet smirk, "We're about to see how the other half live."

CHAPTER TWENTY

He parked some distance away from Doris Chisholm's house in Middleton Road and made his way there on foot by way of what he considered to be a circular route. He had briefly considered some sort of disguise, but discounted the idea as foolish, his own egotism causing him to believe himself to be too well known in the area and did not want to attract attention. However, he did decide to carry his medical bag in the belief that if anyone did see him and recognised him, well, they would simply believe it was the good Doctor Mayhew out attending to a patient and he inwardly smiled, for these days Geffrey Mayhew didn't do house calls. Unless it was a patient of some influence, that sort of nonsense was left to his junior partners.

Approaching the house, he was almost overcome by nerves and wondered again if this was a good idea.

Bracing himself, he took a deep breath and turned into Middleton Road, his eyes darting towards the front door of the mid-terraced house that was some forty metres distant.

To his surprise there was no police officer at the door, no sign of any blue and white police tape and seeing no police vehicles parked in the street, concluded the body had not yet been discovered.

He involuntarily stopped dead and stared towards the front door, his mind in a whirl and his pulse racing.

Should he take the chance, the opportunity to return to the house and search it to ensure he had left no trace of himself?

Hesitating, his attention was drawn to a young woman who was walking from the far end of Middleton Road along the path in the green landscaped park area opposite the mid-terraced houses.

Though she was still some distance away, he could see she wore a multi-coloured scarf, dark coloured jacket, jeans and carried what looked like some sort of backpack.

His mouth dry, he busied himself first looking at his wristwatch, then patted at his jacket pockets as though searching for something, but all the while watching the young woman who then stepped from the path and crossed the narrow one-way street towards Doris Chisholm's house, where she appeared to knock upon the front door. As he continued to watch, the young woman disappeared, presumably into the house.

That decided him. Turning away he began to quickly retrace his steps but had gone no more than ten yards when he imagined he heard what sounded like a piercing scream.
****

Alice Mayhew placed her cutlery neatly onto the plate and said, "That was delicious. Thank you."

"How about a sweet?" Tommy asked with a grin.

"No, thank you," Alice waved away the suggestion, but both turned when Marcy piped up, "I could manage an ice-cream."

Calling the young waiter to him, Tommy requested two coffees and a bowl of ice-cream, "…for the wee monster here," he nodded towards Marcy.

"Hey, I'm not a monster," she scowled with a petted lip.

"Well, you've got a monster appetite," he countered with a smile. They sat in silence until the waiter returned with the tray and placing the bowl in front of Marcy, Tommy and Alice exchanged smiles as the little girl set about the ice-cream with gusto.

"I like your friend, Peasy," she said at last, idly stirring her coffee.

"Well, he's your friend now," Tommy replied. "After all, what was it he said," Tommy frowned, then adopting Byrne's quiet voice, said, "I'm not doing it for you, I'm doing it for Alice and the wean."

She laughed then asked, "What's a dunderhead?"

"According to Peasy, I'm a dunderhead. It's his way of reminding me I'm not as bright as him."

"But he's joking, yes?"

He sipped at the scalding coffee and nodding, replied, "I hope so. You could say it's a term of affection or as much as the big guy will admit to. We've been friends for far too long for either of us to say anything that will offend the other. That and he acts as my sensible conscience. Keeps me right when he thinks I'm about to make a fool of myself," then for some unfathomable reason, found himself blushing.

Alice smiled and intuitively asked, "By conscience, I presume you mean when it comes to women?"

"Aye, something like that," he coughed to hide his embarrassment, then hoping to change the subject, turned to Marcy and asked, "How's the ice-cream?"

"Delicious," she grinned at him.

But shrewdly, Alice wasn't fooled. Tommy Burke, she thought, lacks confidence around women and though she couldn't know it, correctly guessed that sometime in the past he had formed a relationship with a woman that didn't work out. She thought it must have occurred between his wife's death and now for she couldn't believe him to have been unfaithful. She inwardly shuddered for she was the first to admit she wasn't any kind of expert in relationships, not after thirty years of living with Geoffrey behind her, but somehow an inner sense told her that Tommy just wasn't the type of man to cheat on his wife.

Now why couldn't I have met someone like him, she wondered.

"Why are you smiling?" he asked, his eyes betraying his curiosity.

"Am I?" she raised a hand to her mouth and her face flushed with the worry her thoughts were evident. "I didn't realise I was. Just," she paused and continuing to smile, added, "thinking about something nice."

After settling the bill then waving away Alice's protest and joking, "I'll get the food. You can pay for the foreign holiday," the three made their way back to the car park.

Helping Marcy into the rear seat, he watched the little girl yawn and said, "Early night for you, my wee lassie."

She smiled and reaching her arms forward to encircle his neck, whispered in his ear, "I like it when you call me your wee lassie."

Taken aback, Tommy stood perfectly still until Marcy released him then smiling at her, said, "Well, my wee lassie, compliments or not, early night for you."

Climbing into the driver's seat, he stopped and thoughtfully glanced at Alice who stared at him.

"Ever driven one of these beasts?" he asked.

"What? Your jeep you mean?"

"Aye, my *Defender*," he smiled.

"Eh, no. Nothing as big as this. Why?"

"Well, now's as good a time as any to learn," he grinned and waving her to him, stepped out of the vehicle. "It's still light, the Sunday traffic will have eased off so on you come, change places with me."

"Tommy! I can't!" she wailed.

"Go on, Gran. Drive the big car," Marcy, now fully awake, gleefully cried out to encourage her from the rear seat.

"Oh, heavens," she raised both hands to her face. "If you're sure?"

"Course I'm sure," he encouragingly smiled. "Oh, you're not banned for reckless driving or being drunk or anything, are you?" he smiled.

"No, of course not," she pretended indignation.

"Well, then," again he waved her to come to the drivers side.

He stood and held the door then when she was seated showed her how to adjust the seat and briefly run over the controls. "Same as your wee Toyota you were telling me about, only much larger," he opened his eyes wide, pretending to frighten her while in the back, Marcy giggled.

When he was buckled into the passenger seat, she nervously started the engine, but over-revved and promptly lifted her hands off the steering wheel.

Smiling, Tommy said, "This is a Land Rover Defender, hen. There's not much you can do to damage it. Just take your time and pull away when you're ready."

To the amusement of a couple of elderly men sitting on a nearby bench, she stalled the engine twice before pulling away in jerky movement from the car park, yet within a few minutes of anxious driving, began to relax and enjoy herself.

Apart from the odd occasion when she slowed for sharp corners, Alice drove the big four by four skilfully and at a constant, though moderate speed.

Soon they were driving through Lamlash and then onto Brodick where Tommy said, "Can you pull into the Cooperative? We need more milk."

"No problem," she replied and teeth biting gently at her lower lip as she concentrated, turned into the car park in front of the store where she stopped in a bay.

"I'll just be a minute," he said and got out of the vehicle.

Watching him walk towards the entrance, Alice breathed a sigh of relief that she had not failed in his confidence of her, had not let him down.

"That was great, Gran," said Marcy from behind her. Glancing in the rear view mirror she saw the little girl yawn and smiled before replying, "Thank you, sweetheart, and Tommy was right. Bed for you when we get home."

The words were hardly out of her mouth when she gave a slight gasp. When we get home. My God, what am I thinking?

Her thoughts were interrupted when she saw Tommy returning to the vehicle, a plastic carrier bag weighing heavily in his hand and a sheet of paper in the other.

Getting into the car he placed the plastic bag at his feet and said, "I've asked them to reserve two bottles of wine and told them you'd collect them some time later."

"Wine?"

"Aye," he cheekily grinned at her. "My fee for putting up with you two devils. Now," he handed her the sheet of paper, "they had a sign taped to the inside of the front door. They're looking for part-time staff, so I took the liberty of getting you an application form. Is that okay?"

"What? Yes, of course," her eyes lit up and she stared at the form.

"Right then, Jeeves," he pointed forward through the windscreen. "Up the road for a cuppa."

****

Returning to his car, Geoffrey drove straight home, his mind in a whirl.

Who was the young woman, he wondered then decided that as she felt comfortable enough to enter without being invited into the house, she must be a relative or a friend of Doris Chisholm.

Well, he grimly stared through the windscreen, the cat's out of the bag now.

****

The two police officers who responded within ten minutes of the hysterical young woman's phone call to the emergency services, arrived at the house in Middleton Road.

Getting out of the car, PC Davie Fletcher and his partner, PC Alan Whittinghame were met at the front door by the tearful young teenage woman who told them she was Brenda Chisholm, Missus Chisholm's granddaughter.

Ushering her back into the hallway, Fletcher said, "Right then, Miss, tell me what's happened? Where's your grandmother?"

"In there," the young woman said, her hand pointing shakily towards the lounge. "There's blood everywhere and she's dead," she wailed.

"Look after her, son," Fletcher instructed his probationary constable partner and opening the door to the lounge, startled at the sight that met him.

Gagging at the strong smell of blood and loosened bowels, he decided there was no need for him to check for a pulse, that clearly the old woman had fallen and cracked her head open on the coffee table.

Returning to the hallway, he saw that Whittinghame had manoeuvred the granddaughter into the kitchen where she was now seated, sobbing into a white handkerchief the young officer had given her.

Beckoning with his head that Whittinghame join him in the hallway, Fletcher closed the kitchen door and sniffed, "Looks like an accidental death to me. The old bird has tripped and fell backwards then struck her head on the coffee table."

Puzzled, the younger officer replied, "How can you be sure, Davie? Shouldn't we get the CID in to check? I mean…"

"Listen, son," Fletcher raised a hand. "I've been doing this job for twenty-five years now and you're in what, three months? I've seen it and done it and bought the T-shirt, Alan," he boasted, "so stand on me. It's accidental. Besides, those clowns in CID would only make a mountain out of a molehill and have us standing outside the front door in the freezing cold all day and night while they ponce about making themselves seem important. No," he winked, "I've an indoor bowling tournament tonight and it's a straight forward accident. So while I get a brew on to calm the girl down and write up some details, you call in the casualty surgeon to pronounce life extinct and we can get this wrapped up in a couple of hours, okay?"

Though unhappy the CID were not to be informed, Whittinghame reluctantly nodded, aware that he was in no position to argue with his tutor cop, for Fletcher was also responsible for writing monthly reports that would determine whether or not the younger officer would complete his two-year probationary period and finally be appointed as a fully fledged constable.

Had he known that Fletcher was considered by the Inspector to be the laziest man on the shift, that his appointment as a tutor constable had been made in the belief it might at last motivate Fletcher into doing something useful, PC Whittinghame's concern might not have been as misplaced as he believed. However, unaware of Fletcher's reputation the young officer did as he was instructed.

Reaching for his handset though still unable to shake off the feeling that this was wrong, he slowly inhaled then called the station.

****

After moving the four detained individuals back to Padiham nick, DI Sandford arranged that Monty Reid be brought to the interview room where she sat with Terry Goodwin.

No sooner had Reid, his hands now unbound, been escorted into the room than he said, "I'm saying fuck all till you get my brief gets here."

"Your lawyer has been contacted, Monty and should be here any time," Sandford smoothly replied, "but before he arrives, tell me. Who's the bird we found with you? Says she's only twenty. Bit young for an old nark like you, isn't she?"

His eyes flashed and he venomously hissed in reply, "Who are you calling a nark, you black bitch!"

Seated beside her, Goodwin readied himself and though wouldn't admit to it, relished the thought that Reid might again consider lunging at Sandford and give Goodwin the opportunity to punch him in the mouth. However, he did wonder where Sandford was going with this. Calling Monty Reid a nark seemed bizarre, for after all Reid was the unlikeliest informant he could imagine.

"Well," she sat back and her brow creased when she smiled at him. "Let me explain. It's caused me to wonder that through the years that you have managed to survive so many police operations against you. Admittedly arrested a number of times, yes," she pursed her lips and slowly shaking her head, continued, "but never been convicted, eh? Now," she leaned forward onto her elbows, resting her chin in her fists, "over the last couple of weeks I took the opportunity to research all the operations against you, Monty, and guess what I concluded? You've been getting away with so much for so long, it occurred to me that you are either an amazingly lucky man or you are paying off some very good sources within the police service *or…*"

She stopped and stared at him for a few seconds before slowly smiling. "My very favourite opinion is that you're being protected. Are you being protected, Monty? Are you being permitted to continue your business while grassing up your fellow drug dealers? Is that how it works?"

Goodwin glanced from Reid to Sandford, his brow knitting as he thought, where did that come from and what the *hell* is she thinking? But when he turned back to stare at Reid, he caught his breath.

There it was, the slightest flickering of Reid's eyes, so faint as to be almost imperceptible.

"I have no fucking idea what you're on about," he snarled before adding, "You cow!"

She didn't react other than to give a slight sigh, then said in a soft voice, "Is that the best you can do? Name calling? Come on, Monty, we both know that within an hour, I'll probably get a phone call from someone in authority to tell me that my interest in you is to be discontinued, that you are not to be questioned by me. Isn't that right? So," she quickly continued before he could interrupt, "while it's just me and you and my silent partner here," she gave a slight nod towards Goodwin, "tell me; who's really pulling your strings?"

Sat beside her, Goodwin hardly dare breathe, afraid that any interruption by him might break the tension in the room; the invisible but rigid connection that kept Sandford and Reid's eyes locked together.

"Monty," she said, her voice low and steady as though speaking with an errant chid, "we both know that I've worked it out, don't we? We both know that you'll walk out of this room without me being able to charge you with anything; not even that small amount of personal use coke we discovered in your bedside cabinet. However," she continued to smile, "what you *don't* know is that if you don't give me the answers I need, I'll become very loose tongued. I mean," she gave a deliberate girlish snigger, "you know what us women are like for gossiping, don't you? I'll let my pals in the CID and anyone else who cares to hear that you *are* being protected, that in payment for this protection you are firing in some of your serious criminal associates who are now languishing in prison. Criminal associates, may I remind you, who likely still have considerable pull here in the outside world. Now, how long do you think it would take for that gossip to reach the ears of some of your old pals?"

Reid turned a ghastly pale colour and to Goodwin's surprise, beads of perspiration began to form on his forehead.

"You're bluffing," he said, his voice shaking. "You can't do that."

"There's a difference between can't and won't, Monty. Like I said, give me the answers I need and you can keep on informing on whoever you like." She shrugged and added, "I'm not concerned about who is protecting you or what else you're getting out of it. All I want is answers to my inquiry. Nothing more."

Reid's head dipped and Goodwin watched as Reid's throat tightened. Raising his head, he stared levelly at her and said, "You can't do this! For fuck's sake, you're the fucking cops! Do you realise what you're saying, that you could get me killed? Don't think I won't be telling anyone about this…this fucking *blackmail!*"

"No," she smoothly replied, "you won't be telling anyone, Monty, because what we discuss here will never come back to you. No one outside these four walls will ever learn that it was you who gave me the answers I need."

Turning to him, she said, "Isn't that right, DS Goodwin?"

"Correct, Ma'am," he croaked, his eyes steadily fixed on Reid.

Reid raised his head to stare at the ceiling then shoulders slumped, quietly said, "What do you need to know?"

CHAPTER TWENTY-ONE

The young Polish locum who arrived at Middleton Road in response to PC Whittinghame's radio call had qualified just two years earlier and only been in the UK for seven months.

Desperate for work, she had been fortunate to be taken on by a local practice who were contracted to provide Lancashire Constabulary with out of hours' medical assistance that included the seizure of blood samples from suspected drunk or drugged drivers, assessing or treating minor injuries to prisoners or in this case, attending at sudden deaths to pronounce life extinct.

Slightly overawed by the middle-aged police officer who greeted her with a wide smile and seemed to know what he was doing and who led the nervous young woman into the lounge, she quickly agreed with him that the poor woman was dead and, eager to please, agreed that it looked like the woman had fallen over and struck her head.

Fetching the certificate from her medical bag, she signed the formal form that pronounced life extinct.

"Right then," PC Fletcher courteously led the doctor to the front door, "me and my lad will arrange for the funeral director to get here to remove the body, doctor. Now, is there anything else?"

While he asked the question, his eyes told her that she was dismissed and with an edgy smile, she shook her head and left.

****

Arriving at his daughter's house in Bellshill, Peasy Byrne led his small dog wee Chic along the path and at the door greeted his daughter with a hug, but declined the offer to go in for a cuppa.

"Now, you're sure you don't mind?" he asked.

"Course not, dad. Now, are you away for one or two nights or more?"

"I'm not certain yet, but I'll phone to keep you updated."

"Well, as long as you let me know you're okay, then this wee lad," she bent to lift the dog who immediately began to nuzzle at her, "can stay over for as long as he wants."

"Thanks, hen, I'll away because I want an early start and I've a bag to pack."

Patting the dog on the head, he returned to his car and made his way home.

****

At Alice's bidding, Tommy Burke carried the sleeping Marcy upstairs to the bedroom and gently laid her down onto the bed.

"I'll be down in a minute," Alice smiled and began to undress the child.

Down in the kitchen, Tommy set the kettle to boil and thought about his day.

He couldn't help but feel relaxed and found himself involuntarily smiling at the memory of Alice driving the Defender back from Kildonnan.

"What you grinning at," he turned to see her standing in the doorway.

"Oh, you driving the Defender, the big *jeep*," he mocked her with a smile. "Now, cuppa or maybe a glass of wine?"

"Eh, tea will be fine, thank you Mister Burke. You never know, I might have to drive again sometime this evening to fetch your ego back from Kildonnan."

"My ego?"

"Yes, well, isn't the Defender a *man's* vehicle and there's me, a mere woman, driving it?" she pretended snootiness.

He smiled and shaking his head, replied, "I have to concede you handled the beast like a pro, Alice. Well done. Now, away into the lounge and get yourself a seat and I'll bring in the tea."

She saluted him with a smile and a nod and left him in the kitchen.

He slowly exhaled, for though he couldn't explain why, he had felt a little awkward that now with Marcy asleep in bed it was just he alone with Alice and wondered what kind of conversation they might have. Stood with his hands resting on the worktop while the kettle boiled, his mind raced for after all, much as he liked her; well, really liked her if he was honest with himself, it wasn't as if she was a woman that he could pursue, not with her being married.

The kettle switched off and he poured the water then set the teapot on the gas ring to simmer.

Occupying himself setting a tray with mugs and a plate of biscuits, he didn't see Alice return to the doorway, but turned when she quietly said, "I'm glad it's just the two of us, Tommy. I think we should have a bit of a chat."

****

Geoffrey Mayhew stood with his back to the closed front door as though the solid wood and walls of the house would protect him from any intrusion and from the police who would now be hunting for the killer of Teddy Meiklewood.

He gave no thought to Doris Chisholm, having now convinced himself it was her own fault that she was dead, but still worried that if he *had* left anything of himself in her house the police might not see it that way.

Slowly, his heart stopped racing and forcing himself to be calm, he stepped into the hallway and took his jacket off, carelessly throwing it onto the banister of the stairs.

He had not given much thought to Alice or the child, but now wondered again where they might have gone.

That's when he remembered the scrap of paper with the phone number and the STD code for Arran.

In the lounge he poured himself three fingers of whisky then settled down into his favourite chair.

If the police connected him to Teddy Meiklewood, if they discovered Meiklewood had supplied him with the Brown Speeders, then he was certain to be interviewed and probably charged. Of course, he would deny all knowledge of the performance enhancement drug and suggest that it was Meiklewood himself who had supplied that idiot Jonathan Archer. However, the merest suspicion of association with Meiklewood's drug dealing would taint him and he could kiss goodbye to the Chair of the rugby club, not least the damage it would do not only to his reputation and status in the community, but the worst of it was it could lead to him being struck off.

He sipped at his whisky and licking his lips, then considered Doris Chisholm's death.

Confident as he was that he had left nothing of himself in her house, if by bad luck somehow the police associated him with her death…

No, he shook his head as though to clear it. The only connection he had with Chisholm was her friendship with Alice.

Alice, he sipped again at the whisky, a sudden anger overtaking him.

She had the packets with her, of that he was certain.

She had the means with which to not only discredit him, but have him arrested too.

She had to be stopped, of that too he was convinced.

And if stopping her meant…well, by any means necessary he decided, but worried how he was going to go about that particular matter.

Throwing back the last of his drink, he placed the glass down onto the table by his chair and getting to his feet, realised that by using his computer he could research the island of Arran and perhaps even discover where she and the brat had gone to.

****

Stood together in the corridor outside the interview room, they watched Monty Reid who deliberately ignored them, being led off to be returned to his detention cell.

"Do you believe him, Ma'am?" Goodwin asked her.

Sandford didn't immediately respond, but then slowly replied, "Even criminals sometime tell the truth," then slowly nodding, added, "Yes, I believe him. I also believe he was too shit scared of me spreading the word he's a police nark and the consequence of what might happen to him if the word did get out."

Goodwin turned to her and his face expressing his curiosity, asked, "Just where did you get the information he is a nark, anyway?"

Sandford smiled before replying, "Let's just say it was a lucky guess and leave it at that, shall we?"

"Ma'am?"

She turned to see Lucy Carstairs behind her.

"There's a phone call for you in the CID room. It's the Area Commander and he says…" Carstairs paused before continuing, "He asks that you are to speak to him without delay."

Nodding in acknowledgment, Sandford glanced at her watch and tightly smiling, reminded Goodwin, "I believe I said within the hour, didn't I? I make it fifty-six minutes, so I wasn't that far off," then with a frown, added, "Wait here for me."

Turning, she began to make her way towards the CID office.

Goodwin stared after her then inquired of Carstairs, "Is that what the AC said? Without delay?"

"What he *said* was tell DI Sandford to get her arse onto the phone this minutes and added a few expletives while he did so," she grinned, then asked, "What was that about, fifty-six minutes?"

****

It was fortunate that the mortuary attendants of the firm contracted to the local Coroner were engaged in a genuine accidental death and thus were not immediately available to remove the body of Doris Chisholm from her home, for their delay gave the duty Inspector the opportunity to call at the house. The newly promoted officer had been warned about the slothful attitude of PC Fletcher and though he did not really suspect anything to be amiss about Fletcher's apparent accidental death, made the decision to attend and ensure the older officer was properly tutoring his twenty-two-year-old partner.

Met at the door by Whittinghame, the stocky built Inspector, a former Detective Sergeant prior to his promotion to his uniformed rank, greeted the young probationer with, "Where's the body then, lad?"

In the hallway before entering the lounge, the Inspector could hear Fletcher speaking in the kitchen and raising his eyebrows at Whittinghame, was informed in a whisper, "It's the woman's granddaughter, sir. Her names Brenda Chisholm, she's eighteen and a student. She's the one who found the body and she's in a bit of a state," he apologetically added. "Davie…I mean, PC Fletcher, he's trying to calm her down and get some details for the death report."

"And the shell for the body is due when?"

"Anytime sir, according to the control room," Whittinghame shrugged. "The doctor has been and pronounced life extinct," he helpfully added.

"Okay, then let's see what we've got," the Inspector turned and pushed open the lounge door.

The smell that assailed him was one he recognised, but it was the twisted features of the dead woman that attracted his attention and his shoulders slumped.

Slowly breathing through his mouth, he turned to Whittinghame and in a flat voice, slowly asked, "Have the CID been informed?"

"The CID, sir? No," Whittinghame shook his head, but alerted by the Inspector's expression his heart sank for unless he was way off the mark, Davie had made a mistake.

"Can you tell me why the CID were not informed?"

"Eh, no, not really sir," the younger man gulped. "When I suggested it to Davie…PC Fletcher I mean, he said there was no need for the CID, that it's a straight forward accidental death, that the woman has fell backwards and hit her head on the table."

"So," the Inspector deliberately kept his voice neutral when he stared at Whittinghame and asked, "PC Fletcher decided of his *own* volition that this woman's death was accidental?"

"Eh, yes sir. It *is* accidental, isn't it, sir?"

The Inspector didn't immediately reply, but first turned away to stare down at the dead woman then with a sigh, said, "Step outside the front door, lad, and call this into the control room as a suspicious death. Request the presence of the CID and nobody, but nobody," he leaned forward and stared at the young officer to emphasise his point, "gets through that door unless I say so. Understood?"

Whittinghame felt a chill run through him and stomach suddenly clenching, his mouth went dry. Nodding he understood, he made his way to the front door, but as he did so he heard from behind him the Inspector calmly calling out, "PC Fletcher. Can you join me in the hallway? I need a word. Now, if you please."

****

Sitting facing each other in the lounge, Tommy watched as Alice poured them tea then leaned across to hand him his mug.

"So, what do you want to talk to me about?"

She sat back down and inhaling, replied, "I'm so very grateful for what you have done for Marcy and me…"

"But?" he interrupted.

She tightly smiled and continued, "But we can't continue to accept your hospitality like this."

She bit at her lower lip then said, "You can't imagine what it's like to be able to trust someone, not when you have lived the kind of life I have, but I do trust you, Tommy. You and Peasy. I don't know many men," she admitted with a tinge of a blush, "but you have both been so kind I just don't know how I can ever repay you."

"Repay us, Alice?" he pretended to be stunned and screwed his face in surprise. "Are you kidding me on? Peasy needs something to do and I'm enjoying the company here, so what's to repay?"

She smiled at his attempted humour and replied, "You know what I mean, Tommy Burke,"

then paused before continuing, "We can't go on living as we are, being fed and cared for by you. Marcy and I need to find our own place and I need a job. Furthermore, she will need schooling too."

"So, what do you suggest?"

Alice shrugged, then said, "Tomorrow when the weekend tourists leave I will need to try and find some accommodation and a job here on the island. If not, then I'll need to return to the mainland and try somewhere there."

"Okay, I won't try to change your mind," he shook his head and held up both hands, "but what I *will* suggest is that you let me help you. Besides, you'll need to be handy for when Peasy gets back to us about his inquiry down in Preston. I mean," he grinned, "the big guy won't be a happy chappy if he finds out everything you need to know and you're not here to take the information from him."

"I'll be very grateful if you will help me, Tommy," she smiled shyly at him before adding once more, "though I don't know how I can ever repay your kindness."

Outwardly expressing support and agreement with Alice, Tommy could not but help feel that he should say something, anything that would make her and Marcy stay, yet his ingrained sense of decency and courtesy prevented him from speaking out.

Instead, he nodded to her mug and said, "Let me top you up."
****

When she returned to the corridor where they both stood, DI Sandford's face was hard to read though she curtly said, "Let's get back to our own nick and I'll brief the team there."

The return journey to the Preston office was made almost in total silence and only broken when Goodwin cheerfully asked Carstairs, "What's planned for tonight, then Lucy?"

"Well, if that hubby of man can get his arse off the couch after watching the sports I'm kind of hoping he's got dinner prepared, then the kids to bed, a lazy bath and a glass of chilled white wine. You?"

It was common knowledge that Goodwin and his partner of five years had recently split, so she was surprised when he replied, "I'm meeting Derek for dinner though we've not yet agreed a time or a restaurant. Likely Chinese though. Yeah," he absent-mindedly added, "I fancy a Chinese tonight."

At last Goodwin turned the CID car in through the security gate of the Preston office where Sandford wordlessly led them to her office on the second floor.

Opening the door, she saw the rest of the team were already assembled and who stopped speaking when she permitted Carstairs to enter the room ahead of her; however, Sandford raised a hand to stop Goodwin and then with them both still in the corridor, called out to the team, "We'll just be a minute."

He stared curiously at her until she said in a low voice, "I want us to be on the same page in there when I give the briefing, so just nod in agreement no matter what I say. Got that, Terry?"

He nodded and followed her into the room, though slightly confused, but not at what she asked.

No, what surprised him was that the rank conscious Sandford had never before addressed him by anything other than DS Goodwin. Terry? Well, he thought, that's a first.

Settling herself behind her desk, she stared at the team before beginning, "As you are all aware, we detained Montgomery Reid earlier this afternoon and conveyed him and three associates to the Padiham nick. Upon our arrival at the nick DS Goodwin and I interviewed Reid under," she paused and cast a glance at Goodwin before continuing, "what you might call informal circumstances prior to Reid's brief arriving. However, while I regret that Reid told us absolutely nothing and refused to admit to even his name until the arrival of his brief, I also received a phone call from the Area Commander."

She paused again and prepared herself for the lie.

"The AC was able to inform me that intelligence has arrived from an non attributable source that indicates Monty Reid is not the supplier of the Brown Speeders, that he is himself a hands off middle man who arranged for the Speeders to be supplied to Teddy Meiklewood."

"Do we know who the supplier is, Ma'am?" asked a young detective.

She smiled, a ghostly smile and holding up her police notebook, replied, "The AC provided me with full details of the supplier and where the current batch of Speeders are being stored. It seems a Turkish coffee shop in the Metropolitan area is the drop-off place so it is my intention to pass the details to the Met's drug squad and have them raid the place."

There was some curious glances before the same detective asked, "Why didn't the AC just pass this himself, Ma'am?"

"I had a word with him and he agreed that the information should come from us because like me, he agrees you guys have worked hard on this inquiry so it is both our belief you deserve the kudos."

There were smiles all around, though more than a few were surprised at Sandford's appreciation of their efforts.

"What about Meiklewood's murder, Ma'am?" Lucy Carstairs piped up.

Sandford sat back in her chair before responding, then carefully said, "The AC has information that though Reid's arrangements did ultimately result in the Speeders being supplied to Meiklewood, that is something we will never prove and will not pursue because it might cause problems for the source. However, it seems the source reported that Reid believed Meiklewood to prospectively be a regular customer for the supplier and had no reason to murder him and Reid was apparently surprised he had been killed. What the source also told the AC was that Meiklewood purchased the Speeders with the intention of selling them on to a customer who is apparently a well know figure. Regretfully, the source did not know the name of this individual."

"Could that well known figure be our suspect, Doctor Mayhew, Ma'am?"

"Perhaps," Sandford pursed her lips and staring at the younger officer, continued, "but until we gather evidence, DC Carstairs, it's speculation only at this time and don't think that I'm not aware how pleased you would be if it *is* Mayhew."

She turned from Carstairs to glance at each of the team in turn and then concluded with, "In essence, once I've made the call to the Met drug squad, the ball's in their court. We have done our job." Tapping a manicured forefinger on her notebook, she continued, "We've identified the suppliers of the Brown Speeders and once the suppliers are arrested it's up to the Met to interview and charge them with the deaths of the six young people…"

"Possibly seven, ma'am," interrupted a female DC with a raised hand. "There was a report on the radio late this afternoon that Cumbria Police are making inquiry into the death of a player who collapsed on the field at a junior football match. I took the liberty of calling the local nick and their first indication is that it's drug related, though of course they can't confirm at this early stage it's due to Brown Speeders."

Sandford didn't respond, but stared at the young DC before slowly lowering her head and quietly muttering, "Seven. Shit!"

The unusual exclamation of emotion from the DI took those present aback and an uncomfortable silence settled on the room.

They watched as the DI reached into her handbag and withdrew her cigarettes and lighter that she placed on the desk in front of her, though made no attempt to light up.

"Either way and as you say, Ma'am," Goodwin broke the silence and nodded, "we've done our job."

"Yes," she nodded then sighed, "we've done our job. As for Teddy Meiklewood's murder and as you all know, the AC has warned us off from investigating it, so it's down to the Force's MIT to deal with that. What we'll do is pass on what little we know to the DCI of the MIT regarding Meiklewood's customer here in Preston who," she raised both hands and using her fingers as quotation marks, added, "is a 'well know figure' and our suspicions regarding the good Doctor Mayhew."

Glancing at Carstairs, she smiled and further added, "I should say our *credible* suspicions."

Exhaling, she continued to smile and said, "Now, it's Sunday, it's early evening and you guys have homes and families to go to. I'm instructing that I don't want to see any of you till at least ten o'clock tomorrow morning, so go home…"

She didn't finish for the desk phone rang. Raising her hand to prevent them leaving before she finished thanking them, the team saw her frown and her eyes narrow. Taking a deep breath, she grabbed at a pen and make a note on her desk pad. Replacing the phone into its cradle, her brow furrowed before she spoke.

Staring first at what she had written, she raised her head and said, "I was about to dismiss you for the night, however, that was the control room. It seems we have a suspicious death in Middleton Road."

CHAPTER TWENTY-TWO

The uniformed Inspector met DI Julie Sandford on the street outside the house as her CID car came to a halt in Middleton Road. A second car and like the first car, carrying four officers, stopped behind Sandford's vehicle.

Before approaching the door, she glanced with approval at the sterile area the Inspector had organised with blue and white police tape and uniformed officers keeping back inquisitive neighbours and members of the public. However, and to her distaste, she saw that some people were already filming the comings and goings of the police on their mobile phones.

Instructing her team to wait outside the house, she and DS Terry Goodwin first struggled into white Forensic suits and donned nitrile gloves before following the Inspector past the sullen faced constable on duty at the door.

Goodwin squinted at the constable, recognising him as PC Fletcher, a particularly lazy bastard who he knew persistently ridiculed and undermined his CID colleagues.

At the front door of the house, both she and Goodwin gave their names to Fletcher who sullenly noted them and their time of arrival in his notebook.

What Sandford did not know was prior to her arrival, the Inspector, a seasoned former CID officer, had taken the decision not to inform the DI of PC Fletcher's dreadful decision of failing to notify the CID of the death, reasoning that other than the loss of almost two hours of inquiry, nothing else had contaminated the scene.

Besides, he had inwardly argued, relations between the two departments had recently been strained and he did not wish to exacerbate an already tense situation. No, Fletcher's actions would be the subject of a discussion the Inspector intended having in the morning with the stations Chief Inspector, who he suspected was already seeking an excuse to remove the indolent officer from any further street duties or contact with the public.

"This way, Julie," the Inspector, wearing nitrile gloves but not a Forensic suit, led Sandford and her DS into the hallway and without stepping into the room, used a hand to open the lounge door to permit Sandford and Goodwin to see the body.

"And as far as you are aware, the room's sterile?"

"Other than the granddaughter, who's in the kitchen behind you there," he nodded to the closed door, "Fletcher, who is on the front door and the attending doctor who confirmed life extinct, nobody else has been in the room since she was found."

"Who's with the granddaughter?"

"One of my younger cops, PC Whittinghame, but he assures me he did not step into the room."

Sandford, staring at the body, slowly nodded then turning to Goodwin, said, "Right then, let's get started, Terry."

****

"Do you want to take a drink with you to bed?" Tommy smiled before adding, "I don't mean alcohol. Milk or a hot chocolate or something."

"No, I'm fine. Thank you."

She stood a little anxiously by his chair and stared down at him, uncertain how to end what had been a nice, relaxing evening, sitting together and talking about everything and nothing at all.

Inwardly, nervous, she took a deep breath and leaning down towards him, said in a soft voice, "Goodnight, Tommy," and lowered her head even more to kiss him on the top of his head.

He fought the urge to pull her down towards him, to hold her on his lap and kiss her fully on the lips, but knew to do so would harm if not completely shatter any trust she had in him, so instead he smiled tightly and replied, "Goodnight to you, too, Alice."

She had been gone just a few minutes when he let out a long sigh and raising his head to stare at the ceiling, thought, "Peasy. Where the hell are you when I need your advice?"

****

After issuing her instructions to her team, Terry Goodwin had said, "Can I have a quiet word, Ma'am?"

Walking together, they stood by the second parked CID car and that gave her the opportunity to light a cigarette. Tearing off the filter that she placed in her trouser pocket, she drew deeply on the fag before saying, "What's on your mind, DS Goodwin?"

"What you said in the office, about the Area Commander giving you the heads-up info about Reid and the Turkish suppliers. We both know it's all bullshit, that it was you who burst him into giving you the information. Why the hell are you not taking the credit for it? Jesus," he shook his head, "these Brown Speeders deaths are a high profile media issue. You've solved it and could end up being promoted for what you did, so why the *fuck* let the team think it's that dickhead of an AC who gave you the info?"

She shrugged and replied, "Look, we both know he's obviously made a deal with one of the bosses, though to be honest, I don't believe it's the Area Commander. No," she shook her head and her eyes narrowed as she considered her words, "the AC is too wrapped up in his own career advancement to concern himself with running a tout. He's probably being given his orders by someone higher up in the food chain." She scratched at an itch on her chin then said, "I'm of the opinion that Reid has made a deal with someone who has real pull, maybe even someone who is working as high as in the Chief's office." She sighed and continued, "So, let's say I tell the team the truth, then sure as God made little green apples, sooner or later one of them will inadvertently let it out that Reid's a nark and we both know what would happen if his former associates learn that he's responsible for setting them up."

She drew again on the cigarette, feeling the strong tobacco rush into her lungs. "Reid certainly won't admit to his handler that we burst him for information because that would dilute his usefulness and likely without his protection, he'd be hung out to dry. However, it suits me to have Reid dangling on a string and what he knows about who's doing what in the Preston area," she softly smiled, "might come in useful in the future."

She stared thoughtfully at Goodwin. "So, with more to be had from him, now that he's already rolled over once, I think I made the right decision. Yes," she held up her free hand to forestall his protest, "I know and admit that he'll continue to conduct his business, but it's the old argument, isn't it? We turn a blind eye and let him supply his drugs locally, but he gives us the main suppliers who are doing the real harm." She flicked ash from the fag to the ground and staring down at it and waited for Godwin's outburst.

"Then you're playing a dodgy game, Ma'am, because if it gets out that you've quite literally signed Reid on as your tout as well as…as whoever the fuck is running him," he shrugged and shook his head. But then she astonished him, for she replied, "Nobody will know, Terry, because other than Reid, the only other person who is aware of what went on in that interview room is you. And though I am aware I haven't previously given you cause to know this, I trust you."

He blinked in surprise.

The Ice Queen trusted him?

Bloody hell, wonders will never cease!

"Right, then," she used her forefinger and thumb to nip her butt that she returned to the cigarette packet, then turned her head to watch as the Forensic vehicle pulled up and was permitted into the cordon.

"Let's get back into the house and let the Scene of Crime guys know what we want doing."

****

Geoffrey Mayhew sat in his favourite armchair, flicking between the news channels, but it was as he expected. There was nothing about the discovery of Doris Chisholm's body from the London based news programmes. Using the remote control, he scrolled to the menu then selected the radio channels and clicked on the local North West Radio channel. At that time of the evening it was a country and western show, but glancing at the clock he saw the hourly news bulletin was due.

Time for a top-up, he sighed and reached for the bottle of whisky. Pouring himself a generous three fingers he was about to sip from the glass when the music changed to announce the news bulletin.

His eyes opened wide when the first item broadcast was the attendance of the police at a house in Middleton Road in Preston where a body had been discovered. The reporter at the scene disclosed that according to neighbours, the house was occupied by an elderly woman who lived there alone then added that police were treating the death as suspicious.

He closed his eyes against the throb in his forehead that seemed to have settled there for the past few days.

The news on the radio left him with little choice.

He had to deal with this situation before it got out of hand and if dealing with it meant travelling to this bloody island in Scotland and…he stopped, aghast at where his thoughts had taken him for he knew now he had no choice.

He had to deal with Alice and if it came to it, the brat too.

****

Thanking the neighbour as the young man closed the door behind her, DC Lucy Carstairs took the opportunity to use her mobile phone to call home and in a brief few moments, informed her husband Mike that she was called out to a suspicious death, that he was not to wait up for her, that he put the kids to bed and kiss them goodnight for her and "Yes," she smiled, "I'm absolutely fine, darling. If I'm too late, I'll use the spare room so as not to disturb you when I get in. No, no," she shook her head and absent-mindedly waved off his protest, "just give me a shout before you leave for work and I'll tend to the kids. Honest," she smiled.

She had just ended the call when her partner left the adjoining house and nodding at her, asked, "Anything?"

"Never saw or heard a thing," she shook her head. "All they could tell me is that the elderly lady who lived three doors away occasionally would nod in the passing, but they didn't even know her name. In fairness, they've only lived here for about six years," the sarcasm dripped from her.

"Same at my house," the detective nodded backwards. "See no evil, hear no evil. Had the bloody cheek to ask if in my experience in dealing with such matters, did I think the death might affect the house prices in the area? Morons," he sighed.

"Sign of the times," Carstairs sagely replied as they walked towards the next two doors.

****

Concerned he might waken Alice or Marcy, Tommy quietly tiptoed across the floor of the upper landing towards his bedroom.

He'd thought about bringing his Kindle to bed, but after widely yawning, knew he was ready for sleep.

Or so he had thought.

Getting into bed and no matter how hard he tried, his thoughts kept returning to Alice and her decision to leave the following day. Of course, he would do everything he could to help her find accommodation and a job, but knew in his heart he would be sorry to see her and Marcy go.

Not that he wouldn't stay in touch, he told himself. After all, though widowed he was a single man and while she was married, he had little doubt after what she had disclosed that there was no likelihood of her ever again seeing or resuming her relationship with her husband.

What that might mean in terms of…he exhaled, for he was about to give thought to a relationship between him and Alice. Well, why not, he grinned in the dark and with that happy thought, fell asleep.

****

His bag packed, the car fuelled and ready for the next morning's trip to Preston, Peasy Byrne sat at his desktop computer and turning back and forth in the desk chair, idly stared at the white cardboard packet he held in in his fingers.

Just as Alice had said and if his research on the computer was correct, the typed writing and symbols were the Russian Cyrillic language. As for the name printed on the the blister packs that contained the small brown tablets, nothing came up and not for the first time he wished that he had access to a MIMS, the drug database directory that was held in all the CID offices throughout Police Scotland.

It did occur to him to telephone a former colleague and call in a favour, but glancing at the clock realised it was unlikely his former DCI would be in the office at this time of night and particularly on a Sunday during a local holiday weekend.

Opening the computer, he checked his e-mails and saw that one e-mail from Tommy Burke that had arrived just an hour previously, informed Peasy that Alice had tried again that evening to phone Doris Chisholm, but there was no reply and curiously, the answer machine did not activate.

Finishing with his e-mails, he Googled hotels in Preston and finally settled on the Holiday Inn that was adjacent to the city centre. One phone call and less than ten minutes later, he was booked for two nights, pleased to hear also that there was free parking.

Opening his notebook, he checked again the address for Doris Chisholm and opening the AA's AutoRoute planner, printed off the route from the hotel to Middleton Road.

That done, he decided to call it a night and switching off the computer, headed headed upstairs to bed.

****

Sandford had nipped out of the house for a fag and watched as the CID car with the deceased's granddaughter drove off towards the station.

"I left them to it,", Terry Goodwin nodded his head indoors to the SOC officers as he stepped from the doorway to join her and rubbed his hands together against the chill of the evening.

"Anything yet?"

"Nothing so far, but they're the experts," he replied with a shrug.

The Inspector approached and said, "If it does turn out to be accidental, Julie, I'll stand my guys down. Some of them are well past their finish time and I don't need to tell you about the freeze on overtime."

She smiled and reaching into her handbag pulled out her cigarette pack then offered it to the Inspector.

"No, thanks," he shook his head. "Chucked them when I was promoted," then wryly grinning, added, "but it doesn't mean I don't still crave them."

The three turned when the door behind them opened to disclose a white suited figure who emerged and pulling down her facemask, then pulled off the hood to reveal a mass of curly blonde hair.

"Anything?" Sandford asked.

The senior SOCO, a woman in her early thirties, took a deep breath of the fresh night air and slowly exhaled before replying, "When the old lady fell down onto her back, her cardigan had fallen across the left side of her breast, so we didn't immediately spot it, Ma'am, but yes," the young woman nodded, "we believe there was a struggle before she died. When we moved the cardigan we saw the top button of her blouse was torn away and later found it in the hallway against the skirting board. You guys must have walked past it a dozen times, but in fairness it's a small, pearl coloured button so unless you were looking for it…" she left the rest unsaid.

But then to the Inspector's consternation, the SOCO glanced at them in turn before innocently asking, "We were wondering, didn't the first officer on the scene who inspected the body tell you about the missing button?"

Sandford cast a sharp glance towards the Inspector who calmly said,

"With your permission, Julie, I will deal with that issue."
Suspecting there might be more to it, Sandford stared at him before replying, "As long as you can assure me there is nothing else that will affect my investigation?"

"You have my assurance," he replied with more feeling than he felt. Sensing the tension, the SOCO intervened with, "So, if you were wondering, Ma'am, we definitely believe the old lady fought with someone in the hallway and that's where the button was torn off her blouse, then somehow found herself in the lounge, possibly dragged or pushed there, where she fell to her death. Was she pushed down onto her back and her head deliberately struck off the table to cause the injury?" The SOCO shrugged. "About that we can't give you a definitive answer, but in our opinion the way the carpet fibres in the rug are risen suggest she was propelled backwards into the room with her heels dragging for there is a definite run against the way the fibres should sit in the rug."

"Anything else?" Sandford tightly asked.

They didn't miss the slight hesitation from the SOCO who slowly replied, "We're not pathologists, ma'am, and we're aware the old lady has been lying there for at least a day or more. However, we can see that lividity has settled in or because of her age, maybe it's some kind of condition she had, but…" she licked at her lips.

"But?" Sandford repeated.

"Well, there seems to be some sort of red marks around her neck. We don't know if pressure has been applied or as I say, she had a medical condition. The best we can suggest is that an autopsy will determine if indeed it is marks on her neck."

"But she might have been throttled?"

"Possibly," the SOCO shrugged then added, "There is one other thing you should know, Ma'am. While we were conducting our examination of the lounge, there was an incoming phone call to the landline in the hallway, but we didn't respond. We presumed that you'll be requesting a telephone billing check on the line."

The young woman could not know that the DI wanted to scream at her, why the *fuck* did you not think to answer the bloody phone, but Sandford kept her cool and her stomach clenching, instead, asked, "So, your conclusion?"

"The old lady was assaulted, Ma'am, and we believe in the hallway. From there we further believe she was forcibly taken backwards into the lounge where again, we believe she met her death. Needless to say the autopsy will determine the cause of her death but it is our findings that subject to any contradictory evidence, there is every indication the woman's death was not accidental, that her death likely resulted following a violent struggle. We'll provide you with statements in due course regarding our findings."

With a meaningful glance at the pale faced Inspector, Sandford slowly nodded and said, "So, murder it is then."

CHAPTER TWENTY-THREE

To the relief of the weekend holidaymakers upon Arran, Monday morning dawned brightly with just the hint of clouds.

Mary McKay was busying herself in Tommy Burke's kitchen and humming tunelessly to the radio when she heard the doorbell ring. Wiping her hands on her apron, she hurried to answer it and pulling it open smiled hesitantly at the three young woman who stood there, the taller of the three clutching the hand of a little girl as a local taxi pulled away from the drive.

"Good morning, can I help you…" she began and wiped her hands on her apron, but then stopped and her eyes opening wide in recognition, smiled and said, "Oh, you must be Tommy's daughter's. I'm pleased to meet you."

Surprised, it was Fiona who responded when she recalled her father had engaged the services of a housekeeper and replied, "That's us. Mary, isn't it? You're the lady our dad hired to look after the house?"

"Aye, that's right, dear. I'm Mary and Malky, my man, he's been hired to look after the gardens and do any wee jobs your dad wants done," she replied. Stepping to one side, she added, "Come away in."

As the young woman and Cissie stepped into the hallway, Mary continued to beam and said, "I should have recognised you from the photos Tommy has on the sideboard upstairs, especially you two girls," she flashed a glance at both Fiona and Jenny, "with your lovely red hair. Here, let me take your coats."

As they shrugged off their coats, Mary took them from the women and the little girl and hung them in the hall cupboard. Closing the door and turning she heard Cissie, who glanced around the brightly decorated hallway and asked, "Is my Granddad here?"

"Oh, he and Alice and the wee girl are out at the minute, dear," she cheerfully replied. "They're away looking for somewhere for her and Marcy to stay."

Mary didn't fail to notice the sharp glances between the women.

It was Jenny who asked, "Alice? And a wee girl?"

"Oh," Mary lifted a hand to her mouth, a blush creeping across her face and feared that perhaps she had said something that she shouldn't have.

Seeing the portly woman was not just embarrassed, but also lost for words, it was Fiona who tightly smiled and stepping forward, gently took the older woman by her arm and said, "We came over on the ferry as foot passengers to surprise dad, so a cup of tea would be nice, Mary. Perhaps then you can tell us who Alice and this wee girl Marcy are?"

****

The house was now a crime scene and the Family Liaison Officer explained to Brenda Chisholm that in the meantime she could not be permitted to remain in the house until such time it was deemed no longer to be of evidential value. That, and the officer gently continued, the lounge was cleaned of her grandmother's blood; work that would be undertaken by a specialist cleaning firm.

In the meantime, the police had arranged accommodation for the young woman in a local guesthouse with a sympathetic landlady and now, her appetite gone and having drunk just coffee, she had returned to her room, exhausted and shattered by the previous day and nights events.

Her parents were returning by road from their holiday visiting her sister, who was in her fourth year studying medieval art in Florence. It angered her that after breaking the news on the phone, her father had predictably been extremely upset though her mother, bitch that she could be, had sounded her usual phlegmatic self. Probably more concerned about cutting short her bloody holiday, Brenda unkindly assumed, for her mother had never really got on with her outspoken grandmother and Brenda knew that her parents' infrequent visits to Doris had been a source of argument between them for many years.

Likely, she thought, her mother's main interest would be to know what was in her grandmother's will and who would be left the house. She lay back on the bed, her mind refusing to dismiss the sight and the smell of her grandmother lying dead and she began to hyperventilate, but recognising the signs, forced herself to calm and slowly inhaled and exhaled into her cupped hands.

A few minutes later and with her breathing returning to normal, she remembered the police officer called Lucy had told Brenda that she would call at twelve noon to return her to the police station to go over her statement again. Glancing at her phone she saw she still had almost forty minutes before the detective came for her and rising from the bed, decided to shower.

****

Sober and after a good nights sleep, Geoffrey Mayhew was now supremely confident that the police had no inkling of his involvement in either the death of Doris Chisholm or his murder of Teddy Meiklewood. Checking his hip flask was full and the leather travel bag to confirm it contained enough clothing to serve him for the next few days, he took a final look around the house to ensure the doors were all secured and ignored the mess in the kitchen and the untidiness of the lounge. That was an issue he'd deal with when he returned and with a grin, considered he might employ a live-in maid to tend to it; preferably someone young and willing to tend to *all* his needs.

His final act in the house was to telephone the practice and explain to one of his junior partners that he was taking a couple of days off, that he had some personal issues that he needed to deal with, but would make himself available if he was needed. He had wisely decided there was no need to disclose he intended travelling anywhere, least of all to Arran and by inference let his partner assume he was staying at home.

Locking the front door, he made his way across to the Volvo and placed the bag in the boot.

In the driving seat, he switched on the engine and after glancing at the dashboard to ensure he had a full tank of diesel, set the Satnav's destination for Ardrossan Harbour.

His face turned grim for it was then he fully realised what he was about to set out to do.

He was on his way to hunt down his wife.

He was on his way to recover the drugs she had stolen and stop Alice from ever revealing what she knew, no matter what it took.

****

Peasy Byrne had set off early that morning and as he approached the border, with a weather eye on the road, reached down for the stainless steel mug of coffee.

Draining the last of the coffee he licked at his lips and replacing the mug in the holder, indicated to turn off the M74 into the Gretna Green service station for a toilet break.

****

Guessing she was slightly disheartened, Tommy followed the dejected Alice down the driveway to the gate as Marcy, looking back at the house, held her grandmother's hand and said, "We aren't going to live there, are we?"

"No, sweetheart, not at the rent the woman wants," Alice sighed.

Reaching the defender, Tommy pulled open the passenger and rear doors then helping Marcy climb in, ensured she was properly buckled into her seat before rounding the vehicle and getting into the driver's seat.

"I'm sorry about that," he shook his head. "It's a nice enough wee cottage, but the woman should have been wearing a mask, trying to rob you blind with that kind of rent."

"I don't suppose the rent is that steep, not for living on this lovely island," she replied.

"Aye, it's probably about average. Round here the landlords charge like the light infantry. I could phone the young lassie I dealt with who works at the estate agency. She gave me valuable assistance when I purchased my house. I could always ask if she's got any idea of where you might rent somewhere cheap. The problem is," he shook his head again, "you get what you pay for and let's face it, Alice. You've no job at the minute and no income. Can I ask," he turned to face her, "what money do you have right now?"

Perhaps from anyone else, she might have considered that to be an inappropriate question, but this was Tommy and so she had no hesitation in replying, "I started out with about three-hundred and eighty pounds, but the rail and ferry fares and food for Marcy on the way here cost me…" her eyes narrowed, "about fifty pounds."

"So, you've about three hundred and thirty quid left," he frowned. "Not a lot to do you until you get a job. Not unless…"

He didn't finish, but she guessed what was going through his mind and holding up her hands cut him short when she vigorously shook her head and brusquely said, "No, Tommy, there's no way I'm taking money from you. No way. You have been more than generous to Marcy and me."

He misinterpreted her anger, at first assuming it was directed at him. Alice, close to frustrated tears now and acutely conscious of Marcy in the back seat listening to everything that was said, bit at her lip and staring through the windscreen, slowly exhaled.

He quickly realised her anger was not after all directed at him, but at herself and waited till he thought she was calm.

He knew he had to make his proposal in such a manner that it would save her pride, so quietly told her, "No, Alice, you *don't* know what is going through my mind. What I'm thinking…" she turned towards him, her face pale and eyes bright with unshed tears, "…is that instead of looking for accommodation right now, you look for a job first; maybe submit that application for the part-time work at the Cooperative on Shore Road. In my experience, part-time work isn't really part-time. Employers advertise jobs like that then ask the part-timers to do extra work, so you could end up getting a full time wage."

He let his suggestion sink in for a few seconds before continuing, "In the meantime, I will rent you the room you're using. We can agree a price and when you're settled in your job, you can pay off the back rent at a rate that suits you. That will give you some leeway to find a place of your own and to be honest, I'm not short of a bob or two and I don't really need the rent money, but," he raised his palm towards her, "if it makes you feel better paying it, so be it."

He smiled and added, "It's no hardship for me to let you and Marcy stay in the house. While that's going on, we can try to get the wean into the local primary school. Besides, I probably won't be at the house all the time, so there are occasions when it will just be you and Marcy living there. How does that sound? Would you be interested in becoming my tenant?" he smiled again to try and coax her into agreeing.

She didn't trust herself to speak, but for the hundredth time wondered why this man was being so kind and generous.

Finally, she took a breath and at last, replied, "You will do that for us?"

"Of course I will. Why wouldn't I?" he pretended to be surprised by her question.

She couldn't help herself and at last the tears run down her cheeks. Biting at her lower lip she could only nod and embarrassed, turned her head away to stare through the passenger window.

Feeling unusually relieved, he glanced at Marcy in the rear-view mirror and catching her eye, winked and said, "How's about we head home and see if there's any hot chocolate in the cupboard? Then when we're settled, wee girl, we'll speak with Mary and find out what primary schools there are round about here."

****

DS Terry Goodwin, still half asleep, but pleased that his former partner Derek understood why he had to call off last nights dinner and who had surprised him by instead suggesting they meet meeting this evening. Maybe, he mused, there was still time to salvage their relationship. With that thought in mind, he knocked on DI Sandford's door before pushing it open.

"That's Lucy Carstairs arrived with the victim's granddaughter, Ma'am. Are you wanting a word before Lucy goes over the girls statement again?"

Sandford considered it for a few seconds, then shaking her head, replied, "No, Carstairs is more than competent to deal with the girl. If there's anything the granddaughter has neglected to tell us, she'll get it from her. The only thing I'll ask of Carstairs is that she makes sure the girl is all right, that she's being properly looked after. Oh, and try to find out when the parents are due to return home. I don't want to put that young woman through a formal identification. I believe she's suffered enough."

"Ma'am," he acknowledged with a nod, inwardly surprised at Sandford's concern for the young witness and was about to pull the door closed when he remembered and asked, "Any word yet from the Met Drug Squad?"

"Nothing so far. After I contacted them last night, their plan was to put the suspects doors in first thing this morning so likely if that's happened, they'll be tied up processing their prisoners. As soon as I hear anything, you'll get the nod."

He had gone but a moment when the door was knocked and pushed open by the uniformed Inspector who popping his head into the room, said, "Just to say, Julie, about that wee issue last night. Thanks again for being so understanding. Not only can I assure you that it will not occur again, but the constable concerned has been dealt with and will no longer be assigned street duties or any contact with the public. Short of cleaning the shithouse, his career is in the toilet."

She responded with a tight smile and slowly nodding, replied, "Fine, but not only will it remain between us, but you also owe me. Agreed?"

"Agreed," he closed the door and in the corridor, exhaled with relief.

Tapping the ash from her cigarette into the ashtray, she arched her back and rolled her head to ease the strain in her neck. She had jumped from one major inquiry into a second, but this time it was murder. Now, she picked at a piece of loose tobacco from her lower lip, who would want to murder a harmless old woman and why?

Ten minutes later, she made her way to the general office that now doubled as the murder incident room.

To one side a team of HOLMES operators worked steadily at their computers and she noted with a quiet smile a table in the corner had been stocked with tea, coffee and packets of biscuits.

Terry Godwin, designated by her as the office manager, called the inquiry team to order as Sandford took her place at the top of the room. Five feet ten inches tall, her jet black hair pinned up into a neat bun and dressed in a white blouse, navy pinstriped skirted suit and black patent high heels, the attractive Sandford looked more like a fashion model than a Detective Inspector about to conduct a murder briefing. Stood with her arms folded and her backside resting against a table, she glanced around the room and began.

"First, thank you all for staying late last night. I know it's not easy rubbing the grit from your eyes and dragging your sorry arses in here to hear me speak when you much rather would be elsewhere."

A titter went around the room, more so because it wasn't like the usually acerbic Sandford to attempt humour.

"Right, Doris Chisholm, aged sixty-eight, discovered yesterday by her granddaughter Brenda lying dead with a head injury in the lounge of her home in Middleton Road. No witnesses and no suspects at this time. The granddaughter is currently in an interview room going over her statement with DC Carstairs. The autopsy is to take place…" she turned to Goodwin, who said, "The coroner has agreed two this afternoon, Ma'am."

"Okay, two it is. I'll take you, DS Goodwin, and DC Carstairs with me."

She turned back to face the team and continued, "According to our colleagues in Scene of Crime, there is every indication that the victim has been dead for anything between twenty-four and thirty-six hours. It also seems she was involved in a struggle within the hallway of her home from where she was either dragged or pushed into the lounge where she was found dead. Given that information I am treating her death as murder and have so informed the Coroner who agrees with my assessment." She paused slightly then continued again. "Now, as for the locus. There was no evident sign of a break in so that suggests the victim let her killer into the house. Nothing either to suggest the house had been ransacked or anything stolen, though with the number of ornaments and bric-a-brac lying around, it was nigh near impossible to tell if anything of value has been stolen. Her handbag with her purse inside was in the kitchen, so robbery didn't seem to be the likely motive either. Aside from a tear in her blouse that we assume occurred during a struggle, her clothing seemed to be intact so it seems…" she stopped and raising her hand, continued, "Yes, I know, she was an old lady, but there are some horrible predators out there who don't give a damn about their victims age. However, like I said, apart from the tear in her blouse and with no evidence to the contrary, I'm ruling out any attempt sexual assault."

She paused again, her eyes probing for any questions or disagreement with her decision. When none were forthcoming, she started again.

"The SOC discovery that a struggle had occurred in the hallway seemed to suggest too that the killer was of sufficient strength to drag or at least manoeuvre the old woman into the lounge, for her build seems to indicate the victim was no lightweight. The absence of any attempt at theft or other reason places us at a loss for the motive of her murder. There has to be some reason the old woman was killed. So, ladies and gentlemen," her eyes travelled between the team, "suggestions, please."

A hand was raised by a middle-aged female detective who asked, "Family member, Ma'am?"

"According to her granddaughter, her only son and his wife, who she did not along with, were visiting her other granddaughter in Italy.

There are no known relatives other than those and of course, her granddaughter who discovered her body. Before you ask," she raised a hand, "I am of the opinion her granddaughter is not a suspect."

"Any feedback from the neighbours, Ma'am?" asked another detective.

"Nothing of value," she curtly replied, unable to prevent her upper lip curling and unwittingly giving her opinion of some of the uncaring neighbours who lived near Doris Chisholm.

"Any suggestion she might have been targeted, for say," the young female detective hesitated and pursed her lips, "some historical thing, Ma'am?"

Before Sandford could respond, the door at the back of the room was opened by Lucy Carstairs, who seemingly agitated, raised her eyebrows to catch Sandford's attention.

"Hang on folks," she waved a hand and made her way across the room to join Carstairs who had stepped back into the corridor.

"Ma'am," Carstairs held a brown coloured, hard backed A3 sized book in her hand that she held towards Sandford.

"It's the victim's diary, Ma'am, and I think you'll be very interested in what she wrote in the days prior to her death."

Sandford's eyes narrowed and she asked, "Where did you get it?"

"It was an exhibit, Ma'am, but nobody had the opportunity to read it last night. Brenda, I mean, the victim's granddaughter, she told me that her grandmother always kept a day to day record of what she was doing, so I left her in the interview room to go and collect this from the exhibit room. I went straight to her last entry and that's when I found…" she stopped and excitedly said, "Maybe you'd be better reading it yourself, Ma'am, to see what I mean."

"Summarise for me."

Carstairs could not prevent herself from smiling when she said, "The last entry gives quite an insight into our suspect, Geoffrey Mayhew. Maybe even enough of an insight to also suspect him of murder."

****

Because his daughters had travelled to the island as foot passengers, other than Mary McKay's battered old Ford Escort there was no other vehicle in the driveway to warn Tommy of what awaited him in the house.

Pushing open the door with Alice and Marcy trailing behind him, he was taking off his jacket and cheerfully called out, "Mary, that's us back, hen. I'm putting the kettle on. Do you want a cuppa?"

To his astonishment, Cissie burst through the kitchen door and running towards him, threw her arms around his waist, loudly crying out, "Granddad!"

He felt the little girl's grip on him loosen as she stared curiously behind him at the woman and the girl who stood in the doorway, just as his three daughters stepped out from the kitchen into the hallway.

"Hello, Dad," Vicky said and striding forwards, reached up to kiss him on the cheek.

"Sweetheart," he slowly replied, sensing the tension as the three young women stared in turn at Alice and Marcy.

In the kitchen Mary McKay remained standing by the sink and, cursing her big mouth, raised her eyes to the ceiling while wondering if it might be a good idea to slip out of the back door and phone Tommy later to find out if she still had a job.

"Eh, girls, this is Alice," he half turned towards her, "and Marcy, her granddaughter."

If he were to describe his daughter's temperaments, Tommy might have depicted Fiona as the most sceptical and cautious and the daughter most likely to openly speak her mind. His second daughter Vicky he considered to be the most thoughtful and appraising while of the three, Jenny was undoubtedly the most open-hearted.

So, it did not unduly surprise him when Jenny broke the tension with a smile and greeted Alice with, "Hi there. I'm Jennifer, but I'm usually just Jenny. And you must be Marcy," she approached the little girl, her body bending to Marcy's level, but who shyly tried to hide behind her grandmother."

Thinking, this is bloody awkward, Tommy adopted a wide smile and hands out wide as though to usher them all through, called out, "Like I said, the kettle's going on, so why don't we all move into the kitchen eh?"

Wordlessly, Fiona and Vicky turned about to return to the kitchen, however, to her surprise, Alice found Jenny linking her arm through hers as she brazenly asked, "So tell me, Alice, how did you and Pops meet then?"

Mary had not fled the house after all, but was at the sink, filling the kettle and then trying to avoid catching Tommy's eye, busied herself setting out clean mugs.

While Fiona and Vicky settled themselves on one side of the table, Tommy sat at the head as Jenny almost pulled Alice down to sit beside her.

"Shall I put out biscuits, Tommy?" Mary broke the silence that had settled in the room.

Turning towards her, his face away from his daughters, he grimaced and replied, "No, hen, tea will be fine, then if you want to get away early?" he suggested with a wink.

Taking the hint, she said, "Aye, if you don't mind and I'll see you Wednesday, eh?"

"Aye, of course," he said but unknowingly, to her relief.

After setting the teapot down onto a mat on the table by the milk and sugar, she bid everyone cheerio and left the house by the back door. It was just as she'd left that Alice noticed Marcy had not followed them into the kitchen. She was about to rise from her chair to go and look for the little girl when both she and Cissie, hand in hand, walked through the door.

"Mum," Cissie began, "is it okay if Marcy shows me the house? She says there's a telescope and we will be able to see right across to the mainland."

"Dad?" Fiona turned towards him.

"Of course," he smiled at the little girls who turned and run off giggling.

"So," Jenny asked again, "how did you and Pops meet?"

Alice, pale faced, turned beseechingly to Tommy, who replied, "It's a bit of a funny story about an old suitcase and some luggage straps, so let's pour the tea before we begin."

But to his surprise when he reached for the teapot it was Alice who took up the story.

Hesitant at the beginning, her voice grew stronger as during the following twenty minutes and without interruption, she told the young women of fleeing with her granddaughter Marcy from an abusive marriage, but not of her suspicions about her husband's illegal drugs; of their father's kindness while travelling on the ferry, of her initial mistrust of him when almost distraught, wet and miserable, she and Marcy were unable to find shelter that first night. As her story unfolded, her face softened and she darted a glance at Tommy when she described his kindness and support and finally, of his offer that morning of accommodation while she sought work on the island.

"And so there you are," she smiled at his daughters in turn. "My story and," she raised a hand, "I fully understand your concern that you might suspect me to be the kind of woman who would take advantage of your father's good nature and generosity. I cannot prove to you that my story is genuine nor would I try, but believe me if you will, I will never," she shook her head, "do anything to hurt Tommy and if that means Marcy and I leave this very minute," she paused, "we will."

The silence that followed this statement was surprisingly broken when Fiona turned to her father and said, "I never said to the girls, but I phoned uncle Peasy early this morning to tell him that we were coming across to the island, but he said he was on his way to England to do a wee favour for a friend of yours. Said that if we did come across we might get a bit of a surprise, but wouldn't tell me what the surprise was."

She glanced at Alice and added, "I'm guessing you must be the surprise."

Turning back to Tommy she continued, "There's something else going on, isn't there?"

He glanced at Alice, his eyebrows questioningly raised.

She swallowed and slowly nodded, then said, "My husband is a doctor, the senior GP in a local Preston practice. He's also the Chairman of the local rugby club and always had this driving ambition to be the best." She stopped, her eyes flickering, uncertain how much she should reveal, but then decided no more lies or deceit; these young women who had every right to distrust her deserved the truth, if only for Tommy's sake, and so she told them everything.

"You uncle Peasy offered to travel to Preston to ensure that my good friend Doris is all right, but we haven't heard anything from him yet."

Tommy glanced at the wall clock and interrupted with, "Early days yet. He might still be arriving and booking in."

"And you think your husband might have, I don't know," Vicky shrugged, "harmed your friend?"

Alice paled and bit at her lower before taking a breath and unable to speak, nodded.

"Bastard!" Vicky muttered then turned to Tommy and sheepishly said, "Sorry, dad."

"Well, that's quite a story, Alice," Vicky exhaled, then turning to Fiona said, "I can't imagine that Alice brought enough clothing for both her and Marcy in her suitcase," she stared meaningfully at her sister, "so why don't the three of us take a turn down into the Shore Road with her and get what she needs. Maybe some lunch too."

Before Fiona could respond, Vicky turned to Tommy and added, "You don't mind watching the girls for an hour or so, do you Dad?" He knew what was going through Vicky's head; the girls wanted some time alone with Alice, but he could hardly refuse such an innocently put suggestion. Simply nodding, he could not avoid his eyes narrowing in suspicion.

"That's settled then," she cheerfully smiled. "Right, let's finish our tea, ladies, have a look around the house and then go shopping."

****

Peasy Byrne thanked the helpful receptionist and made his way out the front door of the Holiday Inn to his car. The young woman had said that Middleton Road was a mere fifteen minutes driving and her written directions seemed relatively straight forward.

Approaching his destination, he could see the busy M6 in the distance and finally turned into the small, private housing estate. Parking in an empty bay by some modern flats he checked the hand drawn map and made his way on foot to Middleton Road, but stopped when he saw a uniformed constable stood outside a door in a block of mid-terraced houses. He hesitated, uncertain whether or not to approach the officer, but decided that to do so would necessitate him explaining his reason for being there.

A middle-aged man carrying a plastic shopping bag in each hand slowly approached Byrne from the rear and stopping beside him, stared towards the police officer and said, "Bad business, isn't it?"

"I'm sorry?"

"The murder." He nodded towards the constable. "Bad business," he said again and shook his head. "Can't even feel safe in your own home these days. Probably one of these bloody foreigners the Government insist in allowing into the country."

"Did you know the victim?" Byrne asked, keen to keep the man talking.

"Missus Chisholm? Well," the man shrugged. "Knew her to see."

He stated keenly at Byrne before asking, "You're not from around here, are you?"

No shit, Sherlock, what gave me away, thought Byrne, but instead replied, "No, I'm down from Scotland visiting a cousin. Thought I'd take a look at the area."

"Oh, I thought you might be one of those reporters that was hanging around yesterday. Kept knocking on our doors looking for information on poor old Doris. Rum lot, if you ask me," he sniffed.

"That was the victim's name then? Doris Chisholm?" Byrne felt his stomach tighten.

"Yes, sadly, that was her. Well, must get on," he jovially nodded and continued walking.

Byrne watched the man enter a nearby house and turning, made his way back to the car. He knew there was little point in hanging around the area and nothing to be gained. He had learned that Doris Chisholm had been murdered and decided not to phone Tommy and Alice with the bad news, but instead would first try and track down the second name on his list, DC Lucy Carstairs.

Touching the small cardboard packets in his jacket pocket as though to reassure himself he had not lost them, he realised now the detective needed to know what Alice had told him.

****

Geoffrey kept the Volvo at a steady seventy miles per hour and glancing at the signpost, saw he was now approaching the Gretna Green service station and decided to pull in for a coffee and toilet break. According to the SatNav he had just over two hours of travelling till he arrived at Ardrossan Harbour.

CHAPTER TWENTY-FOUR

Seated at her desk, she nodded that Lucy Carstairs sit in the chair opposite while she read through the murdered woman's diary. At the last sentence, she sighed and closing the diary, said, "I appreciate what your thoughts are, DC Chisholm, but even you must realise that while the victim recorded what she was told by Mayhew's wife, it is third party information and while I admit if it *is* true, he sounds a right bastard, but does not conclusively indicate that he murdered the old woman."

"No, Ma'am, I agree," Carstairs replied, her excitement dulled by Sandford's common sense and strict interpretation of the written account. "But as you say, if it *is* true, doesn't that at least give us the opportunity to bring Mayhew into the office and interview him? Put it to him that the entry in the diary is probable cause for him killing her?"

"Did have you consider that the fact the diary was not taken from the house seems to suggest that Mayhew is unaware of its content. However, if he had known his wife was relating the circumstances of this alleged violent relationship to the victim and she in turn was writing it down, he'd not have left the house without it?"

Deflated, Carstairs replied, "No, Ma'am, sorry."

"Don't be sorry, DC Carstairs," Sandford slowly shook her head. "I'm not annoyed at you and to be frank, if anything, you've given us the only lead that we have in this bloody case and while I remember; have you had any success in tracing Missus Mayhew?"

"No, Ma'am, not yet."

The door was knocked and a uniformed officer carrying a white coloured envelope in her hand, stuck her head in to say, "Sorry to disturb you, Ma'am, but this was just delivered from the telephone company," and placed the envelope on the DI's desk before closing the door behind her.

Sandford lifted the envelope and placed it in her in-file tray, then said, "Right, where were we? Missus Mayhew. IF I recall correctly, you were not aware of her relationship with anyone and certainly not the victim?"

"That's correct, Ma'am," Carstairs nodded. "Alice didn't mention anyone that she was friendly with. In fact, I got the impression she had no friends at all, that her husband strictly controlled her social life."

"Hmm," her eyes narrowed in thought. "Right, here's what I want you to do. Speak with DS Goodwin and have him allocate you an Action to attend at Mayhew's house. You are there to bring Missus Mayhew in for a formal interview regarding her relationship with the victim. If our information about him is correct, he will bluster and try to bully you into disclosing to him why she is to be interviewed, but he must *not* know. Is that clear?"

"Yes, Ma'am."

"However, if she is still not at home, require her husband to inform you of her whereabouts. If he tells you he doesn't know where she is, find out when was the last time he saw or had any contact with her. If he cannot provide that information, ask if he wishes to report her as a missing person."

"And if he does?"

"Take the information and submit it to the PNC. That will give us the lawful authority to search for her as potential witness in the murder investigation."

"If she is there and I bring her in, Ma'am, do you wish to interview her yourself?"

"No, you can conduct the interview, but I will sit in on it." Her eyes narrowed when she continued, "I'm not certain about letting you go unaccompanied to the house," Sandford mused, "but if you are alone, it might not seem so suspicious to Mayhew. Are you okay about attending the house alone?"

"Yes, Ma'am, I don't have a problem with that."

"Right then," Sandford nodded, "off you go and keep me apprised of how you get on."

"Ma'am," Carstairs nodded and left the room.

When the door closed behind Carstairs, Sandford reached for her cigarettes and reopening the diary, begin to read again Doris Chisholm's graphic account of Alice Mayhew's life with her husband. As she read, a cold chill swept through Sandford, recalling her own childhood and the abusive white father who daily tormented and bullied her Jamaican mother; his conduct so reprehensible it led to Sandford's decision that she would never be placed in that kind of relationship with any man, white or black. Her thoughts led to the memory of her school years and being a child of a mixed race marriage, the taunts and abuse she received from her fellow pupils. Yes, she was the first to admit, it had hardened her and the few relationships she had in her adult life had usually fell apart because of her suspicion of men.

Throughout her service she had avoided any personal friendship, ignored the hesitant smiles of the women and the leering glances of the men. Good-looking and shapely, Sandford wasn't unaware of her sexual attraction and on dozens of occasions fobbed off and even on two occasions, fought off attempts to inveigle her into a relationship.

Her attitude was if she avoided men and the occasional woman attracted to her, she would not find herself hurt.

And it's no wonder they call me the Ice Queen, she permitted herself a smile at her office nickname and unusually, decided not to have a fag.

Idly, she opened the white envelope in her in-tray and cast a glance at the list of phone numbers, but her attention was focused on the last eight calls from only two phone numbers and included the call the SOCO heard during the examination of the house.

She stared curiously at the two distinct numbers and pulling a copy of Brenda Chisholm's statement from the file on her desk, read that one of the calling numbers belonged to the young woman's mobile phone. However, the other number seemed to be a landline and using her desktop computer, Googled the STD code then wondered; who the hell was calling from an Arran phone number?

With the list in her hand, she was about to rise and return to the incident room when her desk phone rung.

"DI Sandford," she snapped.

"Ma'am, it's Jim at the front office. I've a Scottish man here looking to speak with DC Carstairs. I'm told she's with you?"

"No, she's just left on an inquiry, tell him to…" her brow furrowed and she glanced at the computer screen that continued to display the Arran STD code. "No, wait. You said he's Scottish. What's he want with Carstairs?"

She listened and heard Jim asking what the man wanted, then to Sandford, said, "He says he has some information that might be of use about the murder in Middleton Road, Ma'am."

"Does he now? Right, bring him up to my office, if you please."
****

In the hallway at the front door of the house, Vicky asked, "Are we walking down to the town? I don't mind, but remember I'm still not that fit after having wee Fergus pulled from me and while walking downhill won't kill me, the thought of walking back up might."

"If your father doesn't mind," Alice said, "I can drive the Defender down and save you having to walk back up the hill."

"He let's you drive that old thing? My, you must be well trusted," she grinned. "Anyway, that suits me fine," Jenny quickly interjected and grabbing the keys from the hall stand that she passed to Alice, then called back into the house, "Pops, we're taking your big motor. See you in about an hour or two."

Minutes later, Fiona in the front passenger seat and her sisters settled in the rear seats, Alice nosed the large vehicle out of the driveway and slowly headed downhill towards Brodick's Shore Road.

She was in no doubt why the girls wanted her alone and away from Tommy. They wanted to find out more about her and her intention towards their father. But as she drove she thought, what more can I tell them?

I do like Tommy, she inwardly admitted; really like him and no man has ever been as kind to me as he has. Yet how can I persuade these young women I have no intention of using him or hurting him; none at all.

It was Jenny in the back who opened the conversation with, "I see you're wearing one of Pop's old jackets, Alice, and trainers on your feet. I think our first stop will be the Arran Active shop on the sea front where we'll get you some proper footwear and a jacket. No offence, but you look like you've popped over here from one of the lower class housing schemes in dear old Glasgow."

Blushing, Alice was about to retort, but taking a breath, brought the vehicle to a halt and applying the handbrake, then turned and tightly replied, "Thank you, Jenny, but I'm afraid your father's jacket and my trainers will need to do for now. I'm working to a very tight budget and right at this time, clothes are really the last thing on my mind."

There was an awkward silence, but then to Alice's surprise, it was Fiona who gently resting her hand on Alice's arm, said, "Please don't be offended. Jenny just went about it the wrong way. It's obvious to the three of us," she cast a reproving glance towards Jenny in the rear seat, "that things have been difficult for you for a very long time. It doesn't really surprise us that our dad is keen to help you. He's been like that all his life, helping others. Yes," she sighed, "I admit we're very protective of him, but more importantly, we support him and try to look out for him and have done since…well, you know, since our mum died. Asking you out with us isn't some kind of plot to get you on your own, Alice. We don't need to know how tight things are, but I suppose you could think of this as just our way of saying hello. The shoes and jacket are on us and we'd be very disappointed if you refused. Besides," she smiled, "if you're letting us take you to lunch, we want you to look the part. I mean," she sat back in her seat and extending her arms as far as the interior of the car would permit, joked, "we want the four of us to look fabulous, don't we?"

Alice glanced at the two young women in the back then at Fiona and lips trembling, smiled with relief as she fought the wave of emotion that threatened to engulf her.

It was then that Vicky, hoping to lighten the atmosphere, said, "Right, now we've got that settled, I'm of the opinion that with Alice's auburn hair, a nice bright yellow colour would suit her. Who agrees?"

****

The SatNav directed Geoffrey from the M74 onto the M77 and called out that he would arrive at his destination in forty-six minutes.

****

Back at the house, Tommy tried to be cheerful and when the two girls asked if they could go and play out in the garden, he sighed with relief and agreed.

However, as he watched them run around giggling, he wondered what was going on in the Defender and hoped that his daughters were not being unkind.

Turning on the radio in the kitchen, he was making himself a coffee when the hourly news opened with the report that an Atlantic storm was approaching the West of Scotland.

****

The first thing she noticed was that the white coloured Volvo was not in the driveway, though the old Toyota sat forlornly to one side with its front nearside tyre seemingly losing air and on its way to becoming flat.

Still seated in her car, she glanced at the house and suspected with the Volvo gone, so was Doctor Mayhew. However, before she went about tracing him to his practice, she still needed to check he wasn't at home and marching up to the door, pressed the doorbell then when there was no response, rapped her knuckles on the door. Again there was no response, but before she left decided to take a look around the back of the house.

Maybe it was her vivid imagination, maybe it was some fear in the back of her mind, she just didn't know; but grinning at her silliness, mentally kept her fingers crossed that she didn't stumble across Alice Mayhew's body in a newly dug grave.

Pushing open the unlocked six-foot wooden gate she saw a paved path that led to the rear of the house.

Licking at her dry lips, she called out, "Hello?" in the faint chance that there was someone in the house who hadn't heard her at the front door.

For such a beautiful house the back garden was not as she expected. The grassed lawn was simply that; grass and overgrown, too. No flower beds, no children's toys, no garden furniture, no potted plants; nothing that indicated a family enjoyed the garden area. Making her way to the patio door, she rapped her knuckles loudly upon the double glazing, but as she expected, there was no response. In the vain hope they might be unlocked, she tried the patio door handles then the rear door handle, but without any luck. She was about to walk off when her attention was drawn to the black bin bag lying at her feet. Idly she kicked at it then lifting it, hoped with a grin it didn't contain body parts. Having gone that far, with a nervous glance about her she untied the yellow string.

Her brow furrowed when she saw the bag contained clothing and a pair of shoes and was about to dismiss her find when she stopped. Sniffing at the inside of the bag she was certain she could detect a strong soap smell and wondered why someone would first wash clothing they intended to discard.

Still holding the bag, her face paled and she involuntarily dropped it back to the paved slab.

Fumbling in her coat pocket, she brought out her mobile phone and licking at her dry lips, pressed the number for Terry Goodwin.

When he answered her call, she gasped, "Terry, it's me. I think I might have discovered something. Can you send me a Scene of Crime team to the Mayhew's house in Spruce Close?"

****

Peasy Byrne was shown into the room where he saw a glamorous woman wearing a pinstriped suit sat behind the desk.

Now, he wondered, why didn't I think that DI Sandford might be a woman and struck by her good looks, had to check himself from staring.

Sandford's eyes opened a fraction wider when she saw the clean shaven, six-foot-tall, strong looking Byrne enter her office and though he was not formally dressed, saw him to be wearing a plaid shirt, cargo pants over polished black walking shoes and a very expensive black coloured hiking jacket. Not handsome in a Brad Pitt way, she decided, but certainly there was something about him.

"I understand you might have some information for DC Carstairs, Mister, eh…?" she opened the conversation.

"Byrne," he softly replied. "Charlie Byrne, but most people call me Peasy," he smiled and with his eyebrows raised, nodded towards the chair in front of her desk.

"Yes, please, take a seat," she said, then continued, "My name's DI Julie Sandford, Mister Byrne. I'm what's known as the SIO, the Senior Investigating Officer in the murder investigation. Did you know the victim, Doris Chisholm?"

"No," he slowly shook his head, "I didn't. I was asked to travel down from Scotland to inquire if she was all right, but when I went to the house in Middleton Road this morning, I saw one of your constables stood at the door and learned of her murder from a passing neighbour."

"So, you're not a local man then, Mister Byrne?"

"Peasy," he reminded her. "No, I live just outside Motherwell." He could see that it meant nothing to her and added, "About twelve miles from Glasgow city centre."

"Ah, yes. I'm sorry, but I've never been to Scotland and so I'm not familiar with the topography of your country. So, two questions…Mister Byrne," she half smiled. "Who asked you to make the inquiry and what is this individuals interest in Doris Chisholm?"

"I was asked to come down to Preston by Alice Mayhew and Doris Chisholm is…" he corrected himself, "was her friend."

It didn't escape his notice that the mention of Alice's name caused the DI's eyes to widen just a little.

"And is Missus Mayhew well?"

"She certainly was yesterday."

"And can you tell me what her current location is?"

There seemed little point in not disclosing it and he knew better than most it wasn't wise to piss off the SIO in a murder inquiry, so replied, "She's currently staying with my friend, a man called Tommy Burke, on the island of Arran."

"Arran," she repeated, then glancing at her computer screen, asked, "Do you happen to know the phone number of the place where

Missus Mayhew is currently staying?"

"It's a new landline number," he reached into a pocket of his jacket to retrieve his mobile phone and watched as she lifted a sheet of paper from the desk. Scrolling down his directory, he read out Tommy Burke's house number and saw Sandford nodding.

"That number was recorded on the victim's phone during the time our Scene of Crime examination was being conducted and during the course of yesterday, about half a dozen time thereafter."

"That will be correct," he replied. "I'm aware that Missus Mayhew…Alice…made several attempts to contact her friend. When she couldn't get a reply, like I told you, I agreed to travel down to establish if Missus Chisholm was okay."

"And you discovered she had been murdered."

"Yes."

"That was very good of you, offering to come down all this way to Preston. If Missus Mayhew thought her friend might have come to harm, why didn't she contact the police?"

"And tell them what, Miss Sandford? That she suspected someone might have hurt her friend?"

"DI Sandford. And do you have a name for that someone?"

Peasy leaned forward and locking his eyes onto hers, slowly smiled before replying, "I have, but I suspect you have too, Miss Sandford."

She couldn't explain why, but this man made her feel uncomfortable. Not physically threatened, just…strangely uncomfortable. That and she had the queerest feeling she was enjoying their verbal sparring match.

"DI Sandford," she repeated once more in an attempt to formalise the discussion, then staring at his eyes, his very blue eyes she couldn't help but notice, said, "Yes. We might have the name of someone of interest."

The door knocked and was pushed open by Terry Goodwin who seeing Sandford had a visitor, apologised with, "Sorry, Ma'am, but I need to speak with you."

She stared at Byrne then said, "Excuse me," before joining Goodwin in the corridor.

Before he could speak, she took a breath as though to clear her head then asked, "What?"

In a quick-fire burst, he told her of Lucy Carstairs visit to the Mayhew home where the Volvo was gone and no sign of either

Geoffrey or Alice Mayhew, of the discovery by Carstairs of a black bin bag with clothing that had been washed yet seemed destined for the bin and of Carstairs request for a SOCO team that was now en route to the house.

"And I'm surmising she thinks this clothing and the shoes might have been washed to perhaps what, remove blood?"

"Yes, Ma'am. Says the bag stinks of washing-up powder and the clothes and the shoes seem to be good quality and like you say, thinks the items have been washed to remove evidence prior to being dumped."

"She's obviously also thinking about the doctor's apparent relationship with Meiklewood and I know she's got a bee in her bonnet about Mayhew," Sandford's brow furrowed. "However, our Lucy just might be on to something," she mused.

Hesitating for just a heartbeat, she instructed Goodwin to crave a search warrant for the house with the supposition that there might be evidence of Teddy Meiklewood's murder within the property.

"Ma'am," he acknowledged with a nod and turned away.

She hesitated before re-entering her office, curiously realising she was enjoying the visit from the tall and polite Scotsman.

Resuming her seat, she inhaled and said, "I apologise for that. Now, Missus Mayhew. Why did she ask you to come down to Preston, when she could have travelled here herself?"

"Alice is in Arran with her granddaughter, Marcy, because she's fled from her abusive husband, Doctor Geoffrey Mayhew."

He saw her eyes flicker again and though it was hardly enough to notice, he'd been a detective for a long time and recognised the sign, so said, "But you already know that, don't you, Miss Sandford?"

Caught unaware at his intuitive insight, she half smiled and asked, "And I ask again…Mister Byrne. Why are you here and not Missus Mayhew?"

He slowly smiled and replied, "Missus Mayhew is currently being sheltered by a good friend of mine, the man I mentioned, Tommy Burke." He exhaled and continued, "I have to admit to some initial reservation about her and some scepticism about why she was on the island, but having spoken to her at at length, I'm convinced she told me the truth. Besides," he decided to come clean and stared at Sandford, "I have some experience in this sort of thing."

She caught on immediately and nodding, said, "You're either serving or ex-job?"

"Thirty years with Strathclyde Police," he pursed his lips. "Twenty-two as a detective. I retired a few years back as a DS. Now I'm happily living alone with wee Chic, my Westie dog," he grinned roguishly at her, "so it was no problem for me to come down here as a favour to both her and my friend, Tommy."

The admission didn't surprise her as she thought and in fact, brought her some relief that he wasn't some amateur detective trying to impress her. And why am I pleased to hear he's single too, she wondered and unaccountably found herself blushing.

"What's Missus Mayhew's relationship with your friend, Mister Burke?"

He didn't immediately respond, but then smiling, replied, "How would I describe Tommy? In short, he's one of the most straight forward men I have had the pleasure of knowing and attracts helpless souls like a moth to a bright light. Before Missus Mayhew fled to Arran, she had not met Tommy, but being the kind man he is, he saw her on the ferry across to the island then realising later that she and her granddaughter needed help," he opened his hands wide and grinning, added, "and so he helped her."

She said, "We're trying to trace Doctor Mayhew to interview him. Do you have any idea where he might be?"

"None," Byrne shook his head, then added, "But before we go on, there's something you might be interested in."

From his jacket pocket he fetched out the cardboard packets of Brown Speeders that after carefully taking them from Alice, had prudently placed it into a zipped plastic food bag.

Leaning forward to lay them on her desk, he fetched his notebook from an inside pocket of his jacket and said, "Let me relate what Alice Mayhew told me about these."

TWENTY-FIVE

He arrived at the Ardrossan Harbour and parking his Volvo in a bay outside the booking office, stepped from the vehicle to stretch his aching muscles. A covered walkway led from the road towards the main entrance and ensuring his wallet was in the inside pocket of his jacket, began to make his way across to the front doors.

That's when he noticed the member of staff carrying a handful of black bin bags towards a large, green coloured wheeled bin and stopping, muttered, "Shit!"

He'd forgotten to dispose of the black bin bag from the rear door, but knowing that nobody had any reason to visit the back of the house almost immediately dismissed his forgetfulness from his mind.

The reception and waiting area was brightly lit due to the wall of glass windows and smiling at the young woman behind the counter, Geoffrey inquired about booking his vehicle onto the next afternoon sailing.

"Will that be a day return, sir?"

He hadn't considered that his search for Alice would take much longer than a few hours and had thought, how hard would it be to search a small island like Arran?

Better be safe than sorry, he decided and booked a sailing for that day with a return the following day. It shouldn't be too hard to find overnight accommodation, he thought.

"You have thirty-five minutes till the ferry arrives and then departs, Mister Mayhew," she smiled as she issued his return ticket. "If you drive your car to the gate and give the gateman the ticket," she pointed out the door, "you can join the queue waiting to embark. If you need tea or coffee, there's a wee stall just around the corner in the waiting area."

Brusquely acknowledging her help, he bought himself a coffee and returning to his vehicle, drove to the boarding gate and joining the queue of vehicles, settled down to wait.

****

Alice Mayhew sat at the square, wooden table in The Brodick Bar and Brasserie with Fiona seated opposite, Vicky on her left and Jenny occupying the chair against the wall on her right. The remains of their lunch lay before them.

She was surprised to find that her nervousness had completely gone and that Tommy's daughter's had seemingly accepted that she was not as they had at first suspected, a threat to their father. To her embarrassment, the young women had been as good as their word and ignoring her protests, insisted on purchasing a number of items that included the bright yellow coloured and the warmer waterproof hiking jacket that now rested on the chair behind her as well as the new walking boots on her feet.

"After all," Fiona had used her elbow to nudge at her sisters, "it's not as though we're short of a bob or two and what our husband's don't know, we won't lie about."

"Besides," Jenny had continued as she stared at Alice, "it's good to see Pops taking an interest in something, even better because it's a woman!"

To Alice's continuing embarrassment, the comment not only made her blush but caused Jenny's sister's to burst into good natured laughter.

Seeing her discomfort, Vicky explained, "You have to understand, Alice, our mum died over four years ago and dad, well, he's been lonely for a long time now…"

"Even though over the last couple of years we've been trying to steer him towards an affair…" Jenny giggled.

"But not that we're suggesting you're the affair," Fiona choked back a laugh, then continued, "It's just that after he sold his business, it made dad quite a wealthy man and me and the girls," she turned to nod at her sisters, "we've been kind of keeping an eye on him; making sure that nobody takes advantage of him."

The last few weeks had seen Alice develop an inner strength she never realised she had and now her face flushed not with embarrassment, but annoyance as she crossly replied, "As I said I would never…"

However, she was stopped from continuing when Fiona reached across the table to gently grab at her hands and interrupted with, "We know that now." She smiled and with a grimace added, "But we had to make sure, you understand?"

Alice visibly relaxed and calmer now, returned her smile with a nod. A short awkward silence fell upon the table, but then Vicky asked, "Tell us about your wee granddaughter Marcy. She looks lovely. Are her parents not wondering where she is?"

Alice stared at the young woman, realising that in her brief account of why she and Marcy had fled from Geoffrey, she had omitted to disclose the death of her daughter Gemma and son-in-law Peter. Minutes later, her story concluded, she was surprised to see that Fiona was pale faced while both Vicky and Jenny were close to tears.

"I'm so sorry," she began and sighed. "It wasn't my intention to upset you."

To her surprise, her hands were grasped tightly on either side by the two young women while Fiona, unaccountably angry at a situation that was not of her making and the most inherent of her mother's fiery Lewis temper, stammered, "Bollocks to coffee. We can leave dad's big motor here for the night," then turning to the young man behind the bar, loudly called out, "Hello there, can we have four glasses and a couple of bottles of red over here, please?"
****

On her way back to the office, DC Lucy Carstairs could hardly contain her excitement. Not only had she discovered the bag of clothing at the rear of the Mayhew's house, but driving from there to his practice, she learned form her phone call that earlier that morning Geoffrey Mayhew contacted to inform his partner he was taking time off for some personal issues and though had not actually told his fellow doctor, implied it was Mayhew's intention to remain at home. If that was the case, then she was certain the DI would authorise a team to standby the Spruce Close house to await his return and fervently hoped she would be one of the team.

Arriving at the office she made her way to the incident room to discover a cheerful hive of activity.

"What's going on?" she asked Terry Godwin.

He grinned and replied, "We've just had news from the Met Drug Squad's Detective Chief Inspector. This morning, they put in the doors of the addresses we gave them for the cache of Brown Speeders and the suppliers. They've recovered what they said is a significant amount of the drug and arrested eight individuals he believes to be concerned in the supply and distribution of the Speeders. According to the DCI, one of the main players has already been asking about turning Queens Evidence. In short, it's a bloody good catch, Lucy," he grabbed her by the arms and to her surprise, whirled her around.

Caught up in his enthusiasm, she grinned, but then when he'd stopped she asked, "Any news about the search warrant for Mayhew's house?"

"Being craved as we speak," he continued to grin. "Oh, and one more thing. Your missing woman, Alice Mayhew. The DI has just informed us that she's alive and well and on some island up in

Jockland with her grandchild."

"Jockland? Oh, Scotland," she pretended to scowl at his poor humour. "What the hell is she doing up there?"

"Apparently she got on her toes to get away from your number one suspect, Geoffrey Mayhew. The DI is in her office at the minute, speaking to some Scotch guy who came down here at Missus Mayhew's request to check on her friend, Doris Chisholm." Carstairs wasn't taking it all in, though there was a number of questions she wanted to ask.

That and she believed the teams main objective should now be finding the whereabouts of Geoffrey Mayhew.

"And before you ask, we can't get a team to watch the house," Goodwin shook his head with a petted lip. "The DCI from the Force's Major Investigation Team has persuaded the Area Commander to turn over the surveillance guys to assist him with his murder inquiry." He leaned in close to add, "I heard a whisper that the AC and the DCI are golfing buddies, so guess who's getting the priority there?"

Her brow furrowed and she asked, "But doesn't the AC know that we now have a suspect for the murder of Meiklewood? Geoffrey Mayhew?"

"Politics, my dear Lucy," Goodwin tapped the side of his nose. "Our DI is keeping that little titbit under her tight little bun for now. Following your discovery in the dead woman's diary and what you found today in the plastic bin bag, and," his brow furrowed, "though I don't want us to get overly optimistic, if fingers crossed it proves to be evidence of Mayhew's culpability in the Meiklewood murder…"

"And Doris Chisholm's too," Carstairs interjected.

"And fingers crossed again, Chisholm's too," he agreed with a nod, though inwardly thought that might be stretching their luck, "then it will be major kudos for us and a slap in the kisser for the AC. Teach the bastard to steal our murder inquiry," he bitterly added.

She shook her head. It didn't make sense to her. After all, weren't they all supposed to be on the same side, working together towards giving the bad guys the jail?

A thought struck her and she asked, "What if Mayhew doesn't return home tonight? What
happens then?"

"Well," he shrugged, "as we both know, a lot will depend on the result of the Forensic test on the items you found in the bin bag. If they prove negative for any evidence of Meiklewood's blood or DNA, quite frankly we're back at square one. If as we hope, however, they prove conclusive for Meiklewood's blood or DNA then we're seriously looking at Mayhew for murder and it will be all hands to the pump to find him."

"Have we made any start on that? I mean, we have his vehicle's registration number. Can't we at least issue a lookout and try to trace him for interview?"

He stared at her and slowly shaking his head, said, "Interview him about what? Yes, he's been a right bad bastard to his wife and likely a domestic abuser too, but like the DI said, what we know is third party information. Missus Mayhew hasn't made any complaint about being assaulted by him and all we have is the written record of a murder victim; a record that if had been in her house and known about, he would have destroyed. No matter what you or I suspect, Lucy, there is no direct evidence at this time that he's murdered anyone," he raised his hands, palms down as though to calm her. "No, we wait for the result of the Forensic test."

The door behind him opened to admit Julie Sandford who was closely followed by Peasy Byrne.

She didn't bother introducing him, but stepping to the top of the room called for the attention of the team and holding up the zipped food bag containing the cardboard packets of Brown Speeders for all to see, began, "I've just received information from Mister Byrne here that Alice Mayhew took these from her husband's medical bag. They haven't been tested, but I'm certain they are Brown Speeders. DS Goodwin," she sought him out in the crowd, "please raise an Action for someone to contact Police Scotland and request they have Missus Mayhew formally interviewed at her current location. Mister Byrne here," she turned to Peasy, "will provide you with her current address on the island of Arran."

The mention of the island had more than a few heads turning and eyebrows raised in surprise.

"Now, while most of you are probably aware, earlier this afternoon DC Carstairs discovered a black bin bag at the rear of Mayhew's home that is currently being examined to test if the clothing discovered in the bag has any residual blood or DNA on it. While we await the result of the Forensic examination for the clothing and from the information received from Alice Mayhew via Mister Byrne, I am issuing an alert to detain Geoffrey Mayhew as a suspect for possession of and possible distribution of an illegal substance, the Brown Speeders."

She paused to permit the muttered comments to abate, then her eyes settling on Lucy Carstairs, she directly addressed her with, "Lucy, well done today," and gave her a wide grin.

Taken aback, Carstairs returned Sandford's grin with her own smile and turning to Goodwin, coyly said, "About that lookout request for his car?"

****

The four women had just left the Brassiere and chatting together, were approaching the Defender when Vicky saw the young woman who holding a briefcase in her hand, stood beside it, peering curiously into the front passenger window.

The thin young woman in her mid-twenties wearing the cream coloured jacket startled when Fiona brusquely said, "Can I help you?"

"Oh, sorry," the woman turned and blushing furiously, said, "It's just that I thought…"

She stared at the women and then as if recognising Fiona, asked, "Isn't this Tommy's big car? And you're his daughter, too. I thought I recognised you," she cheerfully added.

Fiona glanced at Alice before replying, "I'm sorry, you are?"

"Oh," she smiled, "I'm Shona Mulveigh. I'm the estate agent who handled the sale of the house in Glencloy Road. We met that day when you came to the island with Tommy. I mean, your father."

"Oh, yes, of course," Fiona politely smiled, then turning, introduced her sisters and glancing at Alice, hesitantly said, "and this is my father's friend, Alice."

"Nice to meet you all," Mulveigh replied. Embarrassed now, she began to turn away, but not before adding, "Tell Tommy I said hello and if he's needing anything else?"

It was when they were climbing into the large vehicle that Jenny giggled from the rear seat, "That's you all over, Fiona. You have this way about you, scaring the shit out of people."

****

Tommy Burke was growing anxious about what was happening

between his daughters and Alice and frequently glanced at the kitchen clock.

His attention was distracted when arm in arm, Marcy and Cissie marched into the kitchen to ask if they could have something to eat. Sitting the two girls down at the table, he prepared toast and beans then when serving them with their glass of juice, heard the crunch of tyres on the driveway.

A moment later, wearing her new jacket and footwear, Alice was led into the kitchen by his smiling daughters who he could see were all slightly flushed from drink.

"Had a good time then, you ladies?" he grinned at them.

"We did," Vicky replied, "but Alice insisted on staying sober because she said she needed to drive us to catch the last ferry. I think she's just being silly, dad, because you could have taken us down to the ferry, couldn't you?"

"Course I could have," he smiled, but the cheerfulness in his voice was not as his daughters thought, but relief that they seemed to have accepted Alice as the good woman she is.

Any further thoughts were halted when the phone in the hallway rang and excusing himself, Tommy closed the door behind him, smiling as he did so at the banter that continued in the kitchen.

"Hello?"

"It's me," Peasy Byrne said. "Are you alone? I mean, Alice can't hear you?"

"No, she's in the kitchen with the girls. They arrived this morning to surprise me," he sighed and unconsciously shook his head at their boldness. "How did you get on with her friend, Doris?"

"Bad news, I'm afraid, Tommy. I'm calling from Preston police office. Doris Chisholm was found murdered yesterday evening."

"What? God almighty," stunned, he slowly reached out his free hand to lean against the wall.

"It's a long story, but it seems that Alice's husband has been under suspicion for some time for being associated with a drug that has been circulating in the North of England. The Detective Inspector who is running the inquiry," he glanced at the seated Sandford, "informs me that Geoffrey Mayhew might also be responsible for the murder of one of his associates."

"What about the Chisholm woman. Did he kill her too?"

"That's an open question at the minute and there's nothing of evidence to suggest that, but the police down here discovered a diary belonging to Missus Chisholm in which she recorded Alice's treatment at her husband's hands. According to what the dead woman wrote in her diary, everything Alice told you is God's truth, Tommy, so look after that lady."

"Yes, of course I will," he spluttered, still reeling from the news of Doris Chisholm's murder, then asked, "Have they arrested this man Mayhew?"

"Not at the minute. DI Sandford and her team are building a case against him as we speak. I won't go into details, but they're awaiting the result of Forensic tests, so as soon as that's received, we'll know more. In the meantime, DI Sandford has arranged that the local cops be contacted to take a statement from Alice, so I've given her your home phone number and ask that you break the news to Alice as best you can and to expect a call from the CID."

"Are there CID on Aran?"

"I don't think so," Byrne smiled, "so likely they'll phone first then travel over from the mainland some time tomorrow."

"Well, they might be lucky to get here," he glanced through the window at the front door. "There's reports of a storm brewing and due in from the Atlantic. It could affect the ferry sailings."

"DI Sandford needs the statement, but if it takes a day or so to get it, then there might be nothing we can do about it meantime."

"Are you finished down there or is there anything that I can do from here?"

"Not much more I can offer the local police," Byrne shrugged, "so likely I'll head back up the road tomorrow. I'll come straight to the island and give you the full story when I arrive."

"Okay, anything else, give me a phone," Tommy ended the call.
He turned at the sound of the kitchen door opening to see Alice holding a mug of tea that she offered to him, but when she saw his pale face, asked, "What?"
****

In DI Sandford's office, Peasy Byrne slowly exhaled then getting to his feet, cocked his head to one side and said, "I can't think of anything else you might need from me, but a thought did occur," he began. "When I booked into the Holiday Inn earlier, the young guy at the reception recommended a local restaurant for this evening, Coco's Soul Food. I know you'll probably be tied up for quite a while, but when you're clear, how would you feel about meeting me there for dinner? Maybe you can update me as to how your investigation is coming alone?"

Taken aback, she could feel her face reddening, but then replied, "Why would I feel the need to update you on my investigation?"

He smiled and shrugging, replied, "I might be retired, but in return for the information I brought, you could call it a professional courtesy. So, how about it?"

She couldn't explain it, but felt something, some kind of sensation in her that she had not felt for a very long time. She stared thoughtfully up at the tall man before coyly asking, "Is it the fact that I'm a dusky skinned maiden that prompts you to invite me to a Caribbean restaurant, Mister Byrne?"

These days he wasn't used to asking good looking women...or truth be told, any women to dinner and so stone-faced, paused before replying, "Actually, it's the fact I'm told the restaurant sells good food and that I find you very attractive, DI Sandford, and that's what prompts my invitation. So, how about it?"

The Ice Queen hesitated, then surprising herself that she would even consider his offer, a slow smile crept across her face before she replied, "It might be later this evening before I can get away. Tell you what, why don't I phone you when I'm, say, fifteen minutes away from finishing here and meet you there?"

****

He returned to his Volvo upon hearing the announcement that drivers return to their vehicles and in line with the other traffic, slowly drove off the ferry.

Waved through the harbour by the ships crew, he found himself on the Shore Road and ignoring the wrath of the driver of the van behind him, braked without indicating and turned sharply into an empty parking bay to get his bearings.

Switching off the engine, he twisted his head back and forth as he glanced along the road at the row of shops and the large number of pedestrians and vehicles who passed by the rear of his vehicle.

Shit, he thought. In his naivety and unaware it was a local public holiday and that most of those he saw were tourists, he did not for one minute imagine Arran to be so occupied and cursed his failure to properly research the island when he had the opportunity to do so back at the house.

Reluctantly accepting that it was likely going to take longer than he thought to find Alice and the brat, he decided that his best option would be to find accommodation and that's when, less than 200 metres away, he saw the brightly lit Douglas Hotel set back from the road.

CHAPTER TWENTY-FIVE

They sat in the small lounge, he in one armchair while Alice occupied the other and quietly sobbed into the handkerchief he had given her.

"That's as much as I know," he softly told her. "Peasy is returning tomorrow and will give us the full story. I'm so very sorry, Alice."

The door behind him opened to admit Jenny who wordlessly carried in two mugs of tea that she placed on the coffee table then left, gently closing the door behind her.

"It's all my fault," Alice sniffed. "I should never have left. He killed Doris because of me," she wailed, her shoulders heaving as she cried.

He was about to say that they couldn't be sure that her husband was responsible, but thought better of provoking an argument and remained silent. However, he couldn't help himself and rising from the chair, moved towards her where kneeling in front of Alice, he offered his arms and she fell forward into them, her head on his shoulder while he soothed her as he once did his children.

He was unaware that the door was again opened just a fraction by Fiona, who seeing her father on his knees comforting Alice, withdrew without disclosing her presence.

Returning to the kitchen, she slumped down into the chair and said to her seated sisters, "She's taking it very badly."

"No wonder," gasped Vicky. "That poor woman has been through the mill. What kind of life must she have had living with her husband?"

To the young women's surprise, her question was answered from behind them. Turning, they saw that the two little girls had come in from the garden and it was Marcy who quietly said, "My grandfather is not a very nice man. He's *supposed* to be a doctor and doctors are *supposed* to help people, but he hits my gran and shouts at her all the time. She's very frightened of him."

Her head lowered just a fraction as in a voice that was almost a whisper, she added, "And so am I."

"My God," muttered Fiona, "out of the mouth of babes."

As they watched, they saw Cissie throw a protective arm around Marcy's shoulder's, then nod and tell her, "But your gran will be okay now. My granddad will look after her and nobody will *ever* hit her again. He's great," she enthusiastically added.

The three women glanced at each other, but none of them spoke. Cissie had said it all.

****

The pretty young blonde receptionist flashed Geoffrey Mayhew a professional smile, but thought what a sleazebag.

When she turned to lift the room key from the board behind her, she could almost feel his eyes gawking at her and involuntarily shivered.

"You're very fortunate, Mister Blackwood. The double room is the all we have available and was booked, for but some unknown reason was cancelled late last night. Room 23 on the first floor, sir," she continued to tightly smile, but thought 'in your dreams, you fat git,' before politely asking, "Do you require a hand with your bag, sir?"

"No, I'm *more* than capable," he winked at her and turned away, but stopped and turning, said, "I'd like to book a table in the restaurant for this evening, say seven?"

"That will be no problem, sir. Many of the weekend guests are leaving after the holiday. I'll arrange the reservation. Is it a table for one?"

"It is, unless you'd like to join me," he leered.

She felt a cold shiver run down her spine and choking back her response, instead icily said, "Thank you, sir, but it's against the rules for the hotel staff to fraternise with guests. Will there be anything else?"

"Ah, no," he smiled at the obvious rebuff, though the smile did not reach his eyes and began to make his way towards the wide staircase.

In his room, he fetched the bottle of whisky he'd brought from his bag and poured a generous three fingers into a glass he took from the en-suite. Removing his shoes and balancing the glass on his chest, he lay down on the Queen size bed to collect his thoughts.

How the hell was he going to find Alice, he pondered. He had, to his inner anger, completely underestimated the size of the island and wondered if a single day would suffice. No, he mentally shook his head and accepted that it might quite possibly take several days to track her down.

Again he contemplated phoning the number he had noted from Doris Chisholm's phone and informing her that he was here, on Arran, and wanted to meet with her, but realised if she had already fled from him once there was little chance she would agree to meet him. No, more than likely she would take off again and he'd never find her.

It still confused him why she had chosen Arran. To the best of his recollection, Alice had never even visited Scotland, let alone this rock in the middle of the bloody water; and who was she staying with, who had offered her lodgings? It certainly wasn't any family member because he knew for a fact she had none. And what money did she have other than the couple of hundred pounds she stole from his wallet? How was she managing to live? His query with the bank had discovered the fifty odd quid she'd taken from the ATM had occurred in Preston, but knew that wouldn't last long either.

It wasn't another man; of that he too was certain. Yes, admittedly Alice had been a looker when she was young, but my God, she was what now, fifty-one or two?

His thoughts turned to what was happening back in Preston.

By now the police investigation into Teddy Meiklewood's murder and the death of Doris Chisholm would be in full swing, but he was satisfied that there was nothing to tie him to either Meiklewood's murder or that old woman's death. Yes, he found himself smiling, he had got away with them both.

Now all he had to do was tie up the loose end.

Alice.

Nobody knew he was on the island. He had used cash to pay the ferry fare and signed the register 'George Blackwood,' his father's forename and his mother's maiden name; that and he intended using cash to pay the bill, so there would be no credit card trail.

Admittedly his vehicle's registration number was logged on the ferry's manifest, but the girl at reception had not asked for it and it was unlikely anyone and certainly not the police, would have any reason to check; particularly with so many vehicles visiting the island during what the girl at reception downstairs had said was a holiday weekend.

Growing in confidence, his imagination took over as he contemplated the many ways he could deal with Alice then dispose of her body. First he would make her hand over the packets of Brown Speeders she stole. Then after he dealt with her, perhaps put her in the sea surrounding the island, but discounted this idea almost immediately for there was always the risk she might wash up on the shore. He could bury her in the hills he saw when the ferry approached the island, but without knowing the lie of the land there was every possibility that hill walkers might stumble across her, so also deemed that as far too risky.

But then he smiled, for he had the perfect solution. He would return to the mainland with her body hidden in the rear of the Volvo. That would afford him the the time and opportunity of disposing of her corpse wherever he chose. That way if whoever she was staying with reported her missing, the police would search the island, but not the mainland for there would be no record of her travelling back on the ferry.

Yes, he nodded at his own cleverness, he would find her and deal with her just as he had dealt with that fool Meiklewood.

His brow furrowed.

The brat. He had almost forgotten about her.

Taking a deep swallow, he all but drained the glass.

With a sigh he realised that when it come down to it, it was either his life or the lives of Alice and the brat and really, there was no choice. He must always come first.

****

Her phone rang and lifting it, she said, "DI Sandford," then listened as the senior Forensic scientist at police headquarters, having testing the clothing discovered by Lucy Carstairs in the black bin bag, began to speedily relate his findings.

"Hold on, you're going too fast," she said, "I need to write this down." When she was ready, she snapped, "Go ahead."

Five minutes later, the sheet of paper in her hand, she quickly made her way through to the incident room and beckoning Terry Goodwin to her, said, "Call the team together. That was the Forensics on the blower with a result of their examination."

Doing as he was bid, he fetched officers from the canteen and from the rear yard where some had gone for a quick smoke then, when they were all assembled, Sandford said, "Quiet, please."

She glanced around the room, savouring the moment and sensing the apprehension.

"First of all, I regret to inform you that the house search of the Mayhew's home did not disclose anything of evidential value." She ignored the quiet groan of disappointment and continued. "The only positive thing, though obviously not conclusive evidence, is that though the clothing in the bin bag did not have name tags attached, it does physically match the sizes and clothing of our suspect, Doctor Geoffrey Mayhew and the labels on the shirt and trousers are also the same make as on the clothing. However, from his en-suite bathroom, we obtained hair follicles whose DNA I'm pleased to say matches the DNA lifted from the black bin bag. When we finally get the opportunity to interview Doctor Mayhew, he will provide a sample of DNA that I am confident will tie in with those from the bathroom and the bin bag. Now, as DS Goodwin might have already divulged, I spoke less than ten minutes ago with the Forensics who told me that they completed the examination of the clothes in the bag discovered by Lucy Carstairs."

There it is again, Carstairs thought; the use of my forename. Wonders will never bloody cease and unconsciously willed Sandford to just bloody get on with it!

"According to the scientist I spoke with, the shoes and gloves that were wrapped in the trousers and the shirt were *not* cleansed as thoroughly as the other garments and presumably because they were wrapped so tightly in the trousers and shirt. Therefore, the soap powder was unable to get at these items," she glanced at the paper in her hand, "namely the said shoes and the gloves. Must've been a man that did the washing," she smiled at the sudden outburst of laughter.

She took a breath, conscious that all eyes were on her, the room so quiet she imagined she could almost hear her own heartbeat.

"I'm pleased to inform you that from the threads of these the shoes and the threads of the gloves, the Forensics managed to obtain some blood samples from which in turn they extracted DNA that positively matches that of our murder victim, Teddy Meiklewood…"

She got no further for a spontaneous cheer, handclapping and cries of 'Yes!" went up from the team. Holding her hands up to quell the noise, she could not but help herself from grinning. Finally, the group calmed and she continued, "But that's not all the good news." There were several curious glances before she said, "Besides the blood on the gloves, the Forensics also lifted some epidermis…skin cells to the uninformed among you," she cracked one of her very rare jokes, "that I'm also *very* pleased to tell you they have matched to our recent victim, Doris Chisholm."

There was a sudden intake of breath, some exclamations and gasps from the team at this sudden and very unexpected development, but then a portly detective raised his hand and asked, "That seems to be good evidence in our murder inquiry, Ma'am, but what about that Major Investigation Team lot who are working on the Meiklewood murder? Will they take over our case? I mean, aren't they *our* detections?"

"Let them try," she snarled, then to more cheers, widely grinned. When the noise again calmed down, she clapped her hands and called out, "Right, still lots to do. First, we need to arrange a watch on Mayhew's home for his return from wherever he is and Terry," she glanced towards Goodwin, "put out a lookout for his vehicle on the PNC that as soon as he's found, he is to be detained and we are to be informed. Okay then, folks," she glanced around the room, her eyes encompassing every member of her team, "let's find this bugger, Geoffrey Mayhew and nick him."

****

Peasy Byrne, wrapped in just a bath towel, finished his phone call to his daughter to inform her he was returning home the next day and threw the mobile onto the bed. In the en-suite he shaved then turning on the shower, stepped in, his thoughts filled with the bad news he had disclosed to Tommy Burke.

He could only imagine how difficult it must have been for his old pal to break such devastating news of Alice's friend's murder, but knew that she was in good hands with Tommy.

Like Tommy's daughters he had made it his business to look out for his long term friend and of course had been initially suspicious of Alice Mayhew. However, even he had to admit the woman had won him over and Charles 'Peasy' Byrne was not a man easily fooled.

No, he smiled as he ducked his head under the running water, Alice was a good woman and if things worked out as he hoped they would, Tommy might do himself a favour and keep a hold of her.

His thoughts turned to his own life and he wondered how tonight would go.

It had been a long time, a very long time, he smiled, since he had felt such attraction for a woman. He had been scrupulously faithful during his married years and like most men had admired other women, though never felt the urge cheat on his vows.

But Julie Sandford? Well, she was something else.

He wondered if she felt the same attraction then turning off the shower, stepped onto the bath mat and involuntarily nodding, decided she must have for why else would she agree to have dinner with him?

His brow furrowed.

One thing bothered him; her crack about being a dusky maiden. Was Sandford embarrassed or self-conscious about being of mixed race?

Towelling himself dry he decided that issue was something he would sort out right away, for though he had dealt with it in his working life, never had Byrne any opinion about prejudice other than that those who practised it should be hung, drawn and quartered.

But then he grinned for being a fanatical Celtic supporter, he disliked Rangers football club, though not their supporters, the team followed by many of his friends and former colleagues.

"Well, I suppose that makes me sort of prejudiced," he muttered with a grin then got down to the business of choosing his outfit for his dinner that night with Sandford from the few items of clothing he had brought with him.

****

It had taken some time to calm Alice and now with dinner concluded and while the two little girls said their farewells in the small lounge, here she was, still very pale, with Tommy and his daughters in the large lounge and wishing them the very best for their trip home.

"Have you ever visited Glasgow?" Vicky asked.

"Other than passing through the railway station to catch the ferry train, no," she smiled.

"Well that's settled then, pops," Fiona butted in. "Bring them both over next weekend. Phil and I can keep Marcy for a sleepover with

Cissie while you take Alice out on the town," she grinned, then reached forward to hug her.

Vicky and Jenny did likewise then while Fiona called on Cissie, her two sisters made their way outside towards the Defender.

When the three young woman were settled in the vehicle with Cissie strapped in between her two aunts in the rear seat, Tommy climbed into the driver's seat and started the engine.

Alice and Marcy waved as the vehicle was driven through the wooden gates.

"She's my new best friend," Marcy solemnly told her as Alice closed the front door behind them.

"Yes, you seemed to get on well with her," she smiled in reply.

"Can I tell you a secret, Gran?"

"Of course you can, but can you do it while I'm clearing away the dishes?"

"Yes," she replied and continued in a low voice, "Cissie says her granddad likes you very much."

Alice fought to refrain from smiling, but replied, "And I like Tommy very much, but let's not read into anything, eh?"

"What does that mean, not read into anything?"

"Well," she slowly drawled as she pulled on an apron, trying to work out how to explain to a eight-year old that life is more complicated that she imagined, "Tommy is a very nice man, but because we like him a lot and he likes us, it doesn't mean we're going to be a family, Marcy. You do realise that, don't you?"

"Oh," she huffily crossed her arms. "Does that mean we won't be living here for ever?"

Alice could see how disappointed Marcy was and bending down, drew her granddaughter into her arms and tried to sound encouraging and cheerful before responding, "No, we won't, sweetheart. But if things work out what we will do is I'll get a job here on the island, find somewhere for us to live and a new a school for you and we can remain friends with Tommy, just like we planned. How does that sound?"

"I suppose it will have to do," Marcy sighed.

"Right then," she got to her feet, "why don't you hand me those plates while I load the dishwasher then we'll get the kettle going for Tommy coming back."

****

He parked the Defender in a bay on the Shore Road and walked his daughters and Cissie to the Harbour where he saw the ferry was already loading both foot passengers and vehicles.

"Will you be okay, Pops?" Jenny asked, her face etched with concern.

"Course I will," he grinned, then the grin faded as eyes narrowing, he asked, "About what?"

"Well, you do have a tendency to wear your heart on your sleeve and let's face it, Alice and her granddaughter are an attractive wee couple for an old romantic like you."

"It's not like that that," he tried to protest, but couldn't help the flush that spread across his face.

"Maybe not," Vicky interjected as she leaned forward to kiss his cheek, "but whatever you decide, you have my approval."

"And mine," Fiona added as she took his face in her hand and kissed his other cheek.

"Make it three," Jenny gave him a crushing hug before he scooped Cissie into his arms to kiss her cheerio.

"Let me know you girls get safely home," he insisted while watching them make their way through the throng of weekend holidaymakers returning home, up the covered gangplank.

Once on deck, the four stood by the rail and waved as the ferry departed.

He watched them for a few minutes, seeing them leave the deck presumably to enter the lounge then turning away to return to his vehicle, glanced at the dark and threatening clouds overhead, feeling the first few drops of rain on his face and hands.

He didn't immediately start the engine, but took a few minutes to contemplate and consider how the day had gone.

The elation of his daughter's acceptance of Alice and her granddaughter was tempered by Peasy Byrne's news of her friend's murder and he worried how it might affect Alice.

Would she as she threatened, decide to return to Preston to face the man for whom now she bore such hatred?

He hoped not and though he had not broached the issue, promised himself that if she did come to that decision and despite any protest she might make, he was going with her.

****

Crowded though the ferry's passenger lounge was, Fiona, Vicky and Cissie managed to find a bench seat against a bulkhead and a table while Jenny fetched three coffees and a juice from the on-board Coffee Cabin.

When she returned, Fiona fetched an Enid Blyton book from her shoulder bag to occupy Cissie then glancing at them in turn, asked her sisters, "So, what do you think?"

"About what?" replied Vicky, sipping at her disposable paper coffee cup.

Fiona drew her a sarcastic glance before sharply adding, "Alice, you idiot."

It was Jenny who answered when she said, "I like her and before you ask, I think she'll be good for Pops."

"Certainly impressed me," Vicky nodded. "Can't imagine what her life must have been like living with that husband of hers."

"Aye, he sounds a real bas…" with a grimace and a guilty glance at Cissie, Jenny caught herself just in time.

Vicky, her eyes narrowed, stared at Fiona, the more cynical of the three before asking, "Why, what are you thinking?"

She didn't immediately respond, but then holding up a hand, slowly replied, "Look, I like Alice. I really do and yes, I appreciate she's gone through a really bad time with her husband. But girls, this is our dad. I just don't want him to get hurt and I think he's fallen for her, head over heels. What worries me is, does Alice feel the same about him? I mean, I'd like to think so, but…"

"But nothing, Fiona!" Vicky sharply interrupted. "We've tried for years to protect him since mum died, you more than Jenny and me. Besides, you're always joking that it's about time he found a woman. I like Alice too and yes, I think she's a good woman and that she would be good for dad. So, what do I think? I think it's about time we let dad get on with his life. If he and Alice *do* get together, we let them. It's got absolutely nothing to do with us anyway for after all, he's a grown man and the three of us know how good he's been to us and our families, so…" she run out of steam, but her sister Jenny took up her argument when she said, "Vicky's right. The three of us like Alice and I for one do not believe she would hurt dad."

"Alice likes granddad."

They stopped and turned to stare at Cissie, her book lowered onto her lap as she stared at them.

"What was that, darling?" her mother asked.

"It's supposed to be a secret and we *did* make a pinkie promise, but Marcy told me her gran told her that she wished she'd met someone like granddad a long time ago, that she *really* likes him."

Fiona bit at he lower lip then quietly replied, "Well, we won't tell anyone what Marcy said, darling, will we girls?"

Turning to her sisters, she added, "What was it I said before? Out of the mouth of babes?"

****

Peasy Byrne, having brought just an overnight bag of clothes, had little choice other than to dress in a clean, light blue dress shirt but no tie, navy blue corduroy trousers, his black walking shoes and his black coloured hiking jacket.

He had phoned ahead to book a table and arriving at Coco's Soul Food restaurant, was surprised to discover it doubled as a small, takeaway shop and just inside the door at the counter were five fixed tables and bench like seating. On the two opposing walls each bore a large mural of a Caribbean scene.

His heart sank.

Here I am, he thought, for the first time in as long as I can remember, trying to impress a good looking woman and I bring her to a takeaway shop.

However, to his surprise, when he gave his name at the counter the very helpful staff cheerfully directed him upstairs to 'Marleys,' the dining area of the restaurant where soft Caribbean music played and a large mural of Bob Marley covered one wall overlooking the more intimate tables for two.

Settling himself into a chair that gave him a view of the stairs, he ordered a beer, but learned the restaurant didn't serve alcohol and had to content himself with a daiquiri 'mocktail.'

He had been seated for less than ten minutes when he saw Julie Sandford coming up the stairs.

He could see she had obviously returned home to change for she had allowed her hair to fall in soft waves about her shoulders and instead of her business suit now wore an olive green, tightfitting one-piece dress to just above the knee with thin straps on her bare shoulders and black high heel shoes. In her hand she carried a short black dress jacket and a black clasp bag.

He was stunned at her good looks and rising to his feet, rounded the table to pull out the chair. As she sat down, he inhaled the faint of fragrance of her perfume.

"My, and I was thinking there were no more gentlemen left," she softly smiled at him as she took her seat. As if by magic, a waiter appeared to take her jacket from her.

"I regret, when I was recommended this place, the young man forgot to say it wasn't licensed," he apologised.

"Oh, I knew that," she waved away his protest and added, "I'm not much of a drinker anyway. You?"

"I admit to a glass of vino and a few beers now and then," he pursed his lips, "but no, I'm not what we call a heavy bevy man."

"A heavy bevy man," she smiled at that. "I thought all you Scots were heavy drinkers?"

"That's a bit like saying all you English are kind and generous people," he smirked at her.

Her sharp retort was cut short when the waiter arrived to take their order.

As they waited on their food, she leaned forward on the table, her chin resting on her clenched fists and peering at him, said, "So before we discuss my investigation, tell me a little of yourself, Mister Byrne."

"Oh, I'd much rather hear about you, Miss Sandford," he smiled at her.

"There's not that much to tell. I'm married to the job. End of," she sighed.

"I refuse to believe that such a good looking woman like you could be married to police work. Yes, it can be a compelling profession, but there is life outside polis work."

"Polis work," she teasingly mocked his accent, then sitting straight back in her chair, peered at him as she asked, "Why did you ask me to dinner? Is it to find out more about the investigation?"

He didn't immediately respond but then leaning forward, replied in a quiet voice, "I'm not what you might call a ladies' man, but when I saw you today," he paused and shrugged, then staring at her, shook his head and said, "I don't ever think I've been as attracted to a woman as I am to you."

His reply took her by surprise and blinking, she intuitively knew he was being truthful.

She surprised herself by blushing and gulping to hide her discomfort, said, "Well, let me tell you how we got on today and then we can maybe learn something about each other."

Her account of the day's investigation began as the food arrived and took just ten minutes and after concluding that she and her team were now actively looking for Geoffrey Mayhew for interview regarding two murders, Byrne widened his eyes and said, "Phew! You guys have been busy."

"We'll get him, don't worry about that," she confidently predicated. "It's just a question of time."

"I'll give Tommy and Alice a phone tomorrow morning and apprise them of your information and hopefully, your forthcoming arrest," he toasted her with his glass.

"Now, tell me about Julie Sandford."

CHAPTER TWENTY-SIX

Tuesday morning arrived as did the violent Atlantic storm that caused havoc as it swept across the west coast of Scotland, battering down trees and telephone poles and causing flooding throughout the coastal areas. Trains and flights were cancelled as were the ferry crossings to the Western Isles that of course included Arran, stranding most if not all the weekend holiday makers who were obliged to remain in their booked accommodation or shelter in their tents.

On the island, the stoic locals continued with their daily routine and glancing at the dark skies, shook their heads and settled in to endure and accept a couple of days of isolation.

****

Geoffrey Mayhew awoke to the sound of rain battering against the window and for a second, wondered where he was.

Lying back on the bed, he softly exhaled and belched, tasting again the remains of the whisky he had consumed before falling asleep.

Glancing at the digital clock on the bedside cabinet, he decided to lie for a little longer before rising.

An hour later, shaved and showered and dressed in a plain, sky blue coloured dress shirt and jeans that were uncomfortably tight about his waist, convinced himself before making his way downstairs the jeans must have shrunk when that fool Alice washed them.

However, before making his way into the near empty restaurant for breakfast, he spoke to the young assistant manager and booking a further three nights at the hotel, made a down payment in cash.

It was while he was eating and admiring the pert bottom of the young Polish waitress that he had the idea to shake things up a little. Now returned to his room he sat on the edge of his bed and reached for his mobile phone.

****

While Tommy walked hand in hand with Marcy to the bakers on the Shore Road for morning rolls and giggling as they fought to stay upright against the strong winds, Alice busied herself in the kitchen preparing breakfast and stared curiously but with a smile, at the square sausage and the Stornoway black pudding so beloved by Tommy.

But then the phone in the hallway rang.

Conscious the police were due to call and make the arrangement to attend the house and note her statement, she lifted the phone and said, "Hello?"

There was a few seconds pause, but then her heart sank and her blood turned to chilled ice when Geoffrey said, "Hello, my dear wife. How are you?"

He had found her.

Her instinct was to slam the phone down, but gripping it so tightly it hurt her hand, she replied in a shaky voice, "Geoffrey. Why are you calling me here?"

"I just wanted to say hello, my dear," his voice, calm and unruffled, oozed charm.

She could hardly breathe and thought she might pass out, but her self will forced her to maintain standing and her voice a mere whisper, she asked again, "Why are you calling me here?" then eyes narrowing in suspicion, added, "How did you get this number?"

"Where is here, my dear? What I mean is," his voice sneered, "what hovel have you found to hide on this shitty little Scottish island?"

Her free hand grasped at her throat. He had said 'on this shitty little island.' Did that mean he was here too?

Her body shaking and mouth so dry she could hardly speak, at last she said, "Where are you, Geoffrey?"

"More to the point, my dear, where are you? Oh, I know you're here on Arran, but why don't we meet? You and I? Somewhere we can talk?"

'Here on Arran,' he had said. That confirmed it for her; he *was* on Arran!

"Why…" she had so very little spit in her mouth and tried again, "Why do you want to meet with me? It's over. I've left you."

"Oh, I realise that, Alice, but before you left me, you took something from me and I want it back. The small cardboard packet from my medical bag and the other one from my coat pocket. We both know that you might suspect me of something and I can't have you holding that over me, can I? Now, listen very carefully to me, Alice. All I need is for you to hand the packets over and then you and I are finished, you can go on your merry way. You have my word. You and your granddaughter. Now, I'm not asking anything else of you, only that you hand over the packets," his voice soothingly said. "That doesn't sound too difficult, does it?"

It was the mention of Marcy that steeled her, referring to the child as Alice's granddaughter; the certainty that he still did not nor would ever accept the little girl as his own flesh and blood.

She had never been a woman who used bad language, never cursed or blasphemed, but his patronising attitude and certainty that she would simply comply maddened her into replying, "Fuck you, Geoffrey!" and slammed the phone down.

She suddenly stood back, aghast; her hands at her mouth and stared in horror at the phone as though it would somehow transfer Geoffrey here, to the hallway.

She had to get away, take Marcy and flee.

But to where?

Her next thought surprised her for she wondered, Tommy, where are you when I need you?

****

In his hotel room, Geoffrey smiled. He had rattled her. Of that he was certain. Now all he had to do was find her and with all the holidaymakers due to leave the island, it made his job that little less difficult.

****

She awoke and for a few seconds in the room lit by the daylight coming through the crack in the curtain, stared at the strange ceiling and wondered where she was.

Suddenly conscious she was naked beneath the sheets, she turned her head slightly to see the sleeping man beside her and inwardly groaned. As she watched she saw the greying hairs on his chest rise and fall as he breathed and could not help but smile.

After their meal, he had invited her to return with him to the hotel bar for a drink, accepting his arm as they walked to the Holiday Inn. A bottle of wine later, they both realised what was going to happen and moved from the bar to his room where one thing followed another.

It had been a very, very long time since she had given herself to a man, but though he could not know it, he was as she expected; a considerate lover, undemanding and gentle.

Still, she sighed, that was last night and now it was the morning and she had work to go to.

As quietly as she dared, she slipped from the bed and bending to collect her clothes from the floor, was about to tiptoe to the en-suite when Byrne whispered, "Thank you for last night."

Startled and self-conscious at her nakedness, she half turned to see him propped up on one arm, smiling at her. Clutching her clothes to her, she returned his smile before making a dash for the door.

Closing it behind her, she blushed furiously and grinning at her foolishness turned on the shower while she made her toilet.

Reaching out a hand to test the temperature of the water, she was about to step into the shower when the door was knocked and Byrne loudly said, "Julie, phone."

Opening the door just a fraction, he handed her mobile through to her.

She saw it was a missed call from Terry Goodwin and switching off the shower, called him back.

"Ma'am, I came into the office early. Where are you?"

"I, ah, stayed over at a friends house last night," she impulsively replied. "What's up?"

Before replying, Goodwin smiled for he had always seriously doubted Sandford had any close friends nor did he miss her hesitant pause either and with a smile, wondered about the big Scotsman that had arrived yesterday.

"There was a message just come in twenty minutes ago from the Automatic Number Plate Recognition office in response to our lookout request for Mayhew's Volvo. They wanted to know if we wished to continue the lookout. It seems that yesterday about midday, his vehicle was recorded driving on the M6 and crossing the border into Scotland."

"Yesterday? When did our lookout request go live?" she angrily asked.

"Yesterday evening, Ma'am," he replied and she knew from his voice there was more.

"So, they received our request yesterday evening and recorded him travelling into Scotland and didn't think to inform us as soon as they had that information?" she hissed.

"They did inform us, Ma'am. I mean, not our incident room," he slowly replied and envisaged her anger. "When they got a hit they sent the result to the Major Investigation Team. I asked why didn't they send the information to us as the issuing incident room. Well," he took a deep breath, already imagining her anger, "it seems when the MIT's DCI learned that we had identified Mayhew for Meiklewood's murder, he instructed that all sightings of Mayhew be forwarded to *his* incident room and that's why we were not immediately informed. Told the ANPR people that Teddy Meiklewood is his murder investigation."

"So, the bastard hijacked our lookout request and might have cost us valuable time in catching Mayhew?"

"To be fair, Ma'am, he probably didn't know about Missus Mayhew being in Scotland. That's what you're thinking, isn't it? That Mayhew's gone after his wife, that somehow he's found out she's on the island of Arran."

"That's *exactly* what I'm thinking, Terry," she raged, her voice rising, "and Mayhew probably thinks if he can recover the packets of Brown Speeders she took from him, we won't have any evidence of his drug dealing with Meiklewood. Particularly if he kills her too! It's more than likely he doesn't know we have evidence of him committing two murders and that *fucking* DCI is playing politics and one-upmanship with someone's life!"

"Oh, and I've had a thought about that too, how he knew his wife is on Arran."

She forced herself to be calm and brow furrowed, asked, "What do you mean, you have a thought?"

"I was wondering how Mathew would know his wife was in Arran then it occurred to me. If Mayhew was in the victim's house when the second last phone call was made to the house from Arran…"

He didn't finish for she interjected with, "Then he would have heard the call and got the last number called from the phone. But that would only give him the STD code and from that he could identify the area she was calling from, but not where she is."

"Exactly," he agreed, "so even if he *is* on Arran, he might not know where on the island his wife is staying."

"And that might give us some time to get her to safety," she snapped. "Good work, Terry."

She slapped a hand to her forehead as she tried to think, then said, "Get onto Police Scotland with his vehicles registration number and inform them he is a suspect for two murders.

We've a photograph of him too, haven't we?"

"Yes, Ma'am."

"Send a copy to the Scottish police as well as telling them he might be heading for or maybe even already arrived on Arran. I'll tell Alice Mayhew's friend Peasy Byrne to phone her and get his friend to take her somewhere safe."

"When will I see you in the office, Ma'am?"

"I'll be there in say," she screwed her face and added, "twenty minutes," before quickly ending the call.

Hastily, her mind preoccupied by what had to be urgently done, she pulled open the en-suite door to see Byrne, dressed in a pair of white coloured football shorts and a plain black tee-shirt, stood at the table as he prepared two mugs of coffee while the kettle boiled.

She raised a hand and sharply called out, "I'll explain later, but right now we need to go and you need to phone your friend and tell him to take Alice Mayhew to somewhere safe. Her husband might be on the island."

He stared at her then with a quiet grin, replied, "I'll get right onto it, Julie, but can I make a suggestion?"

"What?" her eyes narrowed.

"Lovely as you are, you *might* want to put on some clothes."
****

As soon as he and Marcy returned to the house, soaked through but uproariously laughing and giggling as they continued to struggle against the strong wind, he looked at Alice and knew something had happened; something worrying.

However, though her body trembled she kept it together for the few minutes it took to get Marcy dried and then after ushering the little girl through to the small lounge to watch cartoons, broke down in the kitchen front of Tommy.

Shocked, he reached out to comfort her, his hands on her arms and asked, "What is it?"

"It's Geoffrey," she stammered, her body shaking, "he's here, on Arran!"

"Has he been here, to the house?" he sharply asked, more sharply than he intended.

"No," her nose running, she tearfully sniffed, "he phoned me I don't know, about twenty minutes ago? He didn't say where he is, but he inferred he *was* on the island."

He felt himself go cold and his hands tightened slightly on her arms when he asked, "Where is he? Where on the island?"

"I don't know!" she vigorously shook her head and sniffed. "He called the house number and said he wanted to meet, that he wanted me to return those small packets of drugs. That if I did that he would let me go, that it would be the end of us."

"And do you believe him?"

She stared at Tommy and her throat tight, shook her head, before replying, "If he has killed Doris and that man like Peasy said, why would he simply let me walk away when I just know that he is probably the one who gave those drugs to that young lad in the rugby club? It doesn't make any sense that he'd come all this way just to collect the packets, does it?" she stared fearfully at him.

"No, Alice, it doesn't," he quietly agreed with a shake of his head and let his hands slip from her arms. "What did you tell him?"

"I told him…" her lips trembled and licking at her dry lips, she took a deep breath before adding, "I told him to fuck off."

He couldn't help himself and suddenly grinned before telling her, "I bet you've wanted to say that to him for a *very* long time."

She smiled through her tears and nodded.

Staring keenly at her, he said, "You told Peasy that Geoffrey drives a large white coloured Volvo, didn't you?"

"Yes. There's the old Toyota too, but I can't see him coming all this way in such a small car."

"So, it's likely then he'll have driven north in the Volvo. Are you aware if he knows anyone who lives here on the island?"

"No, I don't think so," she shook her head. "Why? What are you thinking?"

Before he could respond, the phone in the hall rang.

Leaving her in the kitchen, he made his way into the hallway and half expecting it to again be Geoffrey Mayhew, snatched at the phone and snapped, "Yes?"

"It's me," said Byrne. "Can you speak?"

But Tommy had already guessed why his friend was phoning and rubbing at his forehead to ease the sudden ache, replied, "Yes. This about her husband being on the island?"

Startled, Byrne said, "You know? How? And he's definitely on the island?" Byrne quick fired the questions.

"Oh, he's here right enough. Bastard phoned here to the house about twenty minutes ago, Peasy. Wanted to meet her and get the wee cardboard packets of the drugs from her. Said if she handed them over he'd go away and leave her in peace, or words to that effect."

"Jesus, Tommy, she's not agreed to meet him, has she?"

"No, of course not," he scoffed.

"Good, the bastard is far too dangerous. I've a wee update for you. Right, you're up to speed about him being wanted for the two murders. Well, the latest is that he's likely got it that Alice is on Arran from when he was at the old lady's house and did a check on Missus Chisholm's phone. That's where he'll have got the STD code, but not your address; just your landline number. You're a new number too so you won't be in any phone book just yet. They've assessed down here that he doesn't yet know he's wanted for the murders, so he will still be thinking this is all about the drugs, that if he gets them back and," he paused, bit at his lip and continued, "silences Alice, he'll be safe. The advice from the DI here and I agree is that you lock your doors and stay inside till the local cops get there."

"Local cops, Peasy?" he smiled despite himself. "This is Arran, pal. There's no crime or problems on here. The local cops will be a sergeant and a couple of constables and they'll be up to their neck in it attending to calls for assistance because of the storm."

"A storm? Oh, I didn't know about that," Byrne grimaced, "but I'm not talking about the Arran cops. I mean there's CID officers who will coming over from the mainland to take Alice's statement. DI Sandford," he turned and unable to help himself, stared admiringly at her as with her back to him, she slithered into her tight dress, "has arranged for Police Scotland to be made aware that Mayhew is wanted for the murders and they'll be sending some bodies across to look after Alice."

"Well, that's all fine and dandy, Peasy, but in the meantime I take it you don't know about the really bad weather up here at the minute? What you're telling me is we've just to hole up here at the house till they arrive?"

"What do you mean, the bad weather?" Byrne stepped across the room to fetch the television remote control and switched on the set.

"We're getting pounded by an Atlantic storm, so it's unlikely there will be any sailings today or maybe even in the next two days. There is no way the CID can get across here. We're cut off for the time being."

"Bugger!" Byrne snapped in his ear, his stomach tensing as his eyes darted across the screen while the BBC twenty-four-hour news reported the storm on the scrolling ribbon at the bottom of the screen.

"Look," Tommy said, "I'll keep Alice safe in the meantime, but as soon as you can arrange for the CID to get here, do it."

"Will do, wee man, so keep your head down and..." he hesitated, knowing his pal from many years of friendship, then added, "don't go looking for this guy, Tommy. I mean it."

"Don't worry," he replied with a smile, "I'll do what's necessary," and ended the call.

And that, Byrne grimly thought, is what worries me.

Turning, he saw Sandford was now dressed and ready to leave, stared enquiringly at him.

"What did he say?"

He sighed and nodding towards the television screen before replying, said, "As you can see, there's a bad storm hit the west coast up there and that includes the island. They're cut off for at least two days. Tommy told me that Mayhew phoned Alice and is apparently on the island," then recounted the conversation.

"But she won't meet him, surely?"

"No," he shook his head, "she's too wise for that and besides, Tommy wouldn't let her go."

"Then if he doesn't know where they are on the island, they can simply wait out the storm until assistance gets there?"

"That's what I suggested and *that* is what concerns me," he shook his head. "Tommy Burke is no shrinking violet, Julie, and was brought up in a hard area and worked most of his days on the building sites. He's a good and decent man, but if he thinks Mayhew is a threat to Alice or the wee girl," he didn't finish, but shook his head.

"But he's certain that Mayhew is on the island?"

"Mayhew didn't exactly say so to Alice, but it was inferred and besides, he asked to meet her on the island so, yes, I would say it's fairly certain he's on Arran."

She stared at him and all her feelings for him aside, made a decision. Glancing at her wristwatch, she said, "Pack your bag and we'll go via my home then you can drive me to my office. I have an idea."

****

Lucy Carstairs was about to kiss her children and husband goodbye before travelling to work when her mobile phone rung.

The screen indicated the caller to be Terry Goodwin and she answered with, "What's up?"

"Are you still at home?"

"Yes, I'm just about to leave."

"Well, before you do, change into travelling gear and bring a bag with you for say, at least two overnight stays."

In the office he glanced again at the television screen and said, "No, better make that three."

"Three overnight stays? Where the hell am I going?"

He grinned before replying, "Where are *we* going, Lucy. Me, you and Ma'am. We're going to Jockland."

****

He sat her down and pulling his chair alongside hers with their hips almost touching, said, "It's the only way, Alice. We need to know where he is. He doesn't know where you are and doesn't have this address, so as long as you and Marcy stay indoors and lock all the doors, you'll be safe. If what you said before is true, then he won't know Arran, not like I do. If he doesn't know anyone on the island then it's more than likely he will be staying in accommodation somewhere and the way you describe him, it's unlikely to be a B and B. No, I'm guessing your husband…" he stopped and grimacing, added, "your former husband, will be in a hotel somewhere and again I'm guessing if he doesn't know the island, it will likely be here in Brodick."

"But what do you intend doing?" she stared at him, her lovely features drawn with concern.

"Well," he shrugged, "if I find his Volvo, I've found him. I can then contact the local police and inform them of his whereabouts. If they get him, they can lock him up till the weather abates and the CID get here."

"You promise me, Tommy, you won't confront him? I couldn't bear it if…" she didn't finish, but slowly raised one hand to her throat and the other to gently touch his cheek.

He tensed, then with his own hand, covered hers as she continued to stroke at his cheek.

"I'll be sensible and I've got my mobile with me," he smiled with more confidence than he felt.

They both turned to see Marcy standing in the doorway, her lips trembling. "Can I come in here with you, please? The rain's scaring me."

Alice held open her arms and he watched as the little girl run into them, then to his surprise, she shyly reached for his hand too.

"How long will the rain last, Tommy?" she asked.

He held his hands wide and with a grin, replied, "This long."

Marcy giggled and said, "No, I mean what *time*."

He made a point of glancing at the clock and said, "It's half past ten."

She continued to giggle and then pretending to be huffy, said in a serious voice, "Will the rain last much longer?"

"About two days I think," he replied, pointing to the small television set on the wall in the corer where on the screen, the BBC weather forecaster was indicating a chart behind her.

"At last," she rolled her eyes at the foolishness of adults.

"Right," he abruptly stood and staring down at Marcy, smiled and said, "I've a wee job to do for an hour or so, so I need you to do something for me."

Little did he know, but had he asked her the little girl would have walked on hot coals for Tommy Burke and so she eagerly nodded. "Make sure your grandmother locks all the windows and the doors when I'm out. I don't want to come home and find the place flooded, do I?"

"Okay, Tommy," her brow furrowed and she solemnly nodded as behind her, Alice mouthed 'Thank you.'

He nodded and then staring at Alice, gave in to his impulse.

To both their surprise, Tommy stepped forward and leaning over Marcy, took Alice's tearstained face in his hands and kissed her before turning and heading back out the door.

****

Peasy Byrne agreed to run Julie Sandford to her home in Grafton Street not far from the Preston railway station where, while he waited in his car in a bay outside the mid-terraced town house, she went in to fetch her bag and change.

Less than ten minutes later she was out and hair now pulled back into a tight ponytail, was dressed in a black coloured polo shirt, blue jeans, a dark coloured quilted anorak and a pair of stout walking boots.

"What, never seen a woman ready for bad weather," she grinned at him as she threw her tan coloured leather holdall into the rear seat. "I'd have invited you in," she continued, "but I had the strangest feeling if I did I might have taken the opportunity to tear your clothes off again."

Surprised, Byrne almost stalled the car. To the best of his recollection, no woman had ever said *that* to him before and grinning, gunned the engine as directed by her he sped toward the police office.

Just over ten minutes later and again directed by Sandford, he parked in her dedicated bay at Preston police then followed her upstairs to the incident room where she found both Terry Goodwin and Lucy Carstairs similarly dressed to travel and with packed bags.

It was to Goodwin's credit that surprised though he was by Sandford arriving with Byrne, he made no comment, though his mind was ticking over.

"Right people," she loudly announced her presence by clapping her hands for their attention, "here's what's happening. I know while I've been getting here DS Goodwin has updated you with the latest information we have on the whereabouts of our suspect Geffrey Mayhew, so here's a further update. It is my intention to travel with DS Goodwin and DC Carstairs and Mister Byrne, as our pressganged liaison with his former Police Scotland colleagues, to go north and arrest Mayhew."

There was a curious glance from Goodwin who interrupted with, "Don't we need to run this past the Area Commander first, Ma'am? I mean, we're not just going into another Force area, we're going into a completely different judicial system in Jockland."

He turned to Byrne and and with an self-conscious grin said, "No offence, mate."

"None taken," Byrne tightly smiled at him.

"That's why I intend travelling with Mister Byrne," she smiled. "En route to catch the Arran ferry from Ardrossan, he will introduce me on the phone to his former colleagues who are still serving and I hope to smooth out any legal difficulties with them as we journey north."

News to me, Byrne thought, but wisely made no comment.

"As for the Area Commander," she continued and smiled again, "I'll speak to him from the car and explain that this is a time critical operation. In the meantime," she singled out the portly detective stood in front of the team, "DC Wellbright, I want you take on the role of Acting Detective Sergeant meantime and continue running the incident room and ensure that all outstanding Actions are completed. Once that is done, oversee the day to day running of the office and issue criminal inquiries as they come in. Any problem with that?"

"No, Ma'am," the startled detective flushed at the responsibility, but privately wondered if he would get an upgrade in his pay during the period he performed the acting role.

"Good. DS Goodwin and DC Carstairs?" she was about to indicate they depart, but was stopped when Goodwin interrupted with, "Can I have a private word, Ma'am?"

His face flushed, he nodded towards the corridor.

Curious, she nodded in return and beckoning that he follow her, opened the door that led to the corridor outside the incident room. When they were alone, he began, "Look, I think you're going way out on a limb here. If the DCI for the Major Investigation Team finds out what you're up to…"

"Fuck him!" she raised a hand and snapped back. "We're having to travel north because he hijacked our investigation and quite probably put Alice Mayhew's life at risk, so I'm not concerned about him. As for the Area Commander," she shook her head, "if he tries to stop us pursuing a killer and preventing a woman's murder, then I'll go above him and expose him for the cowardly, two-faced, back-stabbing, conniving…"

She got no further for Goodwin raised his own hands in surrender and with a grin, said, "Okay, enough. I get the message. You won't be talked out of this so, maybe we should just go."

She stared at him then permitting herself smile, told him, "I don't say this often enough, but thanks, Terry. You keep me grounded when I go off on one and I'm grateful for it, believe me," she sighed. "Right," she briskly added, "You take a car with Lucy and I'll travel with Peasy Byrne and meet you for a comfort break at the first service station just over the border, where hopefully I'll have an update for you after my phone calls to the Police Scotland Force."

CHAPTER TWENTY-SEVEN

Not for the first time, Tommy Burke was grateful for the purchase of the Defender as he wound his way down the rutted road for the big, heavy vehicle made light work of the storm that lashed its fury against the windscreen and the sides. He easily manoeuvred the heavy vehicle while he dodged and rounded the debris that was being tossed about by the wind and reaching the Shore Road stopped at the junction.

He was about to turn right towards the Douglas Hotel to commence his search, but suddenly recalled Alice telling him that had been the first hotel she had visited for accommodation, but it had been fully booked with weekend holidaymakers.

It was to his later frustration and everlasting regret that he decided to turn left to drive slowly towards where he knew the first hotel on his mind was located and did not turn not right.
****

In their home, Mary McKay and her husband Malky sat in their lounge, the television switched off and the radio tuned to the weather station as it broadcast the latest updates for the storm that swept across their island.

"Will the boat be okay do you think?" she asked with a worried frown.

"She's beached, hen, and that new canvas covering her is tightly tied and weighted down with heavy stones so don't worry, she'll be fine," he confidently replied as he dry-sucked at his old briar pipe, for Mary was quite rigid that there would be no smoking in the house.

Malky's pride and joy, a fifteen foot Vimar open fishing boat that permitted him to enjoy his passion of fishing and the occasional hire by tourists keen to see the seals that abound the island, had been purchased as a near wreck and loving restored by him.

She didn't miss the worried crease in his forehead and asked, "What?"

"Just a silly thing," he sighed. "I don't know if you noticed that old tree with the branches hanging over Tommy's back fence near to the garage. I'm a bit concerned for when I had a look at it last week, it seems to me that rot has settled in near the trunk and with these high winds," he cast a wary glance out of the window and sighed, "there's every likelihood it might just come down and if it does topple over, it could take his fence down and maybe even the garden shed."

"Can you not phone Tommy and ask him to have a look at it? It would save you having to go out in this weather," she shuddered."

"I did try, but our phone's down. Must be the line again, same as the last time, do you remember?"

"Aye, I do" she sighed, recalling the nuisance caused by the previous years storm. "What about his mobile number? I've got that. You could maybe tell him what to do over the phone."

"No," he abruptly raised a hand. "The man has been good enough to employ me to take care of his grounds, so I'm not going to have him doing what is my job, Mary, and that's final."

She stood there, glaring at him her hands on her hips and replied, "And what exactly do you you think you can do, Malky McKay, with the sort of weather that's raging out there? Are you mad, man? You could get yourself hurt."

He didn't immediately respond, but she saw and recognised that look on his face and with an exasperated groan, said, "No matter what I say, your mind's made up, isn't it? You're going up to have a look at that tree?"

"Mister Byrne…" he stopped and smiled, "Tommy, I should say, will be there too, so we can both have a look at it and if need be he can give me a hand. There's plenty of rope in the boot of our car. If it comes to it, I'm certain we can secure the tree to one of its neighbours for the time being or at least until the wind dies down."

"Then I'm going with you," she crossly muttered and began to untie her apron strings. "I can't have my man running around in this weather without me being there to look after you, can I? Besides, if we're going out, we can call in on old Jessie in her bungalow down in Alma Road. I know she can be so blinking independent," Mary said, the nearest she ever came to an expletive, "but she's in her late eighties now and I worry about her."

"Aye, well, we can do that on the way," he nodded.

"I just hope that Tommy's daughters got away all right," she grimaced.

"What, after you dropped that bombshell on them, you think you might still have a job after all?" he grinned at her, then quickly ducked to avoid being hit by the flung apron.

****

They were making good time and it was only after they left the Gretna Green services they began to encounter the bad weather, the driving rain that lashed against their vehicle windscreen.

In the lead car, Peasy Byrne's mobile phone activated and he pushed the button on the dashboard for the hands free.

"Hello?"

"Peasy? It's Cathy Mulgrew. I hear you're looking for me."

"Miss Mulgrew," he smiled and with some relief, genuinely pleased to hear from the Police Scotland Detective Superintendent.

"You're on speaker, Cathy," he informed her. "I'm travelling north in my car about six or seven miles away from the border and I have with me Detective Inspector Julie Sandford of the Lancashire Constabulary. It's a long and convoluted story, but to summarise I travelled down yesterday to Preston on behalf of a friend and inadvertently wandered into a murder investigation being conducted by DI Sandford. We're now travelling towards Ardrossan with two Lancashire detective officers in a car behind us to catch the ferry over to Arran. If you don't mind, I'll pass you to DI Sandford and let her explain further and the request she has."

"Right, Peasy. Go ahead DI Sandford."

"Ma'am," Sandford acknowledged and with a hesitant glance at Byrne, spent the next ten minutes providing Mulgrew with a background to the investigation, the information that her double murder suspect is likely on the island of Arran and her fear that if he finds her, Geoffrey Mayhew might intend to seriously harm his wife or worse."

Mulgrew permitted Sandford to speak without interruption, then asked, "And you are satisfied that this man Mayhew is probably guilty of both these murders?"

"The Forensics doesn't lie, Ma'am, so yes; I am satisfied Geoffrey Mayhew is guilty of both murders."

"And your Force has not authorised this trip into the Police Scotland area, DI Sandford?"

"No, Ma'am," she swallowed and trying to sound as confident as she could, continued, "I took the decision to travel north with two of my team and, well," she glanced and grimaced at Byrne, "it's my belief if I'd waited for the paperwork Missus Mayhew might have come to serious injury or worse. I have tried to contact my Area Commander to inform him of my decision, but he is not immediately available."

There was a few seconds pause during which both Sandford and Byrne thought they might have lost the connection, prompting him to ask, "Are you still there, Cathy?"

"I'm here, Peasy. Sorry, I was making some notes. Right, here's what I suggest. Continue towards Ardrossan. I'll have my people try to arrange transport across the water, but to be frank with the weather conditions as they are, we might be pushing it for as far as I'm aware the ferry crossings are off. In the meantime, I'll arrange to have the police on Arran contacted to attend at this man Burke's house to provide protection for Missus Mayhew. You have to know, DI Sandford that you will not be permitted to make an arrest here in our area, that will be down to us. However, I'll need some paper authorisation from your Force so I'll get right onto that and if I can swing it, you can take your suspect back to England with you."

"Yes, Ma'am, that would suit me fine," she agreed.

"Okay then. I'll also inform your Force of the time critical decision you made. Peasy?"

"Yes?"

"What's your best estimate for arriving at Ardrossan?"

"The weather is closing in so I estimate, say," he pursed his lips, "one and a half hours."

"Right, that gives me some sort of time frame and listen, in future you old bugger, try to give me some better notice when you start involving yourself in another Force's murder investigations."

"Will do," he grinned at her black humour then ended the call.

****

Detective Superintendent Cathy Mulgrew, the Police Scotland Head of Intelligence Services, tore the sheet of paper from her pad and leaving her office in the state of the art Scottish Crime Campus at Gartcosh, hurried across the walkway to where Detective Inspector Danny McBride was located.

Pushing open his office door, she rushed in and without any preamble, held up a hand to prevent any questions and said, "Long story cut short. We have three Lancashire Constabulary detectives travelling north with our former colleague Peasy Byrne and about one and half hours from Ardrossan Harbour. They have a double murder suspect on the island who might be there with the intention of injuring or murdering his wife. What we have to do is contact the cops on Arran and have them attend at this address to protect the wife."

She laid down the sheet of paper and stabbing her manicured forefinger at it, added, "Peasy's mobile number is on there too. Now, how the hell can we get them across to the island in this weather?"

McBride frowned then softly exhaling, he lifted the sheet of paper and staring at it, smiled.

"Remember that Maritime Counter Terrorism exercise at Faslane naval base that we participated in with those mad buggers from the Royal Marines? The guys with the wee fast boats, what do you call them…" he snapped his fingers as he tried to recall, then said, "The raiding craft. That's what they called their boats. Remember how they almost flew through the water?"

"Yes," she nodded. "They were the Special Boat Squadron mob," she said, but didn't add anything about the Marine captain who tried in vain to talk her into going out with him, albeit she explained she was gay.

"They guys are trained for all sorts of foul weather boating," he pursed his lips in thought, before continuing, "What's the chance if I give them a call they might be able to assist?"

"Worth a shot," she agreed then added, "You go ahead with that and I'll contact Lancashire and explain we're willing to participate in a mutual in a cross border arrest of their murder suspect."

He stared curiously at her, prompting her to ask, "What?"

"You're taking a lot on here, ma'am, without any paperwork or official notification from the Lancashire cops other than what you've been told. You're absolutely certain we're doing the right thing?"

"Peasy Byrne was a first class detective, Danny, and you've met the guy. He believes he's doing the right thing, so, would you trust him?"

He didn't immediately respond, but then a slow smile crossed his face and lifting his phone, he said, "I'm on it, Ma'am."

****

The miserable Scottish weather was far too foul to be going outside, Geoffrey decided and with a glance through the bedroom window at the dark sky and the driving rain made his way to the bar downstairs. About twelve to fifteen hotel guests sat in small groups at the tables quietly talking, some with luggage at their feet, most hunched forward as though fearful the wind was going to snatch their drinks from them while the wind gusted and the rain beat a tattoo on the large windows that looked across Brodick bay.

The thin built waitress with the mousey fair hair tied back with an elastic band into a tight bun who wore her black metal name tag on her light blue coloured uniform shirt, smiled broadly when she served Geoffrey the first of his double Dalmore whisky's.

Watching the young woman, he thought her to be quite plain featured and guessed her to be in her mid-twenties, then idly contemplated what she'd be like in bed. Upon being served his second whisky, he glanced at her name tag and said, "Shona. What a lovely name. Are you a local girl, Shona?"

None of the other guests needed immediate attention, so leaning on the bar she smiled and replied, "Born and bred, sir. And you? Where are you from?"

"Oh, I'm one of the old enemy from down south," he smiled, cautious not to say too much and again using his maternal grandfathers name, extended his hand and added, "George Blackwood."

He held onto her hand just a fraction too long, enough to cause her to be surprised, but then releasing his grip, said, "Seems I'm trapped on your island for a couple of days anyway, Shona, so what does a man do around here for entertainment."

A little uncomfortable at his touch and her face face reddening, she replied, "Oh, I don't get too much time to myself, sir…"

"George," he stared at her with what he believed to be a beguiling smile.

"George," she repeated. "Like I say, I don't get a lot of free time. I hold down two jobs you see," then as if disclosing a secret, added, "I'm saving up to trade in my old car for a new one."

"So, bar keeping isn't your full time occupation then?" he feigned interest, but his eyes were taking in the faint swell of her breasts. Besides, he thought, he needed something to occupy his time while the weather outside was so fiercely atrocious.

"No," she shook her head. "I'm a trainee estate agent," then proudly added, "In fact, quite recently I sold my first big property to a man from the mainland."

"Oh, really?" he sipped at his whisky, disinterested in her story but conceitedly confident that with a little charm he could quite easily bed this young barmaid.

"Yes," she gushed, then as though considering the sale, added, "It was funny, really. It's a large family home, but there's only him living there and only part time too." Leaning forward, her elbows on the bar, she quietly smirked, "I think it's a love nest, somewhere for him to bring his girlfriends to."

He smiled at her, but was thinking if he kept her talking, it wouldn't be too difficult to persuade this unsophisticated young woman to come to his room and particularly if as she said, she needed to make some money. Ordering a third double, he watched her turn away to pour it from the bottle on the back counter, noting how the fabric of her skirt tightened across her buttocks as she leaned forward.

When she handed him his whisky, he said, "Put it on my bill. I'm in room twenty-three on the first floor. You *do* know where that is, don't you Shona?" and again stared into her eyes.

Blushing, she stammered that yes, she did know and wishing to continue the flow of conversation, he asked, "So, you believe this client of yours has a love nest. Why do you think that?"

"Oh, I think I met one of his lady friends yesterday," she bit at her lip, naively uncertain of this old mans motive and why he would have such an interest in telling her what room he was in other than to add his whisky's to his bill.

"Really? And was this a glamourous courtesan?" he smiled tolerantly at her.

Shona didn't wish to admit she had no idea what a courtesan was, so slowly replied, "She was English, like you."

His glass raised to his lips, he stopped dead, some inner instinct telling him this might be useful, but then slowly replied, "I'm certain there must be a lot of English people on the island, particularly during the holiday weekend. Was this a young woman you met?"

"No," she shook her head and pursed her lips, "she was definitely old, in her forties I think."

"Blonde?"

"Blonde? No, dark haired. Nice enough though. Tommy's daughter…" she stopped. "Tommy, that's the name of the man that bought the house. His daughter Fiona introduced me to the girlfriend," she casually added. "Well, I say girlfriend. He'd told me he was widowed, so I just assumed she was a girlfriend," she shrugged.

"Introduced you? To the woman? Don't suppose, my dear, you can recall her name?"
 his eyes bored into hers and with growing certainty, he could feel that this was important.

"Her name? Yes, course I can. It was only yesterday," she grinned. "Alice. Her name is Alice."

It never occurred to Shona that the guest, this man George, might have some ulterior motive nor was she astute enough to notice when his lips tightened and his eyes widened.

What she did hear was him say, "So, you're an estate agent, Shona. Tell me, if I was interested in buying a house on the island and wanted to see the kind of property that you sold, say, like to this man Tommy, where would I see such a house?"

****

Struggling against the wind, Malky McKay and his wife got into their old Ford Escort and buckling their seat belts, he took a breath and turned the key, only to hear a click.

"Bugger," he muttered, knowing that once again the battery terminal must have come loose.

"Wait here," he told his wife and pushing the door open against the wind, struggled out into the rain to try and reconnect the terminal.
****

No wonder there's nobody out walking, Tommy Burke thought and shook his head as his windscreen wipers fought against the driving rain.

His search of the hotels to the north of Brodick proved fruitless for a white coloured Volvo and he wondered, am I being too hopeful?
****

In her office, Cathy Mulgrew took the internal call from Danny McBride who gave her the result of his phone calls, that the Royal Marines agreed to assist and would have a boat at the Ardrossan Harbour within the hour.

"What, as quick as that?" she expressed surprise.

"Apparently they are on permanent stand-by at Faslane, Ma'am, and it's not as if they're driving to Ardrossan. They can make better time on the water than a car can by road."

"True enough," she agreed, then brow furrowed, asked, "When you say a boat, Danny. What kind of boat are we talking about here?"

When he told her, she took a deep breath and thought, better you Peasy than me.

Exhaling, she thanked McBride and checking her pad, called Byrne's mobile.

"Where are you now?" she asked.

"I reckon we've just under an hour to travel," he replied.

"Am I on speaker?"

"Yes."

"Right, then here's what I've got so far. The bad news is radio communications with the three Arran cops is down. According to the control room on the mainland, they were tasked earlier today to assist in the search for a missing man on the west side of the island, some place called Pirnmill. A tourist who hasn't been seen since yesterday evening. Anyway, they can't be contacted. However, you'll be aware the ferries are not running because of the weather, but the good news is," she couldn't help herself and grinned, "how do you feel about small boats?"
****

When he got back into the Ford Escort, Mary McKay told her husband, "Heavens, Malky, you're soaked through."

"No, I'm all right. These waterproofs are just the job."

"Aye, maybe for keeping you dry," her voice dripped with sarcasm, "but the cloth seats in this wee car will be smelling of dampness for days to come."

He mentally crossed his fingers and turned the key, then smiled with relief when the engine burst into life.

"Right, let's crack on and find out how old Jessie's coping," he grinned.

****

He was just about to turn the Defender onshore Road when his mobile activated and pulling into the side of the road, saw on the screen it was Peasy who was calling.

"Tommy, thank heavens," Byrne said. "I've been trying to get through for hours."

"It's the damned weather, Peasy. It buggers up the communications throughout the island. Where are you?"

"Right now, we're about half an hour from Ardrossan Harbour on our way to you. You don't sound like you're in the house."

"No, when I heard that Alice's husband might be on the island, I left her and the wean locked in the house and I'm out scouring the hotels car parks for his car, but no luck so far."

"Right, here's an update," Byrne hurriedly continued. "One of my old bosses is arranging for a boat to get me and some Lancashire detectives across to you. As far as I'm aware, she's also trying to contact the local CID in Ardrossan and hopefully they'll travel over with us. What we need you to do is…" the line went dead.

"Tommy? Tommy! Bugger…" he irritably snapped.

"You concentrate on your driving and I'll try to contact him," Sandford said and punched in the numbers for Tommy's mobile.

****

The satellite signal for the television had gone dead, so Alice and Marcy were cuddled together watching a DVD when a small branch was torn free from a tree and carried by the wind to whip against the window, causing them both to cry out in fright.

Taking a deep breath, they stared at each other, then both began to giggle.

"Come on," Alice said, pulling at Marcy's hand, "let's go into the kitchen and make some hot chocolate. Would you like that?"

"Yes, please," Marcy leapt up from the couch and skipped ahead of her grandmother.

****

Sitting in the CID office in Glencairn Street in Saltcoats, Detective Constable Jimmy McGuire was bored. Worse than that, he was hungry. The only CID officer on duty, McGuire was on an eight to eight shift and wished he had brought more than a couple of rolls of cold meat. The bad weather had closed down several nearby shops and the local takeaway had still to open and right now and more than anything, he fancied a fish supper.

Six feet one of skin and bone, as his wife frequently cracked, the lanky twenty-eight-year-old, dark haired young detective had just finished his six-month probationary period in the CID and so was the DI's first choice for the unpopular shift that stormy day.

Balancing his feet on his desk, he yawned and was about to reach for the porn magazine one of his colleagues had confiscated from a twelve-year old, when the desk phone rang.

"CID," he answered in a bored voice, but his eyes widened when the female voice curtly said, "This is Detective Superintendent Mulgrew from the Crime Campus at Gartcosh. To whom am I speaking?"

He gulped and shot up from his chair to his feet before replying, "DC McGuire, Ma'am."

"Well, DC McGuire, I understand from my phone call to your DI that you are on your own, today, so here's what I want you to do."

****

Driving south on the Shore Road, Tommy loudly cursed the break in communication with Peasy Byrne and in disgust, tossed his mobile phone onto the passenger seat.

Right, he thought, better safe than sorry so let's try the hotels nearer the harbour.

He was about to pass the putting green on his left when he saw a green coloured, plastic council bin being hurled by the wind across the road in front of an oncoming small dark coloured car.

Instinctively, the driver of the car swerved to his right to avoid striking the bin, but to the driver's horror, made straight for the front of Tommy's Defender.

"Shit!" Tommy cried out as he pressed hard on the brakes, but was unable to avoid the smaller car striking the Defender.

After the collision, he sat for a few seconds then staring through the windscreen, saw the driver of the smaller car, a Nissan Micra he now realised, was an elderly man who with his equally aged wife, stared with shocked faces at Tommy.

Switching off the engine and the four way indicators on, Tommy jumped from the Defender into the pouring rain, his first thought the safety of the elderly couple and was relieved to find that other than them suffering what seemed to be mild shock, both were uninjured.

He glanced at the crumpled bumper and wing of the Micra, unconsciously noting that his Defender had escaped with a very minor dent and some paintwork scraped.

Upon hearing the collision, Tommy was joined in the road by a middle-aged man and two young women who had rushed to help from the nearby Bank of Scotland.

Between them, they helped the shaken couple from the car and brought them into the bank while Tommy, with the help of a couple of nearby shopkeepers, moved both vehicles to a safe parking spot.

Just what I bloody need right now, Tommy angrily thought, though his anger was not directed at the elderly driver, but to himself.

****

Geoffrey Mayhew could hardly believe his luck.

The young barmaid, Shona, unwittingly had almost landed Alice right into his lap for he was in no doubt it was *his* Alice, the the errant wife he had come to find.

Believing him now to be a prospective client seeking a property on the island, she had provided Geoffrey with a local map of Brodick from a stand at the reception and helpfully marked the map with a cross, indicating the house she had sold and where Alice was staying.

Back in his room he had sat in the easy chair to reflect on what he had been told and taken the time to consider his options.

This man, this Tommy Burke she was staying with. He might have to be dealt with too.

His thoughts turned to what he must do and, having convinced himself that Doris Chisholm's death was her own fault, pondered that he had already killed once and believed himself more than capable of doing it again; particularly as it was now his life, his career and his reputation that was at stake.

He could not, must not fail.

He turned to the side table by his elbow and lifted the bottle of whisky in one hand, the chunky glass in the other and was about to pour himself a double when burping, he tasted the whisky he had already consumed and stopped.

No, he thought, I've already had enough, but then decided it would do no harm to refill his hip flask and take it with him.

The time for whisky is when I get back; when it's done.

His eyes narrowed. If this man Burke was at the house too, he would need something to protect himself, some kind of weapon. Something heavy or sharp to carry out his plan. He began to smile, but then frowning, stared at his right hand and flexed the fingers. Yes, it was fine now, the cut almost healed but decided that he would not risk using a heavy weapon, that he needed something light and easy to handle.

And he knew from where to obtain such a weapon.

Taking a breath, he eased himself to his feet and fetching his waxed, waterproof jacket from the wardrobe, slipped it on then opening the door, began to make his way downstairs.

The reception desk was unattended and with a glance along the corridor, he slipped across the hallway into the dining room and saw that the tables had been set for dinner.

More importantly, the room was empty.

Quickly, he cast an eye at the tables, but couldn't see what he needed.

At the waiters' station, he saw a narrow table upon which rested a wooden cutlery tray. Holding his breath lest he be challenged by a member of staff, he glanced into the tray and smiled.

In one of the compartments lay a number of black handled steak knives with bright and sharp, silver coloured serrated blades. With a nervous glance about him, he lifted two of the knives and thrusting them into the jacket pocket, hurriedly made his way out of the room and through the hotel front entrance towards the car park.

CHAPTER TWENTY-EIGHT

Following Cathy Mulgrew's instructions, Peasy Byrne, closely followed by Terry Goodwin driving the CID car, drove towards the

Ardrossan Harbour and slowed to a crawl, his and Julie Sandford's eyes searching for their contact.

"There," she pointed through the heavy rain to a group of men standing by the harbour wall where three of the men wore bright yellow coloured fluorescent police jackets and upon seeing the two vehicles in convoy, one of the three waved towards them.

Pulling up alongside the five men, they saw two of the group were uniformed police officers who held their caps in their hands and two men who wore military camouflage waterproof uniforms and wore olive green coloured Kevlar safety helmets.

The fifth man who had waved approached the car and because of the noise of the wind, loudly greeted them with, "DI Sandford? I'm DC Jimmy McGuire."

He turned and indicating with a nod, added, "This is Constable's Mark Fraser and Willie Johnstone. I'm instructed by Detective Superintendent Mulgrew to place myself and these guys at your disposal, Ma'am."

Sandford nodded and staring at the military men, asked, "And these are?"

The taller of the two men approached with his hand extended in greeting and cheerfully shouted, "Sergeant Tommy Burnside and Corporal Ian Mackie. We're your drivers, Miss Sandford."

"Drivers?"

He beckoned she step forward and pointed downwards.

Looking over the low harbour wall she saw concrete steps that led down to the bubbling water and where a green coloured boat with an open cockpit bobbed furiously in the sea.

"That's what we'll be driving," Burnside continued in a loud voice. "It's an Offshore Raiding Craft, what we call an ORC. It's 9.1 metres long, has an aluminium hull, twin 250 horse power engines and can go like shit off a hot shovel, if you pardon the expression."

Sandford, with Byrne, Goodwin and Carstairs stood beside her, stared down into the boat, then loudly called out, "I really don't think we'll require those machine guns mounted at the front though, Sergeant Burnside."

"We're Royal Marines, Miss Sandford," he leaned in close so she could hear and grinned at her. "Always prepared. Now, the bad news is we brought enough spare life jackets for six, so one of your party will need to drop out, I'm afraid."

Without hesitation, Sandford turned to the group and gathering them to her, said, "Anyone not keen on the idea of going out into that maelstrom in this small boat?"

To her surprise, it was Goodwin who replied, "Only a bloody idiot would go out in that weather in such a small boat, but if you think I'm letting you go out there without me, Ma'am, you can think again."

Carstairs, both hands holding her hood tightly about her head, loudly called out, "Goes for me too."

Sandford took a deep breath, inwardly grateful at the unexpected support from her team, then exhaling turned to Byrne who anticipating her question, raised his hand and said, "It's my pal who's over there, so I'm going too."

"Gentlemen?" she turned to stare in turn at the three local officers. Though not keen on the idea of travelling across the water in such conditions and feeling queasy at the thought, McGuire felt obliged to nod that he too was going and turning to his colleagues, said, "Sorry, lads. Do you want to toss for it?"

It was Fraser who quickly replied and said, "This old bugger gets nauseous travelling in a panda car, so it looks like it's down to me."

"Hey, now hang on a minute," Johnstone began to protest, but was stopped by McGuire who raising a hand, suggested, "If you don't mind, Willie, you can let the Coastguard know we're going out on the water and ask the control room to keep trying to contact our lads on the island."

Then, with a nervous glance down at the boat, he leaned in close to add, "Just in case this goes ape shit, tell the wife it wasn't *my* fucking idea."

"Aye, okay then," replied Johnstone who inwardly delighted he wasn't about to risk life and limb, tried his best to look disappointed. Sandford again looked over the low wall and saw that they'd need both hands just to get down to the boat, then told her team, "We won't be taking our bags, so if we get stuck over there make sure you've your bank cards with you if we need to buy anything."

Once they were fitted with their green coloured, military lifejackets and checked over by the two Marines, holding hands for safety, the group carefully made their way down the rain lashed steps and were helped into the bobbing boat by the Marines who showed them where to sit.

Crowded together in the seats that were forward of the cockpit, they couldn't help but notice the two grinning Marines seemed to relish the thought of travelling in such dangerous conditions.

Seated beside Goodwin, Carstairs instinctively grabbed for his hand when the powerful engines started and then forced back into their seats as the boat surged forward, they were off.

****

Satisfied that old Jessie was comfortable and wanted for nothing, Mary and Malky McKay, holding on to each other against the force of the wind, were making their way back to the car when Mary said, "Oh, I forgot. I've left my handbag in Jessie's house. Give me a minute."

Raising his eyes to the sky, Malky wordlessly nodded and continued towards the car.

In the drivers seat he turned the key, but to his frustration, again heard the click and realised that the battery terminal had once more worked itself loose.

****

The couple had been given a hot mug of tea and now seated together on a couch in the managers office, listened as Tommy Burke, kneeling beside them, patiently explained that there was nothing to worry about, the damage to his Defender was minimal and no, he did not wish to take their insurance details for he did not intend to make any kind of claim.

"That's awful good of you, Mister Burke," the elderly lady replied before turning to her husband and using her elbow to dig him in the ribs, said, "Isn't it, Archie? Tell the man how grateful you are after bashing his motor like that."

"No, really, there's no need," Tommy interrupted and rising to his feet, added, "I really have to go now, so take care, eh?"

Stood by the door, the manager smiled and in a quiet voice, said, "You're being very generous, Mister Burke. The old bugger shouldn't be driving at his age and certainly not in this kind of weather."

"Aye, maybe so," Tommy sighed, then reaching into his wallet extracted a twenty pound note and said, "If you can call them a taxi to get them home to Sannox, they don't need to know who's paying for it, eh?"

Surprised, the manager nodded and taking the note, replied, "I'll see they get home and I'll send one of my staff in the taxi with them. Thanks, Mister Burke."

Outside, he stared up at the black sky and returned to his vehicle where grabbing the mobile phone from the passenger seat, he called Alice on the house landline.

"It's me," he began. "Everything okay with you two? Got the place locked up tight, I hope?"

"Yes," Alice smiled into the phone. "Are you okay? I mean, you haven't found him or anything?"

"No, I kind of got diverted, but I'll tell you about it when I get home. I'm just about to head south towards the harbour area. There's a couple of hotels on the Shore Road and the Douglas Hotel is the last on my list. I know it was full when you tried to book in, but I'll check it anyway and if I can't find his car then I'll come back up the road."

He glanced at his wristwatch and added, "I'll see you guys in about fifteen, maybe twenty minutes and I'll definitely be ready for a cup of tea."

"Good," she breathed a sigh of relief then almost shyly added, "Please don't be long. I…I mean, we miss you."

He smiled and ended the call.

****

With both engines going full pelt and hurling the raiding craft through the water, it took the Marines just over twenty minutes to traverse the sea between Ardrossan and Arran, twenty minutes during which the light aluminium boat, more used to calmer waters, was buffeted by the strong waves and would have been tossed about like flotsam, but for the efforts of her two-man crew who fought to not only keep the boat on an even keel, but to maintain their speed.

Twenty minutes that saw both Terry Goodwin and Jimmy McGuire one after the other, retch then vomit onto the deck.

"Sorry," white faced, Goodwin gasped at Carstairs who herself experienced seasickness, but managed to stave off from puking.

Sandford, her hand firmly clasped in Peasy Byrne's, felt a rap on her shoulder and turning, saw Sergeant Burnside leaning across from the cockpit, his head as close to her ear as he could make it.

"Can you hear me?" he bellowed at her.

She nodded and gave him a thumbs up.

"It's too risky to try and dock at the harbour. Mackie and me will beach the boat onto the sand and let you guys off onto the Shore Road across from the Douglas Hotel. Pass the word to your team and let them know what we intend doing. Your man McGuire will know his way from there. Got that?"

"Will you be able to get back off the beach?" she literally had to scream her question.

She saw him grin and jerking a thumb over his shoulder, he loudly replied, "I've got five hundred horse power back there. No problem."

Again, she gave him a thumbs up and turning into Peasy Byrne, her lips almost against his ear, related what she had been told and added that he pass the message on.

****

He stopped on Glencloy Road and staring through the storm lashed windscreen, breathed a sigh of relief. He wasn't used to driving in such bad conditions and cursed the foul weather, Arran and all things Scottish.

It was now very dull under the black clouds and switching on the interior light, he pored over the map with the cross marking the man's house.

His head snapped up and he saw that the girl Shona had been spot on. The house was directly in front of him, a mere sixty or seventy metres away.

From his jacket pocket he fetched out the hip flask and took two quick nips, just to bolster him against the cold, he told himself. However, the truth was Geoffrey was nervous and if he were totally honest, a little anxious about what he intended for Alice. There was no doubt in his mind that she would not present any kind of physical problem. No, it was the unknown that worried him, the man called Burke who might present the problem.

Almost without thought, he lightly taped at the other jacket pocket as though to reassure himself that the two knives were still there.

Deciding to leave the Volvo parked where it was, he pushed open the driver's door, no mean feat as it was buffeted by the wind, then almost bent double with his hair whipped back as the rain drove at him, made his way towards the house.

****

Malky McKay closed the bonnet of the Ford escort and with a mild expletive, struggled to get back into the drivers seat.

"Is it fixed?" Mary asked.

"Fingers crossed," he tightly grinned at her and turning the key, heard the engine burst into life.

"Phew," he exhaled and with a smile, started to slowly drive towards Glencloy Road.

****

Stumbling across the sand towards the Shore Road, Peasy Byrne wrapped his arm around Julie Sandford as did Lucy Carstairs with Terry Goodwin, then accompanied by the Scottish officers made their way to stand between the cars in the parking bays and stopping to catch their breath, turned just in time to see the two Marines back their boat off from the beach and race off into the waves at a breathtaking speed.

Drawing Sandford close to him, Byrne pointed and hollered in her ear, "I suggest we head into that hotel across the road and I can try to phone Tommy from there."

"Agreed," she nodded.

Lurching across the road like shipwreck survivors with Carstairs continuing to assist the still nauseous Goodwin, the group began to stagger their way to the hotel.

****

He arrived at the house and pressing himself against a tree, glanced into the driveway. To his relief there was no sign of the big red Land Rover the barmaid said Burke drove, but seeing two tandem garages wondered if it was in one of them.

His mouth was dry and his palms sweaty, but he chose to believe it was the whisky he had drunk rather than nerves. In an attempt to bolster his courage, he thought, I'm a man that's faced down a scrum and taken more than my fair share of knocks.

Fuck this guy Burke, he snarled, his breath coming in spurts. I'll gut him if he tries to stop me.

He could see lights on in the house and licking at his dry lips, pushed open the gate and began to creep into the garden.

****

In her office at Gartcosh, Cathy Mulgrew was reading through an intelligence report and using a red pen, commenting in the margin any points of interest.

The desk phone rang.

"Ma'am, it's me," said McBride. "I've just had a call from the Marines base at Faslane. Their guys have radioed in that they dropped DI Sandford and her team off on the beach at Brodick and are returning to their base. Said to tell you we owe them big time, but that a couple of cases of lager might settle the bill."

She smiled with relief that their initiative had not drowned Peasy Byrne and the Lancashire detectives and asked, "Any news from the Ayrshire Divisions control room about contacting the local uniformed officers?"

"No, Ma'am, other than the local CID guy, a DC McGuire and a uniformed officer have accompanied DI Sandford to make the arrest if they manage to trace the suspect."

"Right, thanks, Danny. Ask the Ayrshire control room to keep trying to contact their Arran officers and keep me apprised of any developments."

"Ma'am," he ended the call.

****

Alice and Marcy sat facing each other across the kitchen table, the little girl enjoying her hot chocolate and now much calmer.

"How long will the storm last, Gran?"

"Oh, I don't really know," Alice replied, "but I suppose it must blow itself out before it stops."

Marcy giggled. "Blow itself out? Like a candle, you mean?"

"Just like a candle," she smiled and with her attention taken by Marcy, was unaware of the face at the window who keenly watched them.

****

He had completed a full circuit of the house and as far as he could see through the windows in the brightly lit rooms and the absence of the red coloured Land Rover, there was no sign of the man Burke and that seemed to indicate he was not at home. His glance through the garage window also proved the large double garage was empty. Unaccountably, his legs were shaking and his hands trembling as a rivulet of perspiration slowly worked its way down his spine.

He guessed that with the foul weather and the high winds, the all the doors would be locked tight, but he knew that somehow he had to get into the house.

To calm his nerves, he took yet another swallow from the hip flask. That's when he saw the shed at the foot of the garden and treading carefully, made towards it.

Pulling back the heavy bolt to open the unlocked door, he was almost clouted by the wooden door when the wind swung it viciously towards him, but managed to side step before it hit him. Peering inside he saw a variety of garden tools from which he selected a new, wooden handled spade that still had the paper wrapping on the blade.

Carrying the spade with him, he ignored the banging of the shed door as it swung in the wind and returned to the kitchen window where he saw Alice and the brat still seated at the table and laughing their heads off.

His eyes narrowed and his brow furrowed. In his alcohol addled mind, he believed she was laughing at him.

Laughing at having made a fool of him.

His grip tightened on the spade handle and fuelled by the whisky he had consumed, his anger increased.

****

As he slowly drove past the white coloured Volvo, Malky McKay stared curiously at it and wondered who would be so foolish as to leave the vehicle lying out in Glencloy Road in this weather instead of parking in their driveway.

****

With no trace of the white coloured Volvo in the Douglas Hotel car park, a disappointed Tommy was turning the Defender to return back to the house when to his astonishment, he saw Peasy Byrne running from the front entrance and waving his arms to attract Tommy's attention.

He jerked the big vehicle to a halt and getting out of the driver's seat, saw two women and three men, one a uniformed police officer, following Peasy from the hotel steps.

"What the hell…" he began, but was stopped by a breathless Byrne who gasped, "Have you found him yet? Where he is?"

"No, not yet. How the hell did you get onto the island?"

"Long story and I'll give you the nitty-gritty details later, but right now," Byrne exhaled and asked, "Is Alice safe?"

Tommy nodded, but before he could respond further, Byrne was joined by one of the woman and said, "This is Detective Inspector Sandford from Preston. She's here to arrest Mayhew."

"Alice is at the house," Tommy said at last, darting a glance at Sandford and the rest of the group who crowded around her. "I told her to stay there and lock her and Marcy in until I get back. I've been round the car parks of the local hotels, but I haven't found him yet, her husband I mean."

"Right," Byrne turned to Sandford and with a grin, said, "I suggest we all pile into this old heap and get back to Tommy's house and work out our plan from there."

"Let's do it," she grabbed at the front passenger door handle and climbed in.

****

While the little girl remained seated, Alice arose from her chair and lifting Marcy and her own mugs, moved across the kitchen to the dishwasher.

She bent to open the door of the machine when to her shock, there was a loud smashing noise from the kitchen door.

Turning, she saw to her horror that a man…

Oh dear God, no!

She realised it was Geoffrey and he was using something to break in the window in the door.

The spade gripped in both hands, he swung it back and forth to batter at the glass and heard Alice scream. Grimacing, his hair in disarray and his face contorted in hatred, he continued to hammer the spade forward until the shattered glass fell inwards and throwing the tool to the ground, reached in through the enormous hole he had made, his fingers groping for the lock.

To Alice's dismay, she saw she had left the key in the door and turning towards her granddaughter saw the little girls face pale, her mouth wide as she loudly screamed.

Alice run to Marcy and took her by the hand, but in her terror the little girl, her hands clasped tightly to her ears against the noise, refused to move and continued to scream.

The few seconds that had passed allowed Geoffrey to open the door and throwing the spade to the floor beside him, he reached into his jacket pocket and removed one of the knives that he loosely held in his right hand.

His body shaking with exertion and a fine sheen of sweat on his forehead, he slowly moved towards his wife and granddaughter and sneeringly hissed, "You thought I wouldn't find you, didn't you. Well, I'm here now," and holding out his left hand, said, "Give me the packets you stole from me."

****

Malky McKay drove slowly through the gate and stopped the car. Even though the wind noisily howled, he could clearly hear the garden shed door banging and knowing for certain that it had been secured by the bolt, wondered how it had got open or, his eyes narrowed, who opened it and why it hadn't been closed again.

****

Alice, too frightened to even reply, stared at the knife in his hand and thought her legs were about to give way, but then to her own surprise, a cold fury overcome her.

She moved to stand in front of the still seated Marcy, one hand protectively behind her on the little girl's body and the other reaching forward as though to beseech him and croaked, "You don't need to do this, Geoffrey. I'll give you whatever you want. Just leave Marcy be! For God's sake, she's your granddaughter!"

He wished he had taken the time to pee for he badly needed to urinate, so badly he could almost feel his bladder bursting, but right now he had to do what he had come to do.

Collect the packet of Brown Speeders and deal with Alice.

Her and he realised with an inward shudder, the child too, for she could not be permitted to live and reveal what he was about to do. Now no more than a few feet from Alice, he thrust the knife towards her and growled again, "Where are the packets!"

****

At a speed that was bordering on reckless, Tommy willed the old Defender to go even faster. Crammed between Peasy Byrne and Tommy in the front passenger seat, Julie Sandford reached forward to brace herself on the dashboard and turning, stared curiously at Peasy's friend, wondering for the umpteenth time what caused him to shelter a woman on the run from her husband.

****

"Please, Geoffrey," she continued to implore him, her eyes darting from the knife to his face, "Just let Marcy leave. She doesn't know anything about the drugs."

He startled at that. The drugs.

So, perhaps Alice isn't really as stupid as I always thought, he frowned and hissed, "Just tell me where the packets are, my dear?"

****

He had never served in the military, wasn't a police officer and was a man completely devoid of any type of guile, yet Malky McKay had a funny feeling, a stirring he later called it, that something was amiss. He couldn't explain it then nor could he later, but firmly told Mary, "Stay in the car, dear."

When she tried to protest, he sharply repeated, "Stay in the *car*!"

Now, here he was, limping on the path around the house against the wind and making his way towards the garden shed when to his surprise, he saw the spade lying at the open kitchen door and the ground littered with glass that brightly glittered in the rain.

****

Geoffrey glanced at Marcy and said, "I *need* the packets, Alice," then in one swift movement belying an unfit man his size who was badly out of shape, quickly moved forward and grabbed her arm.

Pulling her close to him, he hissed, "Fetch me the packets now!"

Pushing her from him, he reached forward and dragged Marcy from the chair by the collar of her sweater, then clamped his free hand about her neck and held the knife loosely at his side.

****

In the rear seat of Tommy's Defender, Terry Goodwin, Jimmy McGuire and the uniformed cop Mark Fraser held tightly onto Lucy Carstairs who was lying awkwardly across their laps and being bounced around while Tommy Burke drove the big vehicle across the rain filled ruts in Glencloy Road.

Then they heard him cry out, "It's the Volvo! Dear God, he's here!"

****

Alice screamed and was about to attack Geoffrey, but stopped when he lifted the knife and threateningly held it inches from the sobbing little girl's throat.

"Let's not be foolish, Alice," he smirked, knowing that as long as he threatened her little darling, he had won, that she would now do exactly as he wanted.

"Fetch me the packets!"
****

Hearing the little girl scream, he risked a peek into the kitchen and not for the first time since the accident Malky cursed the loss of his left leg. Then, as quietly as he could, he bent to lift the spade from the ground.

That done, he licked his suddenly dry lips and with the spade held tightly in both hands, prepared himself.
****

Sitting in the passenger seat of the old Ford Escort, Mary McKay heard the screech of brakes and turning, saw Tommy Burke's big red motor coming to a halt almost beside her. To her surprise she watched as Tommy burst from the driver's door, closely followed by a man and a woman from the front passenger seat then, to her astonishment, it seemed like a bus load scrambled out of the back doors.
****

She wanted to cry out, take me, do what you will and leave my granddaughter alone, but knew that in his crazed and controlling state, there would be no arguing with Geoffrey.

She also knew that though she no longer had the packets, whether she had or not he intended killing her, just as he had killed her only friend Doris.

She felt helpless, knowing that she could not overpower him.

If she could distract him, even for a few seconds, it might be enough to allow Marcy to run.

Her life meant nothing if he hurt Marcy, but then a sudden resolve gripped her for she knew what she had to do.

Steeling herself, she launched her body at him, her hands reaching to grasp the knife and screamed, "RUN!"

Geoffrey instinctively flinched as their bodies collided and released his grip on Marcy.

Taken aback, the little girl fell to the floor stunned, her eyes fixed on her grandmother.

In that heartbeat as Alice and her husband struggled together and though she were a lot slighter than Geoffrey, the momentum of her attack and the whisky he had drunk combined to throw him off balance and together they fell in an untidy heap to the floor with Alice on top of Geoffrey.

"I'll fucking kill you!" he screamed at Alice as using both hands and finding a strength she did not know she had, she tried to wrestle the knife from his grip.

But then he screamed again, "I'll kill you! Both of you!"

Malky McKay, with the spade raised, seized the opportunity and hurriedly limped the fifteen feet across the kitchen to the struggling pair just as Geffrey broke free from her grip and raised the knife to plunge it into Alice's body.

However, so intent was he on stabbing his wife he failed to see the approaching Malky who smashed the blade against the back of Geoffrey Mayhew's head.

The sudden impact of the stainless steel blade against Geoffrey's unprotected head not only caused him to cry out in pain, but to release the knife that fell with a clang to the tiled floor.

Pushing Alice from him, he turned onto his knees and dazedly tried to rise to his feet, but Malky wasn't finished.

For good measure, he drew back the spade and whacked the blade firmly a second time onto the top of Geoffrey's head then watched as the heavyset man sunk heavily to the floor.

And then the final indignity for Geoffrey, for just as he lapsed into unconsciousness, he felt his bladder uncontrollably release and he peed himself.

CHAPTER TWENTY-NINE

It took almost half an hour for the ambulance to attend from the Arran War Memorial Hospital in Lamlash, during which time the now conscious but stunned Geffrey Mayhew was roughly removed from the kitchen to lie on the concrete floor of one of the empty garages. Securely handcuffed, he was vaguely aware of a police officer who stood leaning against the wall, a cigarette in one hand and who sipped at a hot mug of tea while keeping a wary eye on his prisoner.

Ten minutes after the ambulance conveying Geoffrey and DC McGuire and Constable Fraser as arresting officers had left, Alice, still pale after her ordeal, sat on the couch in the large lounge with a protective arm about Marcy while a solicitous Tommy, seated in a chair in front of her and holding her free hand in his, continued to berate himself for leaving her and her granddaughter alone.

"I'm so sorry, Alice," he shook his head and told her over and over. "I should never have left you and the wean alone. I'm so sorry."

Around Alice were seated Julie Sandford, Terry Goodwin and Peasy Byrne, while Lucy Carstairs busied herself in the kitchen helping Mary McKay prepare coffee and sandwiches.

In the garden shed, Malky, who in his adult life had never raised a hand against another human being, nervously rummaged about looking for a sheet of plywood to effect a temporary repair on the kitchen door and wondered that he'd nearly killed a man.

"It's a matter of territorial jurisdiction, Missus Mayhew," Sandford began to address her, but was interrupted when she said, "Alice, please. I intend reverting to my maiden name and won't be using the name Mayhew again."

Sandford nodded and began again. "As I said, our colleagues from Police Scotland have formally arrested your husband…I mean, Geoffrey Mayhew, but when the Lancashire Constabulary arrest warrant is e-mailed through to Police Scotland, my colleagues and I will take charge and return him with us to face two murder charges in Preston. There is also the issue of his complicity in the distribution of illegal drugs and likely, his involvement in the death of Jonathan Archer too. However," she turned and smiled at Byrne, "I am also reliably informed by my former Scottish police friend Peasy here that after what you and Marcy suffered at his hands, it is also likely he will face charges of abduction and assault; charges that I am confident will be forwarded by Police Scotland and included on the Crown Prosecution Service indictment against him."

"Abduction?" Tommy asked.

It was Peasy Byrne who replied when he said, "In the strictest interpretation of the law, Tommy, when Mayhew took hold of wee Marcy there," he smiled at the child, "he prevented her from going about her lawful business so aye, I think the Crown Office will be more than happy to libel that charge too, against him. Might not stand up in court, but it's just something else to throw at the bas…" he stopped and grimaced.

Alice, slightly confused by the legal babble, said "All I really need to know, Miss Sandford…"

"Julie," she interrupted with an encouraging smile.

"Julie," Alice acknowledged with a nod. "All I need to know is that he will be locked up and will never again be in a by position to hurt me or Marcy."

"I failed you once, hen," Tommy interrupted, then shaking his head growled, "I damn well won't fail you a second time. That man will never come near you or the wee girl again. I swear it."

It was as though there was no one else in the room, for Alice turned to Tommy, seated on the arms of the couch, and softly replied, "You never failed us, Tommy. You saved us. Without you…" her eyes sparkled with tears and her lips trembled as she grasped at his hand and tightly held it.

In her arms, Marcy rolled her eyes and to the amusement of those there, sighed, "My Gran's getting all wishy-washy about Tommy again."

****

It was in the early hours of the next morning the storm finally abated with the promise that by that midday, the ferries to the mainland would resume their sailings.

Later that morning, lying in a private room in the seventeen bed hospital in Lamlash with his right wrist handcuffed to the metal frame and his wounded head bandaged, Geoffrey Mayhew continued to complain loudly and vigorously about his treatment, calling for the senior medical professional to attend to him and reminding all and sundry he was a doctor.

Seated on uncomfortable tubular chairs in the corridor outside, Constable Mark Fraser and a local constable drafted in to assist, idly glanced through old editions of Vogue magazines and pointedly ignored their prisoner.

The door to the private room opened to admit DI Julie Sandford who, accompanied by DS Terry Goodwin and DC Jimmy McGuire, drew up a chair and stared at Mayhew while the two detectives stood behind her.

"And who the hell are you?" he curtly demanded, his eyes flitting from one to another before settling on Sandford.

"I am the woman who intends charging you with two murders, Doctor Mayhew," she smiled at him. "That and a list of other charges that will be included on the indictment against you."

She saw his face pale and his throat tighten as he blusteringly replied, "You have no proof I murdered anyone."

She stared curiously at him and with a smile, leaned forward and in a soft voice politely asked, "Tell me, Doctor Mayhew. Have you ever heard of DNA?"

****

In the kitchen of the house at Glencloy Road, Alice sat with Lucy Carstairs enjoying a coffee while Tommy, Peasy Byrne and Malky McKay worked together outdoors, securing the unsteady tree that threatened to fall upon the fence.

Sitting in the small lounge, Marcy, now seemingly over her distressing ordeal, caught up with her Tom and Jerry cartoons.

"I wish I'd known sooner what kind of life you'd had with him, Alice," Carstairs sipped at her coffee.

She shrugged and sighing, replied with a sad smile, "Well, that's all over now. He will no longer be in any kind of position to threaten or hurt me or Marcy."

Carstairs didn't immediately respond, but then with a soft smile, teased, "Tommy Burke seems to be a very nice man. Seems quite devoted to you…and Marcy too, of course."

"Yes, well, after all this," she inhaled and slowly exhaled, "I think Tommy just might be keen to see the back of us and the trouble we've caused him."

"What trouble's that?" she turned to see Tommy pushing through the kitchen door and removing his heavy-duty working gloves and skipped cap that he laid down onto the worktop.

"Oh, just girls talk," Carstairs replied then with a knowing glance at Alice, added, "I think I'll just see how Marcy's getting on."

When she'd left the room, Tommy asked again, "What trouble is it that you think you've caused me, Alice?"

She blushed and replied, "Well, you know, what, with everything that has gone on…"

He held up his hand to interrupt her and moving towards her, gently pulled her to her feet then wrapping his arms about her waist, drew her close and said with a grin, "I wouldn't have it any other way and for what it's worth, Alice, I'm not letting you or Marcy go out of my life. Ever."

CHAPTER THIRTY

The day following the arrest of Geoffrey Mayhew on the Scottish island of Arran, he found himself being returned to Preston where, following a brief appearance at the local Magistrate's Court, he was transported to the remand wing of the Category A prison at HMP Wakefield.

Almost six months passed before he left the remand wing and only then to be conveyed to the High Court sitting at the Preston Crown Court.

Among the charges that Geoffrey faced was the murder of Edward Meiklewood and Doris Chisholm as well as the assaults committed upon his former wife Alice Mayhew and their granddaughter, Marcy Benson.

Also included in the Indictment were charges from the Scottish Crown Office as well as a number of charges relating to the Misuse of Drugs Act 1971, that accused Mayhew of distributing a Class A drug, namely the so-called Brown Speeders, that ultimately led to the death of a promising young athlete, Jonathon Archer.

The forthcoming trial produced much local excitement and it was widely reported in the popular press that the egotistical doctor had sacked two consecutive Queens Counsel, publicly citing them as incompetent and a waste of his money.

Prominent witnesses in the prosecution case were the former Missus Alice Mayhew, who was now known by her maiden name Carrington and who with her granddaughter Marcy Benson had travelled from their home in Arran to give evidence.

According to a leaked report to the press, a third witness who had travelled with them was a disabled handyman, Malcolm McKay, who was a key witness in the attempted murder of both Alice Carrington and Marcy Benson.

However, on the second day of the accused being called to trial and prior to the commencement of the prosecution case, a third Queens Counsel, on this occasion appointed by the Court and after a careful review of the DNA evidence against her client, attempted to persuade Doctor Mayhew to plead guilty to the two charges of murder, both Scottish charges of assault, but not guilty to the rather flimsy Scottish charge of abduction and the distribution of the Brown Speeders.

Initially reluctant to accept any responsibility for his actions, Geoffrey Mayhew continued to demand he go to trial, haughtily telling the QC, "I want my day in court."

However, when it was patiently explained to the tight-lipped Doctor Mayhew that he could not beat the DNA evidence for the murders nor could he deny the evidence of the handyman, Mister McKay, who had clearly saw him assault the former Missus Mayhew and also heard him threaten to kill her and the child.

The final argument by the QC to her client was that the accused's granddaughter Marcy, now turned nine years of age, would be a totally credible witness for the Prosecution and without doubt evoke sympathy from the jury of fifteen local Prestonians.

"Do you *really* want to put that child on the stand, Doctor Mayhew," the QC slowly stared into his eyes. "You do realise the jury will see you as the grandfather who held a knife to her throat and threatened to murder her?"

Sullenly and with ill grace, he agreed to accept the QC's advice and throw himself at the mercy of the Court.

Happy to avoid the cost of a lengthy and expensive trial and in exchange for the guilty pleas to both the murders and the Scottish related charges of two assaults, the DPP eagerly accepted Doctor Mayhew's not guilty plea to the abduction and drug charges.

The packed court watched as flanked by three prison warders, Geoffrey Mayhew was brought to the Dock where mounting the steps he arrogantly glanced at Her Ladyship.

What the judge could not know it was Geoffrey's privately held and conceited belief that his prominence in the community, charismatic reputation and profession as a doctor would save him from any lengthy sentence.

Staring at the prisoner in the dock, Her Ladyship reminded the court that regardless of his guilty plea, Doctor Mayhew had not apparently shown any remorse for either of his victims and indeed had informed the police during his interview that Doris Chisholm need not have died had she provided Doctor Mayhew with the information he desired; the whereabouts of his wife who he intended murdering.

However, any hope held by him that his guilty pleas in bar of a trial would somehow dilute his sentence were quickly dispelled when Her Ladyship, taking cognisance of his guilty pleas to the libelled charges, finished her sentencing.

In consequence of his actions, Her Ladyship awarded Geoffrey life imprisonment on each of the two murder charges to run consecutively and two years' imprisonment apiece for both assaults; the sentence for each of the Scottish crimes to be served concurrently.

Initially stunned at the severity of the sentencing, Geoffrey paid no attention to the whispered reaction of the crowded court for what really enraged him and caused his frenzied outburst in the Dock was when Her Ladyship concluded her summing up by instructing that he serve no less than thirty years' imprisonment before he be permitted to make application for any early release and in effect, ensured that in all probability he would likely die in prison.

When the final remark by Her Ladyship sunk in, it resulted in Geoffrey subjecting the judge to a torrent of abuse before being dragged screaming and struggling from the Dock by the three red-faced warders.

****

Just under three hours after the sentencing, the former and recently divorced Missus Mayhew or Alice Carrington as she now was, sat relaxed in an easy chair in the spacious guests lounge of the Holiday Inn in Preston City Centre.

On the table in front of her were a number of glasses alongside one empty bottle and one half full bottle of champagne.

In the chair to Alice's right sat her granddaughter Marcy, her brow furrowed and apparently engrossed in a story in her girl's magazine. On Alice's left sat Tommy Burke, his hand tenderly holding that of Alice.

While he chatted to Peasy Byrne who sat opposite him, Byrne's partner Julie Sandford leaned across the table to ask Alice,

"What's your plans now that it's all over? Think you'll come back here to Preston?"

"Well," she shrugged, "I have my part-time job at the Cooperative on the island to return to where I've made some lovely friends and Marcy has settled nicely into her new school where she too made a lot of friends; so no," she shook her head, "I really don't see me returning to live here. That and well," she exhaled, "what happened to Doris would haunt me every time I walked out the door."

"And when we return to Arran," Tommy interrupted with a theatrical wink, "now that her divorce has been settled and she's come into a large sum of money from the proceeds of the sale of her house, I'm thinking of making a permanent move on her."

"In your dreams," Alice grinned at him before coyly adding, "I'm a free woman now, so the world's my oyster," she joked, then frowning, glanced at Tommy to ask, "That's what they say, isn't it?" Before he could respond, they all turned when they saw Malky McKay and his wife Mary, both carrying plastic bags, approaching them from the front door of the hotel.

"Get your souvenirs?" Tommy smiled at them.

"Oh, aye, but my feet are killing me," Mary sighed and nodded as she slumped gratefully down into a chair, but grinned when she was handed a glass of champagne by Byrne. "It's not that often we get off the island and thank you for putting us up in this fancy hotel, Tommy," she beamed at him.

"Least I can do, Mary, and after what you did, Malky," he turned to his friend and nodded his thanks to Malky, who pulled a chair over to the table and sat down beside his wife.

Tommy's brow creased and scratching at his head as though in thought, then continued, "Which reminds me. You know my girls persuaded me to buy myself a new Land Rover Discovery, one of they fancy automatic ones? Well, to be honest I was never keen on automatics, Malky. I still prefer my Defender, bumps and scratches and dented though it might be. So, I was wondering; that old Escort of yours has passed its sell-by date. How would you feel when we get back about taking on the Discovery? Remember, it's got a tow bar fitted that you can use to haul that boat of yours about the island," he added.

Malky's eyes widened and his face split into a huge grin before he replied, "I'd be delighted, Tommy, and you have my word I'll take good care of it."

"Then it's done, but what you do with it is your business, Malky, because you own it now," Tommy smiled, conscious of Alice's slight squeeze of approval on his hand.

"So," Julie Sandford's eyes narrowed as she coyly addressed Alice again, "if I've any need to contact you, I take it you're still living at Glencloy Road?"

She turned to smile at Tommy and nodding, replied, "That's our address now, though during the school holidays and at least one weekend a month we'll probably be over at the flat in Glasgow, spending time with Tommy's girls and grandchildren or I should say," she leaned to ruffle her granddaughter's hair, "Marcy's new aunties, uncles and cousins."

"And Cissie and me are to be a flower girls," Marcy proudly piped up.

"Oh, and who's getting married?" Sandford, poker-faced, asked her. Staring guiltily in turn at her grandmother and Tommy, the little girl grimaced and replied, "Oops."

Tommy shook his head at her and pretending to frown, asked, "What part of pinkie promise don't you understand, Miss Cheeky Nose?"

"Looks like the secret's out," Alice blushed.

"Aye, well I expect to be asked to be Best Man, so I suppose I'll need to look out my kilt," Byrne sniffed and toasted the couple with his glass.

"Oh," Sandford suddenly turned to grin at him and assuming a broad Scottish accent, said, "I like the thought of you wearing a kilt, my handsome laddie."

"Heavens, woman," he resignedly shook his head, "if you're pretending to be a Scotswoman, don't take up acting for a living."

"And you, Peasy," Tommy interrupted as he stared from one to the other. "Are you coming back up the road with us tomorrow or staying down here with Julie?"

"Oh, I think I'll hang on for another couple of days with my Detective Chief Inspector," he smiled and catching Sandford's eye, again raised his glass to toast her recent promotion.

"Well, here's to us all," Tommy reached across to the table and refilling two glasses, handed one to Alice.

As the group sipped at their champagne, Tommy stared at Alice and smiling, leaned across to whisper softly to her, "And thank the heavens for the broken handle on an old suitcase."

He could not know that though Alice returned his smile, her thoughts were of another day; a journey on a ferry when she had likened herself to be just like the old suitcase; broken and unloved.

But those days, she held Tommy's hand even tighter and inwardly sighed, were in the past.

****

Thank you for your support in reading this book.
Needless to say, this story is a work of fiction and none of the
characters represent any living or deceased individual.
As readers of my previous books may already know, I am an
amateur writer and self-publish on Amazon as well as also self-
editing, therefore I accept that all grammar and punctuation errors
are mine alone.
I hope that any such errors do not detract from the story.
If you have enjoyed the story, you may wish to visit my website at:
www.glasgowcrimefiction.co.uk

I also welcome feedback and can be contacted at:
george.donald.books@hotmail.co.uk
Kind regards,
George Donald

Printed in Great Britain
by Amazon

41181434R00185